and she teache

Barb's short

magazines an

Blood Memorie

have also app

Find out mo

Orbit author

By Barb

DHAM

THIEF OF L

STER OF THE D

ATOR TO THE BL

TRAITOR TO THE BLOOD

Barb & J.C. Hendee

orbit

www.orbitbooks.net

ORBIT

First published in the United States in 2006 by Roc,
Penguin Group (USA) Inc.
First published in Great Britain in 2006 by Orbit
Reprinted 2007

A CIP catalogue record for this book
is available from the British Library.

ISBN 978-1-84149-571-2

Papers used by Orbit are natural, recyclable products made from
wood grown in sustainable forests and certified in accordance with
the rules of the Forest Stewardship Council.

Typeset in Bembo by Palimpsest Book Production Limited,
Grangemouth, Stirlingshire

Printed and bound in Great Britain by
Mackays of Chatham plc, Chatham, Kent
Paper supplied by Hellefoss AS, Norway

Orbit
An imprint of
Little, Brown Book Group
Brettenham House
Lancaster Place
London WC2E 7EN

A Member of the Hachette Livre Group of Companies

www.orbitbooks.net

This one is dedicated with much appreciation to our editors Liz Scheier and Jennifer Heddle, our agent Dan Hooker, and our talented cover artists Steve Stone and Koveck.
All novels are collaborations.

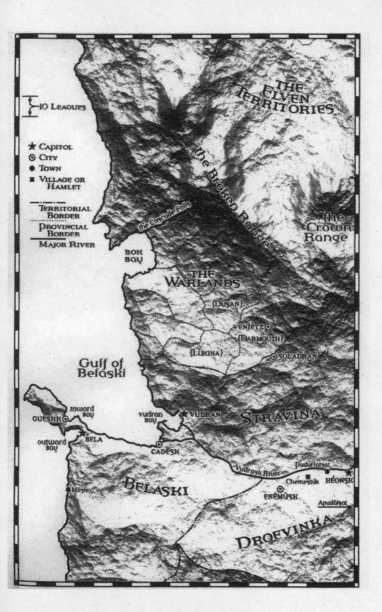

Prologue

A half-elf lay shivering on his bed, unable to get warm. His mother was downstairs in the kitchen, but he couldn't go to her for comfort. Instead Leesil sat up and looked down at his dog lying on the floor.

Chap's silver-gray fur shimmered by the light of a single candle in the dark room. He raised his head, blinked once at Leesil, and whined softly as if to ask what was wrong.

Leesil's stomach churned, and his hands trembled. A feeling he couldn't name crept through his body. He was a spy, an assassin, enslaved to the warlord Darmouth, who owned both him and his parents. He served his lord without question to protect the lives of his mother and father. But this day had been different.

Thirteen days ago, Darmouth sent Leesil to spy on an old scholar named Josiah. The old man had been kind to him; not everyone would have taken a half-elf into his home. Leesil had betrayed Josiah, giving Darmouth a letter the old scholar had written to his sister. There was no malice in it, only concern for the state of the province, but it was enough for Darmouth to claim sedition. Josiah was arrested, and Leesil was paid for his services. Darmouth called it a 'reward.'

Leesil couldn't erase the image of Josiah's smiling violet eyes. His chest constricted with a faint hope that Josiah might be cleared. Perhaps one of Darmouth's ministers would petition for the scholar's release.

He ran a hand over his face, shivering and sweating at the same time. He needed air. He needed to get out of this room, out of this house. He reached for the draw-string pouch of coins that Lord Darmouth had given him, then got up and snuffed the candle before walking quietly into his parents' room. His father was out, and his mother was in the kitchen, so he laid the pouch on their bed.

Few people could step softly enough that his mother wouldn't hear, but she had taught Leesil how. His foot-falls down the stairs were so silent even she would never hear him. Halfway down, he paused and looked back. Chap was there behind him, his paws making no noise either.

Leesil would've preferred to slip out the back door facing the lakeshore, but that meant passing through the kitchen. He didn't want his mother to see him and ask questions. So he went out the front door, opening it silently, and Chap followed.

The moon was high, and Leesil looked about at the city of Venjètz, and up and down Favor's Row, the street on which he'd lived his whole life. The only times he'd been beyond the city walls was in service to his lord or while training with his mother or father. Their house stood among others along the lake's shore, and in those waters rested Darmouth's keep, with its front portal con-nected to the shore by a fortified bridge. Leesil's eyes strayed to the keep's massive basalt walls, and then he stopped breathing.

Hanging from the wall was a body in soiled cream-colored robes, barely visible by the massive fire braziers burning atop the towers.

Master Josiah.

Lord Darmouth hadn't waited to hang the old man.

The world grew dim before Leesil's eyes, and his knees almost buckled as he tried to suck in air.

I did this, he thought. *I am the one who did this.*

On the first gasp of air, he started to run.

Leesil lurched through the streets, not caring who saw him. It was two city blocks before he heard the click of claws on cobblestone that told him Chap still followed. He ran out into the main route and stared toward the city gates before he finally regained control of himself. He slipped behind a shop, watching passing travelers.

The night was half gone, but a few wagons still entered and left the city. What trickle of commerce and trade came to Venjètz often ran both day and night.

This life had to end. If Leesil even disobeyed Darmouth, let alone tried to flee, his parents would be arrested and executed. He had nothing. No money or spare clothing. No water or food. But in this moment, nothing mattered more than escape.

The house that Darmouth had given his parents was no 'favor' but a cage close enough to the keep to be watched. Close enough for Leesil to see Josiah's body each day and night, until it rotted and fell to sink into the lake. Even the old scholar's bones would be lost, mingled among those who'd died before him and lay tangled in the water's depths.

A wagon passed by, heading for the gates with a heavy load covered by a canvas tarp. Leesil dashed after it, and he climbed in the back before anyone saw him, and then waved for Chap to follow.

Chap's shocked expression was almost human. The dog took two hesitant steps as the wagon pulled away. He looked back once into the city, but the house was far out of sight and only the towers of Darmouth's keep were visible above the rooftops. Chap bolted after the wagon, leaping into the back. Leesil pulled the tarp down as they both squirmed deeper among the crates and sacks.

The wagon slowed to a creaking stop as someone called out to the driver.

'Hallo, Vireck. Headed for the south?'

'Better trade down there,' came the driver's answer. 'The provinces are getting thin.'

'See you in a moon?'

'Probably two. But I'll bring you some pipe weed to smoke on your watch.'

'Appreciate it.'

The wagon rolled out of the city gates, and no one bothered to check in its back.

The reality of his situation crept in on Leesil. He closed his eyes and saw the faces of his mother and father. The wagon moved down the road, and he didn't peer upward to see the walls of Venjètz finally blocked out by the night. The only sound was the clop of hooves upon the dirt road.

Chap struggled to gain more room, and a crate toppled toward them both. On instinct Leesil rolled out of its way and slipped halfway out from under the canvas tarp.

'You!' a voice shouted. 'What are you doing in there?'

At first Leesil thought the driver had seen him, but the man only turned about at the voice coming from back down the road. The driver jerked the reins, and the wagon shuddered to a halt.

Leesil still heard the clop of a horse and looked back toward the city.

Three horses came up the road toward the wagon. The lead rider was a tall, slightly built man with reddish hair. Leesil knew him. Baron Emêl Milea was one of Darmouth's nobles and a minister on his council – one of his lackeys.

Emêl's eyes widened. *You*, he mouthed silently and halted his mount. Companion guards pulled their horses in beside their lord.

Leesil had seen this man only a few times. Though his parents were known as only servants to Darmouth, anyone close to the warlord had suspicions concerning their duties. Leesil had his mother's coloring and hair. The baron could easily guess who – if not what – Leesil was.

He'd hoped to be long gone before any but his parents realized it. The coin pouch on their bed would be enough to assist them. They could run before Darmouth learned anything. They could . . .

Leesil's whole world slowed as Baron Milea yelled at his men, 'Take him!'

Leesil rolled from the wagon bed and dashed into the trees, Chap following. His mother's teachings of night ways in the forest filled his head. He ran through the dark, still seeing Josiah's body hanging from the wall, and the eyes of his parents watching him.

Cuirin'nên'a heard the front door click and turned to welcome her husband home. But Gavril's face was strained and nearly white, and the welcome died on her lips.

'Nein'a,' he panted. 'Leesil is gone. He's run from the city.'

Her husband's disheveled hair hung forward across his sweating brow. Gavril was nearly the same height as she, but there the resemblance ended. Plain-featured with dun-colored hair and eyes, he wore a short beard peppered with gray that hid the lower half of his face. No one who met him once would ever remember him. As a spy and assassin, this was but one of his strengths.

Nein'a was his contrast in all ways – tall compared to humans, with silken white-blond hair tied in a coil. More often she wore it loose down her back and tucked it behind her elongated ears whenever she wished to accentuate her strange appearance. Her skin was a golden brown. Almond-shaped amber eyes, larger than a human's, dominated her triangular face. They captivated any human male who stared at her too long. As a spy and assassin, this was her strength.

Nein'a served as a distraction at Darmouth's rare evening events, putting off guard any noble or officer her lord suspected of duplicity. Such men eagerly tried to impress her with whispered words of their affluence in the province, and how much they could offer for her favor. But her whole world had just shifted – hers and her husband's.

Her heart pounded slowly inside her narrow rib cage, and she shook her head. 'Leesil is upstairs, asleep in his bed.'

'No.' Gavril looked in her eyes. 'He is gone.'

Nein'a closed her large eyes. Leesil had abandoned them?

'Darmouth will hang us from the keep walls,' Gavril

said, and he pointed at her. 'Change, and grab weapons. I will retrieve our store of coins.'

Of the three of them, one always remained in the house. The only exception was when she was called to one of Darmouth's evening gatherings and remained under her lord's watchful eyes. Only then were her husband and son both free to leave their home. Gavril sometimes took Leesil to a little inn at the backside of the merchant district. But one of them was always a hostage to ensure the others' obedience. Yet Leesil, her son, had fled the city of Venjètz.

'Where did you hear this?' she asked.

'Byrd warned me and —'

'How did he know?'

'There's no time,' Gavril said too sharply. 'We must run!'

He hurried out of the kitchen.

Nein'a followed him upstairs, but before she ducked into their room she went to Leesil's. It was empty, and the covers lay rustled. Chap was nowhere to be seen. She suppressed panic, turning cold inside, and rushed back to her own room.

She tore open her dress, snapping off buttons, and let it drop upon the floor. Standing naked in the cold room, she looked briefly toward the rear window. Their lord and master's massive keep loomed offshore in the lake. She hurried to gather clothing for a cold night's travel. Then she spotted something lying upon their bed.

Nein'a snatched up the small drawstring pouch. It was full of silver shils and pennies. A sharp pain rose in her chest as if she had been stabbed. Leesil had left this for them. Did it mean he'd been forced to leave? Had he planned for this?

When she glanced back to the open door, Gavril was climbing onto the railing of the stairs to the third floor. He reached for the hallway's ceiling lantern.

When Nein'a had breeches, a wool shirt, and boots on, she kicked the dress under the bed and retrieved a cloth-wrapped bundle from beneath the dresser. The last thing she grabbed was a charcoal wool cloak. By the time she stepped out, Gavril stood before her with another small pouch in hand. He reached out and gently touched her arm.

'Leesil was spotted hiding in a wagon beyond the city wall. The alarm was sounded, and the wall patrol has been alerted. We'll never get out that way. We have to go back inside the keep.'

She knew what he suggested, and the risk was great. 'The guards at the bridge gatehouse may be alerted as well. We will be caught in the open.'

'We have no choice. Our only hope waits in the belly of that keep.'

He was correct, and she knew it.

They slipped out the kitchen door and into the night. Darmouth's keep stood out upon the lake, its tower braziers casting burning reflections upon the water.

'Why would Leesil do this?' Nein'a whispered, pulling her cloak tighter.

Gavril's voice was soft as he gestured toward the keep. 'I think our son could bear no more.'

Nein'a looked up. With her elven night sight, she could see clearly and did not need the orange light of the tower braziers. A limp corpse in a cream robe hung upon the nearest wall. For an instant she felt the cold stab in her chest once again.

'He left us to die because an old scholar was hanged?'

Gavril's softness vanished. 'Leesil wasn't meant for this life, but you insisted . . .'

Nein'a knew the words hanging on his stilled tongue. She had been the one to insist on their son's training, though Gavril would have preferred Leesil remain nothing but a hostage, the leash Darmouth used to bind them. She had trained their son in the ways of her caste, the *Anmaglâhk*.

There was no time left to defend or regret what was past. Nein'a grabbed Gavril's hand and hurried along the water's edge toward the bridge. They fled toward the keep and their only chance of living through the night.

1

'Where is that girl?' Magiere muttered. 'And that conniving four-footer?'

'Wynn and Chap will be along,' Leesil answered. 'The day's almost gone, so we might as well stay in the city one more night.'

Leesil didn't look at Magiere and barely heard her impatient footfalls smack upon the wet street behind him. Instead, he stared out the massive northern gate of Soladran, the northernmost city in the nation of Stravina. As he raised his eyes to the distant snow-covered peaks of the Crown Range, his gaze passed over the forested foothills of Lord Darmouth's province at the eastern side of the Warlands.

He closed his wool cloak against the late afternoon chill as a gust of wind slipped through the stone archway with its massive timber gates swung wide. The wind rustled his hood, and he tucked escaping strands of white-blond hair back into hiding.

Full winter had come during their long trek up the continent. Patches of lingering snowfall marked the ground inside and outside of the city walls, and lightly dusted the shake-and-thatch roofs of the nearest shops and other buildings. The open land beyond the gate sloped down to a wide ice-fringed stream running east to west. On the water's far side, the ground rose to an open field of browned wild grass partially matted by the earlier cold rain. Farther out was the tree line of firs and pines marking the edge of the foothills.

There lay the forested reaches of Darmouth's domain within the Warlands, still and quiet below a gray sky. The naïve might find the sight serene, but it was a deceit to the eyes, and Leesil knew it. Across the border stream waited the haunts of his first life.

Son and slave, spy and assassin.

Never walk backward through your own life. At least, that was the truism Leesil made up for this moment, but he had little choice if he was to continue his search.

No visible road ran out from the gate, and no matching path could be seen on the border stream's far side. Sparse travel and trade came here from the north. None of the Stravinan border guards in their white tabards and fur-trimmed helmets stepped beyond the gate's threshold. The citizens of Soladran didn't even glance out the opening as they went about their daily routines. The opening of the gate each morning was a ritual rather than a necessity to the life of the city.

Leesil was so absorbed that he barely noticed Magiere cease pacing. She peered at him around the side of his hood with an impatient scowl, and then followed his gaze toward the tree-shrouded land and the white-capped mountains beyond. Leesil turned his eyes just enough to watch her search for whatever had captured his attention.

Her wool cloak's hood lay in bunched rolls across her shoulders, and her black hair was pulled back by a leather thong into a dangling tail. She glared out the gate, dark brown eyes in a face too pale for the living. In profile, her nose ran straight and long down to the clean, neatly chiseled wedge of her mouth, lips barely tinted with life compared to her complexion. Her scowl faded in realization.

Magiere's smooth brow furrowed again but not in irritation. She put her hand firmly upon his far cheek to pull his face toward her. Her voice was soft yet firm.

'Quick and quiet, as always. No one will know we passed.' Her hand slid down against the chest of his hauberk. 'I'll let no one out there touch you.'

Leesil tried to smile for her but couldn't.

Fleeing her homeland of Droevinka had been hard for Magiere, much as she openly detested the place. He'd made her understand why they had to leave so quickly.

In a clearing near Apudâlsat, deep in the southeast of Droevinka, Magiere had faced the mad necromancer Ubâd. In all the years since the night of her birth, he'd awaited her return. Ubâd had called up something old and forgotten in the shape of massive black coils like a serpent. By all Leesil could guess, the necromancer's minions — or those of the coils among the trees — still searched for Magiere. And so she'd fled north with Leesil all the way through Stravina.

Now the province of Leesil's old lord and master, Darmouth, lay before them. Leesil knew it was now his time to return 'home' if they were to find passage by land through the untracked Crown Range and into the territory of his mother's people, the Elven Territories. Somewhere in that hidden realm, his mother might still wait. Cuirin'nên'a — Nein'a, as his father had called her — was a prisoner of her own people.

And if his mother survived . . . if she hadn't died

because her son had fled slavery . . . then what of his father, Gavril?

'Leesil?'

Startled, he looked at Magiere. She now faced inward toward the city, and he followed her gaze.

Leesil saw nothing but people on their way to some-where else. They wandered or strode purposefully in and out of shops and stalls along the main way from the gate. But one short figure dodged awkwardly through the others, drawing closer by the moment.

Wynn Hygeorht looked like a younger sister dressed in the oversize hand-me-downs of an elder brother. The heavy sheepskin coat over her short robe was too large for her small frame, and the coat's hood had slipped down. She tried to hold the collar closed with one hand while the other gripped the bunched top of a canvas sack slung over her shoulder. The bouncing bundle threatened to unbalance her small frame as she hopped around puddles. Beside her trotted Chap, breath steaming in the air, paws muddied, and his silver-gray fur damp across his back. The two must have been caught in the morning rain while doing errands.

Street activity increased to a flurry, as if Wynn's passing stirred up an ever-multiplying warren of rabbits. People gathered in clusters, speaking quickly before scampering off to join others. Shopkeepers slipped out their front doors, and hawkers halted their carts. Passersby spoke with them, gestures emphatic, but neither would-be customer nor merchant showed interest in goods or services.

Wynn skidded to a stop before Leesil, and the canvas sack jostled and nearly toppled her into the mud. She caught her footing before Leesil had to grab her. Her round olive-toned cheeks glowed from the cold, and her small mouth was obscured by her hand clenching the coat's collar. Her wide brown eyes blinked rapidly. When she released the collar, Leesil saw the worry on her round face.

'Where have you been?' Magiere asked. 'The day was long when you ran off, and now it's all but gone!'

Wynn's mouth gaped. Her strange fright vanished with a clench of her delicate jaw, and she turned on Magiere. Leesil winced before Wynn snapped out her first word.

'You knew it would take time to find a courier! I have to return finished journals to the guild in Bela, and there are few enough caravans on the move in winter. So what did you expect? Not to mention finding any cartographer who could show us a way through the mountains. And I needed more paper, ink, and supplies for my work.'

Leesil let out a slow sigh, though the two women didn't notice.

Bitterness had grown between Magiere and Wynn. It started in the Apudâlsat forest when Magiere beheaded a vampire named Chane – whom Wynn had foolishly befriended. Since then, Leesil had tried to keep the peace, but sooner or later any 'discussion' between these two erupted into petty bickering. Leesil would pull Magiere aside while Chap herded Wynn the other way, but the long trek and deepening winter had worn Leesil's patience thin. Before he could cut loose with a tongue-lashing, Chap shoved himself between the two women, snarling at both.

Near a guards' hut to the street's side, a chattering

cluster of city folk fell silent and backed away. Two border guards lowered their spears and took steps toward the dog.

'Enough, Chap.' Leesil touched the dog's back and cast a warning glance at Magiere and Wynn. 'I think they catch your meaning . . . or they'd better.'

Wynn clenched her lips, eyes closing, as Magiere looked away with a scoff. The two guards returned to their post as Chap settled to a low grumble.

'Did you find us a map?' Leesil asked. 'Or some clue to a way through the mountains and into the elven lands?'

Wynn rolled her little shoulders, shaking off anger as well as her sack of acquired goods. The canvas bundle dropped to the ground.

'There is a passage into the lower reaches, but few have gone beyond and none of those have ever returned. The master cartographer let me copy what little there was in her records, since no one ever asks for or commissions a map to a place no one wants to journey.'

Wynn pulled a folded parchment out of her coat and handed it to Leesil. He turned it in his hand but didn't open it. Another quarter moon would pass before they needed the map, and judging by Wynn's words, it didn't promise much help.

'That doesn't sound good,' Magiere said.

'And?' Leesil replied.

'I'm not saying . . .' Magiere returned quickly. 'I would never —'

'No one before had Chap along to find a way,' Wynn offered.

Chap huffed agreement, and Leesil looked down into

the dog's crystalline eyes. An old memory from youth surfaced into Leesil's thoughts.

His mother sat upon the bedroom window ledge in their house, wrapped in a thick russet dressing gown. Her white-blond hair fell straight and glistening down her back, and she stroked it slowly with a rowan-wood comb. Slender and tall in the evening light, with the forest across a lake in the distance outside, she looked like a young oak growing alone in a barren field far from the other trees.

Nein'a turned, exposing a sleek triangular face with a narrow chin and a caramel complexion deeper than Leesil's own. She raised one feathery eyebrow above her oversize and almond-shaped eyes, like some lithe and long-boned forest creature trapped in the world of humans. Unearthly, large amber irises like coals in a furnace focused upon Leesil as she spoke.

'*Léshil?*'

Leesil shook himself, clearing Chap's memory play from his thoughts. 'I told you never to do that. Stay out of my head!'

Chap licked his nose.

Given all the time since first discovering the dog's true nature, Leesil was certain it was some rude gesture.

'It is his way of communicating,' Wynn argued.

'It's far more than that,' Magiere grumbled.

Wynn turned another spiteful glare at her. 'He is anxious as well to find Leesil's mother!'

Leesil suppressed a groan as the squabbling began again.

If they'd only get the true matter over with, once and for all, though even that might not settle things. They were both stubborn, or perhaps Magiere's pigheadedness had worn off on the young sage. Either way, Wynn was idealistic to the point of delusion. Her deceit over Chane's trailing all of them into Droevinka wouldn't be forgotten by Magiere – or by Leesil.

'It's no surprise,' came a deep, gravelly voice. 'Except that this time it took so long for them to jump for each other's throats.'

The words took Leesil by surprise. He spun about, wondering who in this faraway place knew his companions that well. Neither of the two men was familiar to him.

'But will it spread, Colonel?' the younger man asked the elder.

Both were dressed as Stravinan border guards in crestless white tabards over padded armor. They wore furlined capes, vambraces, and metal-scaled gloves, as well as plain polished armor for their shoulders and lower legs. Thin prongs of gold sprouted a finger's length above the noseguards of their fur-trimmed helmets – one for the younger and three for the colonel. The only other distinguishing mark was the elder's blue sash running from his left shoulder across his thick torso. His gray chin-beard was too long to be stylish. The taller and younger one's sandy-blond hair hung long across his shoulders out the bottom of his helmet.

'Unlikely,' replied the colonel. 'They've been in civil unrest for a century or more. They're no threat to any beyond their borders, unless they cease squabbling and unify . . . and that's unlikely.'

'If war spreads from there,' said the younger, with a disgusted shake of his head, 'someone else can attend it. Stravina has stood long enough against the Warlands' disorder. Let Belaski face the south, as we've borne enough vigilance for them up here.'

'This is what I tried to tell you when I arrived,' Wynn said. 'Before I was interrupted.'

Leesil turned back to her, at a loss to understand the conversation between the two officers.

'War,' Wynn explained. Her glance at Magiere was quick and nervous. 'Civil war has erupted in Droevinka.'

Magiere's expression flattened.

She turned south, as if her gaze could cut through the city and reach all the way to a small village left far behind.

'Aunt Bieja . . .' Magiere whispered. 'Leesil, I know I promised you, but we have to get to my aunt —'

'We cannot,' Wynn cut in. 'It would take a moon or more to reach Droevinka again, let alone get to Chemestúk amid . . .'

The sage's words faded at Magiere's hardened expression. Leesil slipped one shoulder into Magiere's way.

'What's happened?' he asked.

Wynn shook her head. 'I overheard but a little while bartering with a wagon master from Vudran, Stravina's capital. The Sclävên allied with several minor houses and put the Droevinkan capital to siege. Another major house may have joined them. Rumors say they may succeed in casting out the Äntes and their reigning Grand Prince.' Her next words were slow in coming. 'It started only days after we fled from Ubâd's forest. We stayed so far from settlements that we missed any word of what was happening. News travels too slowly to know for certain all that has occurred.'

Leesil didn't see how their own actions or stealthy

flight connected to the outbreak of civil war, but the timing disturbed him. When he said as much, Magiere's panic increased.

'I have to go back,' she insisted.

'Wynn is right,' Leesil argued. 'It won't help. And I'd wager your aunt is already long gone.'

Magiere's puzzlement was matched by Wynn's, and Leesil touched Magiere's arm as he confessed.

'The morning we left Chemestúk, I gave Bieja a letter of introduction to Karlin and Caleb back in Miiska, with enough coin to get her there. I told her there's a home for her at the Sea Lion tavern with us, though right off she took it as an insult and —'

'Why haven't you told me . . . in all this time?' Magiere asked, and her tone was disturbingly quiet.

Leesil barely turned his cringe into a shrug, wishing her ire were still aimed at Wynn. 'I didn't know if it would lead to anything. The women of your blood are more rigid than a dead deity. But Bieja's cunning. I think she'd follow my advice in the face of what's happening.'

'He is correct, Magiere,' Wynn added. 'Your aunt could well be in Miiska by now, or reach there long before you returned to Chemestúk. There is nothing we can do, and your turning back within reach of Ubâd's people will not help her.'

'And what if they go looking for her,' Magiere replied, 'as a way to find me? Ubâd was there at my birth, and if he —'

Chap rumbled so deeply that they all turned their attention downward. His gaze locked only upon Magiere, and she froze for a moment, then flinched. Leesil suppressed an urge to swipe at the dog.

'You stay out of her head as well!'

'No, it's all right.' Magiere shivered briefly and swallowed hard. 'He's reminding me . . . of the clearing near Apudâlsat. Ubâd probably had my village watched for years and gave up on it long ago. When he learned that I was heading toward him, it's unlikely he'd have told anyone to watch the village again . . . before he died.'

She'd told Leesil what happened in the clearing, from Chap's frenzied slaughter of the necromancer to the massive specter of black coils circling in the forest. In Leesil's own imagining, it was disturbing in many ways how vicious and terrified that apparition had made Chap. In turn, fear for Magiere had ridden Leesil ever since.

Magiere shot him a narrow side glance, and Leesil cringed again.

'I'd appreciate it,' she began softly, tone sharpening with each word, 'if you would stop keeping these little arrangements to yourself!'

Before Leesil fumbled out another excuse, a bellowing tone carried through the air from behind him. A border guard atop the stone wall to the gate's east side blew two more times upon a curved ashen horn. Beside the man stood several comrades and two figures in pale blue tabards over dark wool robes with full cowls. One cowled figure pointed over the wall to the north.

People nearby drifted toward the gate, and several guards politely urged them to stay back. Leesil pressed forward, his companions close behind him. He saw nothing but the still landscape across the border stream.

'What's happening?' he called to the two Stravinan officers.

The elder colonel ignored him, eyes fixed upon the distant tree line as he uttered low commands to his men. The younger officer looked Leesil over, perhaps appraising him as a stranger. Leesil knew his tan skin and amber eyes were out of place, though his raised hood hid his oblong ears and most of his hair.

'More refugees on their way,' the young captain replied. 'The *Sluzhobnék Sútzits* brought word last evening.'

Wynn tugged on Leesil's cloak. 'I do not understand. Why did he call those robed people "menials"?'.

Belaskian was the most common language, even in Stravina, where its own tongue was used only in remote backlands or by old-blood nobles who thought such things mattered. As much as Wynn had learned the tongue surprisingly well, there were still nuances she didn't catch.

'Not menials,' Magiere muttered. '*Sútzit* – minister or servant.'

'The Servants of Compassion,' Leesil added with disdain. 'Priests.'

To Leesil, religion was somewhere between annoying and tyrannical. It was little more than politics shrouded in the trappings of faith and justified by doctrine surrounding a touted deity or patron saint. These 'Servants' were the least offensive Leesil knew of, though he couldn't remember their patron's name. Respected healers, they followed the teachings of a long-dead wanderer from a time when only scant settlements across the land marked where future countries would be born. Leesil avoided religious minions and, at the moment, had less tolerance than usual for sermons. He looked back through the open gate, and a flicker of movement near the distant tree line caught his attention.

A figure surged across the flat grass field – it was a woman in drab peasant garb. Two smaller forms followed. Judging by their height and the way they shadowed the woman, they were children in her charge. A pair of medium-size figures came next, a boy and girl, who rushed ahead of the others.

The younger officer took a step toward the gate's opening. His colonel clamped a hand on the man's shoulder and pulled him back.

'You will not breach the border, Captain!'

The tall captain jerked away. 'Sir . . . I can't stand by and watch this again.'

The old colonel leaned in, growling into his subordinate's face. 'There's war in the south as is, and I won't have you starting one here. This isn't the first time, and it won't be the last, so bite your lip and be still! Until the refugees cross the border, we cannot interfere.'

'Interfere with what?' Magiere called out.

The colonel ignored her, but the captain cocked his head. His long face, reddened by the cold, was clenched, showing that it took all his effort to keep silent and obey his superior. Leesil saw the man's left eye twitch before he looked away, snapping orders to guards now gathered beside the gate.

Leesil watched more figures emerge from the distant trees, running as they came. In his youth within the Warlands, he'd seen people reach for a better life. He'd been forced more than once to take it from them. No matter how he'd sympathized with their plight, there was always Darmouth's hold upon him, his mother, and his father. They . . . he had done things for lord and master that left him with years of nightmares.

'Leesil, what's this about?' Magiere asked.

The first mounted soldier broke from the trees after the escaping prey.

'A slaughter,' Leesil whispered.

Chap watched the chase unfold upon the field. Two full-grown men were among the fleeing peasants, bringing up the rear. The rest were women, children, and an elder boy and girl old enough to run ahead of the pack. Five riders had cleared the trees so far and sped after their quarry. Armored in leather and mail, their shields were slung upon the sides of their mounts, and each wielded a long-hafted mace with a narrow iron head.

A gust of wind blew through the city gate.

It struck Chap squarely in the face. He blinked sharply as his spirit shivered with a declaration. His kin – the Fay – spoke into his being through the chill air.

Do not interfere! This event does not bear upon your purpose.

Not so, or should we keep one from the Enemy – Chap looked briefly to Magiere before his gaze fell upon Leesil – *only to lose the other to his past?*

Leesil stood motionless, staring across the field. The wind pulled at his hood until strands of his white-blond hair whipped around his face.

If need be, then let it be so. The child of the dead is foremost.

Across the field, the lead rider reversed his mace. He struck down with its butt upon the back of one fleeing man, who tumbled out of sight into the grass.

Chap snarled through clenched jaws, but the sound was lost in exclamations from the loose crowd about him. He turned a tight and agitated circle, and then focused on Leesil's cold expression and unblinking eyes. Chap's awareness caught a memory surfacing in his companion's thoughts. Leesil's shame washed through Chap as he saw into a moment of Leesil's past – saw it through Leesil's own eyes.

A nightfall meeting of tradesmen and townsfolk gathered in the shop room of a local tannery. They muttered curses for their suffering, and it was not long before talk turned to how to end their ruler's tyranny. Leesil looked away from their angry faces and deafened his ears to their frustration. It had taken a whole season to gain the trust of a contact and be invited among them at this meeting. A shuttered lantern in hand, he inched toward the tannery's rear door, watching for anyone who might look his way. When he was certain he moved unnoticed, Leesil cracked the rear door and slipped out into the dark street beyond.

He opened the lantern's shutter, freeing its light, and set it on the ground before turning down the nearest side street. A handful of heartbeats passed before the quickening sound of hooves and footfalls grew louder. No one within the tannery heard the soldiers coming until it was too late.

At the sound of the shattering tannery door, Leesil ducked around a stable, pressing himself flat against its timber wall. Steel clattered and the townsfolk screamed. Leesil did not look back nor move until the night became silent again.

A rumble shuddered in Chap's chest as Leesil's memory faded, leaving only lingering misery. There was so much that Leesil carried within, and Chap feared a return to the half-elf's past might break him. Chap followed his companion's blank stare across the field to the struggling flight of the older boy and girl. And Leesil's guilt lingered in him. Chap flattened his ears as he lashed back at his kin.

In the time of the humans' Forgotten, the ancestors of the flesh I wear stood with those who opposed the Enemy. We fought beside them . . . for them.

His kin offered no sympathy.

Only to preserve balance. Only to preserve this world as a whole. This is not such a time – but a blink in eternity – and you let mortality corrupt you. This is no more than Life itself, predator and prey in the cycle of survival. You would save an instant and risk losing all time!

The pounding of hooves carried to Chap's ears.

A lead rider closed on a trailing peasant woman. His mace arced down, and Chap heard the distant crack as its iron head broke the back of her skull. She pitched forward and slammed down limp into the grassy earth.

The mace arced upward, trailing blood and torn hair.

Chap snarled so loudly it drowned all other sounds from his own ears. His spirit threw a spiteful reply back to his kin.

Cower in your Eternity, if you wish . . . I do not agree!

Wynn shuddered, though she did not know if it was from the chill breeze or what she saw upon the field. Even so, spite smoldered inside her toward Magiere. Chane was gone. Magiere, with her irrational instincts, had killed him. Wynn could not let go of her pain.

A gust blew through the gate. The shiver of her small frame increased, and an ache expanded sharply in her head.

A multitude of voices speaking in sync came from too far away to hear – or was she hearing them? It sounded more like the buzz of insect wings or the rustle of autumn leaves through an orchard. It filled her awareness until she became dizzy, like the night that . . .

This had happened to her once before.

Chap paced before her in agitation, fur on the back of his neck standing up. As Wynn watched him, she heard – felt – a lone set of insect wings or one single rustling leaf answer back to the others.

A rider out in the field struck down a fleeing man with the butt of his mace.

Wynn saw Chap's muzzle wrinkle back from clenched teeth, but any sound he made was smothered by the curses and gasps of people in the street. A lone buzz of wing or leaf sounded in Wynn's head as Chap turned in circles that made her vision spin for an instant. What was he doing? She stood still, no longer shivering, and not wishing to move at all in the vertigo passing through her, sickeningly reminiscent of the night in Droevinka when she'd foolishly used thaumaturgy to give herself mantic sight . . . to see the elemental Spirit layer of the world.

Chap's snarl came late behind the curses of several border guards. Ears flattened, the dog lunged forward, and two startled guards backstepped as he spun to face Leesil.

The single leaf-wing buzzed in Wynn's head with a deafening roar.

She clenched her eyes and covered her mouth against a dry heave. A realization fought its way over the nausea turning rock-hard in her stomach. That sensation in her skull, that single thrash of leaf-wing countering the chorus of the others . . .

It had come from Chap.

Chap lunged forward, snapping and snarling. Two Stravinan guards leaning into the gateway jerked back out of his way. He closed off his awareness of his kin and spun to face those in his charge and care.

Wynn stood silent, a hand over her mouth, staring at him in panic.

Magiere's pale features were strained around black-ened irises as she clutched Leesil's wrist in a tight grip.

Leesil's breath came hard and fast.

Chap did not need to dip into Leesil's memories. He still felt shame pouring over him from the half-elf.

'We can't take mounted soldiers in the open,' Magiere warned.

Chap's frustrated bark stuttered into a growl of anger.

Leesil pulled from Magiere's grip and shouted, 'Go!'

Before the word faded from the air, the border stream's fringe ice shattered beneath Chap's paws. He splashed through chill water, racing up the slope and into the field.

'Chap . . . Leesil, no!' Magiere shouted, too late.

The dog hit the stream at a full run. Leesil breached the gate before anyone could stop him, slinging his cloak aside as he ran.

Fear for Leesil flooded through Magiere, but then anger boiled with a hunger rising in her throat as she turned on Wynn. Before Magiere could say a word, Wynn jumped as if startled. She looked pale, almost sickly, but she met Magiere's gaze.

'You stay put!' Magiere commanded, and her own words sounded guttural and slurred.

'Magiere,' Wynn said, eyes wide and round, 'you must control yourself.'

The cloud-streaked sky and the whites of Wynn's eyes burned Magiere's sight worse than snow under a brilliant sun. Everything was far too bright, and she felt tears slide down her cheeks as a dull ache filled her jaw.

'Magiere!' Wynn called.

Magiere backed one step toward the gate. She felt the cold on her face and stripped off her cloak to let it fall. Chill air helped settle her. The clouded sky above the city remained sharp but less bright. It no longer pained her vision as she pulled her dhampir nature under control.

'Stop her,' commanded a rough voice.

A large hand settled on Magiere's shoulder. She instinctively slammed her elbow back, and it sank into padding beneath leather. The man stumbled clear as she veered toward the gate. Two more guards stepped in her way. The first drew his saber, shrugging his cloak back.

'We are not Stravinan,' Wynn shouted from behind Magiere. 'There is no risk of a war declaration if she crosses the border.'

At that, the second guard hesitated and looked with uncertainty to the bearded colonel. The other guard stepped forward with his sword drawn. Magiere readied to charge, and then the young captain grabbed the man by the wrist of his sword arm.

'Captain, you heard my order,' snapped the colonel, and he stepped in behind the first hesitant guard. 'There'll be no proof we're blameless if anyone interferes on foreign soil.'

Magiere caught something strange passing over the tall captain's face. Beneath the front lip of his helmet, his brow wrinkled at his superior's words. For an instant he seemed confused. His expression smoothed just as quickly.

'Too late for that,' he answered. 'The man and that dog have seen to it.'

He heaved his grip upon the guard with the saber, and the man stumbled sideways, off balance.

Magiere rushed forward, shouldering the hesitant guard as she passed. He stumbled back into the colonel, and the two tangled long enough for her to clear the gate. She drew her falchion at a full run.

Chap was well ahead on the field, and Leesil raced up the stream's far slope. Magiere let hunger rise in her throat, and her stride quickened as she splashed through the border stream.

This wasn't the first time Leesil had thrown himself into a dangerous situation for an innocent, but he'd never done so on this scale. And the look on his face as he jerked free of her grip – like a suffering panic had pushed him into blind rage. She'd seen him determined in anger, or most often coldly vicious when necessary. Now he charged blindly at armed riders?

It was stupid madness! What had gotten into him?

Magiere saw the older boy and girl ahead of the other fleeing refugees. Both staggered to a halt in fear at the sight of Chap charging toward them. A rider closed quickly behind them, horse mace whirling at his side. Magiere was about to shout when the girl darted away, fleeing from the oncoming dog. The rider pulled his reins hard against his horse's neck, veering after her.

Magiere looked across the field, searching all directions, but Leesil had vanished from sight.

From all around Wynn, the sounds and sights of imminent battle filled her senses.

Border guards scrambled to assemble beside the gate under the young captain's commands, as the elder colonel glared out to the field, his teeth clenched. A cluster of pikemen came first, followed by archers. The two priests appeared as well, accompanied by a third. The colonel shoved them back as they tried to hurry out the gate ahead of his men. The gathering obscured Wynn's view, and she lost sight of Magiere, Leesil, or Chap.

'No one breaches the border!' shouted the colonel as the pikemen rushed out. 'Hold, unless the enemy enters the stream. Get the refugees to safety once they reach our shore.'

Wynn could not stand there and wait, doing nothing. She snatched up her canvas sack and scurried over to stash it at the base of the city wall. As the priests stepped in behind the archers heading out, she followed. The colonel grabbed her by the arm.

'Not you,' he said sharply. 'It's enough those priests are always meddling.'

'I have some skill at tending the ill and injured,' Wynn retorted, and tried to pull free of his grasp. 'I can help. If this is as dire as you think, then you need all the help you can find.'

'Not you!' he repeated. 'No more outlander nonsense.'

'Let her be . . . sir,' came the young captain's voice.

Wynn twisted about to find him standing within

reach, gaze locked on his superior with only barely contained resentment.

Saber drawn, he now carried a round shield painted white with a slanted blue bar across it. Long-faced and long-limbed, he was so tall beneath his furred cloak that Wynn's head would not reach his shoulder. Blond hair trailed from beneath his polished helm with its gold prong above the noseguard. He appeared like an armored autumn tree, perhaps an ash, like those of Wynn's homeland, and he waited for his thinly polite demand to be answered.

The old colonel's full attention was on his subordinate. 'You've enough to answer for —'

'And so will you, *sir*,' the captain cut in. 'If she's an outlander, then we've no right to stand in her way.'

'Unless she's a threat to the safety of our people.'

'I am no threat to you,' Wynn shouted. 'I must find my friends, and I can help with those fleeing for refuge. Now release me!'

The colonel stared down into Wynn's eyes. 'Your friends caused enough trouble for one day.'

'She had no part in that,' snapped the captain. 'Let her go, sir, or I won't be the only one facing a tribunal when this is over.'

For a moment all Wynn heard was the soft clench of the captain's gloved hand upon the hilt of his saber. He stared so intently at his superior that Wynn could not look away to see the colonel's reaction.

The colonel released Wynn's arm and shoved her forward. She stumbled toward the captain, who took a tense step in her direction until she righted herself and turned about.

The colonel's cold look was for the captain alone.

Abruptly he turned away to the remaining men around the gate.

'Archers to the slope!'

'If you're coming,' said the captain, and Wynn whirled to face him, 'then get moving. But you, girl, stay behind the lines.'

As he headed out the gate, Wynn rushed to join him. 'Thank you . . . Captain. And my name is Wynn.'

The captain cocked one eyebrow. A smile began to form on his lips, but it never quite appeared.

'Stàsiuo,' he returned. 'But my sisters call me Stasi. Now do as I say . . . Wynn.'

Magiere veered left after the girl's blind flight, and Chap and the mounted soldier closed rapidly at an angle. The soldier swung his mace over from the far side, but Chap was well out of reach. The dog leaped at full speed for the horse's head.

Chap's jaws closed on dangling reins below the horse's jaw, but his head slammed into the side of the horse's face. The mount twisted, jerking sharply away from the impact. The sudden motion slung Chap under the horse's neck like a pendulum.

His body arced upward on the far side. The horse screamed in panic and jerked back the other way. Chap's momentum and weight snapped the reins in half, and the sudden release tossed him into the air.

Magiere saw Chap squirm to right himself. He came down, hitting the earth on his back with a yelp. The sudden release from the dog's weight threw the horse off balance, and it lost its footing. The rider leaped clear as the animal fell and skidded over the winter grass.

Magiere passed close to the older boy, who stood staring after his fleeing companion. When he started to go after the girl, Magiere grabbed the back of his coat, spun about, and flung him in the direction of the stream. He tumbled across the ground through a patch of lingering snow.

'Run, you idiot!' she shouted, not waiting to see if he obeyed.

The soldier that Chap had downed was on his feet again, running after the girl. Shouts and other sounds of flight and panic followed behind Magiere as she bolted after the girl and her pursuer. Earth-shuddering hooves grew louder behind her.

As the girl scurried toward the distant border stream, the soldier jerked a triangular battle dagger from a sheath on his hip. His horse mace was still gripped in his other hand. Magiere let hunger drive her, and then a familiar howl filled her ears.

Chap raced by on her right, heading back the way she had come. Magiere didn't break stride at the whinny of a horse behind her, and then the thunder of its hooves faltered. She glanced back once to see Chap clinging to its neck, trying to down it. There was no time to help him or watch the outcome, and she kept on. The soldier closed the gap on the fleeing girl, but when he caught sight of Magiere, he slowed and turned to face her.

His dagger was too high, aimed at her face. He swung the mace, and Magiere caught it at the base of her falchion. When he thrust with the dagger, she slapped it upward with her free hand, then clenched her fist and struck.

The crack of Magiere's fist against his face was so

loud it startled her. The force threw him backward off his feet, and he spun a full turn before landing on his back. She dropped on him, pinning his arms with her knees before he could roll away. Magiere gripped the falchion with both hands, its wide point posed above the soldier's chest.

And she froze.

He was young – too young. No more than a year or two beyond Geoffry, who'd helped serve in her tavern. His face was split across the cheekbone from her fist, and blood had smeared down to his jaw. No anger or fear showed in his eyes, not even resolve for his own death. He lay limp beneath her as if relieved that he no longer had to fight.

Mail vest and underpadding sagged on his thin frame, and were likely made for someone stouter. He wore no other armor, and his leggings were faded and over-patched. Dark rings of fatigue surrounded his young eyes, and his cheeks were sallow and sunken with hunger.

Yet he was here, killing women and children.

Magiere lashed out with her fist, cracking him across the jaw.

His body jerked once as his head whipped sideways, and then his eyes rolled as he went limp. There was no time to wonder what instinct made her to leave him alive. Magiere lunged to her feet and snatched up the horse mace, kicking the dagger out of reach.

The girl still fled for the border, now joined by the boy. Even the young soldier's mount had run off. Ahead of the fleeing children, riders harried the other refugees. Chap's angered howl carried across the field from among them.

Magiere turned away, searching the grassy field for any sign of Leesil.

Wynn shifted from one foot to the other behind the line of six archers upslope from the stream. Below, a matched number of pikemen stood their ground one pace back from the water's edge. Captain Stasi paced behind them, speaking to each with a pat of a shoulder or a nod, but his voice was too low for Wynn to hear. She would have appreciated a few words of encouragement for herself.

At the far left end of the archers stood the priests, the *Sluzhobnék Sútzits*. Two stood back with their cowls down, a middle-aged woman and a young man. The younger shifted nervously like Wynn, while his mature companion remained as still as the third priest in front with his cowl still up. When the woman glanced toward Wynn, her cowled companion noticed and did likewise.

His features were hard to see, but Wynn made out the tuft of gray-white hair above his clean-shaven face. Though tall and straight, he moved slowly with the care of age as he gave her a polite nod and raised a hand in acknowledgment. Wynn returned the gesture, but her natural curiosity for all new things, particularly the people of this faraway land, remained dormant in the face of what lay before her. A distant scream pulled her gaze back across the stream.

'Hold until I say,' shouted Captain Stasi to his men.

A scattered group of women and children raced across the field toward the stream's far slope. Behind and closing were riders with long maces swinging wildly. The archers startled Wynn as they drew and set their first arrows. Her mouth went dry.

She had been with Leesil and Magiere on the road for several moons, yet the fights she had seen were not like this. Waiting and watching was worse in this moment than scrambling through a dank forest trying to save herself from ambling creatures of the dead. War was practically unknown in her homeland of Malourné across the ocean. She felt alone among the soldiers, until the first child nearly tumbled down the far slope and into the stream.

A second refugee splashed into the water, a woman, wailing out for sanctuary.

One pikeman upended his lance and inched forward. His boot toe cracked the stream's fringe ice and sank into running water.

'Keep coming!' he shouted.

He leaned forward, stretching out a gloved hand toward the thin little girl, perhaps ten or eleven. She floundered as her patched skirt soaked in the cold water.

The eldest priest hobbled downslope. His two companions rushed by him as the mounted riders charged over the lip of the far slope. A second woman cradling an infant in a wool blanket waded into the stream, followed by two young boys. They veered right at the pounding of hooves closing behind them.

Wynn could not move. Breath caught in her dry throat.

'Hold the line,' shouted Stasi, but he was already running along the shore toward the woman with the infant.

Wynn fixated upon the mother, no older than herself.

The woman's mouth gaped from gasping air as she trudged to midstream. One of her boys hesitated at the far side, too afraid to wade in. The other clutched his mother's skirt from behind as he sank chest-deep and was pulled sideways behind her by the current.

The flicker of a hand ax tumbling through the air pulled Wynn's gaze skyward. She never saw where it came from, but she called out, 'Captain . . . behind her!'

Captain Stasi charged into the stream halfway between a closing rider and the woman. He stretched upward with his shield. The ax, thrown from somewhere upslope, passed above the shield's edge and it struck the woman square in the back.

The young mother lurched, torso arching as she clutched the infant to her chest. Both boys cried out as she toppled facedown into the water, the infant trapped beneath her. Blood spread through her split sweater from the ax head embedded deep in her upper back.

Stasi's voice rang out over the shouts of his men. 'Let fly!'

Wynn cowered down beneath the thrum of bow-strings and arrows hissing through the air.

Magiere ran for the tree line with falchion and mace gripped in her hands. She passed another downed horse, still kicking. A deep gash had lamed one foreleg. Saddle strap split in two, a long wound opened the skin along its side to expose its rib cage. The animal's thrashing soaked its belly and the grass beneath it with dark red that steamed in the cold air.

The sight brought her a sickening hope. Leesil was still alive out here — somewhere.

Not far off, the dying mount's rider lay facedown. He didn't move, and Magiere hurried on.

Ahead in the distance, two soldiers dressed in motley clothes and armor crouched low on the ground. The tall unmatted grass nearer the trees made it impossible to see what they were doing, and Magiere's fear rose as she ran toward them.

They stood, lifting two bound refugees to their feet. Both captives were the full-grown men who'd been knocked down instead of killed.

Another rider cantered his mount out of the trees to the far right. Unlike the others, he was dressed as a fit officer in a black tabard over a gray quilted hauberk. A flash of white pulled Magiere's attention back toward the two motley soldiers.

Leesil lunged out of the tall grass, both of his winged punching blades unsheathed.

Their forward ends were shaped like flattened steel spades with elongated tips and sharpened edges. At their bases were crosswise oval openings, allowing the weapons to be gripped by their backsides for punching. A gradual wing curved back from the outside edge of each blade head and was the full length of his forearm, ending at his elbow.

He rushed the soldiers with their captives.

'Behind you!' shouted the officer, and he kicked his horse into a gallop, but the warning came too late for his men.

Leesil never broke stride. He drove his right blade tip into the first soldier's side and ripped the blade backward as he passed.

The man screeched as his side tore open. He grabbed

his wound, and his hands turned instantly red as he crumpled. His shrieks filled the air, but all Magiere saw was the frantic jerk and whip of the grass where he'd fallen.

The second man shoved his captive away and swung with his mace.

Leesil caught the weapon's haft on his raised left blade. The blade's wing slammed against his forearm before the mace slid away along the arc. He punched his right blade up below the man's jaw.

The soldier's neck and face split open. Blood splashed out as the blade exited at the back of his jaw. He dropped without a sound not far from his dying companion.

The mounted officer had nearly closed in on Leesil.

Magiere switched her falchion into her left hand, shifting the mace into her right. She threw the mace as Leesil dropped one punching blade and a stiletto appeared in his hand. He whirled with his arm cocked to throw, but Magiere's mace found its target first.

The mace's haft cracked against the officer's forearm, and he veered his mount. When Leesil threw his stiletto, the man was ready. He blocked with a raised shortsword, and the stiletto clanged away into the grass.

A second stiletto appeared in Leesil's hand. Magiere closed in, falchion ready.

The officer's attention shifted quickly between them, and then he glanced across the field toward the distant stream. He scowled with a hiss of breath at whatever he saw and jerked the reins. His mount wheeled, and he kicked it into a gallop toward the trees, abandoning what was left of his men.

Magiere trotted up to Leesil, aware of her pounding heart. She tried to speak but couldn't between panting breaths. His hands and arms were covered in blood. Spatters marked the front of his hauberk and the right side of his face. It streaked his long hair, as if he'd run through a red rain.

Leesil slashed the bonds of the two captive men, and both immediately ran in the direction of the border stream. After sheathing the stiletto, he picked up his fallen winged blade then crouched to snatch up a horse mace. He studied it with narrow eyes, squeezing its haft until his knuckles whitened.

He was quiet, and Magiere pushed aside a chill that ran through her at the sight of him. When she reached out to check him for wounds, he backed away with only the barest glance at the blood on his arms.

'None of it's mine,' he said, and turned across the field at a run for the border stream.

Magiere followed, close and silent.

Wynn lifted her head where she crouched. The woman priest thrashed through the stream after the dead mother's body floating off on the current. The one boy still clung to his mother's skirt and would not let go. Dragged along, he wailed between gulps of water filling his mouth while his little brother stood numbly silent on the far shore. The instant the priest blocked the body and flipped it over, a rider charged over the far slope. Captain Stasi splashed along the stream's far shore, directly in the horse's path.

Wynn ran downslope.

A Stravinan pikeman rushed into the stream as she hit the cold water herself. Her feet and calves numbed except for the painful ache that shot into her bones.

The pikeman pushed on after his captain as Wynn snatched the boy clinging to his mother's body.

'*Indurare'a Iulian!*' growled the priest as she turned frantically about in the stream, searching for something.

It was a language Wynn had never heard, but when she glanced at the overturned body, she understood. The mother's dead eyes stared up at the gray sky. Her arms floated at her sides, and the empty wool blanket clung to one. The infant was gone.

Wynn heaved the boy up as she trudged two steps toward the Stravinan side of the stream. She shoved him toward the shore. A horse's panicked whinny sounded behind her, and she turned. She caught a glimpse of the priest wading for the shore with something wrapped in the woman's arms. Wynn hoped fervently that it was the infant.

A pikeman's lance sliced a horse's neck as he tried to strike its rider. The spear head glanced off the rider's shield, and he struck down with his mace. The lance shaft snapped as the horse lunged forward. Captain Stasi was still in its path, and directly below him at the water's edge stood the other little boy watching his mother drift downstream.

The captain swung his shield, and its edge smashed hard against the horse's long head. The animal veered, and its footing gave on the steep slope, still wet from the morning's rain. Hindquarters pivoted sideways, slamming into the pikeman and flattening him as the animal toppled. The rider pitched forward, straight at the captain. On impact, both fell backward into the stream, and Wynn lost sight of them in the splash of flailing bodies.

And the little boy just stood there.

Wynn surged through the water. At midstream, the scuffle of a horse's hooves made her look up for an instant. Another rider crested the slope. An arrow protruded from his shoulder, yet he drove his mount downward. Wynn focused on the boy.

Each waterlogged step took too long, no matter how hard she worked her numb legs. When she reached out, the boy did not look at her. His eyes were as blank as his dead mother's. Wynn grabbed him by one arm as she heard a loud whoosh in the air. She looked up.

Wynn saw the mace, and the world slowed to silence as she watched it arcing toward her from the sky. Everything lurched back to full speed as something else slammed into her waist.

Her breath rushed out at the impact, and her vision wrenched into a frantic blur as she was thrown backward. Water splashed up around and over her, as her head and shoulders smacked against bare wet earth.

Blank sky was all Wynn saw. She lay half-out on the Stravina side of the stream, submerged from the waist down. Gasping for air, she pawed at her own head and face, but felt no wound, only the dull ache in her skull from falling. The mace had missed her.

Beside her lay the boy, looking back to the stream. His eyes suddenly widened in terror. He scrambled away, screaming as if something in the stream were more terrifying than watching his mother die.

Wynn rolled over to look. It climbed out of the water, feral eyes glimmering like crystals.

Chap shook himself and a cascade of droplets rained down upon Wynn. He had knocked her out of the mace's path. He padded quickly to her side, head swinging as he studied her. He was matted and wet, yet his face was still soaked in blood. His jowls wrinkled around half-open jaws, exposing teeth and fangs as he sniffed her.

Wynn stiffened.

Chap's face was that of a wolf fresh from a kill. He turned and splashed back through the stream under the sound of clattering steel and thrashing men and mounts.

A rider tried to flee upslope on foot until an arrow struck him in the thigh. He stumbled, grabbing the protruding shaft, and Chap fell upon him. The man went down with the dog at his throat. His scream broke and was lost in the waning clamor of the battle.

Wynn shrank back, turning away. The boy crawled up the wet bank on all fours. She climbed to her feet and hoisted him by the waist.

Chap's stained face and teeth mingled with the memory of a single leaf-wing in Wynn's numbed mind. She ran for the city gate without looking back.

Leesil stopped to look down upon the border stream. He heard Magiere right behind him.

Bodies of men and horses lay from one shore to the other, but only three of the Stravinan pikemen were down. One lay crushed beneath a toppled horse that finally went limp, and a young male priest knelt to close the dead man's eyes. The other two wounded border guards were hoisted to their feet by their comrades and supported as they hobbled toward the city gate. The tall captain oversaw the return of his men, his white tabard soaked and grimed, but otherwise he appeared unwounded.

Downstream, a young woman's corpse drifted away on the sluggish current with her slack face toward the clouded sky.

Leesil felt all the years since he'd fled his first life – son and slave, spy and assassin. He smothered that pain until he felt coldly numb inside. It was an old habit of survival now revived once again.

The snort of a horse called his attention.

One rider with a lamed leg heaved himself across a kneeling horse and jerked the reins to make the mount get up. The horse slipped again and again before its hooves dug into the wet embankment. It clambered to the slope top with the rider hunched over in the saddle.

Leesil pulled both winged blades and took two quick steps. Magiere moved into his path and braced her palm against his chest.

'No more!' she whispered harshly. 'Enough.'

He stared at her sweat-marked pale face and black hair. He breathed twice before true recognition settled through the need to finish the last of his task.

Whatever must be done, no witnesses – the first rule taught by mother and father. For the lives of each other, they'd smothered themselves cold inside . . . kept themselves secret and safe at any price.

'How am I to watch over you . . .' Magiere began, and her smooth brow wrinkled with an anger that would've hidden her fear from anyone but him. 'How . . . if you throw yourself into the path of anyone who'd want you dead? No more. You don't leave my side again!'

She hesitated as she lifted her hand from his chest. Leesil saw her white palm and fingers smeared with blood from his hauberk.

His stomach lurched. There was blood on her . . . from him.

'Leesil?' Magiere whispered, and her furrowed brow smoothed.

She looked at him with worry in her dark eyes, as if he were in danger and didn't see it for himself. He felt the spattered blood mixed with his own sweat beginning to dry into his skin and hair.

And he'd put it on her.

Magiere took a slow step toward him.

Leesil backed away. He jogged quickly down the slope, stepped into the stream, and waded toward the Stravinan side. He heard Magiere splash into the water close behind him.

How could he have brought her here, after all she had to bear from her own past?

He wanted to stop in the cold stream swirling around his legs, sink down, and let the icy water wash over him. Let it crush this sudden anguish out of him. But it would not help. For all the water he might pour over his flesh, or wine he swallowed to deaden his nightmares, there had always been blood on him. He could bear that.

But not on Magiere.

Leesil quickened his stride upslope toward the city. This was his homecoming, in the only way it could ever be.

2

Chane reined in his horse on a forested knoll and peered from the deep shadow of his cowl to the snow-patched field below. The sun dipped low behind the clouded horizon. The trees and his voluminous cloak shielded him from the light of dusk, but he still felt its prickle upon his skin. When he opened his senses wide, the scent of blood carried to him on the stiff breeze.

Across the distance to the Stravinan border, he saw the remains of a small battle. Leesil, Magiere, and Chap trudged through the aftermath toward the city. And there was Wynn, waiting within the open gates as her companions entered.

Chane's anxious worry faded upon seeing her; then the city gates swung closed in the dusk.

Welstiel pulled up his horse beside Chane's mount. 'What happened here?'

Chane shook his head in silence.

When they'd first met, Welstiel had meticulous grooming habits. In his early forties by appearance, he was of medium height and build with dark brown hair marked by stark white patches at his temples. Now uncombed locks hung in lank strands down his brow from under his own cowl. His fine wool cloak was faded and snagged from the many days of sleeping outside in a makeshift tent concealed with scavenged foliage.

Welstiel had changed much in the passing moons, but then so had Chane.

His own red-brown hair, nearly reaching his shoulders, hung limp around his face. He pulled at the wool scarf around his neck. Though he'd not seen his own reflection in a long while, he felt what was hidden there, and rubbed at the ridge of a scar encircling his throat. Less than a moon before, Magiere had severed his head. A ghost of that pain still haunted him. No matter how much he fed and focused his will, the mark remained branded on his pale undead flesh.

Welstiel had brought him back from this second death.

Chane's scheming companion had yet to say how. Was it an arcane secret of Welstiel's conjuration, the magics of the spirit side of existence? Or was it a little-known aspect of the Noble Dead that only Welstiel had uncovered . . . somewhere?

Welstiel's chestnut filly pawed the earth in the cold winter air. They had purchased new mounts a few nights past. Both struck Chane as too young, not nearly broken in, but at least they were swift.

'What now?' he asked, and immediately scowled at the sound of his own voice. He nearly had to shout just to make himself heard, and all that came out was a hoarse rasp of air. Where his neck was scarred, his voice was forever altered.

'Magiere will enter the Warlands,' Welstiel responded. 'We should know her general plans for the coming days. Have your new familiar find her whereabouts and see what you can learn.'

Chane's conjuring skill had refined since he'd risen as a Noble Dead. Creation and control of familiars was becoming a particular expertise. He experienced the world through their senses and commanded their actions to a limited degree.

Upon the rump of his horse beneath a draped deerskin was a square lump the width and height of his forearm. He jerked the covering aside to expose a small wooden cage tied to the back of his saddle. A redbreasted robin squatted inside the bars. Chane opened the cage door to let the bird hop onto his wrist, then turned back around. Out of habit, he grasped the tiny brass urn hanging around his neck with his free hand.

Closing his eyes, Chane focused his will until the robin's image materialized in his thoughts. Its head cocked sideways in Chane's mind, with one black avian eye staring back at him. He sent it commands woven into images.

Half-dead and half-elf – black hair with red sparks and white hair that glimmered, the two side by side.

Find in stone and cut wood – the city below, through the trees and across the open field.

Silent, watch and listen – a glimpse of a pale woman's face next to the deep tan of a man with amber eyes.

The robin thrashed its wings and lifted into the air.

Rushing wind over feathers and the ground falling away filled Chane's awareness as his mind clung to the bird's senses. In his early days, these secondhand sensations had been disorienting, then exhilarating. Now he found no delight in them.

The robin crossed the stream and glided over the city walls. Torches were being lit by patrols upon the ramparts. Below were the rooftops of the city, the shapes of buildings barely defined by the light of oil lanterns hanging in the intersections of its roadways. Nearest the city wall was a tall building with a line of figures moving toward a glowing opening at one end.

The robin dove downward, and Chane watched fatigued Stravinan border guards trudging along the side road. Some assisted their wounded comrades as they walked. Peasants in tattered and soaked clothing were among them, as well as several figures in pale blue tabards over cowled robes. All headed for a tall timber barracks, its lower half a mortared foundation of basalt stone. Orange-yellow light spilled from an open door at the far right end, but there was no sign of Wynn or her companions.

A flash of white passed by a window just left of the main door. Chane made the robin double back to light upon the foundation stone meeting the window's ledge. Looking both ways through the pane, he glimpsed a wood archway to the left. Someone in a studded leather hauberk disappeared through it before Chane could discern who it was. The robin fluttered into the air, and returned to land on a sill at the barrack's end farthest from the door.

Chane peered with the familiar's eyes through the mud-speckled window.

Inside were bunks stacked by twos with a path running between them down the long room's center, end to end. Only two border guards were present, seated on top bunks across the way as they stripped off weapons and stowed their gear. To the left at the room's end was an open space with a rickety table surrounded by three stools. On the nearest sat Leesil, his hair and arms streaked in blood. His stained punching blades lay upon the table, piled with a horse mace.

Leesil's narrow features were blank and dull as he dipped his hands into a water pail between his feet and rubbed away blood. Magiere sat on the last lower bunk to the room's far side, studying him with wary eyes.

A cold stab ran through Chane's throat at the sight of her, and the robin shook itself in response. Once he'd found her black hair and porcelain skin enticing. He'd enjoyed fantasies of doing battle with her. Now the pain in Chane's throat was not born of anger or desire. His pure hatred and hunger were poisoned with fear. He no longer cared to make her suffer – only to rip her throat out before she could gasp.

A small figure huddled on one of the bunks. The robin's eyes were not as night-sharp as Chane's, and he pushed the bird forward until its beak touched the window's glass.

Wynn sat with her back against the wall – as far back in the bunk as she could hide. Her boots lay on the floor in puddles, and her pants and coat bottom were soaked through. She shivered with her knees pulled up against her chest.

Chane stared long at Wynn's round olive face and brown eyes beneath the hood of her sheepskin coat. She was watching her companions.

'Take off your hauberk,' Magiere said to Leesil.

Chane grudgingly turned his attention from Wynn as Magiere rose to her feet.

Magiere had already heaped her cloak, hauberk, and falchion in the corner. She stepped around in front of Leesil, rolling up her shirtsleeves. It would've been bad enough if she'd seen pain or anger – or even a hint of madness – that had driven him out into the field this day. At least she might have some notion of what overcame him. But Leesil's expression didn't change as he glanced down at himself. His eyes were empty as he unbuckled the sides of his blemished hauberk and pulled it over his head. The sleeves of his russet shirt were stained, but before Magiere could say anything, he stripped it off as well.

He sat before her, bare and dark-toned to the waist. For an instant she remembered his closeness at night and the warmth of his skin and breath. A strange loneliness filled her at the sight of blood dried in his hair.

Magiere said nothing as she knelt, picked up his fallen shirt, and sank its sleeves in the bucket to wring the blood from them. She took the muslin rag beside the pail and dipped it in the water. When she reached for his face to clean it, he shoved her hand away. A long, narrow bruise ran down the outside of his bare forearm. Magiere grabbed his wrist to inspect it, and Leesil pulled away again.

'You going to tell me what happened out there?' she asked, though she expected little of an answer. 'You dragged us into something that wasn't our concern. And you did it in the worst way.'

Leesil took the rag from her and wiped his own face, but he didn't meet her eyes.

Thumping footfalls filled the room, and Magiere let out a sigh. Whatever Leesil withheld would be hard enough to drag from him if they were alone. Here in the military barrack, there was no privacy. As she came up to one knee and looked down the room's center path, Wynn crawled from hiding to the foot of her bunk.

The little sage looked haggard, but Magiere couldn't find much sympathy. The girl should've never come with them. There'd been plenty of whispered night arguments with Leesil about sending her back to the Guild of Sagecraft in Bela.

A tall, lanky man in padded armor with muddied vambraces and matted long blond hair came down the path between the stacked bunks. It was the young captain who'd pulled his own men out of Magiere's way at the city gate. He carried an iron vessel shaped like a large cook pot with three legs beneath it, and he gripped its arched handle with both hands. He had a blanket tucked under each of his arms. A dull glow emanated from the pot's top and lit up the captain's long features. Within the vessel, hot coals rested in a bed of gravel. Instead of hauling it to the open space by the table, the captain stopped and placed it between the bunks nearest Wynn.

Magiere scowled. Why did this foolish girl, who'd betrayed them, inspire so much sympathy from every posturing man they ran across?

'Wynn?' the captain said, and held out a blanket.

The young sage shook it out and quickly wrapped it around herself. 'Thank you.'

Wynn struggled beneath the blanket and then stopped to look about with an embarrassed frown at everyone present. The captain cleared his throat. He turned first to the soldier bunked above her and then the other across the way.

'Bôska, Stevan,' he said. 'A little privacy, please.'

The soldiers nodded and left.

'Thank you, Stasi,' Wynn said, and scurried back into

hiding, fumbling beneath the blanket to remove her wet clothing.

The captain tossed the extra blanket on Magiere's bunk, and she gave him a curt nod of thanks. He then folded his arms, turned his back to Wynn's bunk, and stood there like a sentry protecting her modesty. Magiere choked back a hiss of disgust.

Captain Stasi's gaze drifted toward Leesil. His long, horselike face wrinkled with suspicion.

'And what fresh misery puts one of you among us?' he growled.

Leesil rose so quickly that Magiere had to scoot out of his way. Trickles of water ran down his forearms to drip from fingers crooked in anger. His blunt ear tips peeked out through white-blond hair hanging in clotted tangles about his face, and his amber eyes locked on the captain with intensity. He was still eager for a fight, not caring who came at him or why.

Magiere stood up as she realized what had set off the captain. Without his cloak and hood, Leesil's heritage was plain to see. This wasn't the first time he'd been mistaken for one of his mother's people.

She started to grab for Leesil, but stopped short, not wishing to aggravate him further. As she stepped in his way, she turned her own vicious attention on the captain. Wynn scrambled from hiding before Magiere could speak, struggling with the blanket to keep covered.

'Leesil is only half-elven,' she said to the captain.

'A half-breed . . . with elven blood?' The captain frowned in disbelief, but his tense posture eased. 'The very notion! As much cold spite as their kind shows us, I can't picture one intimate with a human.'

Magiere heard Leesil shift behind her. She retreated into him, wrapping her arm back around to hold him in place. Before she could spit a retort at the captain, Wynn cut in once again.

'None of us chooses his heritage, Stasi.' She cast Magiere a glance, but then dropped her gaze. 'And none of us is to blame for it. Leesil's mother lived among humans. He knows nothing of her people.'

'Fair enough,' Stasi replied, and cleared his throat as he looked away. 'I've certainly never heard of one throwing himself in harm's way for a human, let alone a pack of defenseless peasants.'

'What do you know of elves?' Magiere demanded. The only one she'd encountered since leaving Miiska had been sent to take Leesil's life.

'Not much to tell, so few are seen here,' Stasi replied. 'Though more have been noted in recent times than are remembered in my father's whole life. Ill fortune sprouts in their passing.' He scrutinized Leesil and sighed. 'But more refugees made the crossing this day than ever before. I have all of you to thank for that . . . as well as the chance to finally spill Warlander blood in payment.'

Wynn's olive features twisted in a grimace at the captain's last words.

'And what was that about?' Magiere asked once again. 'Why did those soldiers slaughter women and children but take the men captive?'

'Collecting conscripts to fill the ranks,' answered Stasi. 'They've no need for any but the men. It's been getting worse since autumn's end. Darmouth's province is directly across the border, so it's usually his men in pursuit as opposed to the other province rulers. Still, I don't know why he now builds up his forces in this desperate fashion.'

'Not new conscripts,' Leesil said. 'Deserters.'

His sudden comment startled Magiere. She pivoted, her shoulder brushing across his chest. Leesil took a hurried step back, turning away, and his white-blond hair hid his face.

'How do you know this?' she asked. It had been many years since Leesil fled his homeland.

'They want the men back,' Leesil answered. 'But there's a price for disobedience.'

His quiet but sharp tone implied she was being dull-witted – and it hurt. Magiere had never heard him speak to her in quite this way. She was too stunned to lash back at him.

'It fits what we know of . . .' Stasi started; then his suspicion of Leesil returned. 'You've been there – inside that warlord's province! That's where your mother . . . where an elf lived among humans?'

Magiere wanted the captain gone. Whatever fed Leesil's harsh words and tone, it had nothing to do with his mother. Or did it? Nein'a had been . . . was one of the *Anmaglâhk*. She'd served Darmouth with her skills – and taught them to her son.

'Wynn, get us some fresh clothes,' she said, still watching Leesil.

'In a moment,' Wynn answered. 'Leesil, what do you mean —'

'Now!' Magiere ordered, turning a meaningful glare toward the young sage.

Wynn met her gaze without moving. She turned slowly away at her leisure, heading down the center path.

'Stasi, I cannot go for our wagon dressed as I am,' Wynn said. 'Could you please help?'

Openly perplexed, the captain followed her, but not without a wary glance back over his shoulder. When Wynn and the captain slipped out the room's far archway, Magiere turned on Leesil.

'What is this?' she hissed at him. 'What price for disobedience?'

Leesil looked at her, and strange emotions played across his face. First astonishment, as if her question were one more bit of foolishness. Then he half closed his eyes in frustration. The edge in his voice remained.

'Have you forgotten what I am . . . was?' he said. 'And even so, do you think you know enough to understand any of this? Those two men tried to desert, and for that their own families were forfeit. That's the way of things beyond the border stream.'

Magiere's confusion fed her anger. The answer was too simple and explained nothing she hadn't already guessed.

'Those riders with their ragged clothes and misfit armor . . . they're the same as those who fled? Conscripts? But they hunt down their own and slaughter them?'

'Yes,' Leesil answered, so quietly that Magiere barely heard it. 'And if they fail, their own kin pay the price.'

'But they're the same,' Magiere insisted. 'And they're killing each other for it? And you . . . you slaughtered those soldiers at the trees.'

'Yes.'

Magiere's lips parted but not a word came out. He was right about one thing: She didn't understand, and he was unwilling to explain it.

Leesil sank down upon the stool. Elbows on knees, he leaned his head into his hands, exposing the long bruise down one forearm.

Magiere knelt down to take his wrist.

'My own blade,' Leesil muttered. 'Its wing hit my arm when the mace struck and didn't slide off. Something I hadn't thought of when I designed them.'

'It's not bad,' she said, though she wasn't certain. She grabbed the rag and wrung it out to stretch it along Leesil's arm as a compress. 'It'll take a while to reach the mountains, and you're not leaving my side again. You try throwing yourself into anything, and I'll club you down before the second step!'

'We're not heading for the mountains,' Leesil replied. 'I'm going to Venjètz.'

Magiere stiffened. 'Darmouth's city . . . in the heart of his province?'

'They both had to flee when I came up missing long ago. Any clues to what happened to them will be in Venjètz.'

'Both?' Magiere's confusion grew. 'Them?'

'My parents.' Leesil paused, and it seemed to take great effort for him to continue. 'If my mother survived to be captured by her people, then my father may have escaped as well. I have to start at the beginning. And that's in Venjètz.'

Magiere bit down a shout of denial. She'd dragged him into Droevinka looking for her own past. What she'd found had cost them both, and something old and dark was looking for her. Leesil put aside guilt for his mother – and father – to stay with her every step. It was supposed to be her turn to watch over him.

But this was all insane, and fear drove her to selfishness. How could she keep him alive if he walked into the reach of a warlord who'd kill him whether his parents still lived or not?

'You swore more than once that you wouldn't die on me.'

'I won't,' he said tiredly. 'I'm not that easy to kill.'

'Liar!' Magiere's voice cracked. 'You'll just get yourself killed. We go find your mother, and that is the surest way to learn what happened to Gavril.'

'What if she doesn't know?' Leesil returned. 'Do you really think her people would let a human go with her in the elven territory? What if he's still here, somewhere across the border stream? And even if he is dead, I have to know.'

'What of the artifact that Welstiel seeks?' Magiere argued, trying any argument to turn him aside. 'Once we find out what happened to your mother, we still need to look for whatever so concerns the sages.'

'Welstiel can't get it without you,' Leesil answered coldly. 'And I agreed with your reasons for first going into Droevinka – before we came looking for my mother.'

Guilt stifled Magiere long enough for Leesil to cut her off.

'We need to find out who we are,' he went on. 'Why the Fay chose to bring together a dhampir and a half-elven assassin. That artifact is safe until we're ready to go after it, and we won't be until we have all our own answers . . . or at least more than we have now. That leaves my father, and there is only one place to learn what happened to him.'

Magiere rose up, backing away until her shoulder hit the post of two stacked bunks. Fear for Leesil smothered whatever sense was in his words.

'I shouldn't have brought you here,' Leesil said, as if talking only to himself. 'I didn't think this through. Perhaps we should've sent Wynn home – and you as well. If I'd done this on my own, you might have been safe for a while until I returned.'

Magiere's hand closed tight upon the bunk's post, until its corner edge bit into her palm.

'You think I'd let you?' she snapped. 'And sit halfway across the continent waiting to hear how you died? I was right about Wynn. She let that monster Chane follow us. Without telling either of us! We can deal with your mother's people without that little sage's language skills.'

'Enough.' Leesil sighed. 'I won't argue this anymore. Wynn is here, and she's suffered enough for her mistake.'

'You've played nursemaid to her once too often.'

The edge returned to Leesil's voice. 'You don't have to remind me how wrong she was. But you saw her collapse over Chane's body. She was broken inside. Can you imagine what that feels like?'

Yes, she could. Magiere saw Leesil alone in the Warlands, dead at the hands of Darmouth. She shook her head slowly as she backed down the path between the bunks.

'I promised to help you seek your answers, as you did for me. That's our way . . . you and I. But how much harder are you going to make it for me keep you safe?'

She turned away, heading for the wooden archway at the room's far end.

Leesil's voice rose behind her.

'Make some kind of peace with Wynn,' he called. 'She's been through enough, no matter what her mistakes. And neither of us is pure enough to sit judgment on her . . . as you have.'

Magiere's pace increased as she grew desperate to be out and away. She hurried through the adjoining room of stacked bunks, ignoring soldiers settled there or talking among themselves. Before anyone spoke to her, Magiere rushed out the next archway and into the barrack's common room.

The two men whom Stasi had asked to leave were there, but most of the few small tables and stools were taken up by refugees and the priests tending to them. The room was so packed that Magiere had to slow to keep from making contact with anyone. The girl she'd saved huddled on the floor before the back wall hearth. Her companion crouched behind her with his arms wrapped about her shoulders as both stared into the fire.

Wynn sat at the hearth's far side. She faced into the room, not seeming to notice the adolescent couple nearby. Instead, she looked toward a shimmer of silver blue-gray beneath a table where a woman priest cradled an infant in a blanket. Magiere was desperate to be alone, but for an instant she wondered why Wynn sat such a distance from Chap.

The dog lay silently out of everyone's way, likely not wishing to be stepped on with so many people stuffed into the small room. He didn't notice Wynn's peculiar study of him and looked up at Magiere with perked ears.

It seemed odd to Magiere that Chap was still filthy. His muzzle was stained from the fight. The young sage always fussed over the dog, grooming him with a scolding at every stop they made on the journey north. Not that it mattered to Chap. He would be no better for it after his next day of wandering the underbrush along their way.

But Wynn now sat before the hearth, far from Chap.

Magiere couldn't face any more puzzles this night. She jerked the barrack's door open too hard, and it slammed into one rickety table. Gasps and exclamations arose, but she was outside and heading blindly up the road without noticing whom she'd startled.

'Magiere?'

The soft, high voice made her stop. Wynn stood in the open doorway, clinging to her blanket against the cold.

'The captain should be back with our things soon,' Wynn said. 'Where are you going?'

'None of your —' Magiere started in a threatening tone.

She caught herself as Leesil's words ate into her. In the half-light spilling through the open door, Wynn's expression clouded with resentment. Magiere began again, forcing herself to speak calmly.

'Please ask one of the priests to look at Leesil's arm when they're done with the others. I'll return in a while.'

She whirled about with a shuddering breath.

'But . . . you are without even a cloak,' Wynn called after her.

Magiere traveled half the barrack's length before she heard the door close.

A thrashing sound in the dark made her sidestep away from the building, instinctively reaching for her falchion.

She realized she'd left the weapon behind with her cloak. Her dhampir senses expanded, and she glimpsed a startled bird fluttering away into the night.

Magiere looked about and saw the foreign city around her settling itself into winter slumber. She wanted to be alone, and though the dark wouldn't trouble her, she couldn't risk becoming lost until morning in this faraway place. She slipped around the barrack's corner. Leaning against the rough stone foundation, she slid down to her haunches.

She'd been alone most of her life, despite the occasional company of others, and had preferred it that way. Perhaps even in the early days with Leesil, along the back ways of the wilderness cheating superstitious peasants. Here on the edge of his past, his first life, the more she fought with him, the more he retreated inside himself to a place she couldn't reach.

Yet the foolish, unexplained choices he now made could kill him – take him from her in a way she couldn't overcome.

It made her feel lonely, abandoned. And that wasn't the same as being alone.

Magiere shivered in the night air but remained stiff and still, leaning against the barrack's cold stone foundation. No one passed by to be frightened by the white mask of her face with full black-irised eyes. If they had, they'd have fled, never noticing the rising steam from tear tracks on her pale cheeks.

Chane lost contact with his familiar the instant the robin fled in panic at Magiere's passing. It didn't matter, as the bird would return on its own. He'd barely heard what transpired after Leesil spoke his harsh admonition to Magiere for what had happened in the murky forest near Apudâlsat.

Obsession, hatred, and even fear had muddied Chane's thoughts for so many nights – but all toward Magiere. He'd not contemplated what Wynn had endured. She had watched him die and collapsed upon his twice-dead corpse.

Did she weep . . . for him?

Chane's eyes were still closed. He was so poised and still that his companion didn't realize the reconnaissance was finished until the robin lighted upon the saddle horn of Chane's mount.

'Well?' Welstiel asked with irritation creeping into his deep voice. 'What have you learned?'

Chane did not answer. He tightened his grip on the horse's mane tangled between his fingers.

'Chane!' Welstiel snapped. 'What did you hear?'

In the early days of their travels, Welstiel never lost his composure. That too had changed.

Chane willed himself to calm, not allowing any thought beyond this moment. This was how he pushed himself forward, how he kept waking every night and climbing back onto his horse.

'Venjètz,' he rasped. 'They go in search of Leesil's father, and then head on to elven territory for his mother.'

Welstiel's face went blank with his lips barely parted, and then his voice erupted. 'Venjètz? What nonsense is that half-blood dragging Magiere into now?'

Chane held his hand up and dismounted. Welstiel followed with impatience. Before his companion could badger him further, Chane repeated as much of the conversation between Magiere and Leesil as he could remember. Welstiel crouched down, running a hand over his face, absorbing all that Chane said.

'The elven lands are too far north,' he finally whispered. 'A distance from what I seek . . . or so I guess.'

Welstiel slowly looked up as if Chane were somehow responsible for this snag in his plans.

'We press on to Venjètz,' he said. 'If Leesil discovers both his parents are dead, perhaps Magiere will turn away from here. There will be no reason for them to go to the elven lands. I see no other option either. Though I do not yet see how to make this happen.'

Chane did not care what they did or where they went. He simply had nowhere else to go. Or if he did, he no longer had a will to see beyond tomorrow. He placed the robin back in its cage and pulled the covering over it, as Welstiel mounted his horse. Chane put his foot in the stirrup and swung into his own saddle.

It helped him to follow one simple action with another.

3

Four days' travel among the Warlands' forested hills left Leesil weary. So much was the same as when he'd fled eight years ago. That alone was enough to drain him, but by all they'd seen and heard so far, things were worse than when he'd left. He let Magiere or Wynn handle the wagon more often and sat alone in the back.

He'd forgotten the beauty of the land, even in its early winter. Thick-trunked spruce and fir trees surrounded the wagon's passage. They often passed through glens, fallow fields dusted with white snow, and spaces where the forest canopy opened to let in the sky. It was almost a welcome change after the dank forests of Droevinka, but any tingle of relief faded quickly. It was all more deceit to the eyes, as hollow and empty as the villages they'd passed by.

'Is this what you remember?' Wynn whispered.

'Yes,' he answered. 'No . . . worse.'

When they'd first crossed Droevinka's border on the northward trek into Stravina, Leesil knew he would have to tell Wynn something about his past. He was reluctant, though not as much as when he'd confessed to Magiere during their hunt in Bela. When he'd finally told Magiere, his love for her had grown so much that he feared she would leave once she learned any part of the truth. But Magiere stayed by his side, drawing ever closer to him.

They were halfway to Soladran when he'd finally told Wynn a little of his youth. She remained silent while he spoke. Hesitant at first, she admitted her own long-held suspicions since helping him and Magiere in Bela. She'd seen the strange way he fought, his weapons of choice hidden from plain sight, and his long wooden box containing more tools of his trade. But Leesil hadn't told her all. The young sage could only face so much. What little more he'd told Magiere wasn't enough for even her to understand his world.

When the wagon had passed the first empty village in Darmouth's province, Wynn's insatiable curiosity blossomed once again. She asked about the land and its people, and Leesil explained in sparse details.

Lord Darmouth's officers had standing orders to maintain the ranks by any means. Paying large numbers of mercenaries wasn't viable. Taxing oppressed people yielded little for the coffers, and any province's wealth wasn't much beyond what it took from its neighbors. Conscription was more cost-effective for a warlord with pretensions of monarchy.

After each fall harvest, any able-bodied male over fifteen years was herded away at sword point. It wasn't uncommon for the previous year's conscripts to be given this task under the watchful eye of an officer. Occasionally a village was passed over for several years, but this didn't happen often, and so . . . far too many women and children watched fathers and sons enslaved by their own countrymen, neighbors, or even kin.

Darmouth ruled a large territory to the southeast of the Warlands, but there were other lords like him who claimed territories to the north and the west. Skirmishes erupted regularly along province borders, and Darmouth's no less than any other. The rulers of the Warlands ceaselessly nipped and snapped at one another to see who was weakening.

In Darmouth's territory, conscripts were clothed and fed, and paid barely enough to care for those left at home. What little they were given sometimes depended on spoils and supplies taken in raids. This practice made them easily led astray by high-ranking officers or Darmouth's appointed 'nobles' into private armies for attempted takeovers. Most insurrections ended with the traitor's sudden death, the would-be upstart often dying before his scheme sprouted.

Deceit and betrayal thrived in this land, and everyone lived with the threat and promise of war that might come with the next dawn. This had been Leesil's first life and his youth.

As the wagon jostled along the empty road, he found himself viewing another empty village. Starvation was common, but the people had grown thin in number as well.

Magiere said little but glanced back at him every so often. She'd done this before in their time together, but instead of a scowl, there was something else in her face. Leesil hunched down in the wagon and stared out the back. He remained expressionless, offering her no reaction, but her gaze hurt him.

Was it fear he saw when she looked at him?

The nights grew so cold that they slept indoors whenever possible. Near dusk of the fourth day across the border stream, they reached a small village with decently thatched roofs. It was the first they'd found all day that wasn't deserted.

A young boy with a dirt-streaked face swung himself awkwardly on makeshift crutches down a side path through the village. He was missing his left leg from the knee downward. He froze at the sight of the wagon, and his face filled with alarm, like a yearling rabbit who'd wandered carelessly into the open and found himself facing a fox.

Magiere's falchion was stowed in back. She was dressed in breeches, a wool pullover shirt, and a heavy cloak, but not her hauberk. Wynn pulled back her coat's hood and smiled at the boy, her light-brown hair hanging loose about her face. But Chap and Leesil held the boy's attention the most.

At times Darmouth's press gangs used dogs to bring down runaways or sniff them out of hiding holes in the villages. Leesil pulled his cloak hood back, exposing the gray scarf tied over his hair and ears, then pushed Chap down in the wagon's bed. He didn't feel like smiling, but he could fake any expression when necessary.

'Hallo,' he called. 'Is there a place to sleep tonight? We can pay in coin or food.'

The boy blinked twice. His smooth brow wrinkled in suspicion, but he wobbled slowly toward the wagon.

'Willem!'

A woman in a patched wool skirt and ragged cape bolted from the doorway of the nearest hut. She grabbed the boy around the shoulders and backed toward her hiding place. Her hair was so dirty that Leesil couldn't guess its color beyond a dull brown. She glared at him, and Leesil much preferred her anger to fear.

'They just wanna place outta the cold, Ma,' the boy said. Several teeth were missing on the left side of his mouth. 'Said they'd pay with food.'

Magiere shifted uncomfortably on the wagon bench. 'We're headed for Venjètz, but the nights are too cold. We have dried goods to trade for shelter.'

At the mention of stores and fair trade, some of the woman's mistrust faded. She looked at Port and Imp and pursed her lips in thought. Both horses were healthy and bright-eyed, with thick, gray coats.

'We can hide 'em,' Willem said.

Willem's mother lifted her chin at Magiere. She moved and held herself as if in her late twenties, but strands of gray stood out in her matted hair. There were soft lines around her eyes and the corners of her chapped lips. 'We'll put you up, but do as my son says, or you might not find your horses come morning.'

Magiere dropped down from the wagon's bench. Leesil climbed out behind her and took Port and Imp by the halters. As he led the wagon through the village on foot, he saw no other animals. Not a stray chicken, pig, or cow, and not even the goats or sheep more commonly kept in these northern territories.

The woman glanced at him, guessing his thoughts. 'Soldiers took 'em. And any that come'll take your horses.'

'They can try,' Magiere replied with the cock of an eyebrow.

It was difficult to guess her age.

A few more villagers came out of hiding, taking cautious steps at the sight of strangers. All were women and younger children but for one old man, thin and bony. The short crop of his white hair and beard suggested he might be one of the few who ever lived to serve his time at arms and be released to go home. He wore a vestment of furred hide, and the ridge of an old scar ran down his right forearm to the back of his hand.

'Who do you have there, Helen?' he asked in a cracked voice.

'Lodgers that can pay.'

'Best hide those horses,' he said with a steady gaze. 'And the wagon.'

Helen didn't answer. Perhaps she did not care to be reminded of something she already knew.

A wide main way ran through the village's clustered huts, with four crossing paths that were barely more than muddy trails. Leesil spotted a communal smokehouse for drying meat, but it wasn't in use this late in the year. The only dwelling alive with activity was a rickety structure with bundles of ash tree branches piled out front beside an entrance covered with a deer-hide curtain. Three elder women sat there on a bench, splitting and trimming feathers.

'You make arrows?' Leesil asked.

'We can't do the heads anymore,' Helen said. 'My father was the smith, so the soldiers let him stay here when I was a girl. He taught me to make proper shafts. I taught the others. Captain Kévoc arrives in a few days, as he does once a moon. He trades us fair . . . or more so than most.'

Leesil looked back at Chap and Wynn still riding in the wagon. The sage stared about the village. When she looked Leesil's way, her gaze passed beyond him into the distance. She raised a hand to point, and Leesil looked back ahead.

Rounding a bend through the forest near the village's far end, Leesil counted five – no, six – men on foot. Most wore mismatched leather armor, while the lead man wore a chain vest. They were armed with short-swords and longknives sheathed at their waists, the typical armaments given to soldiers. It seemed the village's bene-factor had arrived early, but then Leesil abandoned such a notion. Foot soldiers were one thing, but an officer never walked. All of these men were on foot.

'Forgetful gods,' Helen whispered.

Magiere cast her a startled look upon hearing the curse Leesil so often used. 'Are they soldiers?' she asked.

Chap jumped down from the wagon. As the dog came up beside him, Leesil noticed Wynn digging through their belongings.

'Magiere,' Wynn called softly. She lowered the fal-chion and punching blades over the wagon's side.

Magiere backed toward her, but Leesil kept his eyes on the newcomers.

'Not soldiers,' Helen said. 'Deserters. They just come to take what we have.'

Magiere stepped up behind Leesil, and he slipped one hand behind his back. She placed the handles of his punching blades into his palm. He gripped them both as one.

'Helen, girl,' the leader called out as he passed between the farthest huts. 'You have company.'

Villagers backed away as his men spread out to peer into and between the huts as they came. One behind the leader was little more than a nervous boy carrying the remains of a horse mace, its haft broken off near the butt. The man to the far right kicked open a hut's plank door and leaned halfway in to look about. When he backed out, Leesil saw he had a woman's tattered shawl wrapped about his head, its tail end covering the lower half of his face. A deep furrow of split scar tissue arched from his left eyebrow through the bridge of his nose to disappear beneath the fabric. He grunted at his leader, who didn't acknowledge him.

Tall and lean, the leader wore a shirt of torn quilted padding beneath his chain vest. His black hair was cropped almost to his scalp, and his square jaw was covered in stubble. He remained calm and poised, walking with slow care. There were no visible scars on his forearms, hands, or face, and that made Leesil wary.

Leesil had seen their hardened kind before. But in his youth, marauding bands of deserters had been rare. That they moved so openly meant patrols through the land had become scarce. The way the boy huddled close to the leader gave Leesil pause. The man in the chain vest wasn't old enough to be the father, nor did they look alike, yet there was some bond between them. A litany of Leesil's own father surfaced in his thoughts as he studied the two, and some part of him understood and accepted their way in this hopeless land.

Do what is necessary. Take care of your own. And consequence matters not until it comes.

Chap began to rumble.

Leesil expected the deserters to come straight for the horses, but the leader stopped near the fletcher's shack. The three old women splitting feathers had vanished.

'A new crop of shafts are ready,' the man said.

Helen tensed and pushed Willem off to the side and behind her.

Leesil remained still. These men knew the village's trading schedule. They'd come to steal arrow shafts before they could be traded for winter supplies. The scarf-wrapped man pulled aside the hide on the shack's doorway.

'I wouldn't do that,' Leesil warned.

The leader looked at him without reaction. The man's lack of expression made Leesil shift his feet, feeling the ground for footing. Even the undead, like Ratboy, showed rage or hatred or passion, but this man's eyes held nothing. He was dead and didn't know it yet, or he didn't care either way.

Leesil remembered what that was like, felt it even now.

'Hold your tongue, man,' the leader said, 'and lead those horses over.'

Chap growled, and Leesil sidestepped to the right, letting Magiere move into the open with her falchion in plain sight.

'Turn back and walk out,' Magiere said.

Chap's low growl quickened to a snarl. Leesil lifted his blades in front of himself, both appearing as but one weapon. He heard a click behind him and knew Wynn had managed to load one of their crossbows.

The leader blinked once. That was all the reaction Leesil caught. Perhaps the man did still care about his own death or those under his charge.

'Six to three,' the leader said. 'The odds don't favor you.'

The old man with cropped white hair stepped out

of his hut a few paces behind the leader. Leesil hadn't even noticed him disappear. One of the marauders skidded back from him, drawing a shortsword. The leader turned his head just enough to see what was happening.

The old soldier held a barkless wooden rod the length of his arm and as thick as his wrist. Its smooth surface looked polished. Most likely it had been ground down – boned – with a cow's bone to make the wood hard and tough. He stood quietly, looking to the leader, matching his dispassionate gaze.

To Leesil's eye, there seemed little difference between them other than the choice of what was theirs to keep and protect. The rest of the villagers remained silent, cowering back out of the way. Even the people of Magiere's village had gathered together in their superstitions to face down strangers thought 'unnatural.' It wasn't the same here, where peasants were beaten down one generation after another, and fighting back gained little more than retribution.

As the leader looked back to Leesil, Helen pulled her skirt up and jerked a long iron knife from her worn boot. Another long moment and an elder woman appeared from behind a hut with a woodsman's ax in her hand. None of the other villagers moved, and one woman pulled her two girls farther back against a hut wall. The boy with the broken mace stepped a little closer to his superior, eyes frightened.

'Odds change,' Leesil countered, and he separated his blades so that it was clear he held two. 'That's the way of luck.'

The shawl-masked deserter stepped toward the old

soldier, but the leader raised a hand as if he knew without looking. His man stopped short.

The leader backed up with the same slow and careful steps as when he'd first entered. He reached the village's far end, his men following, and just before he turned he cast one long look at Helen. Everyone remained silent and poised until the deserters were out of sight, and then Helen sighed.

'You just saved us a month's work,' she finally said, now puzzled as she looked over Leesil and then Magiere. 'You'll pay for nothing tonight. Let's hide those horses before they circle back through the woods to find them after dark. We'll lock 'em up in the smokehouse.'

'What if those men come back after we leave?' Wynn called.

Leesil turned to see her standing in the wagon's bed, pale and distressed. He walked over and dropped his blades in the wagon's back. Wynn had seen many things on this journey that were almost beyond her ability to bear. He took the crossbow from her shaking hands and set it down next to his blades.

'We do what's necessary in the moment,' Leesil said. 'That's all there is.'

'That is not enough,' she whispered.

He didn't answer and turned to find Magiere watching him again.

The sleeper rolled, lost inside his dream of glittering stars all around. And the dark between began to undulate.

The movement sharpened slowly into clarity, and stars became glints of light upon massive black reptilian scales. The coils of its body were larger than the height of a man and circled on all sides of him, writhing with no beginning, no end, and no space between.

'Where?' the dreamer asked. 'Show me where.'

This time, no cryptic words came. Black coils faded away.

He found himself standing on a snow-covered slope looking into a valley locked in a perpetual winter. High mountains shot up on all sides like teeth into the cloud-smothered sky. And there in the maw of the valley stood a six-towered castle coated in ice. It was immense in size, but it was dwarfed by the white peaks that surrounded it.

'There?' he asked.

Look deeper. The orb is close.

The words slipped like a whisper into the dreamer's thoughts. He trudged downslope through snow so old it crackled under his boots as he sank knee-deep with each step. When he reached the valley floor, he made out the entrance through the high outer wall.

Twin gates of ornate iron curls joined together at the high top in an arched point. Beyond them were matching-shaped iron doors in the castle's front atop a wide cascade of steps. Mottled with rust, the gates were still sound in their place, sealing in whatever the castle held. Each of the tall towers was topped with a conical spire fringed with a curtain of ice suspended from its roof's lower edge.

As he approached, the left gate swung outward of its own accord on hinges as large as his own leg. Three ravens sat atop the wall staring down at him with pin-prick eyes. One cawed in agitation. Beyond the gate, the barren courtyard was carpeted in snowfall that had crusted with years of cold. Except for the walkway and steps.

The iced stones were cleared all the way from the gate and up the stairs to the towering iron doors. Someone . . . something remained in this place.

He took a step across the gate's threshold.

Welstiel's eyelids opened. The castle faded beyond sight and touch.

'No! Show me more!'

Welstiel rolled to his feet, twisting about as he tried to get his bearings. The previous dawn rushed back to him.

He and Chane had found a deserted hovel and slumbered for the day on its floor, covered only by their cloaks. Broken pottery strewn about was the only sign that anyone had ever lived here. No stools, wooden table, or cook pot had been left behind.

For the first time, Welstiel's dream patron showed him the resting place of what he sought – an unknown treasure that could alter his detestable existence. He was certain, if astonished and more frustrated than ever before. In the past few moons, his dream patron had begun whispering of the treasure by calling it an 'orb.' Welstiel had hoped for further enlightenment.

But this dream had been different from any other. His patron of dreams said little, yet there was this vision. Welstiel had seen an ancient and forgotten stronghold, and would recognize it, if he could find it. But why had the vision been stolen before he stepped in the gate? The waiting and half-hints took their toll upon him.

He stepped to the hut's doorless opening and looked outside. Chane was nowhere to be seen, probably out hunting. Welstiel did not have the strength to go searching for him and squatted down. Since leaving Droevinka, he had awoken nearly every night with the same memory.

In the Apudâlsat forest he had secretly watched Magiere and Chap circle in upon Ubâd, his father's old retainer and confidant. The mad necromancer had cried out: 'Il'Samar! Come to your servant and aid me!'

Coils like waves of vaporous and glinting black earth had appeared in the forest, circling on all sides of the clearing. The name by which Ubâd made his plea was unfamiliar to Welstiel, but he knew those coils as well as his own reflection. He knew its whispering voice in the dark – his patron of dreams. And it had abandoned Ubâd as Chap tore open the withered old schemer's throat.

How the coils had appeared outside of Welstiel's dreams was mystery enough, but how was the conjurer of the dead connected to Welstiel's patron? Most troubling was that the patron had abandoned Ubâd in his final moment of need.

'But it has not abandoned me,' Welstiel whispered to himself.

He believed the voice in his dreams assisted him, guided him. Soon he would never need to feed again – to debase himself with blood. The power of the orb would sustain him somehow. His longing for freedom was an ache that constantly nagged him.

Yet still there was Ubâd, betrayed in the clearing. Welstiel tried to put this aside.

His patron had called Magiere 'sister of the dead.' Welstiel had slowly manipulated her for years to fulfill his plans, and he grew ever more certain of her role to play. The path to the castle doors had been clear of snow, as if something still resided there. Something for which he would need a killer of the dead.

Welstiel stood up, fastened his cloak, and attempted to smooth his hair back as he stepped outside. Tiny snowflakes drifted down through the dusk. It was time to search for his wayward companion.

In the previous night they had passed a few huts off the road among the trees. Chane had likely gone back.

Along with Magiere's frustrating deviations, Welstiel grew concerned over recent changes in Chane. Since rising from his second death, Chane's feedings grew more brutal. He singled out women with coal-black hair and the fairest complexions. The association to Magiere was obvious. Otherwise Chane remained silent and withdrawn. He had not spoken once of the sages' guild and took no further notes in his journals, but also showed neither satisfaction nor quiet euphoria after a kill. Careless in his feeding habits, Chane showed little to none of the resourcefulness Welstiel once valued.

And Chane still wondered how he had risen from a second grave.

Let him wonder.

Chane's begrudging awe helped maintain Welstiel's limited control of the tall undead. And after all, the resurrection was a simple thing, though Welstiel had been uncertain it would succeed until he made the attempt. It had started with little more than a hint acquired years ago, in the very land from which Chane's fledgling sage hailed, where the Guild of Sagecraft was founded. Welstiel had been well traveled in his early years as a

Noble Dead. How else could he have promised Chane a letter of introduction to the guild there?

Gaining that hint, and other knowledge of vampiric nature, had been a dangerous exploit that nearly cost Welstiel his existence. An old vampire living secretly in Calm Seatt, the king's city in Malourné, did not care for his own kind invading his territory.

Pawl a'Seatt – even the old undead's surname was a puzzle. Little more than a reference to the city in which the vampire lived. Welstiel learned bits and pieces from him, such as one scornful proclamation.

Blood is not the life; life is the life.

At first it made no sense, but Welstiel's careful questions gained him more pieces to ponder in the following years. Blood, as an element of the living, was a medium and conduit that carried life energy upon which the undead thrived. The medium was convenient and quick, and nothing more. The very presence of an undead drew life energy to it in slower, unnoticed ways.

If that energy maintained a higher undead, a Noble Dead . . .

If that energy was how one healed its physical form . . .

There had never been a chance to test the theory, until Chane stupidly faced off with Magiere and was cut down.

As with so many folktales and superstitions of the living, beheading was not a permanent way to finish one of Welstiel's kind. Such severe damage merely incapacitated a vampire, placing it into a dark dormancy until enough life was absorbed to heal itself, or its separated parts rotted beyond recovery.

But Chane was suspicious, wary, and even in awe of what mysteries Welstiel seemed to know. This secret was just one of many that Welstiel would keep unto himself.

Welstiel left the horses tied to a tree and made his way on foot. He pushed branches aside and cut through the forest, back to where he remembered six intact huts with cookfires still smoking. Upon seeing the corner of a thatched roof through the branches, Welstiel slowed to listen.

Chane had become more adept at luring victims out of their homes. Welstiel was uncertain how or even why. He almost never caught Chane feeding inside of a dwelling since they had left Droevinka.

Welstiel closed his eyes and listened, letting his senses expand into the night. If Chane would only take more care in disposing of bodies, Welstiel would simply wait for him to return, but Chane could not be trusted anymore. One night south of Soladran, he had slaughtered a young, black-haired woman and her two small daughters right behind the woman's house, leaving the bodies where they fell. Welstiel had cleaned up after his companion once again.

He heard soft sounds, but not the drifting wind or skittering of a squirrel among the branches. He moved silently around the cluster of dwellings and through the forest, and the sounds grew more apparent. Heavy breathing and the thrash of a struggle.

Welstiel rounded the thick trunk of spruce to see Chane in profile.

He had a young woman pressed against the tree with his hand clamped over her mouth and jaw. Her eyes were wild, but her throat was mostly intact beneath

Chane's teeth as he drained her slowly. Pale and cleaner than most peasants, she had long black hair, which was no surprise. From the corner of her eye, she saw Welstiel.

Her weakening expression filled with hope. She doubled her effort to shove Chane away and let out a muffled cry. Chane's hand closed tighter about her mouth. A muted crack of bone silenced her as she stiffened in pain, fingers twitching in the air.

Welstiel let his senses retreat until the darkness masked the detail of what he saw. He stood in silent distaste, waiting for it to end.

Chane must have noticed something, for he pulled his head back from the woman's throat. Even in Welstiel's normal night-shadowed sight, Chane looked like some beast come in from the wild. His cloak and shirt were halfway off one shoulder, and his face was smeared in blood. Some of his hair caught upon his bloodstained lips and stuck there.

Welstiel reached his limit of tolerance with Chane's recklessness. About to step in and end this night's butchery, he suddenly held his place and stared into Chane's eyes.

There was little intelligence or recognition there, but neither was there the savage pleasure Chane took at the end of his hunts. He looked lost to the world, as if not even aware of what he did. It was all a habit he mindlessly clung to.

'Finish it,' Welstiel said.

The words must have registered. Chane wrapped his teeth halfway around the woman's throat and ripped outward. Blood and torn flesh came away in his mouth. He didn't bother to catch the girl as she dropped limp to the ground, flopping over when her shoulder hit an exposed tree root.

Chane spit flesh from his teeth and leaned against the tree. He wiped his lips with the back of his hand, swallowing hard.

Welstiel looked down at the girl lying crooked on the ground. He felt disgust at Chane's need to touch this lowly peasant, to put his mouth on her, but still wondered at Chane's lack of pleasure.

'Did you plan to properly dispose of that?' Welstiel asked.

Chane did not answer.

Welstiel stepped in to pick up the body, then stopped, reaching a sudden decision. 'I weary of this. Bargain or no, either you become useful once again, or leave and find your own way. Clean this up yourself.'

Chane did not look at him, but after a moment he nodded once.

Welstiel turned away, ever more puzzled.

Wynn was surprised when Helen led her into the smith's shop. Leesil, Magiere, and Chap followed, all looking about in mild confusion. Small tables, stools, and one old chair repaired with twine were placed around a crude stone forge. Stalls where horses once had been kept were barren, even of straw. Some stalls had meager stores of piled casks and canvas sacks.

'We've no iron or metal to work anymore,' Helen said, tossing a split log into the open forge that now served as a fire pit. 'We made this our common house. You can sleep here.'

Gazing at the faded tables, Wynn realized these people

had not given up. They scratched out a semblance of community as best they could. Other women and children began coming in. Visitors were unusual here, and, though wary, the people were curious.

Magiere unpacked a change of clothes, ignoring the growing numbers inside the smithy. Leesil settled in the back of the room, seeming reluctant to visit with any of the villagers. He had remained darkly quiet since the battle at the border. Only Chap took to the newfound company, letting the children scratch his ears and back.

Wynn shuddered once as Chap licked the smudges from a small girl's face. The child squealed and giggled over the wet attention of a large silvery dog come to visit. But Wynn heard the remembered buzz of a leafwing instead and turned back to Helen.

'Can I help you prepare supper?' Wynn asked, now that the fire was reviving.

Helen hesitated. 'We'll have more food once we trade the arrow shafts. For now, all we've got is porridge and millet, and all of us ate once today already.'

Wynn felt ashamed for even asking. At least in Droevinka, most villagers had food. Two small girls about four years of age inspected the hem of her sheepskin coat.

'If your men are conscripted . . . taken away,' she said, 'do they come home on leave?'

'Leave?' Helen blinked, then appeared to understand. 'No. We've no grown men shy of forty winters since I was a girl. My father was allowed to stay and make arrowheads for a while, but they took him, too.'

Wynn frowned and pointed at Willem. 'Then where did the children . . .?'

She trailed off, second-guessing the politeness of her question. Helen simply tucked a loose strand of unwashed hair behind her ear.

'Soldiers take more than just livestock and grain. Then leave us with more mouths to feed.'

Helen's meaning sank in as Wynn looked around at all the children. Their narrow, dirty faces and ragged clothing filled her with a need to do something. One little girl's arms were so thin that they reminded Wynn of the arrow shafts the women worked so hard to make.

She hurried toward the smithy's rear door, calling out, 'I will be back in a moment.'

She went to the wagon outside and climbed up into its back. Helen had hidden Port and Imp farther down in the smokehouse. Wynn pulled aside a canvas tarp used to pitch a lean-to tent on the wagon's side and began rummaging through their stores.

Back in Soladran, Leesil had sent her to purchase supplies. Tired of biscuits and jerky, especially since she did not care for meat, Wynn had purchased dried lentils, barley, onions, and carrots, as well as late pears and smoke-dried fish. She acquired a lidded clay pot, a small cauldron, and an iron hook pole for use at a fire. And she found grain and seed-oil for making flat-bread.

At first Magiere was furious over what she spent in coin. But the following night Wynn hung the cauldron from the iron hook and made an herbed lentil soup for supper. She heard welcome sounds of satisfaction from Leesil as he took his first bite. Magiere did not comment, but she said nothing more about the money. This type of cooking was time-consuming, and Wynn tended to make large amounts during the nights. The clay pot was used to store the extra, and it was still half-full from the last meal she had prepared.

But now she dug through the supplies with a different purpose in mind, and hauled all that she could carry back into the smithy.

'Have someone fetch the largest cook pot any of you have,' she told Helen.

'What're you doing?' Helen asked.

'Making supper. There are lentils, onions, and carrots. I have parsley and marjoram as well. We need to get water boiling, as it will take time to make enough for everyone.'

Helen stared at the bounty Wynn pulled from burlap sacks, as if treasure were being poured out on the floor. She shook her head.

'This must be your whole supply. You can't mean —'

'No, she doesn't,' Magiere said, striding over. 'Wynn, what are you doing? We're trading for a night, not settling in until spring.'

Wynn had tiptoed around Magiere until her own anger and anguish got the best of her. She was tired of being polite or bursting into bitter disputes that made her feel petty. In this moment she did not care about broken trust or good manners.

'Oh, yes, I mean it!' she snapped back. 'We need only enough to get us to Venjètz, and we can replace all of this. Look at that little girl. She is having a decent supper tonight, and we will provide it!'

Wynn expected Magiere's assault to begin, but instead she cast a glance toward Leesil and fell silent. Chap trotted to Wynn's side and barked once at Magiere for 'yes.' Wynn flinched, almost pulling away from the dog's closeness before she could stop herself.

'He is on my side,' she said to Magiere.

Helen and the other women looked on in tense silence.

Leesil got up from his stool and came to Wynn, quietly whispering in her ear, 'The next village will be exactly the same. And the next.'

His expression was dispassionate, but the sadness in his eyes washed away Wynn's anger.

'I do not care,' she told him. 'You said we should do what we can in the moment.'

'All right.' He stepped back. 'Magiere?'

'Why ask me? You three have made up your minds.'

Despite Magiere's annoyance, Wynn knew she would help and then never bring it up again.

Wynn turned back to Helen. 'We need knives for chopping as well as the pot.'

The village women set out to fetch the necessary items. No one smiled or muttered thanks, but rather hurried in a way that suggested this miracle might vanish if they did not move quickly enough. Leesil picked up a bucket and went to seek a well or rain barrel for water. Wynn followed him, and, alone outside, she grabbed his arm.

'Why is it so hard for you to assist these people?'

'Because I helped do this to them.' He turned away, and Wynn saw only his tan profile in the dusk. 'And nothing we do here will change anything.'

He pulled free of her grasp and turned his back to her. Wynn watched him walk a slow and even gait down the village's main way. She was silent only because she did not know what else to say.

★　★　★

Chap slipped out the smithy's back door as meal preparations heightened to a flurry. Wynn had returned to oversee the work, but Leesil had not come with her. Sad frustration on the little sage's face made Chap wonder what passed between them while outside.

He circled around their wagon and along the smithy's side until he spotted Leesil walking slowly up the main way. A quick touch upon Leesil's mind found it empty.

Chap could not read thoughts, only memories surfacing to consciousness, and Leesil's mind was devoid of such. Most sentient beings had brief flickers of the past passing just below their awareness at any time. But even those were not present in Leesil. He held them down, shutting out everything.

Which was worse – suppression or immersion – to block all that was past until it welled up to consume one, or to dive into it and drown? Leesil was becoming a danger to himself, and Chap was at a loss for how to care for one of his charges.

Grass and leaves rustling and the sound of clicking branches chattered in the wind.

Chap lifted his head with perked ears and stared across the main way to the woods beyond the village. He felt them again. His kin, the Fay, called for him, demanding his presence among them.

He wrinkled his snout.

More talk was not needed. Perhaps he was corrupted by flesh, as they claimed. How could he not be, living encased in it, limited by it as compared to what he had once been among his kin? Or perhaps he had gained a perspective they did not possess. Either way, now was not the time for more of their admonishments.

Before their presence touched his spirit, Chap clung to the world around him. From sounds the wind made in the trees to the gritty touch of earth under his feet and the smell of the smithy's forge fire, Chap filled up his senses. With these he shut out his kin.

The presence of the Fay thinned and faded from around him.

Chap look backed down the main way. Leesil was gone, perhaps turning aside through the village to wherever the common well was located. Anxious concern over Leesil's foray into his past brought Chap his own memories.

He remembered being 'born' into flesh.

The *majay-hì* were an old breed that ran among the elven forests. Intelligent compared to other animals, and intuitive beyond most, they were marked by long silvery fur of varied shades and crystalline blue eyes. They were sensitive to life and its balance or imbalance, and thereby sensed its unnatural opposite − the undead. But there had not been a *majay-hì* like Chap for so long that even the elves did not remember.

Not since the humans' Forgotten History and the war between the living of the world and the Enemy.

In the conflict's final days, a number of the Fay chose to defend the world of their making by taking flesh. They also wished to keep their presence unknown to most. Some of them entered the unborn young of animals, so they might live in flesh and blood. Among other forms chosen were the wolves of the forestlands. When the war ended, the conflict won but the world in ruins, the born–Fay remained bound in flesh. Some took solace in one another.

For decades they drifted near many forest settlements, and then gradually gravitated toward the varied lands of the elves. Rarely, a small group lingered near an elven clan for a time. One night, a female ready to give birth lumbered into an elven village, and they took her in. Her puppies were not Fay, but neither were they wolves. The first litter was born with coats of varied shades of silver-gray and crystalline eyes, unlike the wolf forms of born-Fay.

And these first ones mated, and the females gave birth to a second generation.

From these descended what were called the *majay-hì*, an ancient elvish word Wynn simplistically translated as 'Fay-hound' or 'hound of the Fay.' The original born-Fay, though long-lived, passed away once their mortal flesh gave out. The descendants of their flesh still thrived in seclusion, roaming the elven forest as one of its natural guardians. Though more than animals, the *majay-hì* were but a shadow and a whisper of the original born-Fay.

Since the Forgotten History, no Fay had chosen to be born in flesh – until Chap.

One moment – or one eternity – he was with his kin, singular and many, all in one. In an instant, the first measure of time in his new awareness, he was a wet, squirming pup struggling against his siblings for a place to nurse from his mother. His birth was his own choice, for once again the Fay needed one of their own among mortals.

Unlike his brothers and sisters, he was fully aware of who and what he was. His first emotion was loneliness. His second was fear in isolation. Though flesh made him one of the litter, he was apart from them in his awareness. And apart from his kin, the Fay, lost in a prison of flesh.

Gonc was his 'touch' upon the essence of any *thing* in existence, to both know and be all that it truly was in its innate nature. He had only this body now. Gone was also his awareness of eternity as a whole, and he lived in 'moments,' one after the other. Even memory of his place among the Fay became mute and cloudy. For a living 'mind' could never hold full awareness of all that was the Fay.

At first his small body seemed so useless. It took many days and nights before he understood the 'how' and necessity of walking on legs. Then he was running before his siblings stopped falling on their snouts. He gained his first reprieve from grief and panic over all that he had given up.

He learned the delight of whipping grass and wind, the joy of mother's tongue on his stomach, and the comfort of sleep and food. There was also wrestling with his brothers and sisters. He learned compassion when he tried not to exploit his greater sentience by winning too often.

Memories were a thing for the living, limited and fragile. Not like the awareness within the Fay that Chap just barely . . . remembered. Like anyone's memories of an earlier past time.

And Leesil hid from his.

Chap stood alone outside the smithy, his frustration mounting. Part of the purpose he carried into flesh was to bring Leesil to Magiere, to save her from the Enemy. But what of saving Leesil?

Intimacy of body and spirit bonded them, but the

bond now grew fragile as Leesil stepped farther into the past. Perhaps Magiere was all there was to keep him from being lost in the past he struggled against. Chap was uncertain how to foster this. And how much could Magiere herself face of what she learned of Leesil in this place the humans called the Warlands?

Something tugged on Chap's tail, and he jumped, startled.

A smudge-faced girl with bone-thin arms grasped at his switching tail with a wide grin. Chap turned about, sticking his nose into her. Beneath her burlap dress he felt the ridges of tiny ribs and the swell of a bloated belly. Prolonged hunger had begun to deform her.

Chap glanced once down the main way, but Leesil had not returned. He pushed at the little girl with his head, herding her toward the smithy's front door and the busy preparations for a hot meal.

4

As Magiere pulled Port and Imp to a stop outside of Venjètz, she wished Leesil had warned them of the markers lining its outer wall.

Heads in varied states of decay were spitted on regularly spaced iron spikes high on the stone. One iron crow's cage hung from the rampart upon a chain, the body within rotted and pecked down to exposed bone. The dangling cage was more unsettling than the other warnings. A dead man's head on a spike was still a dead man. Anyone locked in a crow's cage would still be alive. For a while.

Leesil sat silently beside Magiere on the wagon's bench, as if the heads were common things not worth noting. She looked away from the crow's cage but found herself staring at one skull, denuded of flesh, with hollow black holes for eyes and jaw dangling low.

This is the world my Leesil was born into.

Wynn choked as she averted her face. Magiere wasn't one to coddle the sage, but she reached back to pull Wynn's hood over her eyes.

'Don't look up,' she said. 'We'll be inside soon.'

'Traitors,' Leesil said, watching the crow's cage spin slightly in the low wind. 'Or those he accused as such. Cold weather keeps the stench down. In summer you can smell it before the walls are in sight.'

Magiere knew the 'he' Leesil spoke of was Darmouth.

She kept up her calm front, though she still worried over Leesil's strange withdrawal since entering this land.

'Pull your hood forward, around your face!' she told him. 'Maybe no peasants have mentioned your eyes, but there may still be a guardsman or two left alive who'd remember a half-elf.'

Chap whined and shoved his head across the wagon's bench between Magiere and Leesil.

'Get down,' she told the dog. 'You attract almost as much attention as he does.'

Chap dropped back into the wagon's bed, turned a circle, and curled in the corner below the bench. He lifted his head with perked ears, looking to Wynn, but the young sage had her own head down. When he whined again, she looked over at him. She was strangely hesitant, but then crawled across to cuddle next to him, burying her hands in the fur of his back.

Magiere braced herself to enter the warlord's capital. When she clucked to Port and Imp, and they rounded the curve of the city wall, there was a line of six carts and wagons waiting to enter. As they drew up at the back of the line, she caught sight of vehicles waiting inside to exit. The two-wheeled cart in front of her was filled with grain sacks.

'Venjètz is the center of trade within this province,' Leesil said, his face hidden inside his hood. 'They buy or sell almost anything here, but you need to show reason for entering. Written permission from the military is required to set up residence. Artisans, blacksmiths, carpenters – anyone with tools and a skill – are accepted. Peasants aren't allowed in except to trade their harvest. They're given two days to finish and get out.'

'Why is this?' Wynn whispered.

'The city would be overrun with refugees, more so now, I'd guess. There aren't enough necessities to support thousands with no skills. If you can contribute, you're accepted. Otherwise you're leaving . . . one way or another.'

He fell silent as Magiere drove their wagon up to the gatehouse. A young guard in a leather hauberk with no crest or surcoat approached them. He eyed Port and Imp briefly, running his hand through Port's lush coat.

'Fine horses,' he said. 'What's your business?'

His tone was short but not rude, and Magiere held up an empty canvas sack. 'Passing through. We need to resupply in your market.'

Leesil had told her what to do. She opened their money pouch to show the guard its contents. Leesil had removed most of the coins before they arrived, especially any gold that was left. Commerce bringing currency to the city was welcome, but too large a coin purse would be suspect.

The guard glanced into the purse, nodded, and waved her through. And so they entered the city where Leesil grew up.

Magiere wanted to take his hand but let him be for now. In the last few nights he'd barely touched her as they fell asleep. His thoughts were lost somewhere here in his past. She could follow him to this place, but she couldn't find where he hid inside of himself – hid from her.

They passed a large stable on the left. Straight ahead was a row of eateries, inns, and two taverns, all positioned to be found easily by travelers. Most folk either walked about or traveled in wagons. Motley-garbed soldiers patrolled on foot in twos and threes, while only a few with better armor rode horses.

Venjètz had grown over many decades upon a plateau among the hills. To the city's northeast side, Darmouth's square-block keep rose into sight above the rooftops. The most heavily populated cities, like Bela, were settled upon rocky rises of land with the castle and grounds dead center at the top, towering above all else. Here, Darmouth's keep rested offshore in a large lake, with its front portal connected to the shore by a fortified stone bridge. It would be a hard place to siege.

Magiere glanced over her shoulder as Wynn lifted her head to look about. The sage was still pale but crawled over to sit behind the wagon's bench.

'How did they build a keep inside of a lake?'

'It wasn't built in the water,' Leesil replied. 'More than a century back, a self-titled king named Timeron had it constructed on dry ground. Several streams and a small river up in the mountains were then diverted. Water flooded in to surround it.'

'Oh,' Wynn replied, and looked about the dingy city. 'Where do we begin?'

Leesil fell quiet for a moment. 'My old house by the lakeshore.'

Magiere glanced at him with doubt. 'It's been eight years. Someone else will be living there, if the house still remains.'

'It'll be there, and I need only a moment inside.'

She pursed her lips and hoped he wasn't planning to steal into someone else's home. Chap whined and began pawing at Wynn's pack.

'Wait, please stop,' Wynn said. 'He wants to tell us something.'

Magiere snorted in disgust and didn't pull in the horses. 'Probably about food, no doubt.'

Wynn retrieved the 'talking hide' and rolled it out in an open space in the wagon's back. It was a large squarely trimmed hide on which were painted rows and columns of elvish symbols. To 'speak' with his companions, Chap would point to the correct symbol and Wynn would translate.

'Not necessarily,' Wynn replied. 'He may have advice concerning Leesil's plans.'

Magiere peered over her shoulder as Chap pawed the symbols, and Wynn followed with her eyes.

'Oh, Chap!' Wynn blurted out, and snatched up the hide. 'He smelled sausages back there and wants to stop.'

'What did I tell you?' Magiere said.

'Why do you always think of food at the worst possible times?' Wynn griped at the dog.

Chap returned her a whiny growl and a lick of his nose.

Wynn grew serious again and leaned closer to Leesil. 'Will there be any more . . . anything like outside?'

'Only at the keep walls,' Leesil replied, 'if someone of importance was recently tried and executed.'

'A trial?' Magiere asked.

'A figure of speech,' Leesil answered. 'Bodies left within the city would be a health hazard. Darmouth enjoys warning all who enter, but he wouldn't risk spreading disease here. But be careful, as the military has a free hand in Venjètz. No one questions their decisions, even if a death is involved.'

Wynn huddled back down. In midafternoon, the air was still cold enough that they could see one another's breath, and hers was quick and shallow.

'Head for the keep and the lakeshore,' Leesil said, motioning Magiere forward. 'Then down Favor's Row. It's where Darmouth's favored are housed, meaning those kept close under his watch.'

Magiere clucked the horses into a side street, carefully avoiding citizens walking along the way. It hadn't occurred to her that Leesil might have grown up in the shadow of a keep, as she had in Chemestúk. For some reason she'd pictured him living on the forest's edge, though she'd never asked him about it. It made more sense that he'd remained well within reach of his lord and master.

They passed dwellings and shops, and wove through a small open market filled with croaking hawkers selling wares and the warm smells of meat pies and sausage. Chap groaned in misery, but everyone ignored him as the wagon moved on.

Wynn sucked in a deep breath as they emerged onto a wide cobbled road running around the lake. Magiere frowned at what she saw.

Ahead was a two-story gatehouse to a masoned bridge running out into the lake. Two more high archways marked its span outward to the four-towered block keep sprouting from the water to four or five levels in height. It wasn't the castle of Bela or even the Droevinkan grand prince's stronghold, but it made a weighty impression. The bridge was wide enough for a wagon with room to spare. Where it met the keep's portcullis there appeared to be a lowered drawbridge connecting the fortification to the bridge.

Soldiers paced the bridge, and more were atop the gatehouse and the two arches along its reach to the keep. A few were out along the cobbled road, but none paid undue attention to their wagon.

'Turn left,' Leesil instructed, gesturing with one finger. 'The fifth one down, but don't stop until I tell you.'

Magiere pulled the left rein with a soft snap, and the horses turned down the cobbled road.

There were no buildings within a stone's throw of the gatehouse, but beyond that they were packed along the lake. Dwellings of varied height and make, stone and timber, walled the shoreline. Though not the lavish dwellings of Bela's elite, they were far more than the hovel Magiere had shared as a child with Aunt Bieja. The fifth one was no exception.

A clean gray-stone foundation rose to the sills of the ground-floor windows. The timber plank walls were smooth, not quick-cut, like those used to rebuild the Sea Lion tavern. Whitewashed shutters framed windows with glass panes. At the end of the cobbled walkway up to the house, dormant rosebushes framed a large oak door.

Magiere stared.

Leesil's voice was soft and hollow. 'Not what you expected?'

She didn't answer; nor did she pull the wagon to a halt, but drove past. No, it was not at all what she'd expected for Leesil's home in a place called the Warlands.

'What now?' she asked.

'Turn onto the next side street.' Leesil leaned around toward Wynn. 'Take some pears and go to the front door. Knock to see if anyone is home.'

'But . . .'Wynn glanced nervously at the house.'What if someone answers?'

'That's what the pears are for,' he said. 'Tell them a silver penny for the lot, and take it if they agree. More than likely they'll slam the door in your face.'

The sage nodded apprehensively. Magiere reached the side street and turned the horses. There was barely enough room to fit between the buildings, and she pulled to a stop once the wagon's rear was beyond the corner.

'I am not certain of this,' Wynn said. 'Is this where Darmouth houses people like . . . you and your parents?'

'As we passed, I got a look through the front window. There's a shield on the wall over the hearth. Likely one of Darmouth's officers lives there now. All I need from you is to see if anyone is at home. Take Chap, if you like.'

Wynn nodded hesitantly and gathered pears into a small burlap bag. As she slipped out of the wagon, Chap hopped down to follow, and both turned the corner out of sight.

Leesil quietly climbed over the bench to the wagon's tail, and Magiere followed. They could just see the house from their vantage point. Wynn scurried up to the front door, knocked, and waited, both hands clutching the sack to her chest. Chap paced behind her with raised ears as he looked along the street.

Wynn raised a hand to knock again, but didn't. Instead she stepped slowly around one barren rosebush and up to the front window to peer inside. Chap became agitated, lunging out to the street's edge, turning both ways. He trotted back to snatch the hem of Wynn's coat in his teeth.

'What is she doing?' Magiere whispered.

Leesil tried to step off the wagon, but she grabbed his shoulder, holding him back.

Wynn turned and jerked her coat from Chap's teeth. When he trotted a few paces away, then stopped to look back, she followed him. They both returned to climb up in the wagon.

'No one appears to be home,' she breathed, her face pink from the cold air. 'I do not think anyone has been there in some time. There is a helmet on the floor, and dust has gathered on it.'

Leesil glanced once at the house and then spun on his haunches to unlash the travel chest tied down in the wagon's bed. He rummaged through it and withdrew a long, narrow box.

'Oh, no.' Magiere shook her head. 'You're not breaking into a house less than a hundred paces from Darmouth's keep.'

He ignored her and opened the box. Instead of pulling thin wire hooks from its lid panel, he used a fingernail to pry up the lid's lining and slipped out a small object from beneath it.

'I don't need to break in,' he said. 'I have the key.' With his box hidden beneath his cloak, he dropped out of the wagon, landing lightly on the ground.

Magiere climbed out, wondering why Leesil had kept the key all these years. 'Wynn, you wait here with Chap.'

There was no one in sight along the side street, but Magiere eyed the cobbled road before following Leesil across to the house. He crept down the narrow space between it and the next building, and she kept close as they stepped out at the back.

As Leesil slipped the key into the back door, Magiere saw the lake's edge ten paces off – and the keep looming out of the water. No shed, nor trees, or anything at all blocked her view. They were in plain sight of Darmouth's stronghold.

Magiere crouched low. Before she snatched Leesil to drag him back down the side path, the lock clicked and he ducked inside the house. Magiere followed, shutting the door behind them, but not without a scowl for Leesil's recklessness.

The kitchen hearth was bare of any fire's remains, but it was still warmer inside away from the winter breeze. Magiere's curiosity overrode her irritation, and she looked about the home of Leesil's childhood.

A crafted iron stove stood to one side, likely added after the place had been built with its original cooking hearth. There was a floor hatch in the rear corner to the left of the door. This was all she had time to note, as Leesil headed through the house.

The next room held a table and high-backed chairs of stout walnut. Beneath the thin layer of dust, Magiere judged they were smooth and well finished. A matching cabinet reaching to the ceiling stood against the far wall. The wide archway to the front room was trimmed in the same wood and carved with squared spiral patterns from one side to the other. No other fixtures were present in the meal room.

Sparse but rich furnishings, all tainted with dust. Magiere wondered what had happened to the inhabitants.

'Is this what it looked like when you lived here?' she whispered.

Leesil pulled back his hood and headed through the archway. 'The house is the same, nothing else.'

His voice was too calm. Magiere imagined he'd spent most of his days in this city hidden away beneath a hood or some covering. He looked odd now with his long white-blond hair completely tucked under the scarf, but his narrow face and amber eyes were so impassive.

A braided rug lay in the middle of the front room's wood floor. Below the front window stood a divan. Its dark leather covering was meticulously mounted by an even row of polished brass nails binding it to the walnut frame. Nearby was the steel helmet Wynn had mentioned. A round target shield hung above the small empty hearth. Beyond these remains the room was empty, yet whoever had vacated this place sometime ago hadn't taken the last of their belongings.

Leesil headed for a smaller archway, and Magiere spotted the heavy front door beyond it. He turned around the archway's side, away from the door, and disappeared. She hurried after to find stairs to the next floor, and Leesil already up to the first landing above. She tried to step quietly as she followed. The stairs continued up another level, but he stood in the hallway, staring through a door left ajar.

The long room within was furnished with a large four-poster bed covered in a thick comforter. The other furnishings here, from the dresser and polished silver mirror to the wide chest at the foot of the bed, seemed undisturbed and in place. The last residents had left in a hurry.

Magiere noticed that Leesil wasn't looking at the room's contents. He stared toward the rear wall, and she followed his gaze.

There was a window seat, soft cushions of burgundy in place and heavy cream curtains left open. Through the glass, Magiere saw only the distant forest across the lake. She couldn't tell what kept Leesil there, as if waiting. Then he dropped his gaze with a deep silent breath and turned back to the stairs.

Instead of rounding the banister to head upward, he climbed the rail from the outside, hooked his leg over it, and leaned out to the ceiling above the hallway.

'What are you doing?' she whispered.

Suspended in the hall's center was an oil lamp that could be lowered by a cord tied off at the side wall. Leesil reached for the ceiling mount where the cord passed through an iron ring. He twisted the mount. When it came away in his hand, he lowered the mount and lantern to Magiere, then reached into the ceiling hole.

His expression shifted suddenly to relief and then disappointment. Magiere set the lantern down, stepping under him to peer up, but she couldn't see into the hole even after he pulled his hand out.

'No note or message,' he said, 'but the hidden coin pouch is gone. There's no sign of a hasty search or tampering with the lamp's fixture.'

'What?' Magiere asked. 'I don't understand.'

Leesil unhooked his leg from the stairway rail and dropped down. 'My father kept money hidden here in case of a sudden need . . . such as flight from Darmouth. My mother and I knew of it as well.'

'Then this is good. Your parents took it and fled.'

'We were also to leave a message for anyone left behind. I thought perhaps I'd find . . .'

'A letter from the past?' she finished for him. 'Leesil, they knew you'd left. If they fled together, there was no reason to leave any word for you.'

This wasn't a comfort to him. He hung his head with his eyes closed. As much as he'd kept his distance in recent days, Magiere stepped close, running her hand across his shoulder, down his arm, and to his own hand.

'Remember the dead ends we hit while searching my past? At least you know they took the coin and tried to escape . . . together.'

He looked at her, and after a long moment finally squeezed her hand.

'We need to leave,' she said. 'As long-abandoned as this place looks, we don't want patrolling soldiers to suspect anyone's here.'

Her words spurred him, but not to leave. This time he did round the stairwell rail and climbed toward the next floor. Magiere's own warning became real as she heard muffled voices out in the street before the house.

'We need to go – now!' she whispered sharply.

When he took another step upward, she snatched the back of his cloak.

Leesil turned on her and grabbed her wrist in a tight grip. The look he gave her was no longer passive but cold and poised. It hurt her like a threat. She almost let go.

Magiere's next instinct was anger, but she bit it down. It was difficult for him to leave with so little, but she'd been doubtful that he would find much after eight years.

'Please. We have to go,' she whispered as calmly as she could. 'Now!'

Leesil eased his grip on her wrist, and Magiere backed

down the stairs, watching him until she was certain he followed. She kept along the wall with her eyes on the window as they passed through the front room, then hurried through the meal room, kitchen, and out the back door.

At the end of the narrow path between the houses, she checked both ways. Two soldiers ambled down the street toward the bridge gatehouse. When they were far enough along, she hurried across with Leesil close behind her, and they both climbed through the wagon's back to the bench.

'Did you find anything?' Wynn asked.

'Just that they may have tried to escape,' Magiere answered. 'There's no way to tell when or to where.'

Leesil settled on the bench beside her. He pulled his cloak about himself and did not look back toward his old home.

'What about speaking with their friends?' Wynn asked.

'Friends?' Leesil repeated. A frown wrinkled his brow as if such a notion were naïve.

'Yes, someone here must have known your parents. Perhaps they would have heard something.'

'Assassins don't have friends,' Leesil snapped. He paused, lost in thought, then whispered one word. 'Byrd.'

'What about a bird?' Magiere asked.

'A man, not an animal,' Leesil muttered. 'His name is Byrd, and he owns an inn out back of the merchant district. My father spoke of him something like a friend. I knew him as well.'

A brief flash of relief flooded Magiere, gratitude for any clue that might give Leesil answers. It was quickly followed by nervous caution.

'Can he be trusted?' she asked.

'In a way,' he answered.

Magiere's anger got the best of her this time. 'What does that mean?'

Leesil breathed in and blew the air out slowly. 'He's one of Darmouth's spies.'

Lit braziers of heavy iron lined the keep's council hall where Lady Hedí Progae sat across the table from Baron Emêl Milea. Between them at the table's end was their host, Lord Darmouth. Hedí silently counted the moments until this tense evening would end.

Stuffed pheasants, dried peaches, winter nutcake, and loaves of freshly baked bread were carried in on polished wood trays. All the guests ate from finely glazed plates with silver forks and knives. Hedí had no patience for pretenses of finery, though she did note that the number of Darmouth's trusted ministers had diminished over the years. The only minister present this night was her Emêl. She made polite play with her food in small bites as she watched her host.

Lord Darmouth's brown hair was cropped short, but the front and temples were graying. His blockish face was lined, and there were faint hints of old scars below his left eye. Even at a formal dinner, he wore a steel-reinforced leather breastplate and long daggers sheathed upon his wide belt. Bearded in past years, he now shaved daily, perhaps believing it made him look younger. Pointless, as he was nothing more than an aging savage.

Hedí glanced across the table at Emêl. In his early forties with thinning red hair, he was the one person here this night who understood her false smile of submission.

He had taught her self-preservation, to keep everything inside. Emêl still lived, while so many of Darmouth's entitled nobles and officers ended their days on an iron spike upon the keep's walls. They dangled there until their bodies rotted enough to tumble into the lake and vanish from sight, if not memory.

Each time Darmouth shifted in his high-backed walnut chair, Hedí smelled musk and stale sweat. Reaching for the wine bottle, he brushed his forearm across the back of her hand, and she flinched. His sinewy limb was like knotted cord around a log, and covered in salt-and-pepper-shaded hair. She went rigid to keep from driving her dinner knife through his wrist.

Hedí smiled, demure as always.

Darmouth did not smile back. Instead his gaze moved down her burgundy satin gown and back up to her shoulder-length black curls. Emêl stopped chewing when he noticed Darmouth's wandering eyes.

Emêl had suggested the gown, and Hedí regretted her agreement. Though her attire pleased him, and that was acceptable, it was too low-cut in the presence of a murdering lecher like Darmouth. Pleasing such a man was as dangerous as defying him.

Seven officers were seated at the table, among them Lieutenant Omasta, head of Darmouth's personal guard. Between bites, Omasta tugged uncomfortably at his blond beard and gripped his fork awkwardly like a shovel. Normally these men ate off the same large platter or out of the pots while discussing military matters in the meal hall across the way. This entire dinner display of trays and wine sipped from plundered silver goblets appeared to be for Hedí's benefit alone.

Lord Darmouth gestured to the roasted pheasant ringed in mushrooms.

'Please, my lady,' he said, voice deep and gravelly. 'Have a bit more.'

Perhaps she should be flattered. She could count the times he had used the word 'please' on one hand. Apprehension overcame her revulsion.

'In a moment,' she answered. 'I would like some wine first.'

He fumbled for idle conversation. 'Where are you and Emêl staying?'

'At the Bronze Bell.'

'Yes . . . a fine inn.'

A worthless exchange. They stayed at the Bronze Bell whenever Emêl was called to Venjètz. No visiting noble was lodged in the keep – nor wished to be. Darmouth poured wine into her goblet. Hedí hoped she could swallow smoothly, as he bit into a pheasant leg, speaking while chewing.

'Emêl, I want Tarôvli put down before the winter celebration. I want his head, and I want any officers with him for crow's fodder.'

The words were so casual that for one breath they didn't register upon Hedí. She stiffened and quickly relaxed before giving herself away.

'Of course, my lord,' Emêl said too slowly. 'I've deployed troops and recalled Captain Altani from the north. The matter will be settled before the new moon.'

Darmouth grunted acknowledgment. 'I've enough trouble with that witch, Lùkina, on my western border.'

'Yes, my lord,' Emêl replied more quickly. 'I've placed

most of my own men under your officers there to assist with patrols.'

More patrols, indeed. Hedí knew the growing number of raids across Darmouth's borders was more than the usual feints and jabs the provinces made at one another. The other tyrants of the Warlands watched Darmouth's grip tighten with each year. His hold weakened his own province, with the population decreasing and fewer men to conscript.

Lúkina Vallo was not the only one becoming a threat. There were rumors of Dusan Abosi's forces thickening beyond Darmouth's northern border. And Tarôvli's meager success at treachery from within was another sign of decay. One by one, Darmouth's nobles became starving dogs, turning on one another in desperation to survive. His territory was plagued from within, and the wolves of the Warlands were circling outside.

Hedí had learned of Mikhail Tarôvli, like all other shadowy dealings in the province, from Emêl. The young Count Tarôvli had lured away enough conscripts to ambush a contingent of Darmouth's sparse cavalry. No one knew it was his doing at the time. Some upstart officer was always scheming, but Tarôvli was exceptional or lucky. He managed to build his forces and arms for nearly three moons before his treachery was uncovered. Most never launched their first assault.

Tarôvli was unfortunate, no matter how cunning, for he would not die quietly and quickly in the night. Hedí felt no pity for him.

Sometimes nobles and officers eliminated one another, seizing a rival's plan for their own. Hedí's knowledge of such intrigue was sparse, but lately she had

grown more skilled at gleaning information. Her awareness and hatred grew like an ice-capped mountain constructed one pebble at a time.

Years ago, when Hedí was only fifteen, she, her mother,
and her sisters were invited to a 'ladies' evening' by her
uncle's half sister. It was a long and strangely tense event
of halting empty talk and cards, but they were kept so
late that it was necessary to spend the night. When they
returned home in the morning, the house servants said
her father was still asleep in his chamber. Everyone assumed
he had taken an evening out for himself and been up late
as well. No one disturbed him, even as soldiers hammered
at the manor doors before anyone finished stripping off
their cloaks.

Andrey Progae, Hedí's father, had died alone in his
bed, a thin blade precisely thrust into his skull just above
the back of his neck.

The order had come directly from Darmouth.

Hedí's uncle and his half sister never came under suspicion, not losing their place in this province. They raised
not one finger for their kin. They were never outcast as
the family of a traitor, like Hedí's mother and younger
sisters, who starved to death in the streets.

Hedí had been more fortunate, or so it was said. She
was given as mistress to Emêl for his constant loyalty to
Darmouth.

Emêl was kind, treating her with pity and, later, open
affection. She came to care for him and perhaps even
pity him in return. He was married to a cold-blooded
noblewoman ten years his senior, and there had never
been love between Emêl and his wife, Vàldyislàva. Hedí
was called 'fourth consort,' if referred to at all, though

she was truly the only one. Her predecessors had died in questionable ways, and it took little intelligence to turn a suspicious eye toward Vàldyislàva. So Emêl kept Hedí far from his manor in the west of the province. Through him, Hedí learned and assembled all the pieces of what she now knew.

Emêl promised to marry her, once he was free to do so. A nobleman could retain as many mistresses as he could afford, but he could have only one wife.

Hedí could not fathom why Darmouth insisted Emêl bring her on this evening. Emêl had been recalled to Venjètz six days ago. She had been to the keep with him several times, but never at night. No other women were present, so why was she alone here at a time when Darmouth should be looking to his borders?

Darmouth turned his cold eyes toward her again. He seemed fascinated by her hair. Upon her mother's and sister's reported deaths, Hedí slashed it off at chin length in mourning. When it grew back to her shoulders, it was a mass of black waves that pleased Emêl, so she kept it this length. Some ladies found it unfashionable, but Hedí did not care. Emêl was her only friend.

Her skin was the color of buttermilk, and Darmouth's gaze dropped down to her hands. She kept her eyes on her plate, pretending to be unaware of his inspection. It was not possible that he had serious designs upon her. Darmouth had taken no consort in nearly seven years. It was common knowledge that he saw spies and traitors everywhere, so he trusted no woman within his bedchamber. Even so, she had heard of his brothel visits.

As Darmouth cleared his throat, two slender figures entered the hall with silent steps. Hedí's presence made them pause. She had seen both before but not met either personally, as Emêl had warned her away.

Faris and Ventina were from a northern Móndyalítko clan. Slight and tall, Faris had dusky skin, wild black hair, and eyes to match. He wore his hair long, but this did not completely hide the scars on the left side of his head where his ear had been sliced off – Hedí did not know how this had happened. He spoke with deep, quiet tones and wore silver rings in the lobe of his remaining ear. Ventina looked enough like him to be a sister, or perhaps a cousin, rather than his wife. Her eyes shifted back and forth as she drifted in behind her husband. When her gaze passed over Darmouth, her hatred was too thinly masked. She and her mate skulked in their lord's shadow and did his bidding without question.

Darmouth frowned at their presence.

'My lord,' Faris breathed. 'I beg a word.'

'We are at dinner,' Darmouth rumbled. 'And you enter without announcement.'

Hedí expected Faris to back away, but he stepped closer.

'My lord, there was a skirmish at the Stravinan border over some deserters and their families in flight. A man crossed the border and engaged your troops.'

'Stravinans . . . breach a treaty?' Darmouth straightened with a glower. 'What is this horse piss? Who told you this?'

Faris hesitated, then drew close to whisper in his lord's ear. All the while Darmouth appeared on the edge of striking his servant down. The more he listened, the more attentive he became.

Hedí did not catch much beyond the mention of

white hair and strange eyes. She watched a flicker of alarm pass across Darmouth's features before they clouded with the same viciousness he showed when catching an underling in some minor deceit. He stood up.

'Omasta!' he snapped. 'Double the keep's watch and the contingent at the city walls. Double the length of shifts, if you have to. Any man with white hair, tan skin, and yellow-brown eyes is to be taken alive if possible, and if not, kill him on sight. Either way, bring him to me.'

Hedí's heart slowed as she looked to Emêl. He shook his head once in warning. Then his gaze drifted away.

'Forgive me, Hedí, but I must leave you,' Darmouth said, but he paused in the open arch of the council hall. 'Emêl, you and I will speak alone. See your lady back to the inn, and then join me in the Hall of Traitors.'

Hedí's fork clicked too sharply against her plate, and Emêl turned pale.

Leesil spotted the sign above the two-story inn that read only, BYRD'S. The place hadn't changed much. The walls were a bit more weatherworn, and the shutters over the glassless windows were faded. The shake roof's eaves were jagged and crusted with snow, but the place was strangely a welcome sight compared to all else since they'd entered Venjètz.

If only he'd remembered the cats.

Leesil put a hand on Chap's back. 'Don't you move!'

Chap growled, then whined, and Leesil felt a shudder run through the dog's taut muscles under rising fur.

'You're a Fay,' Leesil said in a low, threatening tone.

'Or that's what you've made us believe, so no doggish nonsense. You hear me?'

Chap's panting quickened, and Leesil gripped him by the scruff of the neck.

There were cats everywhere, sitting on window ledges, ducking around corners, or scurrying in and out of the front door left ajar. Large and small ones. Solid, striped, and spotted, they milled about the inn's front as if they were its common patrons.

Magiere stood at his side. 'Leesil?'

'I told you Byrd is . . . a bit odd,' he replied.

Leesil kept his hood up and forward, shadowing his face. They'd agreed Magiere and Wynn would do the talking, until he decided whether or not to reveal himself. While Byrd was part of Darmouth's web of spies and informants, he was the only person besides Leesil's mother to whom Gavril had shown any trust. Sometimes the two had sat up talking through a whole night or just played cards.

'Look at all of them,' Wynn said in wonder, and stepped up to the doorway to scratch a slender gray calico behind the ears. 'Where did they all come from?'

'Everywhere, miss,' a baritone voice called from inside. 'And they pass the word along that there's a home to be found here.'

Wynn stiffened upright with a quick backstep and bumped into Leesil coming up behind her. Looking through the cracked door, Leesil saw a few felines within, but his attention settled on the man standing near a belly-high bar with no stools before it.

His bright red shirt contrasted oddly with his ruddy complexion. It was impossible to tell the color of his hair beneath the faded yellow scarf tied around his head. He was in his midforties, of medium height and stocky build. He looked the same as Leesil remembered. Well, perhaps a bit paunchier.

'Welcome,' he said, smiling openly at Wynn. 'Do you need rooms? We've plenty, as business is slow of late.'

Leesil ushered Wynn in ahead of himself. Indeed, the cats were the only patrons for the evening. The dimly lit little common room was stuffed with nothing more than empty chairs and tables. Magiere followed, now the one gripping Chap's scruff. The dog shook visibly with restraint, and his silvery coat bristled all over.

Byrd frowned at the sight of Chap. 'Sure you want to bring him in here?'

'He'll behave,' Magiere answered.

'Ha, it's not him I'm worried about,' Byrd added. 'He's well out-numbered.'

Leesil glanced down to see two small kittens toddle out through the legs of a rickety chair. The leader was a slender orange tabby, while the follower was a roly-poly brown with a rather dim expression on his round, bushy face. Without a hint of fear, the pair sniffed Chap all over, or as high as their little noses could reach. They proceeded to dance through his legs while rubbing against him.

Chap made a sound like he'd choked on his own yowl, and Wynn leaned down into the dog's face.

'Do not touch them!' she ordered. 'They are babies, and they do not know any better.'

Byrd smiled widely as he scooped up the tiny tabby and handed it to Wynn. 'This is Tomato, the smart and sassy one. Her brother there is Potato, affectionate but none too bright.'

Wynn held Tomato close, and Potato began thumping his head on Chap's leg, demanding attention. Magiere slowly released her grip. Chap huffed but did nothing more than shuffle about trying to evade Potato's head butts.

A hissing and spitting came from around the bar's far end, and Chap stiffened with his ears drawn back.

The largest cat Leesil had ever seen sauntered out of the kitchen and into the common room. Dirty cream-colored with green stains on his back, the cat had a wide stomach that nearly touched the floor. His left ear was tattered and several teeth were missing, but his claws grated the floorboards as he padded up behind Byrd.

Chap growled, looking anxious over an opponent willing to fight.

'Stop that. These are guests,' Byrd said to the new arrival, and offered Wynn an apologetic shrug. 'This is Clover Roll, my partner. He'll not plague you as long as your dog behaves.'

'Clover Roll?' Wynn repeated.

'Look at his back,' Byrd said. 'He never tires of rolling in the grass.'

'By the size of his gut,' Magiere said, sounding openly tired of discussing Byrd's pets, 'I'm surprised he can roll at all. How much for two rooms, and where can we stable our horses?'

Leesil watched Byrd's expression, remembering the few nights his father had brought him along on an evening of tea and stew and cards. Gavril once told him that Byrd could be trusted to do the right thing. It'd meant little to Leesil at the time, for he'd learned to trust no one but his parents. Now his stomach knotted over memories resurfacing after the years he'd kept them buried. From inside his hood, he looked into Byrd's eyes, and the older man tensed, taking a step closer.

'Do I know you?' Byrd asked.

This man hadn't changed, always direct and open, or so it appeared. A good front, if nothing else. His father's only friend was all Leesil had left for a lead, though he still didn't know why Gavril had ever trusted another servant of Darmouth.

Leesil pulled back his hood.

Magiere tensed, dark eyes locking on Byrd. Leesil caught the shift of her cloak that told him her hand was on her falchion. He stood quietly waiting.

For a moment Byrd's face went blank in disbelief. Much time had passed, and Leesil's hair was still under his kerchief.

'Lad?' Byrd said. 'It can't be . . .'

'Yes, it's me.'

Byrd didn't lunge to embrace him nor call out a welcome. Instead he braced a hand against the bar. Magiere jerked her falchion from its sheath.

'Call for soldiers or try to leave, and you won't reach the door.'

Clover Roll burst into a hissing fit. Chap answered him with an even louder snarl.

'Magiere, put it away,' Leesil said. He hadn't expected Byrd to be glad to see him. 'Byrd, I know it has been a long time, but hear me out.'

There was no anger or blame in Byrd's face. He looked as if someone had punched him in the stomach. 'Oh, no, lad. You don't need to . . . Are you hungry? Have you eaten?'

Leesil backed away and sank down in a chair. When Magiere refused to move, he reached out to brush her aside. She stepped around him, finally sheathing her blade, and settled a protective hand on his shoulder.

'We came to ask after his parents,' Magiere said, and there was still a hint of warning in her voice. 'Do you know what happened to them . . . after Leesil left?'

Byrd looked Magiere over from head to toe, staring briefly at her black hair and again at her well-made leather boots. He ignored her threatening glower and turned back to Leesil.

'This is your woman? Trust you to pick a fierce one.' He cocked his head at Wynn. 'That one looks easier to live with, but your father liked the fierce ones, too.'

Magiere's fingers tightened slightly on Leesil's shoulder. Wynn looked up at Byrd as if she wasn't sure whether to be flattered or insulted.

Words stuck in Leesil's throat. Indeed, his father would have been fond of Magiere, though Leesil wondered what his mother would think if . . . when they found her. He breathed in slowly.

'What happened to Gavril? And my mother?'

For the first time, a hint of anger registered in Byrd's voice. 'It's a bit late to be asking.'

Leesil abruptly stood and turned for the door, pulling up his hood in shame. He shouldn't have come here. Friend or not, Byrd didn't deserve old wounds opened by Leesil's own sins.

'No, wait, damn you!' Byrd called, then grumbled something under his breath. 'You had no choice. You weren't meant for your father's life, and no one understood that better than him. Now sit down.'

Leesil stopped. 'Where are they? Are they dead?'

'Sit — your woman, too,' Byrd said, and he waved Wynn over as well. 'Come, girl.'

When his guests were settled, he left for the kitchen and quickly returned with a pot of hot water, biscuits, and four mugs. He dropped tea leaves in the pot and sat down at the table to gaze at Leesil.

'You look so much like her, but you act like him.' His eyes dropped to the table. 'I don't know what happened to them. When I heard you bolted, I sent word to Gavril. I'd have gone myself, but I feared being spotted. I thought he and Nein'a would make their way out of the city somehow.' Byrd paused to lace fingers together as he leaned on the table. 'The gods only know why, but they ran for the keep. Pure madness! They were seen inside heading down into the lower levels. I tried to find out more but . . . For a year I kept searching for answers, believe me.'

Leesil's mind and stomach both churned. While he'd been drinking himself to sleep every night, this man had been searching for his parents.

'Why would they run into the keep?' Wynn asked, still holding the purring Tomato in her lap. 'There must be some reason. Leesil?'

Leesil tried to focus on the moment. 'I can't think of anything. I rarely went there myself unless ordered to. My father went to give reports, and my mother was sometimes called to attend an evening gathering that Darmouth hosted.'

'Your mother was the loveliest creature I ever saw,' Byrd said. 'But you've done all right for yourself, too.' He stood up, ignoring Magiere's scowl. 'I'll dish us some supper while we talk, but you need to keep hidden. Eyes are everywhere, and these days it takes even less coin or threat to loosen a tongue.'

As little as Byrd knew, Leesil wondered how and where the man had acquired the strange detail of his parents' flight into the keep. He watched his father's only confidant round the bar and disappear through the kitchen's curtained doorway. Indeed, Darmouth's spies could be found in the most inviting places.

Darmouth stood in the center of his forefathers' crypt in the keep's belly. To either side of him, stone coffins rose from the floor to waist height. This was the Hall of Traitors, a name coined by the fearful after his father's death, though it had nothing to do with the occupants of the two tombs.

Four braziers mounted in iron brackets glowed from pillars to either side of the center space. Once three separate storage rooms, the walls had been opened into repeating archways to convert all three into one room. In the far back wall were series of arched cubbies carved into the stone from ceiling to floor. The braziers' light didn't reach far enough to illuminate them, and they remained black pockets of darkness.

Darmouth laid his hand on the tomb to his left. His fingers grazed over the carved image of a face not unlike his own, but with a long beard and thick mustache. Here rested his father, placed within the stone coffin after his death. His grandfather's remains had been exhumed and placed in the other tomb. He only wished he could locate the body of his great-grandfather, who'd taken this province from Timeron a hundred or more years ago.

Kings believed in lineage and the honored crypt of an unbroken family line. Bloodline was immortality, leaving a piece of oneself in a son, who in turn passed it on to his heir. When he was young, Darmouth never dwelled on this. As the years passed, he obsessed more and more over the gray in his hair and growing weight of his sword.

He hadn't kept these lands only to lose them to a traitorous upstart or some rival province leader. Not one of them was strong enough to take what he held. If by pure luck one ever did, this province and those around it would descend into chaos. No, Darmouth's people needed him, the only one strong enough to maintain order in the face of the petty warlords of the other provinces.

Footsteps echoed through the crypt's open door from the outside hallway. Darmouth looked up to find Emêl standing in the opening between two of Omasta's armed men. The bodyguards looked to Darmouth for approval. He nodded, and they stepped aside.

Emêl, who lacked true strength of will, couldn't even rid himself of an unwanted wife. The arranged marriage was intended to give him sons of older blood, but the match failed to produce an heir. Still, Emêl was dependable, one of Darmouth's few old friends and the last of his ministers. He deserved fair treatment, had earned it, but all who served Darmouth needed to be reminded where their loyalties lay. This was why he held such meetings in the tomb of his forefathers, where he passed judgment on both the true and traitorous.

White-faced and silent, Emêl remained in the doorway, slender in his simple brown breeches and a black tunic over a white shirt. Although unarmed, as required here, he was the best fencer Darmouth had ever witnessed. His skill with a straight saber was unequaled.

'Enter,' Darmouth commanded.

To his credit, Emêl didn't hesitate. It was whispered that Darmouth sometimes executed traitors himself in this place. True enough, as Emêl had witnessed twice.

'My lord,' Emêl said. His voice was calm, but fear flickered in his green eyes.

'I'm giving you Tarôvli's holdings. You know his region of the province well enough, and the income will increase your coffers.'

'My lord?'

'You've earned it,' Darmouth went on. 'And I know how little you stay at your own estate these days. A second home would be useful, and something few can boast of.'

He could see Emêl's thoughts racing, waiting for the catch.

'You're also the first to know I've decided to marry,' Darmouth said, looking down upon his grandfather's tomb. 'Someday I'll rest here myself. I need a strong son to hold this land and continue my plan to unify the Warlands under one rule. I choose you to stand as my second and sword-bearer in the marriage rite.'

He paused. Emêl must be flattered to hear his lord's private thoughts, and honored to be the one to stand with him on the wedding day.

'I need a legitimate heir,' Darmouth continued. 'It's late in life for such things, but I've been occupied with holding the province together. Now my duty is to sire a son with the same strength.'

Emêl took one step closer, now smiling with thin lips. 'Good news, my lord. Who is the lady you have chosen?'

'Hedí Progae, most certainly.'

Blank confusion passed across Emêl's features.

'She's unwed and from noble blood that I titled,' Darmouth went on. 'Though small, she's strong and healthy, and young enough to bear me sons.'

Emêl faltered. 'No offense intended, my lord, but she is the daughter of a traitor.'

'The years since Progae's death have made her respectful and accepting of her place,' Darmouth replied.

He liked her black wavy hair and hoped his son – or sons – would inherit it. All the better to sire more than one to see which emerged the strongest. This too was best for his people, his province . . . the nation he would forge in this region that outlanders named the Warlands.

'But . . . my lord,' Emêl stammered. 'She has been with me for years and produced no child. If you seek an heir, perhaps another might be a better choice.'

Darmouth's voice hardened. 'It's you, my friend, who've produced no heir. Not with your wife, nor any of your mistresses.'

Emêl went silent, his expression unreadable, but Darmouth knew him well.

'Of course, my lord,' Emêl finally agreed.

'You can give her this good news,' Darmouth said. 'The marriage rite takes place before the winter feast, once Tarôvli is put down. We'll celebrate the traitor's end and the future of my lineage for the sake of the country I'll make here. You're dismissed.'

Emêl's green eyes dropped from Darmouth's face to the twin tombs. He bowed and backed out of the crypt.

Darmouth turned away into the depths of the room. Though his own bloodline, past and future, was still in his thoughts, another unwelcome threat surfaced to plague him. Faris's news at dinner was disturbing, more so for coming now, of all times. He wondered if this were another ploy of Lùkina to the east or Dusan to the north. Perhaps even one of the more distant provinces had sent this long-absent traitor back to Venjètz?

Darmouth lifted a brazier from its pillar mount and placed it on the floor before the rear wall. Its light rose up to illuminate the tops of numerous cubbyholes.

Within each was a skull, boiled or burned clean of its forgotten flesh. They rested here like enslaved guardians of Darmouth's forefathers. At the wall's center were the most noteworthy of traitors. Here was the reason for the name of this place – the Hall of Traitors – and why some of the bodies hung headless from the keep walls.

Darmouth reached out to take one skull in his large hand. The bone was smooth and glistening, the lower jaw bound shut with steel pins.

'How does it feel, old friend, to know you still serve me through your daughter?'

He ran his thumb over the cheekbone and, with a smile, pressed it into the hollow eye socket of Andrey Progae's skull. When he placed it back in the wall, his gaze caught on a double-wide cubby to the right.

There were two skulls set as a pair. The only ones placed together, and Darmouth's smile faded.

One was round and large, that of a human male, but the second was an oddity, and differed from all the others present. It was slightly smaller, marking it as female, its eye sockets large and the facial structure narrowing to the chin. In life, her face was triangular in shape, the eyes large and slanted below arching eyebrows. She would be . . . was unnatural but deeply alluring compared to any human woman.

This pair – human male and elf female – had been in Darmouth's mind as Faris had whispered in his ear.

A man with white hair, dark skin, and yellow-brown . . . no, amber eyes.

Darmouth snatched the skull directly below the pair and tossed it aside, reserving a place for the new occupant soon to come.

5

Wynn sat on the bed in Leesil and Magiere's room while Tomato and Potato wrestled in her lap, tiny paws and jaws struggling for a better grip. Tomato was winning, which was no surprise, though her pudgy brother outweighed her.

Wynn felt overfull of Byrd's turnip stew and warm cinnamon milk. The lingering taste brought memories of communal meals among the sages in the guild barracks at Bela. Perhaps that was why she had eaten too much.

The bed was soft and fitted with a sheepskin cover over a thick wool blanket. The mattress smelled a bit of stale hay. Heat from the common room hearth and kitchen rose up to warm the floorboards. She could not remember the last time she felt this content in her surroundings.

Byrd had given his guests two rooms upstairs for as long as needed and refused any payment. This bothered Magiere, which was no surprise to Wynn. On one hand an incredible skinflint – Leesil's way of putting it – Magiere was habitually averse to being obliged to anyone.

Leesil scooped up a lanky tabby from the room's little side table and carried it toward the door while scooting a stocky gray along with his boot. When Chap got up to assist, Wynn silently pointed a finger at him. He slumped back to the floor with a grumble.

'These two can stay,' she said, stroking Tomato's ears. 'Chap will not mind.'

Chap cocked his head with a whine, then belly-crawled to her pack, where the talking hide was stored.

Wynn ignored him as she scratched Potato's stomach. 'We will talk later.'

Chap growled and dropped his head on his paws.

'You're right about Byrd,' Magiere said where she sat on the floor. 'A character for certain, but you didn't mention he could cook.'

'Don't let him fool you,' Leesil warned. 'He's skilled in putting people at ease, as was my father.'

'And you,' Wynn added.

Leesil glanced at her. He had many faces, and Wynn had not forgotten his blood-streaked hair and empty eyes when he came in from killing at the Stravinan border.

One of Wynn's tasks for the Guild of Sagecraft was recording all she learned of Magiere, the only dhampir known outside of folklore. Wynn had done so faithfully, including what was uncovered of Magiere's bloody heritage at the keep above Chemestúk, deep in Droevinka. She had gone so far as to steal bones from the corpses of the five *Úirishg* found there. These she included in her last package to Domin Tilswith, as proof that the other three races, besides the dwarves and elves, were more than myth. Somehow one of each had been found and sacrificed to make Magiere's birth possible. What this meant, Wynn could not guess, and Magiere knew nothing of Wynn's careful records. Wynn had no intention of telling her.

But Leesil? Wynn watched him settle on the floor beside Magiere and place one hand on her thigh.

Leesil had been a friend on this long journey. In the nights following Chane's death, he had brought Wynn tea, covered her with blankets, and assured her the world would seem brighter again, someday. Wynn would not forget these small acts – even for what she had seen at the border stream.

He was the only half-elf she had ever heard of. In her own land, the elves were known to mate only among their own kind. Secretive and shamed by his own life, Leesil had told her of himself and his parents in confidence. There were moments she considered recording details of him as well as Magiere, but she did not. It felt too much like betrayal.

Magiere never willingly told Wynn anything and reluctantly allowed her to follow on this journey.

'Do you have thoughts on our first step tomorrow?' Wynn asked.

'What about Byrd's comment?' Magiere replied first, and hesitated as she looked to Leesil. 'Why would your parents run for the keep?'

Leesil shook his head, rubbing one temple with a finger.

'They weren't fools and must have had a strong reason, but it makes no sense.' He glanced at Chap before raising his eyes to Wynn. 'Translate for Chap. He lived with me and my parents long enough that he might know something.'

Wynn plopped Tomato and Potato on the bed, pulled out the talking hide, and dropped down to the floor to unroll it.

'You know what I'm after,' Leesil said to Chap.

Chap stood and began pawing out words upon the hide.

'Noticed how he's changed since Droevinka?' Magiere said, lifting her chin toward Chap. 'He practically threw himself in front of the wagon to stop us from finding *my* past.'

Leesil nodded but made no other reply.

Wynn scowled but kept her attention fixed on Chap's touches upon the elvish symbols. He finished, and Wynn pursed her lips for a moment.

'He does not know why your parents went to the keep, but he remembers the word "down" that —'

'Yes,' Leesil interrupted. 'They were seen heading down below the main floor.'

'Chap suggests they might have known of something in the lower levels to help them escape.' Wynn tried not to sound reluctant. 'So, we search another keep?'

Leesil raised his eyes to Wynn with a disapproving glare. 'I don't think so! There's no bolt-hole to sneak through, and we'd be dead before we crossed the bridge. Even if it were possible, none of you are going near Darmouth.'

'What about Byrd?' Magiere suggested. 'Couldn't he seek an audience, then look about the keep as much as is safe?'

'People like Byrd don't speak directly with Darmouth,' Leesil answered. 'Byrd is one set of eyes among many. Neither he nor Darmouth wants that known to anyone without reason. Besides, whatever informants Byrd has couldn't tell him much, so there's little he'd gain by nosing about himself.'

'If he told us all he heard,' Magiere added.

'Yes,' Leesil agreed. 'There is that.'

This time Wynn grudgingly acknowledged Magiere's

habitual suspicion. 'Then we start with any city records we can gain access to. Perhaps military logs of death warrants or . . .' She bit her lip as Leesil winced. 'I did not mean . . . we must at least look, verify that your parents were not legally executed before we go further.'

'Warlords don't care about records,' Leesil said, and got up. 'Some pretense of protocol exists, simply for jus-tification – or it used to. Byrd might be able to help with that, but I'm too tired. We'll leave it until morning.'

This was Wynn's hint to leave. It had been a long day for Leesil and not a hopeful one in the least.

She rolled up the hide, shouldered her pack, and was about to call Chap when she noticed how tangled his fur had become. He was a mess. She had not groomed him since the night before the border skirmish. When she looked at him, she could still hear the buzz of a leaf-wing in memory and saw the image of his blood-covered face as he crouched beneath the table in the Stravinan barracks.

'Come, Chap,' she said weakly, then scooped up Tomato and Potato. 'They can sleep with us.'

Chap groaned as he followed her out.

Wynn set down the kittens in the hallway. Potato dropped on his haunches, staring up at her in wide-eyed confusion. Tomato trotted after her, much to Chap's rum-bling distaste, and Potato finally waddled along behind.

As Wynn opened her room's door and the kittens scurried in, she heard voices drift up the stairs from below. One was Byrd's deep baritone, and the other's strange cadence was oddly familiar.

The accent was not right for the Belaskian tongue spoken most places in the north of this continent. The speaker clipped his words and syllables with strange pauses, his speech lyrical and guttural all at once.

Eavesdropping was impolite, but when they had all retired, no one else had come to the inn. Who would come by so late for a chat?

Wynn closed the door, keeping Tomato and Potato in her room, and crept to the top of the stairs. She crouched there to peek through the banister's railings. Chap shoved his head in under her arm, startling her.

Byrd stood by the bar, but unlike his relaxed demeanor at dinner, his shoulders were straight and square. He was tensely poised at the visitor's presence.

His visitor was tall, with a cowled head that nearly brushed the low rafters of the common-room ceiling. Solid in build, he wore a long gray-green cloak that hid his form and features. Only his hands were visible, and they were dark-skinned and narrow-boned.

Again the visitor's lyrical accent drifted up to Wynn's ears.

'My source tells me the lady wishes urgently to see you. Await her behind the Bronze Bell Inn. She will come soon, so do not delay.'

Wynn swallowed hard.

The strange accent was one she had heard in her faraway homeland of Malourné.

Byrd's night visitor was an elf.

Chap tensed at the sight of an elf below in the common room. And not just an elf.

He had seen the forest-gray cloak and cowl more than once. The last time was in Bela. An elf called Sgäilsheilleache – Sgäile – invaded the sages' barracks, intent upon killing Leesil. Below in the common room was another of their kind.

Anmaglâhk. An elven assassin had come to the very inn where Leesil stayed.

'She wants to meet outside at night?' Byrd asked of his visitor. 'Alone?'

'One of mine watches over her,' the tall elf replied, 'though she does not know this.'

A flash of surprise crossed Byrd's ruddy features. 'You have orders to watch over her?'

At the mention of 'orders' a face appeared in the elf's mind. Chap focused on the memory and examined what he saw there.

Aoishenis-Ahâre.

Chap knew this was less an elvish name than a title. In his brief time among the elven people, he had seen this face, heard these words – in the memories of others. 'Most Aged Father' would be as close as Wynn might have translated it. The face in the visitor's memory was aged and withered, with sunken cheeks that sharpened its triangular shape and made the cheekbones jut outward. Yet the skin was light for an elf, as if not touched by the sun in decades. The whites around the cloudy amber irises were faintly yellowed. His long hair was so white it seemed translucent.

Most Aged Father was patriarch to the elves of this continent, as well as the leader of the *Anmaglâhk*. Along with this face, Chap sensed troubled dissent in the elf standing before Byrd. Even fear. This one was hiding something from *Aoishenis-Ahâre*, his superior.

'Brot'an, really,' Byrd said when his visitor remained silent. 'This isn't at all how I do things.'

The elf's name seemed familiar, though Chap could not recall where or when he might have heard it. Byrd's voice pulled Chap's gaze, and he caught a flickering memory of a younger Leesil from years past that surfaced in Byrd's mind.

Byrd turned his head with a puzzled frown, eyes lifting toward the stairs.

Wynn quickly shoved Chap back and ducked low.

All memory images vanished as Chap lost sight of both men. He heard a rustle of fabric and quick footsteps. By the time he ventured to peer below, as did Wynn, the inn's front door swung shut. Byrd and his companion were gone.

The presence of an *anmaglâhk* in Venjètz was a complication with unknown consequences. That this first sighting was within earshot of Leesil left Chap deeply disturbed.

Since being given to Leesil as a pup, Chap had met few elves in his life. Most such encounters ranged from uncertain to dangerous. Nein'a, Leesil's mother, had been secretive and guarded, though on a few occasions Chap had seen Most Aged Father's face in her memories – and felt the same discontent in her that he had sensed in this Brot'an here tonight.

Whatever Byrd's reasons for involvement with elves, Leesil should be kept far from them. Difficult at best, since he might have to be told of their presence – but not yet. There was some small hope of brief peace for him, alone with only Magiere for this night.

Wynn scrambled over the top stair and ran down the hall. She reached Magiere and Leesil's door before Chap realized her intent.

He raced after her and squirmed around her legs, trying to block her way. Before he could shove Wynn back with his head and paws, she reached out and pushed the door wide.

'Get up! We must search this place – now!'

Wynn's eyes widened, and Chap groaned in frustration as he looked into the dark room.

What little light filled the space from a single candle exposed shoulders and a back of pale, flawless skin over smooth muscles. Magiere sat naked in Leesil's lap upon the bed, her legs and arms wrapped about him. She turned her head enough to glare toward the open door with one dark eye.

Chap backed up with a hard swallow, and Wynn spun away, eyes clamped shut as she cringed against the hallway wall.

'Damn you, Wynn,' Magiere growled. 'Not again!'

Chane climbed from the bathtub and used a dressing gown left by the maid to dry himself. Welstiel had procured rooms at the Bronze Bell, reputed to be the finest inn Venjètz offered. The accommodations were decent. Nothing close to the standards of Bela, but the bed was covered in a green comforter and the aged furniture was well kept. His room contained two porcelain oil lamps and a small table and chair.

When Welstiel requested they both have a bath, servants carried tin tubs into each of their rooms, filling them with buckets of hot water. Later, the tubs would be laboriously emptied and removed.

Chane remembered the rooms Welstiel had rented in Kéonsk, the luxury of sleeping in a bed, and the fat candles by which he wrote all through the long night. Looking about at his current surroundings, he should have recaptured some pleasure in the finer things, but he felt nothing at all.

He combed his red-brown hair back behind his ears and dressed himself in a pair of spare breeches and a tan shirt. The rest of his clothing had been taken by a maid for laundering. He had not given up his cloak and brushed this out himself. He strapped on his longsword, donned the cloak, and stepped across the hallway to knock at Welstiel's door.

'It's me,' he said with a rasping voice.

'Come in,' Welstiel called.

Chane found Welstiel sitting on the floor with the domed brass plate before him and a knife in his hand. These were the tools Welstiel used to scry for Magiere's whereabouts. He and Chane excelled at differing methods of conjury. Welstiel was an artificer who created objects to work his magic. Chane relied primarily upon ritual, though he used spellwork if urgency required it.

He stepped in and closed the door. 'You wish to locate her tonight?'

His companion looked much improved. Bathed, groomed, and properly dressed, Welstiel was a striking figure, distinguished white patches at his temples visible now that his hair was combed back. He no longer wore his black leather gloves, and Chane's gaze strayed to the missing end of Welstiel's left little finger. It bled black fluid from a fresh cut, and Chane saw one dark droplet upon the brass plate's domed backside.

'Only her general whereabouts,' Welstiel replied.

Speaking of Magiere was difficult for Chane. Since

the night his robin had listened in at the Soladran barracks, his thoughts had become confused concerning Magiere . . . and Wynn.

'I'm going out,' he whispered.

'Out?'

'I'll return by sunrise.'

'Be cautious,' Welstiel said with a disapproving frown. 'Here the city's soldiers appear to do anything they wish.'

Chane left without response. The last thing that concerned him was a pack of mortals who thought they had power over their fellow cattle. As he crested the top of the plush staircase, movement in the foyer below caught his attention.

A slender woman in a burgundy gown donned a charcoal cape, fastening it with a silver clasp. Soft black curls hung to her shoulders around a pale throat and face. Her features were small and lovely down to her tiny red mouth. Her expression was calm, but Chane sensed urgency both in her eyes and her controlled movements.

He gripped the railing, and the wood creaked beneath his fingers in answer to his hunger.

In the last village, he'd lured out a woman of similar make. A mere peasant compared to the one he now watched, but both women's features hinted of the one prey he wanted most of all. Before Welstiel had interrupted him behind the hut among the snow-dusted trees, he'd tried to find solace in tearing warm flesh. Even with blood between his clenching teeth, a missing memory left an ache in him he couldn't smother.

He couldn't remember Wynn touching him in the murky forest of Apudâlsat . . . after Magiere took his head.

He must have fallen immediately, prone upon the

ground as his head rolled away. But surely it hadn't been so quick that he remembered nothing of Wynn falling upon him in sorrow. Some touch, or just the pressure . . . and not being able to do anything for her.

All he remembered was the brief pain of Magiere's blade through his throat and then waking among blood and corpses with Welstiel sitting impatiently nearby.

And behind that forest hut, he'd bitten deep into the peasant woman's throat as if digging for a memory lost between those two moments. He squeezed the outcry from the woman's mouth until her jaw cracked under his hand. There was the rush of life filling him, and the distant euphoria it carried in the wake of the kill – and nothing more.

And still there was Wynn's pain . . . caused by the hatred between himself and Magiere.

Chane forced himself to wait at the top of the inn's stairs and followed the cloaked woman only after he heard the inn's front door close. Outside, he expected to find her heading down the street toward any other place still alive with activity at night. Perhaps to an eatery more suitable to her upper-caste appearance.

But she was gone. He let his senses open wide.

Footsteps. To the left. Resounding from frozen earth.

Chane saw the space between the buildings around the inn's left corner. He slipped into it, stepping softly toward the inn's rear, and glanced around the corner.

His prey stood in the alley with her back turned, and she was not alone.

A man waited for her, half leaning and half sitting on an emptied ale barrel. He pulled his cloak's hood back, exposing a yellow scarf tied over his hair.

Chane held his place, watching two figures of such different social castes meet in the shadows.

'Wynn!' Leesil snapped, more threateningly than he'd intended, and grabbed the blanket's edge. Magiere squirmed in his arms, but he held fast and pulled the blanket up behind her to cover them both.

'That's it!' Magiere shouted. 'You're going home on the first caravan out of here! I don't care if I have to sell our horses to pay for it.'

Wynn peered hesitantly around the door's frame as Magiere thrashed out of Leesil's lap to a more digni-fied – and better-covered – position. Wynn did not back away, though her embarrassment made her voice unsteady.

'Byrd was downstairs talking to an elf,' she said.

Leesil stared at her. Any brief escape from the world that the sage had interrupted washed away. Even Magiere paused at struggling to reach her breeches lying on the floor.

'They left together,' Wynn added softly. 'And they seemed well acquainted. They were meeting a woman, and Byrd reacted as if this were a change in some pre-vious arrangement.'

'An elf?' Magiere asked. 'You're certain?'

Before Wynn answered, Chap reappeared and nearly knocked Wynn over as he bolted into the room with the talking hide clenched in his jaws.

'Wynn, turn around,' Leesil said, and grabbed Magiere's clothes from the floor as he retrieved his own.

By the time he and Magiere finished dressing, Chap

had rolled out the hide with his nose and paws. The instant Leesil said he was dressed and Wynn turned about to peer in, Chap began pawing at the elvish symbols. Wynn scurried in to watch the dog's movements.

'*Anmaglâhk,*' Wynn whispered. 'How would Chap know?'

Leesil sat on the bed, hands planted firmly on its edge. One of his mother's elven caste of assassins was here in the city? And how, for a fact, would Chap know, unless this one dressed the same as . . .

'Was it Sgäile?' Magiere demanded first, and crouched before the dog. 'Was it that butcher sent to kill Leesil in Bela?'

Chap barked twice for 'no.'

Magiere looked up at Leesil. 'You said we could trust Byrd. What's he doing with one of them?'

'Byrd was my father's friend, not mine,' Leesil returned. 'And I never said we could trust him – any more than anyone in this city.'

Leesil's thoughts were too thick with suspicions. Of all places and people, why was it here with Byrd that he ran across more of his mother's kind and caste? He turned his attention back to Chap.

'He was an *anmaglâhk*?' Leesil asked. 'You're sure?'

Chap barked once to confirm this.

Leesil remembered Wynn's outburst when she'd first intruded. Byrd was up to something more than walking a thin line in service to Darmouth. They did need to search this place.

'Start downstairs,' he told Wynn. 'Look for letters, scrap notes, or anything out of sorts for an innkeeper. Anything that looks like it doesn't belong. If Byrd comes back, say you were hungry and went to the kitchen. Say it loudly, so we can hear you.'

Wynn nodded and headed for the door, pausing once. 'And I am not leaving on any caravan, Magiere.'

Leesil waved Chap out, and the dog went after the young sage.

Magiere's anxious expression told Leesil that she wanted to leave, drag him out of this city and never return. Leesil shook his head slowly, and she sighed.

'Let's find Byrd's room,' she said.

Her hair hung down around her ivory cheeks, and Leesil turned his eyes away to keep his emotions in check. Sgäile was the one who'd hinted at Nein'a's fate, that she might be alive. If anyone knew more of her or what had happened to Gavril, it would be the *Anmaglâhk*. One had been right here in the inn, and he'd missed his chance.

'We'll get the answers,' Magiere said, and put a hand upon his shoulder, leaning close. 'But don't you even think about going after that elf.'

She kissed him on the mouth. Leesil pulled away slowly. This place — this city of his first life — was a pit he'd toppled them all into. He couldn't afford another distraction, even if Magiere thought it best he forget for a little while. Leesil dug out his tools from their chest.

They checked each door on the upper floor, and he wasn't surprised to find one of them locked.

'Pick it or break it?' Magiere asked.

Leesil frowned.

It was unlikely that Byrd arranged surprises for anyone snooping about. The risk of a wandering patron stumbling into the wrong place was too great. But when he began studying the door instead of the lock, Magiere backed to the side, understanding his caution.

Leesil started with the hinges and then checked the entire frame before carefully inspecting the latch. Finally convinced it was only a locked door, he took a thin hookwire from the toolbox's lid and slipped it into the keyhole. A *click* answered his efforts.

Byrd's room was ordinary at first glance. Not much different from any at an inn where someone might settle to stay for a while. The belongings seemed sparse, but Leesil remembered how few possessions he'd had in his life with his parents. Beyond a wide trunk, there was no more in the room than could be taken in flight. This was also the way he and his parents had lived, even if leaving were but a wishful thought.

The bed was made, and clothes were neatly folded inside the large trunk. The small table and chair were solid, with no hollows to hide anything. Leesil found no openings or edifices in the walls or the shuttered window. Magiere paged through leather-bound papers left on the table as Leesil dropped down to study the floor. No cubbies or holes, not even a loose board, were there to be found, but this meant nothing with people like Byrd and his parents. Leesil searched the bed and mattress, though he knew Byrd would never hide anything in so obvious a place.

'Nothing,' Magiere said. 'Ledgers and stores lists.'

And not a thing remained to inspect in the room.

Leesil crouched before the chest and started on it for the second time. He emptied it completely, piling the clothes on the floor and lifting out all the trays within supported by side rails. He fingered the interior sides and then the bottom, which flexed when he leaned too hard on it. He could smell cedar beneath the linen lining adhered to the wood. The fabric was folded and sealed continuously across all edges and corners, leaving nothing that could be lifted or pulled away without splitting the lining. And there was no split.

He leaned against the side and stared into the empty trunk.

'There's nothing here,' Magiere said. 'And I can't see him hiding anything in the other rooms, if patrons are housed there. We should help Wynn downstairs.'

Leesil repacked the trunk, got up, and headed for the door behind Magiere. He still felt the lingering flex of fabric-covered wood on his fingers. Magiere disappeared out into the hallway, and he stopped and looked back.

Flexing wood in a stout travel trunk?

He returned to the trunk and began pulling everything out for the third time.

'Leesil?' Magiere called, her voice carrying from the hall.

He was halfway to the bottom when he heard her come up behind him.

'You've done that twice already,' she insisted. 'There's nothing there.'

Leesil reached the bottom and pressed his palm firmly against it. The wood gave beneath the fabric. The trunk's sides were thick and solid, so why the thinner bottom? He placed his other hand on the outside floor. The distance down to floor and trunk bottom was noticeably different.

A false bottom. But how was it opened if the fabric was solid throughout the interior?

'Leesil!' Magiere said, her voice growing more annoyed.

He ignored her and shoved the trunk over backward. The lid slammed on the floor as the vessel toppled. He stared at its bottom, solid and flush to the edges of its side walls. There were six brass knobs that served as legs along the bottom edges, one for each corner, and the last two placed midway along the front and back edge. These were held in place with small brass nails.

He picked at one with his fingernail. It was loose. Magiere crouched down, as Leesil slipped a stiletto from his wrist sheath and began popping out brass nails. Only the front knob legs came off, and the trunk's bottom fell open.

Leesil found himself staring at a pile of flattened parchments. The first depicted the charcoal-drawn layout of a four-towered keep in crude lines. The sheet below this was an interior map of the same structure. He touched it. Part of the rendering smeared slightly, while the rest seemed set and clean. The whole of it was unfinished, with notable areas still blank within the structure's outline.

'Recently drawn,' he said. 'Or parts of it.'

'Is that Darmouth's keep?' Magiere asked. 'Why would Byrd have drawings of the keep?'

Leesil paged through more parchments. There were eight, each depicting a different area or level. All were incomplete, with at least three that had almost nothing added within the outline of the outer walls. Two were of the towers' interiors, with inked marks and lines that might indicate paths walked by sentries.

'A better question . . .' Leesil said, almost to himself.

'Why have drawings of the keep and be meeting with an *anmaglâhk*?'

Magiere didn't answer but reached out for his wrist. 'What are you going to do?'

'Ask him. I'm going to sit downstairs until he returns.'

'I'll wait with you,' she said, and it wasn't a suggestion.

'He won't talk unless I'm alone. Gather up Wynn and Chap and go to bed. I'll tell you everything I learn.'

Magiere heaved on his wrist, jerking him around to face her. For all the rage in her face, he could feel her shaking through the grip on his wrist. Leesil had no patience for a fight over this.

'Just do it, Magiere!' he snapped. 'I know what I'm doing — and you don't.'

A long silence followed as she stared back. Magiere turned away without a word. Leesil rolled up the drawings, stuffed them into his shirt, and followed her downstairs.

Wynn was stunned when the search was called off. Of course she refused, until Leesil explained that he was going to speak with Byrd rather than tear the inn apart. Something must have slipped into his voice or expression, because she nodded and did as he asked without another word. He didn't show her the drawings, or he'd never get rid of her. Magiere ushered Chap and Wynn upstairs to their rooms, but Magiere never looked back at him.

Leesil turned down the lanterns and settled in the chair near the front wall to watch the door. He unfastened the catches on his wrist sheaths.

His father and mother, contrary to Byrd's acquaintance,

had taught him many things in this city. Beyond blood ties — and sometimes those included — there were no friends here. There were only those who hadn't yet betrayed you, and those you hadn't yet betrayed.

Tomato and Potato were asleep on the bed, so Wynn was alone with Chap in her room. She sat cross-legged upon a braided rug, brushing his fur in long strokes to carefully work out his mats and tangles. She could not always read Chap's expressions, but he appeared relieved by her attention. With her hands once again in his silvery fur, she remembered the strange chorus of leaf-wings she had heard while watching him before the battle on the Stravinan border.

Part of her felt guilty for avoiding the dog . . . Fay . . . *majay-hì*. . . whatever or however she should think of him. He was all of these things, all at once, though this merely made it more confusing. He had also been her constant companion on this journey. One part of her took solace in his presence, but another part was frightened by the mysteries behind his presence. She knew too little of his agenda, and why he had left his existence among the Fay.

Was that what she had heard in her head as Chap grew angrier and more savage before the battle? And how or why had it happened to her, for that matter?

Chap whined and pushed his head against her folded legs. Wynn wrapped her arms around him.

There were moments such as this when he seemed no more than her four-legged traveling companion. He pulled his head back and whined again, then perked his ears in a quizzical expression.

Wynn grew hesitant. There were other moments when his canine form seemed a deception for his true existence — a Fay in flesh.

And everything in Wynn's vision turned blue-white.

Her stomach lurched, and her dinner rose in her throat. The room became a shadowy version of its former state. Overlaying all was an off-white mist just shy of blue. Its radiance permeated everything like a second view of the room coloring her normal sight. Within the walls, the radiance thinned, leaving shadowed hollows in the planks. The glimmer thickened within the sleeping forms of Tomato and Potato curled together in a tangle of little legs upon the bed's end.

Wynn lurched back, pulling away from Chap, and the sudden movement sharpened her vertigo. She stared at Chap in fear.

Unlike all else in her tangled vision, he was the only thing that was not permeated with the blue-white trails of mist. Chap was one image, one whole shape, glowing with brilliance. His fur glistened like a million hazy threads of white silk, and his eyes scintillated like crystals held up to the sun.

Wynn cringed and blinked.

The room became dull and dim again. Before her was Chap, silvery gray and furry. He cocked his head, staring at her.

Wynn's panic rose until she shook. This had happened only once before.

In a dark forest in Droevinka, she had dabbled in thaumaturgy to give herself mantic sight. A foolish act, and in the end only Chap had been able to free her of the wild magic she could not control. With it, she had seen the elemental Spirit layer of the world in order to track the undead sorcerer Vordana, so Magiere and Leesil might free a town of the monster's influence.

Why had this happened again? Why had she heard the strange leaf-wings in her head when she had watched Chap at the Stravinan border? And mostly, what had been revealed to her that she did not yet understand?

Wynn took long breaths, looking back into Chap's curious eyes, until her shudders faded.

She needed to put aside the form she saw before her, to talk with *him*, but she hesitated. How could she ask after the nauseating leaf-wing sounds in her head, or tell him of her revulsion at his blood-soaked jowls? She laid aside the brush, pulled the talking hide closer, and unrolled it on the floor with honest purpose in mind.

'Chap,' she began. 'At the border, before you ran for the field to save the refugees, what were you doing at the city gate? Something happened that we did not see.'

Chap wrinkled his snout briefly. He quickly sniffed at her as if checking for something, then barked twice for 'no.' It was low and breathy, like a whisper, and too quick and dismissive.

Perhaps it was that Wynn knew him well, for all the time they had spent together. Or that Chap was not a good liar when confronted.

'I saw you,' she said, 'and I heard . . . felt something. It made me sick and dizzy, like back in Droevinka, when you licked away my mantic sight. I heard whispers while I watched you. What were you doing?'

She hoped he would understand − trust enough to help her to understand.

Chap stood on all fours, dipped his head, and then

leaned forward to lift his muzzle at her. His eyes locked on hers and a low rumble came up his throat. One of Chap's jowls rose slightly to expose teeth, and his crystal-blue eyes narrowed.

Wynn stiffened and leaned away.

He remained there so long in watchful silence that Wynn's shoulders and back began to ache from clenched muscles. She did not believe Chap would hurt her, but the questions had upset him more than she anticipated.

Chap swung his head down to the hide, his gaze leaving her only at the last instant. He pawed the symbols, and Wynn translated his words in her mind.

What did you hear?

She slowly sat upright. 'Not words . . . and not in my ears, as no one else appeared to hear it. It was like leaves in a swirling wind and a flight of insects buzzing inside my head all at once.'

Chap made no response by expression or movement.

'When they fell silent,' she added, 'a single leaf-wing answered back . . . What were you doing?'

Chap dropped on his haunches. He cocked his head again, and it remained there at that odd angle, his narrow eyes studying her.

Wynn felt naked under his scrutiny. Was she being judged?

Chap let out a rolling exhale, like a growl without voice. To Wynn, it sounded like a weary resignation. He pawed again, hesitating over the symbols he chose upon the hide. Some part of what he told her now was difficult for words.

Spiord . . . aræn . . . cheang'a.

'Spirit . . . one-as-one, or collective . . . speech – no, communication?' Wynn whispered.

Beyond their differing dialects of Elvish, there was the more frustrating challenge that Chap did not think like mortals. At least not from what Wynn had reasoned out. Sometimes he grew frustrated in trying to express himself, while other times he was just reticent.

Elvish was a language of 'root' words to be transformed into nouns, verbs, adjectives, and adverbs, as well as other elements of language. Chap now used pure 'root' words, and perhaps transforming them could not render his full meaning.

'Spirit . . . as one of the five elements?' she asked.

Chap huffed twice for 'no.'

'Then spirit, as in spiritual . . . as opposed to physical or mental aspects of existence?'

He huffed once for 'yes,' then quickly added two more. Three total meant 'maybe.'

'Spirit . . . collective . . . communication . . .' Wynn rolled the terms together in her mind and drew a breath. 'Commune? You were communing with the Fay?'

It was the closest meaning she could find. Instead of barking once, Chap nodded, but then pawed two specific Elvish words on the hide – 'yes' and 'no.'

Wynn's translation was close enough but not completely what he meant or what she had 'overheard' in her mind. And more realization came to Wynn.

To banish her mantic sight in the Droevinkan forest, Chap had touched her after all the flowing blue-white trails of mist had joined in his flesh. He had touched her while joined with his kin in some way that was even deeper than his communion at the Stravinan border. Something more had happened in that instant that even Chap could not account for.

His expression went flat, and he backed away.

'The mantic sight . . . it is still with me as well,' she whispered. 'I saw you a moment ago as I did that night in Droevinka.'

Chap did not answer, but his crystalline eyes looked at her with a hint of sadness. Wynn realized that what was happening to her was a mistake that worried him. Still, a weight had lifted from her. She knew what she had heard at the border, and she held out her arms to him.

'I did not mean to . . . did not know. If you wish, I will not tell anyone of this. I promise.'

Chap moved closer. Leaning in, he sniffed again as if testing her scent.

His tongue flicked out across her cheek, and Wynn closed her arms around him.

6

Magiere reached the inn's room she shared with Leesil and slammed the door behind her. Chap and Wynn were safely tucked away in their own room. Frustrated, she just stood in the dark.

'I know what I'm doing,' she muttered, repeating Leesil's last words to her. 'Yes, and it's nothing to do with sinking into your past . . . you witless mule!'

Each thing Magiere learned of Byrd raised more questions, more suspicions, and fewer answers. All of it kept coming back to Leesil, his parents, and Darmouth's keep. All of it centered on Byrd. Now Leesil sat, alone, waiting in the common room for someone he hardly knew.

She went to the small side table, struck the sulfur stick across its underside, and lit the candle lantern resting there. Placing the lantern's glass down around the flame, she settled on the bed.

Taking Leesil head-on was her first instinct, and it was a mistake. She didn't want to be one more weight upon him, shoving him over the edge of good sense.

Magiere unsheathed her falchion and rested it across her knees. She reached over the bed's end into the travel trunk and pulled out a scrap of soft hide permeated with oil. Within its folds was a smooth basalt stone, and she began cleaning and sharpening the blade.

She fingered the steel, from its wide curved tip to its

cross-guard, and her gaze slipped down the hand-and-a-half hilt to the strange glyph engraved in the pommel. She still didn't know what it meant, but the blade's power against the undead suggested much.

Magiere paused in her work and lifted the weapon in her grip.

Made by her half brother, Welstiel Massing, it had been wielded by three women of the same blood. First her mother, Magelia, had tried to defend herself against Magiere's father, Bryen Massing. Aunt Bieja had used it to defend an infant Magiere against a village elder trying to cast the misbegotten child into the wild. And lastly, Magiere herself carried it for her own defense . . . and for those she chose to defend.

It wasn't much of a heritage, tainted with bloodshed and suffering, but it was hers. As she stared at the blade, it gained new meaning. More than some arcane device made for a destiny she neither wanted nor understood.

Her own 'parent,' bad-tempered Aunt Bieja, had tried to keep her safe with this weapon.

Magiere settled the falchion on her knees.

There'd been no way for Leesil and his parents to flee together. She wondered if Nein'a and Gavril had even considered it. Leesil had been raised in his mother's ways. To Magiere, this seemed worse than what she'd endured as a child, and it begged a question.

Why had Nein'a done this to her own son?

An elf among humans, Nein'a had married one. That in itself was bizarre, from what Magiere had learned of this reclusive and dangerous people. Nein'a kept Leesil ignorant of her kind and her caste, and even her native language. It made no sense. It was a puzzle Magiere never heard Leesil mention himself.

Gazing at the steel wielded by three women, Magiere couldn't imagine why any mother would do that to her child. But for all Leesil now faced, she wouldn't put it in his mind.

Not yet. Not until they found Nein'a. If Leesil lived that long.

Magiere sat still and silent, and looked to the room's door as she listened intently. Not a sound reached her ears from anywhere in the quiet inn. Below in a dimly lit common room, Leesil waited blindly for a piece of his past to come for him.

She slipped the falchion into its sheath, stepped to the window, and shoved the heavy curtains and shutters open. The drop to the alley behind the inn wasn't difficult. Magiere would not let Leesil out of her sight, whether he knew it or not.

Hedí turned the corner at the back of the Bronze Bell and spotted a hefty man in the alley leaning back on an empty ale barrel. Even in the dark, she made out the yellow kerchief around his head and knew it was Byrd. His brow was wrinkled in concern, though he wore a half smile on his pleasant ruddy face. In a world of false smiles, Byrd's meant little to her.

'My lady,' he said with his usual wry twist of the title. 'An alley at night is no place for you . . . or me, if I'm seen.'

Three years had passed since Hedí was first visited by one of Byrd's less savory confidants. Not long after that she began spying for the Vonkayshi, would-be rebels of which Byrd was her main contact. She dreamed of Darmouth's death long before then and found she was not alone in that desire. She'd seen many attempts on Darmouth's life. Those involved tried, failed, and died as traitors. Byrd was not to be trusted with anyone's safety or agenda besides his own. His heart was made of ice, but he was the first one to make Hedí believe Darmouth could be dealt with.

To assist him, Hedí took mental notes or quick diagrams on scraps of paper, if she had time, whenever she went with Emêl into Darmouth's stronghold. She fed Byrd these details, bit by bit and drop by drop, as she gathered them like a small scavenger in the shadows. She knew she placed herself – and Emêl – in great danger, but if Darmouth died, the risk was worthy.

'Shhhhh, and listen,' she said. 'Tonight Faris interrupted Darmouth's little dinner party with an urgent message. Darmouth immediately ordered the guards on the keep and city walls to be doubled . . . and for any man with light hair and dark skin to be arrested or killed on sight.'

Byrd lost all semblance of pleasantry and lurched upright, but he remained composed as he spoke. 'Why? What did you overhear from Faris?'

'Only scant pieces,' Hedí returned with a shake of her head. 'There was a skirmish at the Stravinan border. The man they seek crossed the stream and attacked Darmouth's troops running down deserters and their families.' Panic crept into her voice. 'If the soldiers are to arrest anyone who resembles an elf, we are ruined! What was your fool of an associate doing out there?'

A hint of confusion passed across Byrd's face, and

then quickly vanished in some sudden realization. He shook his head. 'Where is Baron Milea?'

'Asleep inside,' she said.

She did not like Byrd asking questions about Emêl and had not risked herself for this meeting only to have her own questions avoided. She stared at him, silently waiting.

His gaze was steady. 'Do you remember a married couple in Darmouth's service from before your father died? The woman was elven.'

Another absurd change of topic. Was he being deliberately evasive or did he not realize the magnitude of Darmouth's new orders? She remembered the woman, for who could forget an elf living among humans, let alone in this accursed place?

'Yes. I only saw them a few times.'

'They had a son.'

She did not recall this, but her family had lived outside Venjètz and seldom attended events except the winter feast. 'I don't remember him. Now please, what about the —'

Byrd held his hand up. 'It was their son at the border, not one of my associates.'

'Then he is responsible for fouling our plans?'

'In a sense. He is staying with me at the inn.' Byrd dropped his gaze in reflection. 'But I've wondered if anyone could scale the keep without being seen. My elven associates were the only possibility we had . . . until now.'

'I do not understand,' Hedí said. 'What has changed?'

'This elven woman and her husband were forced to flee years ago, but they ran inside the keep instead of trying to slip out the city gates or over the wall. I don't know why, and it's a riddle I've never answered or put aside. Now their wayward son wants that answer, and if he finds it . . .'

'So you still think our efforts might —'

'I'll wait and see. The plan may be altered, but it's far from ruined. Be patient. We'll get one of the elves inside those walls. Darmouth will be dead before the winter feast.'

A slight relief, but Hedí's satisfaction was incomplete. Byrd wore many faces, and he would sacrifice anyone – including her – to meet his end goal. Her own determination for assurance made her bold.

'Why are the elves helping us?' Hedí asked. 'What are they getting from this?'

'I don't know, and they're not saying,' Byrd answered, and glanced warily about the alley. 'As troubling as that is, we've no one else for the task. And don't call me this way again. I'll contact you when I know more.'

Hedí nodded and whispered, 'For our people.'

'For our people,' Byrd repeated, and disappeared out the alley's end.

Hedí pulled her cloak tight against the cold night. The inn's rear door was within reach, but it was better to reenter from the front and attract less attention from the staff. She headed for the corner and the side way to the inn's front.

A tall figure stepped from the shadows to block her way.

Welstiel sat on the floor of his room after Chane left, continuing his task of locating Magiere. He had fashioned one of the amulets she wore from the bone of his own little finger. He set the knife down, focused his will to heal the cut on the stub of his finger, and watched the drop of his own fluids on the center of the brass plate's dome. The droplet quivered and spread slightly south.

She was here in the city.

He wiped the plate and tucked it away in his pack. When he stood up, he paused at his own reflection in the narrow oval mirror beside the room's door. His recent doubts about his ability to manipulate Magiere subsided.

Bathed and groomed, in freshly brushed clothing, he was himself again. He would stay in control so long as he kept Magiere from following Leesil into the elven territory. He must convince them that Leesil's parents were dead or block them from their course.

The city's south side was mostly mercantile and not large. For now Welstiel would find Magiere and keep track of her. Hopefully Chane would be sensible while hunting. After Welstiel's last warning, he had shown some attention to concealment.

Before leaving the room, Welstiel opened a small jade box and removed a brass ring with tiny symbols etched around its inside. He rarely took it off these days except when bathing, as he had done this evening. He slipped it on the first finger of his right hand.

The room wavered briefly in his sight like the horizon across a desert plain at noon. Then it settled again.

Though he could be seen and heard, his nature and essence would be masked from all extraordinary means of detection or observation, as if nothing existed where he stood. Not Magiere or the topaz amulet that Welstiel had created for her, or even her dog, would sense his presence as that of Noble Dead.

He stepped quietly into the hallway, closing the door behind himself, and headed downstairs. The evening had grown late, there was no one below, and he slipped out the front door unnoticed.

A woman's cry filled the night.

Welstiel glanced both ways along the street, senses widening, but he detected nothing. He heard a heavy thump against wood and he turned about, staring first at the inn and then saw the side passage around it. He stepped along the street and peered between the inn and the next building. A nagging alarm grew in Welstiel.

Chane would not . . . not so close to where they stayed?

He hurried down the passage to peer into the back alley. There was Chane with a small, well-dressed lady pressed against the inn's rear wall. He had her wrists pulled up and pinned with one hand while smothering her mouth with the other. He pushed her head back to stretch out her pale throat.

Welstiel's anger grew. Was Chane so far into madness that he would kill right outside their inn? And a noble-woman at that?

Chane opened his mouth with a savage snarl, exposing elongated teeth, but he did not bite down yet. He appeared to be absorbing her fear for the moment. He put his face directly in front of hers and drew his lips farther back. The woman's eyes widened, and her scream was stifled by Chane's palm. Chane looked lost and dis-satisfied rather than triumphant, as he sank his teeth into her throat.

Welstiel froze in uncertainty. Perhaps he could cloud her mind enough, if Chane left the inn and never let this one woman see him again. He took one step, ready to clutch Chane by the hair like a dog.

A gray shadow dropped from above and enveloped Chane.

Welstiel lurched back against the inn's wall, glancing to the roof's edge as the shadow drove Chane to the ground. The noblewoman was dragged down the wall in his grip. Chane lost his hold on her, and she scrambled away toward the inn's rear door. He pitched his attacker off and rolled to his feet, drawing his longsword.

'Help!' the woman shouted with no hysteria in her voice. 'Guards! Help!'

Before Chane raised his blade, two metallic flickers shot at him through the air. He swatted the first one aside, but the second struck the center of his chest. He stared down at the stiletto hilt protruding from his torso.

In the alley stood a slender man, slightly taller than Chane. His breeches, shirt, and tunic were all monotone deep grays or perhaps greens. The calf-high soft boots and hooded cloak were darker still. The cloak's corners were pulled up and tied across his waist, holding the cloak to his back and out of his way. A scarf wrap hid his features within the deep shadow of his hood.

Welstiel's sight opened to the fullest, and he saw a hint of yellow-orange glint from the man's large eyes. His slender hands were deeply tanned.

Neither the woman nor the mysterious guardian noticed Welstiel's presence. She had already called for guards, which meant some retinue was within earshot.

Welstiel retreated to the side passage, preferring not to be dragged down in Chane's lunacy.

Chane's lithe opponent reached back inside his tied-up cloak. The woman fumbled with the back door, but it would not open.

'Emêl!' She cried out.

She fled down the alley beyond Chane's opponent before she stopped to look back.

Chane jerked the stiletto from his chest and rushed forward. His opponent whipped something thin and glinting out of the lashed-down cloak and charged to meet him. Chane swung, twisting his blade's path into a thrust. He connected with nothing but night air. The gray-clad man had already leaped sideways to the alley wall at full speed.

Narrow feet stepped once, twice, three times sideways along the building across from the inn. His hands passed on both sides of Chane's head as he dropped to the alley floor again.

Welstiel saw the garrote wire as the man pivoted behind Chane and pulled it tight.

Instead of gasping, Chane pushed off with both legs and threw himself backward. The gray-clad man tucked up his knees against Chane's back.

The assailant's shoulders hit the alley floor, and he flipped Chane over himself, following on the momentum. Chane's sword clattered from his grip as he landed facedown on the packed dirt. The assailant ground his knees into Chane's back as he pulled the wire tight.

Chane pushed up on all fours. His opponent pulled harder on the wire. Black fluid seeped around it down

Chane's throat as he reached back to grab for the fingers holding one of the garrote handles.

Welstiel pulled his own sword, for things had gone too far.

The inn's rear door swung inward and two men in yellow felt tabards over chain vests rushed out, wide-bladed sabers in hand. Welstiel pulled back again.

'You, there!' one guard shouted at Chane. 'Stop!'

Two more men appeared at the alley's far end, coming up next to the noblewoman.

Chane's opponent released one garrote handle and jerked the other as he thrust with his knees. The wire lashed Chane's throat as he was propelled forward, skidding facedown in the alley. The gray-clad man turned and fled the opposite way.

One guard closed in, trying to pin Chane down with his boot. Chane rolled away against the alley's far wall and kicked out into the man's stomach. The guard's feet left the ground as he slammed back into his companion. Both men hit the inn's half-open door, and it tore from its hinges as they toppled into the rear hallway.

Chane snarled at them. When he saw the other two near the woman, he fled down the alley in the wake of his opponent. One guard with the noblewoman began to follow.

'No!' she ordered, and he immediately halted. 'Get me inside and wake the baron.'

Welstiel waited as the woman was escorted into the Bronze Bell. Soon the alley was empty. An unknown guardian had been watching over this woman. Welstiel wanted no part of this. All he wanted was to keep Magiere under his control. Chane's erratic behavior had created unwanted attention. He slipped down the alley to track down his lunatic companion.

Leesil sat at a table in the common room of Byrd's inn, where he could face the front door.

Anmaglâhk had come to Venjètz, the home of his youth, just as he himself had come looking for his past. Of all places and people, they'd come here to Byrd the very night Leesil had arrived.

One too many coincidences, in a land where happenstance made the wise wary.

Few of the cats were still about. Night was the time for such creatures — and others — to prowl about their business. Leesil stared at the drawings, trying to speculate upon their many missing details, and the front door's latch creaked.

Byrd stepped inside. He froze at the sight of Leesil, then quickly closed the door.

'Couldn't sleep either, eh?' he said, and casually tossed his cloak atop the bar.

Leesil shoved the drawings to the table's center. 'What are these for?'

Byrd remained relaxed, perhaps contemplating a response. Leesil watched the man's hands as much as his eyes. His cuffs were rolled up twice, exposing thick wrists bare of anything up his sleeves.

'Been nosing about in my things,' Byrd observed without answering. 'Not many could've found those.'

There were no signs of Leesil's own training in Byrd, though there was something in the way the man planted himself before the table. The last eight years since Leesil's escape felt as if they'd never happened.

He'd never left this land any more than Byrd had. They were both part of the world Darmouth and his father had made. Across the table from Leesil stood a cunning friend, a deceitful enemy, or most likely both. Few but the two of them understood that it wouldn't matter either way. Not when the moment came to kill Byrd.

'Why were you talking to an *anmaglâhk*?' Leesil continued. 'Have they been watching for me . . . reporting to you?'

Byrd paused too long. Long enough for Leesil to see he understood what the question *said* as clearly as what it *asked*. Byrd knew more than he shared, perhaps playing Leesil to some end from the moment he'd arrived.

'You've a high opinion of yourself,' Byrd answered. 'Do you think you're the only one of interest to them?'

Leesil realized his error. His second question revealed he had a history at odds with these particular elves. In turn, Byrd's answer said much as well.

Byrd hadn't questioned the strange Elvish term Leesil used, so the man was well aware of what these elves were. This begged another question. How had Byrd made their acquaintance and gained their assistance for . . . whatever . . . when they detested humans?

Tension held fast beneath the pretense of polite conversation.

'What should I think?' Leesil asked. 'Why else would they be here?'

Byrd cocked his head ever so slightly. He slipped his right hand behind his back slowly enough that the movement would be clearly seen. When he withdrew it, a wide blade protruded like a squat spade from across the knuckles of his fist.

Leesil relaxed all tension in his body.

Most people tensed when threatened, but tight muscle didn't react quickly enough in the final moment. Leesil had spent his entire youth altering his instincts, shaping them. He lazily shifted one forearm beneath the table, tilting it between his thighs, until a stiletto hilt slid into his hand.

Byrd stepped to the table, remaining noticeably out of arm's reach. He pressed the blade's tip slowly into the table's surface. When he released his grip, it remained poised there, tilted toward him as he pulled out a chair and sat down across from Leesil.

'So what's your gripe, lad?' he asked like a concerned father giving all his attention to an angry son.

Still relaxed, Leesil glanced at the blade.

Wide and long as a hand's palm, it resembled a skinner's blade for working hide. No guard, with a short 'hilt' ending in a crossbar, it was gripped in one's fist to cut, stab, or gouge a target. The naïve would see its open display like raising empty hands or releasing one's weapon in good faith.

Leesil knew better what it meant. Byrd was an infighter.

Not like Leesil, with thin stilettos used for surprise or lethal subtlety or the weaponless ways taught by his mother. Byrd would come straight in with speed, weight, and muscle for a close encounter. He wouldn't care what it cost him so long as he finished his opponent first. Brutal efficiency in place of cunning precision.

Whatever Byrd chose to do, it would be backed by determination few possessed and most wouldn't care to face. He did not attack; instead, he sighed.

'I didn't know you were coming,' he said, 'and these drawings have nothing to do with you. None of this has to do with you, lad.'

'Back in Bela, I met one of these elves,' Leesil said. 'His name was Sgäile, and he hinted that my mother was alive, imprisoned by her people. Did your friends tell you —'

'Nein'a alive?' Byrd asked quickly, and his surprise appeared genuine. 'You heard this from one of them?'

'Not exactly.' Leesil wondered if this might work in his favor, if Byrd began questioning his associates, but it seemed just one more risk of betrayal. 'There was enough implication in Sgäile's words, and, if true, I needed to know if Gavril survived as well. So I came here. Did you know she might still be alive?'

Byrd shook his head as he growled back. 'I didn't know! If I had, I would've —'

'Perhaps you were preoccupied,' Leesil countered with a quick glance at the drawings, hoping to keep Byrd off balance. 'With too many missing pieces.'

Byrd's voice took on an open, hard edge. 'Did you even look at the state of these lands – of the people – on the way here?'

'Yes.'

'Would you help them, if you could?'

'That's a pointless question.'

'Would you?'

Leesil suddenly felt like a fool. A second-rate one, at that, as pieces of Byrd's scheme started to become clear.

Whoever was getting the details for Byrd's drawings did so piece by erratic piece. As if there was no telling when, how, or where the next scrap might be acquired. Byrd's informant wasn't a regular or confidant of

Darmouth's close company, but someone who gained rare and limited access within the keep. Such an undependable source meant all other avenues were closed to Byrd, or Darmouth had grown so paranoid that no one close to him could be enticed. It also meant the informant was someone desperate, perhaps fanatical, who had succumbed to the delusion of revolution – Byrd's delusion.

Leesil knew of such. He had betrayed many in his youth. And though it was mostly guesswork, there was the other hint they'd already discussed – the *Anmaglâhk*.

'How much longer will it be,' Leesil asked, 'before you're ready to kill Darmouth?'

Not that he cared, since it would be no help to him. Every question Byrd ignored strengthened this new realization as well as Leesil's first suspicion. Byrd might play any side to get what he wanted, even the son of an old friend.

'I know nothing more of your parents,' Byrd said flatly, as if Leesil had never asked about Darmouth. 'Nothing more than what I've told you.'

'Do you think removing Darmouth will change anything?' Leesil continued, offering his father's old friend one more chance to talk. 'How many officers and so-called nobles wait eagerly to take his place? It's how Darmouth's own grandfather came to power.'

Byrd continued in his own conversation, still ignoring Leesil's questions. 'But don't stop looking for your parents on my say-so. I've not much but guesses and scant facts concerning Nein'a and Gavril, but perhaps those drawings might give you some leads.'

He stood up.

Leesil sat upright, feet flat on the floor, and spun the

stiletto in his palm. He lifted the blade until the point was just below the table's edge. One slap of his free hand would flatten and pin Byrd's blade to the table as the man reached for it. And that movement would provide a clear opening to pierce Byrd below the jaw . . . slide the stiletto tip up along the spine into the base of the skull.

Byrd turned away, lifted his cloak carefully from the bar, and trudged toward the stairs.

'I'm going to bed. You should do the same. I'll let you know if I need the drawings, but best you don't leave them lying about.'

Leesil stared after the man he'd been waiting to kill. The little he'd uncovered hadn't settled his suspicions, and still he'd hesitated when the moment came.

Perhaps he should take Magiere, Wynn, and Chap and head straight into the mountains to find a way to the elves' homeland. But what if Sgäile had lied? He'd be leading his companions into an unknown territory, where humans would be unwelcome, and all for no reason. What if his father was alive, somehow, locked away beneath the keep?

Byrd disappeared at the top of the stairs.

The moment had passed, and Leesil looked down at the squat blade in the tabletop and the unfinished drawings of Darmouth's keep. Indecision began to build to despair as the front door's latch creaked once again.

Leesil reversed the stiletto, grasping the blade as he swung his hand wide, ready to throw. The door opened, and the common room's low light spilled outward to reveal a pale face in the dark.

'Put that away,' Magiere said.

She stepped in, closing the door. Her black hair hung

loose across the shoulders of her hauberk, which was buckled down and fitted for combat. Her falchion was unsheathed in her grip.

Leesil felt an unexplained chill at the sight of her. 'What were you doing out there?'

'I don't trust that man,' she said. Her irises turned dark at the sight of the blade stuck in the tabletop. 'What happened here that I didn't see?'

'You were listening?' Leesil replied. 'I told you to stay away. I'll handle Byrd my —'

'Your judgment has been . . .' Magiere snapped, but never finished. 'I told you, you're not leaving my side. And don't fight me about it again.'

Leesil looked away. Magiere tried to play bodyguard, yet couldn't see that she was the one who needed protecting. She didn't understand this world. Leesil's hand shook as he slid the stiletto back into its sheath.

'Go to bed,' he told her, trying to sound calm. When she was about to argue, he added, 'I'll be along once I've gathered the drawings and put out the lanterns.'

Her gaze shifted sharply to the wrist where he'd just sheathed his blade. She sheathed her own sword and headed up the stairs.

Leesil sat back, and his hands trembled.

Magiere had been outside the whole time.

He'd come here prepared to kill an old acquaintance. That was just the way of things, and there was nothing to feel about it. When it happened . . . if it had happened . . . at any sound of struggle, Magiere would've rushed in to protect him.

Only to see him murder a man in front of her.

* * *

'You fool!'

Welstiel had no trouble following Chane, and waited until he was certain that Chane was alone in an alley before closing on him. As Chane spun about, Welstiel grabbed him and slammed him against a stone wall to the alley's side.

Chane did not resist. His neck still oozed black fluid from the garrote line just above the scar of his beheading. His eyes were vacant and desolate, as if he did not know where he was or did not care.

Welstiel released his grip and stepped back. Common sense told him it was time to get rid of Chane one way or another, but he did not wish to. Not yet.

'Now you do need to feed,' he said. 'We will go to the east side, far from the main gates and our inn. Some market area where refugee peasants try to hide.'

Chane looked down at the black stains on his shirt where the stiletto had struck. 'They plan to assassinate Darmouth. That was an elf that attacked me.'

Welstiel stepped in close. 'What? Who is planning this?'

With halting words and rasping voice, Chane recounted what he had seen and heard between the noblewoman and a man called 'Byrd.' Particularly that a homecoming half-breed stayed at the man's inn, which meant Magiere was there as well.

Welstiel listened carefully, anger fading. 'It's not safe for you at the Bronze Bell. Those guards or the woman might recognize you. But I need to go back quickly, before the panic subsides. We passed an inn nearer the gate, the Ivy Vine. Do you remember it?'

Chane's composure returned, and he pulled his cloak over his wounded chest. 'Yes, I saw it.'

'Go and feed, but be cautious. Then get to the Ivy Vine and stay out of sight.'

'What are you doing?'

'Go! I will gather our things and join you in a while.'

Welstiel trotted down the alleyway, not bothering to watch which direction Chane took. He hurried back through the winding alleys, but stepped out to the main streets before approaching the Bronze Bell. He smoothed his hair, brushed at his cloak, and pulled on his black leather gloves before entering the front doors, like any wealthy patron with a purpose.

He was relieved at the sight of the yellow-surcoated guards still in a commotion. In the back foyer, the noble-woman sat upon the edge of a hardwood bench with red cushions a bit too worn. She held a white hand-kerchief to her neck. A slender man with reddish hair, perhaps ten or fifteen years her senior, sat protectively at her side, barking angry questions at the guards around them.

'What do you mean, "he just ran away"? Why didn't you run him down?'

Welstiel pushed between two guards and stepped directly before the noble couple.

'Forgive me. Is the lady all right? I tried pursuing the villain myself but lost him in the alleys.'

The woman and her protector displayed mild surprise at his sudden intrusion. One guard even stepped in to push him back. Welstiel held up his open hands and proffered a curt but respectful bow of his head to the couple.

'Pardon me. I am Viscount Andraso. I was returning to my room when I heard the lady cry out. When I entered the alley, your men were already at her side, and I saw the creature flee.'

'Creature?' The red-haired nobleman blinked and stood up, offering the short nod of a superior to a lesser or unknown noble. 'I am Baron Emêl Milea. This is the Lady Hedí Progae. You said a "creature" attacked her?'

'It was a man,' Lady Progae said calmly, shifting the cloth at her throat. 'Some madman.'

Lady Progae's shoulder-length hair curled like black silk around her pale face. Her nose was so small and narrow that Welstiel wondered how she could breathe through it. She grew lost in thought, and the longer she lingered there, the more doubt filled her refined features.

'He . . . his teeth were . . .' she began. 'He was so strong.'

Another guard, too young and obviously unsettled, nodded to the baron. 'It's true. I saw him just before he kicked Tolka into me. He wasn't right, with teeth like an animal, not a man.'

A stocky and scruffy guard snorted and pushed the young one back.

'Don't start again, Alexi, or you'll frighten Lady Progae,' he warned, then carefully appraised Welstiel. 'Your attempt at help is appreciated, sir, but we'll handle this.'

'I do not think so,' Welstiel replied, noting that Lady Progae hardly seemed frightened. 'And I pity any of your men who catch up with this thing. Have you ever hunted an undead . . . a vampire?'

'What . . .?' the stocky guard sputtered angrily.

'What nonsense are you suggesting?' Baron Milea interrupted. He looked down at his lady, but her eyes were fixed on Welstiel.

'You know I am correct,' Welstiel said. 'They saw its face. They can attest to its strength, as well as the lady. And how else would you explain her throat? Tell me, Lady Progae, how did his touch feel? Cold, perhaps?'

'It's a winter's night,' Tolka insisted, but behind him young Alexi looked more and more unsettled.

Hedí Progae remained silent a moment. 'I will not jump to conclusions, but I admit he was unnatural.'

'What about the other?' Tolka asked. 'The tall one fighting with him who scampered off first?'

'He was trying to help me,' Lady Progae said quickly. 'Just a passerby who became frightened by so many guards. Focus your efforts on the . . . this madman before he harms anyone else.'

'They will not find him,' Welstiel said with a slow shake of his head. 'No one will find him except a hunter of the dead, a dhampir.'

Silence followed. Folklore and superstitions of the undead were not uncommon. Some of Welstiel's listeners might infer his meaning, if any of them had heard tales of such a hunter, let alone a dhampir. Welstiel kept quiet, letting his words sink in. A third guard listening from the archway sighed and stepped nearer.

'Much as I hate agreeing with the whelp,' he said, cocking his head toward young Alexi, 'I saw those teeth, too. It wasn't a man.'

Baron Emêl Milea settled down beside Lady Hedí Progae and gently took the cloth she held, lifting it from her throat. Welstiel noted that the white handkerchief was only slightly stained. Chane must have just broken her skin when he was assaulted from above.

'Are you . . .' the baron began as he looked up at Welstiel. 'Do you know how to hunt such a thing?'

'No, but there is someone within the city who does,' Welstiel replied. 'Her services and those of her confederates can be costly, and she requires a free hand. She would need to be retained by the lord of the city before agreeing.'

The baron leaned close to his lady. They spoke softly to each other, and then he returned his attention to Welstiel with a curt nod. 'I will try to arrange an audience for tomorrow.'

Welstiel returned a courteous bow. 'My schedule will not be free until after dusk. Oh, and city business requires me to change inns. Have word sent to me at the Ivy Vine.'

Polite farewells were exchanged, and Welstiel turned up the stairs toward his room. Finding Magiere would not be difficult armed with the information Chane had given him, and he would soon regain control of her. He almost smiled.

Chap lay on the thick rug beside Wynn's bed as she slept, and the kittens, Tomato and Potato, were curled around her on the pillow. Their rumbling purrs were louder than Chap thought possible for such annoying little things. Even so, he would not have rested if the room were silent.

Something had gone wrong in the Droevinkan forest, when he had tried to cleanse wild magic from the young sage. Instead, her mantic sight had merely gone dormant and now began to remanifest in new ways. Though this bothered him deeply, it was not why he remained restless and unable to sleep.

Each time he closed his eyes. Chap saw images of Nein'a and of her mother, Eillean. And he remembered the name Byrd had used for the elf who had come in the night. The name had been shortened, which was why Chap had not recognized it at first.

Brot'an. *Brot'ân'duivé ácäräj Leavanalhpa Én'wire gan'Daraglas*.

Like all elvish names, it marked identity, lineage, and place in the world.

Dog in the Dark . . . born of Bending Elm (and) Joining Waters . . . from the clan of the Gray Oak.

Chap barely remembered the man who had accompanied Eillean when she had taken up a young *majay-hì* pup as a gift for her half-elf grandson.

As a pup, Chap had almost forgotten himself in his new existence among the brothers and sisters of his litter. Until his kin came to him, and then he relearned sorrow for the life in the forest he would set aside. His kin whispered into him through a dragonfly's buzzing wings as he chewed on the heads of wild grass beside a rippling stream.

It is time . . . the moment for your beginning . . . to go to the one caught between two peoples, two worlds. You will be with him . . . guide him . . . to one day steal the heart of the sister of the dead.

Chap let go of the grass, though some of its seeds stuck to his nose. He tried to 'remember' what more there was behind the words of his kin.

This task was part of why he had taken flesh – to steal the sister of the dead from the Enemy – but other memories were hazy and faded. His new flesh, mind as well as body, did not hold all the awareness he had shared as a Fay. Flesh had severed much of the knowing that they shared as one. He had to trust in his kin for what he no longer remembered.

But he understood that they now reminded him of why he had freely chosen to be born.

Chap scampered back to the glen where his 'mother' and siblings roamed the village.

Few of the elves were about. Most would be busy with the day's labors or out gathering sustenance from the deep forest. In nearly three moons of 'life,' Chap had learned much of their language. Their strange sounds – words – brought flickering memories with each utterance. It was how he learned their speech, though language seemed such a limited way to share meaning.

Their domiciles were a mixture of shaped living things. Hollows were nurtured in the growth of massive trees until spaces within their wide trunks formed warm and dry places to sleep. Ivy and briar bushes tangled in low tree branches to create walls for exterior spaces where family and friends rested midday or gathered to share meals. Yellow-green moss covered the grounds within the village, where Chap often lounged or tussled with his siblings.

He curled up before an arch made of twining primroses that formed an entryway to a cedar with a cultivated hollow. The tree was wide enough that the outstretched arms of a dozen men could not encompass it. The place provided a home for one family. There

Chap waited, ignoring the taunts of his siblings wanting him to come play.

An elder woman came at dusk.

Her cowl, cloak, vestment, and breeches of soft wool were a deep green that sometimes seemed the charcoal gray of shadow. Her expression was flat and hard. Faint lines around her large eyes and small mouth suggested she was old for her kind, though still shy of a hundred years. Chap looked in her eyes and sensed worry, determination within regret, and scarred-over pain.

A young elven girl and boy, their hair tucked behind narrow peaked ears, peered out from the cedar tree's hollow.

'Eillean!' the girl whispered with adoration and awe.

The woman glanced over at the two children with a soft smile. Chap saw it was only a polite response that hid an inner emptiness.

A memory surfaced in the young girl, and Chap saw her playing make-believe alone in the forest, mimicking Eillean's imagined exploits. The girl had picked an old oak to pretend at presenting herself to *Aoishenis-Ahâre*, Most Aged Father. She would take up service to her people like the great Eillean.

It puzzled Chap why anyone would want to be someone other than who they were, which was impossible. He looked at the elder female elf through the girl's surging memories – which told him more than words could. Not just *who* the woman was, but *what* she was.

Anmaglâhk.

Stealthy warriors, guardians, and agents of Most Aged Father, they sacrificed hearth and home, leaving behind the elven sanctuary in order to keep it safe. A caste unto themselves, separate from the clan structure, they worked in secret within the human lands to ensure nothing there could ever send harm toward their people.

Before Eillean stopped in the village's open space, the soft sound of her steps upon the moss carried another message from Chap's kin, the Fay.

This one will take you to the boy.

Eillean, whose name meant 'Sandpiper,' watched Chap's siblings tumble about the moss carpet. When her gaze fixed on Chap, a memory from Eillean washed over him.

He saw a half-elven youth with white-blond hair crouched behind a lakeshore house. Eillean's grandson, Léshil, whose name meant 'Colored with Rain' or 'Tint of the World's Tears,' had never met his grandmother. When passing through the land where he lived, she stopped to watch for him from across the lake. A stone fortification sprouted from the water, and the boy looked up, quick and furtive, before slipping inside the house.

Eillean glanced once more at Chap's siblings, then crouched down before him.

Chap sat up, staring into her large amber eyes.

His presence brought a childhood memory of her own, watching a yearling *majay-hì* run through the forest. Chap took that memory and repeated it to her, over and over, alongside the one of the lone half-elven boy. The two memories linked.

No elf would take a *majay-hì* from the forest, as they were free-willed creatures of the land. Chap knew he could force her, dominate her will, but he did not.

Eillean scowled, her eyes narrowing at the small pup before her. The more she stared, the more what she saw began to form a memory.

Chap saw his own image surface in Eillean's thoughts. He took it and repeated it alongside the one of the boy named Léshil.

Eillean frowned, looking troubled, as if what she contemplated were immoral.

Chap rocked up on his haunches, putting his paws on her knee where she crouched before him. He stuck his nose up at her brown, triangular face and barked once.

One of Eillean's delicate and slanted eyebrows raised. Chap rolled the memories through her awareness once more with a bark. She lifted him in her slender dark hands.

Her touch felt cold and betrayed no love or affection. But Chap's memory-play would have worked only if some compassion and warmth were buried deep within her. She pulled up the loose fabric wrap around her neck until it covered her lower face. Chap felt a stab of loss, longing for the touch of his mother's tongue or the press of his siblings at night, as Eillean carried him away from the village.

She did not go alone. She stopped in the forest and waited. Another came to join her.

Brot'ân'duivé.

'Dog in the Dark' dressed the same as Eillean, and only his large eyes and the bridge of his long nose were visible above his face wrap. Chap saw more of him through Eillean's memory, and his thin-lipped mouth was nearly always held in a stern line. Silvery hair marked him as old, though younger than she was. Standing half a head above Eillean, he was tall even for an elf, and more solidly built than most of his people.

Chap sensed inner turmoil in the elder male elf, as if he too had grown weary and disillusioned with his place in the world. It made him feel alone among the *Anmaglâhk*, except perhaps for Eillean.

Their journey was long, passing through the elven forest and into desolate and cold mountains. Chap's companions spoke little at all along the way. It seemed there was nothing to say, or whatever lay in their thoughts was so akin in guardedness that words were unnecessary. Chap lost count of the days and nights, shivering in Eillean's arms, as at times the snow was too deep for his short legs. On the mountain range's far side they entered wooded foothills, staying clear of roads that appeared now and then. When they finally reached their destination late one night, Chap recognized it immediately.

The lake and keep within Eillean's memory.

Bright red-orange fires burned atop its four corner towers, and Chap smelled decay and death for the first time. It stung his insides as well as his nose.

They circled halfway around the shore, until the keep stood on their left in the lake and the city houses were visible beyond it. Brot'an waited silently as Eillean cradled Chap in one arm and pulled a silver mirror from inside her vestment. She looked up, and Chap followed her gaze to the bright moon free of night clouds.

Eillean caught the moon's light upon the mirror, then angled the bright surface toward the lakeshore. It seemed impossible to Chap that the moon provided enough light, but she continued flashing the mirror until three answering sparks appeared in one house's upper window. The same house Chap had seen in her memory. Not long after, soft footsteps approached through the forest.

A young elven woman appeared in dark breeches and shirt beneath a charcoal cloak. Her resemblance to Eillean was clear to Chap. White-blond hair hung loose around her tall, narrow frame. Her amber eyes were as hard as her mother's. Eillean held Chap out, speaking in their native tongue.

'Cuirin'nên'a, my daughter . . . for the boy.'

Cuirin'nên'a – 'Water Lily's Heart' – took Chap, and he felt a difference in her hands from those of her mother. She pulled him carefully to her chest to warm him. Hidden tenderness in her touch belied her cold gaze, and this tenderness deepened as Chap caught the daughter's memory of her own son. She had another name for the boy – Leesil.

'Thank you,' she said. 'A companion may keep him whole in the face of what we must do to him.'

'He has a task ahead in his life,' Eillean answered sharply. 'One for which he cannot be influenced by our people's ways. This pup is small compensation, but spare Léshil nothing in training. There is no room for compassion if he is to learn the ways of his father and those of our caste.'

Chap's ears perked up. He did not understand what was behind these words. There were images that lashed through Cuirin'nên'a's thoughts, but she crushed them so quickly that Chap saw little. No more than bone, blood, stained blades, and silence in the dark. Chap remained quietly still.

These three were *Anmaglâhk*, yet they spoke of a plot unknown to the rest of their own kind. Subversion seemed a strange and unfamiliar thing for the guardian caste of the elves.

'I am not so certain,' Brot'an added quietly.

Eillean turned on him. 'I stood for you, when it came time for you to join us in this . . . to be a part of our plan. We need a better way than that which Most Aged Father demands in his fear. If you had doubts, you should have said as much before we allowed you among us.'

'Mother, enough,' Cuirin'nên'a said. 'He only voices the doubts we all have at some time. And no matter what the necessity, it is my son we prepare like a tool. I will never stop aching for him.'

Eillean shook her head slowly and gave her daughter no reply.

'Most Aged Father has waited many years,' Brot'an said to Cuirin'nên'a. 'He grows suspicious of the reasons we bring him for why you have not dealt with Darmouth by now.'

'My reason remains the same,' she answered. 'It is true that Darmouth's death would throw his province into turmoil, but the other Warlands provinces still fear facing one another in open war. And open war is what Most Aged Father wants, not just an internal conflict over who will rule in one province.'

'There may come a time when Most Aged Father will not settle for this answer,' Eillean said.

'Then keep him distracted with his plans elsewhere,' Cuirin'nên'a replied. 'If war among the humans is to be seeded here, then Darmouth must die at a time of unrest throughout the Warlands. Otherwise he will be quickly replaced by one of his own scheming nobles.'

Brot'an shook his head. 'We have already counseled this —'

'Then do so again,' Cuirin'nên'a snapped. 'Let Most Aged Father continue to think that turning humans upon one another is the only way. He is intent upon crippling them, for fear that they will be the waiting forces and minions of this ancient beast he believes will come again.'

'Perhaps he is right,' Brot'an added. 'I only wonder if a choice between his way or ours is necessary. Weakening the humans might be wise as well.'

'So we hack at an unseen monster's body,' Eillean spit at him, 'instead of severing its head? We have been over this countless times before you were even among us! We must train Léshil to take that head!'

'We can see the monster's body,' Brot'an replied, 'in the human hordes spreading across this world. We have yet to see its head. We know nothing of this ancient adversary Most Aged Father dreams of.'

'Only because he refuses to tell us,' Cuirin'nên'a finished. 'And the rest of our caste still follow him in blind faith.'

Chap began to tremble. These three planned to kill an unseen enemy from the deep past, though they had no concept of what they sought. Only that their patriarch feared its return and that the humans would be its engine of war. Chap understood what they toyed with in their ignorance.

It was the Enemy. Chap had taken flesh to seek out and steal its creation, the sister of the dead. It was now clear he was not the only one trying to use Leesil for a hidden purpose. Perhaps his own scheme would at least save the boy from a hopeless fate at his own mother's hands. Chap squirmed and whined.

Cuirin'nên'a looked down, folding her arms closely about him.

'The reason Darmouth still lives remains the same,' she said to the others. 'It is not the correct time . . . and Most Aged Father must have enough patience to accept this.'

Brot'an took a slow breath, then finally nodded. Eillean reached out and touched her daughter's cheek in farewell.

Cuirin'nên'a carried Chap into the stifling city of dark smells and dark corners. She took him to the house on the shore below the stone keep. She fed him goat's milk and shredded partridge. After, he lounged in her lap near the kitchen hearth as she stroked his back. And Chap waited.

When dawn arrived, a bleary-eyed young Leesil came down into the kitchen and saw Chap in his mother's lap. There was so much delight in his face that he tensed with a shudder, as if such a feeling were rare and startling. Chap forcefully wagged his tail, not allowing mother or son to know that he was anything more than a new playmate. Leesil wrestled with the pup upon the kitchen floor under his mother's silent and watchful gaze.

Chap's heart eased a bit. He had not lost a mother and siblings after all. He had a brother to watch over – to guide. And in the years that followed Leesil's flight from home, Chap kept hidden the few hints he had of Nein'a's plans.

Lying sleepless in Wynn's room, he wondered again at the reappearance of Brot'an. Leesil must never meet this man.

But Chap also wondered over the fate of the mother who had taken him in.

Nein'a should not be his main concern, as his own path was crucial to the world as a whole in guiding Magiere and Leesil. But he could not turn from this search, as Nein'a's fate mattered much to Leesil.

It mattered to Chap, as well.

7

Wynn sat on the floor of her room late the next morning, examining the drawings Leesil had brought her. She was still annoyed he had not shown them to her the night before. And there was something more he was keeping from her, of that much she was certain. She could not believe how obtuse Leesil acted regarding this entire situation. Or perhaps he did understand the implications and did not care.

'Byrd left these with you?' she asked. 'After you searched through his belongings without his permission? He just handed them to you and said, "Here, show your friends"?'

'Wynn —'

'Where is Magiere?'

Leesil sighed. 'Downstairs with Chap and Byrd. Putting out breakfast, I believe.'

'Get your cloak,' Wynn said, and stood up, gathering the drawings. 'And Magiere's. We need to speak alone.'

'We don't need to go out. I'll call Magiere and Chap up —'

'No! I am not saying anything with one of Darmouth's spies nearby, who appears to have his own agenda. There is no telling what Byrd will do with any information he might overhear.'

Leesil crossed his arms. Wynn stood there waiting until he realized she would not budge. He finally turned and opened the room's door.

'Meet me downstairs.'

Wynn tucked the drawings under the bed. She put on her sheepskin coat and shouldered the pack. She felt something shift in her pocket and reached inside, remembering the cold lamp crystal she had placed there. Lifting it out, she examined it for a moment, feeling wistful for Domin Tilswith and the Guild of Sagecraft. Alchemists among the sages, artificers who practiced thaumaturgy, created the crystals. The stone glowed brightly when warmed by human hands. She sighed and slipped it back into her coat pocket.

She lifted Tomato and Potato from her bed and carried them downstairs. Byrd had placed a bowl of milk near the kitchen doorway, and she settled them there. Tomato began lapping milk immediately, but Potato sat on his brown rump, blinking sleepily. He noticed his sister's busy tongue and sniffed about until his squat nose led him to breakfast.

Magiere pulled aside the doorway curtain and stepped out from the kitchen, a ratty old hand towel over her shoulder. Her black hair hung down her back over a white linen shirt. Wynn noticed how seldom Magiere bound her hair back these days.

'Did you look at the drawings?' Magiere asked without a 'good morning' or a 'sleep well?'

Wynn did not answer. Leesil came down the stairs wearing his cloak and carrying Magiere's.

'We need to go out for supplies,' Wynn said. 'All four of us.'

Magiere glanced at Leesil and back to Wynn. 'What do we need that we don't have already?'

Wynn grasped Magiere's forearm. 'We *need* to go out for supplies.'

Magiere looked at her for a moment, then lowered her voice. 'How long? Byrd's busy with a late breakfast.'

'Tell him to keep it warm,' Leesil said.

Magiere turned back around the bar's end, headed for the kitchen doorway.

A loud hiss and an angry snarl came from the kitchen. The doorway curtain snapped and curled up as something low to the floor raced under it. Tomato scrambled away through Wynn's legs, but the confused little Potato lost his footing and tumbled onto his face.

The white blur of Clover Roll boiled from around the bar, and Chap came through on the cat's heels, sending the milk bowl splashing off through the table legs in the common room. Clover Roll jumped for a high table, and Chap charged after, sharp teeth snapping.

'Chap! Stop it!' Wynn rushed in before Leesil could move.

She wrapped her arms around the dog's chest, but he was much stronger than she. Her grip slid down to his haunches. His next lunge pulled her feet out from under her. Wynn landed on her rump as Chap got his front legs on the table. Clover Roll's back hunched almost as high as his belly hung low.

Byrd came running out with a bowl of eggs in his hands. 'Clover! You flea-bitten bag of bile!'

Leesil grabbed Chap by the neck so Wynn could get up. Clover Roll hissed and spit, his wide belly swaying back and forth. Wynn saw that Chap's face was bleeding below his left eye.

'It's not the dog's fault,' Byrd said. 'Clover bush-whacked him from a cupboard. Must have been waiting there all morning for the chance. Swung down, hanging by one paw, and swiped your dog before he knew what was coming.' He wagged a finger at Clover Roll. 'You can quit this victim's act. You're the perpetrator here, and if that dog needs a healer, it's coming out of your share this month!'

Leesil pulled Chap down to the floor. Wynn rummaged in her pack for a jar of salve and applied some to the dog's face. The wound was minor, and certainly no healer was required.

'We need to go out for personal supplies,' she said to Byrd, ignoring Chap's low grumble. 'It will not take long.'

Byrd cocked his head in puzzlement as he lifted Clover Roll off the table. 'Dress warmly, as it's bitter out today. And Leesil, keep your face and hair covered, and put some gloves on those hands.'

Wynn thought Leesil hardly needed reminding, but she let go of Chap to pull her own gloves on. The four companions left the inn and walked up the side street to the thoroughfare of the merchant district. Light snowflakes blew past them and twisted gently around the buildings in the breeze. Even Magiere, who seldom seemed to feel the cold, shivered briefly.

'Someone want to tell me what we're doing?' Magiere said, and looked directly at Wynn.

'Not yet,' Wynn answered.

Chap was more settled, now that they were away from the cats, and trotted with his tail in the air, unmindful of the cold weather.

Wynn noticed that the mood and health of the people living within Venjètz was a stark contrast to those of the villages. Shops and inns bustled with activity, though more subdued than the great city of Bela or even the dark streets of Kéonsk, the capital of Droevinka. But unlike the villages of this province, here no one clung to their horses and goods in fear. There was no shortage of motley soldiers about. Armed guardsmen patrolled the streets in twos or threes at regular intervals, yet no one appeared fearful for their young sons helping in the market. Perhaps conscription was not allowed within the city walls.

The most notable oddity Wynn saw was the state of disrepair. Few streets outside Favor's Row were cobbled, but unlike the dirt streets of Kéonsk, which were kept carefully grated and smoothed, Wynn found herself walking on frozen mud clumps and wheel ruts, as if the streets of Venjètz had not been tended in years. Some shops and stalls were falling apart, yet the people appeared industrious. Perhaps there were no woodsmen, lumber millers, or ironworkers left to make materials for repairs with so many conscripted for too long. Or were they being employed in other pursuits in a land where war might come at any time?

As they approached the open marketplace, Wynn caught the sound of hawkers' shouts and the smell of overspiced meats. Chap whined pathetically, and Wynn pointed to a small open-fronted stall with smoke rising through a clay chimney on its snow-dusted roof. Half of the place was open all the way to the back wall. Stools were ringed around small tables.

'In there,' she said.

They took a table at the back corner. Leesil sat to

one side, hood pulled forward around his face, and studied the other patrons. Wynn settled in at the back with Magiere to the other side. When customers left the nearest table, Leesil shoved the vacated furniture farther away with his foot to give them more privacy. The buzz of voices all around would help mask anything they said. Leesil called out an order for tea and porridge to a boy hauling away a tray of empty bowls.

Wynn leaned intently toward him. 'You need to tell us what is going on.'

Magiere pulled her hood back and shook out her hair. 'What do you mean?'

'You saw the drawings,' Wynn whispered. 'And we know who . . . what kind of person Byrd spoke with last night. So what does this add up to?'

Magiere closed her eyes and sighed. Leesil rubbed his face and looked away.

'What?' Wynn looked at each of them in astonishment. 'You know what *he* is involved in, and you did not bother to tell me?'

She was reluctant to say 'Darmouth' or 'assassination,' even in a hushed voice.

'When could we, with Byrd hovering about?' Leesil returned irritably.

Magiere frowned at him before turning to Wynn. 'Ordinary elves don't mingle with humans, and I'd guess the *Anmaglâhk* are even more reluctant. So how is it Byrd could get them involved in killing . . .' She did not say Darmouth's name either. 'I know what it looks like, but I wonder if they're up to something of their own that Byrd isn't aware of. Some purpose that has nothing to do with his plans.'

Leesil remained silent, head hanging, and Wynn found no denial in his cowl-shadowed face. He must have pieced together something from the drawings and talking alone with Byrd. His silence confirmed he had suspicions, but he clearly did not understand the repercussions of Darmouth's sudden death.

'We have to stop it,' Wynn whispered.

Leesil lifted his head. Magiere's pale face grew astonished.

'Save a despot?' Magiere growled too loudly, then lowered her voice. 'This has nothing to do with us. What new madness have you got running around in your head?'

Chap growled from under the table, his agreement clear.

'What happens once his death is known?' Wynn whispered back. 'Every noble with armed forces will seek —'

'To take control of the province,' Leesil finished. 'It still has nothing to do with us. I came here to learn what happened to my parents, and Byrd has been little help.'

Magiere's brow wrinkled and she sadly closed her eyes. Wynn could not spare anyone's feelings in this matter.

'We will not abandon the search,' she said. 'But think how many villages will be devastated by a civil war . . . how many people will die.'

'Inside or out, it's the same,' Leesil snapped. 'Conscriptions are up. People flee for the border, as if military service were a certain death sentence. Why does Darmouth build up forces in such a reckless manner? Either he'll assault another province, or he's bracing for an invasion. Insurrection might come in either case. It doesn't matter how it happens – war is coming, from inside or outside or both. If he's dead in the mix, so much the better.'

'Do you not see?' Wynn replied in a low voice. 'Civil war breaks out in Droevinka. An *anmaglâhk* was sent to Bela after you, Leesil. Now these elves assist humans to murder a warlord. It is beyond one more war for this region's namesake. It is not just happening in the Warlands. And Darmouth still holds this province together, no matter how vile he may be.'

Leesil turned slightly toward Wynn, and she saw his face – and his open disdain. Magiere sat back, dark eyes glancing about.

'Why would the *Anmaglâhk* get involved in this?' she asked.

'I don't know.' Leesil remained silent a moment. 'Perhaps that's not their only purpose here.'

A dull-eyed serving maid in a filthy apron pressed through patrons to their table. She thunked down four small bowls and rough clay cups, and a tin pot of brown water that was presumably the tea. Unfortunately, Magiere paid the woman before she looked into the bowls and saw what passed for porridge. When they were alone again, Magiere glanced side-long with concern at Leesil and took a deep breath.

'Do you think Wynn is right about Byrd's plan?'

'Yes,' Leesil answered, and set his own bowl under the table for Chap. 'You heard me question him last night. He didn't answer, and that told me enough.'

'And why is he so willing to let us study the drawings?' Wynn put in.

Leesil shook his head. 'Some nonsense that it might help in my search.'

'He works for Darmouth, yet he plots against him,' Wynn continued. 'He is supposedly the only friend of Leesil's father, yet he works with these elves who have imprisoned Nein'a. And giving his cat a share of the profits . . . indeed! His eccentric acts are just that – an act.'

Magiere raised both pale hands. 'All right, we hear you.'

Chap let out a vicious snarl from under the table, and Wynn jumped in her seat.

Other patrons glanced toward them and then down beneath their table. A few quickly got up and left, and a half-breath later, Leesil jerked up a foot as if struck.

A pottery bowl shot across the dirt floor and bounced between table and stool legs, splattering porridge all about.

Leesil twisted away, ducking his face, as Magiere shrank down, casting glances about at the other patrons staring at them. She turned a glower downward to beneath the table.

Wynn's jangled nerves gave way, and she lightly kicked out the toe of her boot. It collided with something soft but firm, and Chap growled in response.

'I have seen you eat worse,' she whispered harshly. 'Now stop it!'

'Will we ever eat in public,' Magiere whispered with bowed head, 'without causing a spectacle?'

No one answered her.

'I say we keep looking into the fate of Leesil's parents,' Magiere continued, 'until we uncover more of Byrd's scheme . . . and how to stop it without getting hanged from the city walls.'

'Yes, good,' Wynn said, relieved that for once Magiere was clearly on her side. 'Leesil?'

This time he remained silent for so long that Wynn's patience was about to run out, and then he simply nodded.

'Back to Byrd's,' Magiere said. 'No matter what else, at least he can cook.'

No one smiled at her joke. She grasped Leesil's hand, and his fingers slowly gripped down on hers.

'We should purchase a few supplies,' Wynn suggested. 'It would look strange to return with nothing after our excuse of leaving.'

They left the eatery, which was now half-emptied, thanks to Chap's tantrum, and headed back to the open market. Wynn's mind was not on purchasing supplies or taking note of Venjètz and its people. Her thoughts were filled with how to uncover the rest of the tangled web that Byrd had woven around himself.

Chane awoke that evening to Welstiel once again murmuring in his dormancy. He sat up and swung his legs over the bed. His robin drank from a small tin cup on its cage floor, the cage placed securely on the little table in the room.

The Ivy Vine inn was a far cry from the Bronze Bell in both decor and service, though the Bronze Bell, supposedly the best in Venjètz, barely matched the middle-class establishments of Bela. And Welstiel had rented the only room left with two beds. It was clean but shabby, with a chipped water pitcher and basin resting on an uneven table.

Chane did not care. It was still preferable to another day in their makeshift tent covered over with brambles and branches. He wondered where Wynn was on this evening, what she might be doing, and if she was safe. Welstiel murmured again, and Chane stepped closer to peer down at his self-righteous companion.

'In . . . the high . . . ice,' Welstiel whispered. 'Orb . . . never feed . . . again.'

Chane's resentment wavered. For the first time since rising from his second death, he felt something besides rage or hunger or lingering fear – curiosity.

In their travels, he had occasionally caught a few words of Welstiel's dormant mumblings. Something assisted Welstiel in searching for whatever he sought. Chane knew little more, other than that Magiere was somehow essential. Never feed again? Did Welstiel seek something made for a Noble Dead? An 'orb' to sustain him without a need to hunt and feed?

He crouched on the balls of his feet and stared at Welstiel's languid face. Would that be a desirable state? Never to feed again?

Welstiel rolled, and his eyelids half opened.

Chane backed away to his bed, picking up his vestment from where it draped over the footboard. Welstiel sat up.

'What now?' Chane asked, as if the previous night had never happened and this was but another monotonous night in their tagalong behind Magiere.

'For now, you do nothing,' Welstiel answered, rubbing his face with both hands. 'I have an audience with Lord Darmouth. If all goes well, I will turn you loose on the city. You can savage as much of it as you like. That will flush Magiere into the open, and perhaps give me an opportunity to end this wasteful search for the half-blood's past.' He looked Chane over, inspecting him from head to toe. 'We must alter your appearance to avoid anyone providing an accurate description of you. Oh, and I felt it safer to give myself a false name, so I used your family's. Do not forget.'

Chane tensed. 'You gave Andraso as your surname?'

'Yes, is that a problem? Has your little sage heard this name?'

'No . . . not that I remember.'

Chane understood the need for secrecy. He did not know why Welstiel's use of his family's name bothered him.

Welstiel reached into his pack and took out a black knitted cap. When he put it on, it completely covered the white patches at his temples. He donned his cloak and fastened it at his throat, then glanced at Chane as he reached into the pack again.

'I bought something for you,' he said, and pulled out fresh parchment, an ink bottle, and two quill pens. 'You might document the people and land here, as I doubt much has been recorded on them. It might be of future value in trade with the Guild of Sagecraft. If that still interests you.'

Chane stared at the parchment in Welstiel's hand. He did not reach for it. First, he was surprised that Welstiel made such an uncharacteristic gesture. Second, he was surprised that he had absolutely no interest in scribing a single word. Once such intellectual pursuits had been important to him.

'No,' he said.

A flash of disappointment passed across Welstiel's face. He placed the items on Chane's bed. 'I may be a few hours. Do not leave the room.'

The thought of pacing and waiting in this shabby inn was almost more than Chane could bear. He nodded, and Welstiel pulled on his gloves and left.

Chane stood alone in the center of the room. Once contemplative about most anything, he now hated having time to think. His mind always slipped to the same moments.

Fighting Magiere in the wet Droevinkan forest, he stood above her with his sword in both hands, ready to run it through her chest. Wynn rushed forward to shield Magiere with her own body, begging Chane to stop. And he did.

Magiere rose up. Her blade bit through his throat, burning his flesh from the inside. The world blackened in his sight, and that darkness brought terror.

His next awareness was waking in a shallow open grave, covered in dead bodies. Their throats slit, blood spilling over him, soaking into him, saturating his clothing and flesh. Inside, he was drenched in his own fear. The pain still in his throat was so intense it made every muscle in his body spasm.

And from nearby he had heard Welstiel's voice. 'Are you awake yet?'

Welstiel brought Chane back, but Chane had not come back the same. Too much of himself was still lying in that grave. And he couldn't even remember Wynn mourning for him.

Chane reached out and fingered one of the new quills

Welstiel had left, wondering where Wynn was and if she was safe.

Darmouth walked into the council hall with Faris two steps behind him between two of Omasta's men. Darmouth had too many pressing matters and suspects to watch, and now Emêl had begged an audience for some stranger. The baron was the last of his trusted ministers and rarely asked for anything. Dismissing the request out of hand would be rash, and somehow Hedí was involved. This was enough to convince Darmouth to agree.

The wall braziers were lit and fat candles glowed from the long table. Two heavy tapestries hung on the back wall, one depicting his family crest, and the other was a lone, faceless rider on a rearing horse against a black background. Darmouth cared little for art, but the rider appealed to him.

Emêl stood waiting with a pale man in a knit cap. Darmouth crossed his thick arms and looked the stranger up and down.

'May I introduce Viscount Andraso,' Emêl said in a formal tone.

Darmouth offered neither his hand nor a curt nod. Andraso looked about forty years old, of medium height and build. His eyes were strange, nearly colorless, like worthless quartz, and a slight bump widened the bridge of his nose. His clothes were hidden beneath a knee-length cloak, but that was no concern, as Omasta's men would have searched him and removed any weapons.

'Why are you here?' Darmouth asked bluntly.

'Lady Progae was attacked last night,' Emêl said, 'by

a man with misshapen teeth. He bit her throat, but she is all right. We need to track down this creature, and the viscount believes he can help.'

'What do you mean "bit her"?' Darmouth demanded. Being confused wasn't something he liked.

Viscount Andraso held up a gloved hand. 'Baron Milea is still distraught by the events of last night. I assure you that Lady Progae is well, her wound minor and attended. The baron's men intervened quickly, but she was attacked by a vampire.'

Andraso spoke with a distinct accent, and Darmouth forgot his confusion. He distrusted foreigners almost as much as his own nobles. 'You're an outlander. Where are you from and why are you here?'

'Droevinka,' Andraso answered politely. 'Merely passing this way while searching for a friend.'

Emêl pushed a lock of thinning hair back and stepped closer to Darmouth. 'Please, my lord, hear him out.'

'He's mad,' Darmouth answered. 'Vampires? I'm no addle-minded peasant! Throw him out.'

'No, please, my lord,' Emêl said. 'The . . . creature . . . that attacked Hedí was not a normal man, and I tended what was clearly a bite on her throat. Several of my men saw him — saw his teeth.'

Darmouth frowned. Emêl possessed no imagination, which was largely why he remained trustworthy. He was not given to overstatement or nonsense. Faris stepped closer to listen, his slender fingers intertwined.

'I know something of such creatures,' Andraso said, 'as they've been seen in my homeland. A hunter of the dead, a dhampir, is needed to track one down and destroy it.'

Darmouth glanced at Faris, who backed away, and then turned to ask, 'And you're such a hunter?'

Andraso shook his head. 'No.'

'Then why waste my time? If such a beast exists, my soldiers can deal with it.'

Even in concern for his future bride, Darmouth wearied of this stranger's prattle. He cared nothing for some madman loose in the city, as sooner or later his soldiers always found and eliminated any troublemaker.

Andraso stepped closer, his eyes moving from Darmouth's face to his breastplate and back up again. 'How many noblewomen live in the city at present?'

Darmouth's frown deepened. 'Why are you asking?'

'By legend and folklore, some undead develop habits . . . specific tastes. This one tried to take a noblewoman behind the finest inn in the city. How will your nobles react if their women are threatened? Unless their lord takes action.'

Darmouth felt his own face grow hot at the insinuation. Who was this foreigner to try intimidating him?

Emêl stepped between them. 'My lord, this man says a hunter named Magiere is here in the city. If you were to . . . to use official methods to locate her, we could retain her services quietly. If she's half what the viscount claims, she may track the beast down before word spreads, and this entire affair will be quickly over.'

Darmouth looked into Emêl's narrow face and his stifled rage subsided. Emêl might be weak and unimaginative, but he often provided sensible counsel. Nodding slowly, Darmouth turned to one of his bodyguards. 'Get Omasta in here now!'

As the bodyguard hurried out, Darmouth turned on

Faris and didn't care if his dislike for the man showed. Vagabond trash that he was, the Móndyalítko and his wife had their uses — and talents. 'Locate this hunter, Magiere. I want her found tonight.'

Lieutenant Omasta strode through the council hall archway, a clot of gravy caught in his blond beard. 'My lord?'

'Take a small contingency to the Bronze Bell,' Darmouth instructed. 'Bring Lady Progae to the keep for protection.' He paused at Emêl's shocked expression. 'For her safety, until this is settled.'

Emêl nodded and stepped back to escort his guest out. For an instant, no more than that, Darmouth was puzzled. Had something . . . threatening flickered across the baron's plain features?

8

Magiere took another sip of tea and shuffled the deck of cards. Byrd and Leesil sat across from her at a table in the common room.

It had been a long, unproductive day, but late as it was, no one showed interest in heading for bed. Wynn sat on the floor trying to tease Chap's interest in Potato and Tomato's wrestling game. Clover Roll crouched alone atop a table at the room's rear, glowering at everyone.

A few patrons came earlier for an evening meal. Magiere gave Byrd a hand at the bar, missing the nights at her own Sea Lion tavern. She wondered how Caleb and Rose fared in Miiska and hoped Leesil was right about Aunt Bieja heading there on her own.

Magiere's assistance was also an excuse to watch over Byrd. Like Wynn, she thought the man deceitful at best, with designs on Leesil connected to the unfinished drawings he had so casually handed over. She wished they'd never come here, but Byrd might still be the only lead to answers for Leesil. After the patrons left, Magiere sat down to play cards. She chatted politely as she watched over Leesil, hoping Byrd would tip his hand in some way.

Leesil's heart didn't appear to be in the game. He'd stayed upstairs, out of sight, until the last of the patrons were gone. As the night ran on, he grew more restless.

Magiere knew that they must soon decide on some
course of action.

'More tea?' Byrd asked. 'Or something stout? Your
father never drank, but I don't know your habits.'

Leesil hesitated in a way that set Magiere on edge.
'Just tea,' he replied.

Byrd headed off for the kitchen. Magiere wished she
had the man alone. Getting Byrd drunk might yield
something more than Leesil had gotten out of him.

'Leesil, look,' Wynn said. 'Like four little hands!'

Magiere glanced down. Tomato had all four paws
wrapped savagely around Wynn's arm as if locked in a
life-and-death battle. The sage's fascination with the
kittens baffled Magiere, and the attempt to get a smile
from Leesil failed. Chap was merely bored, head lying
on his paws.

Clover Roll yowled.

Magiere tensed, and Chap instantly sprang to his feet.
The cat's mouth opened wide, exposing missing teeth
in a long, grating hiss. As Byrd trotted back in from the
kitchen, clunking the teapot down on a table, the mangy
animal's noise grew louder.

Clover Roll leaped from table to table all the way to
the front window's sill and pushed at the closed shutters.

'What's up?' Byrd asked and joined the fat feline, but
when he cracked the shutter to peek out, he whirled
around, all traces of the witty innkeeper gone. 'All of
you, get in the kitchen, now! Keep quiet and out of
sight.'

Leesil stood up. 'Byrd —'

'Move!' Byrd whispered harshly, and grabbed Wynn's

arm, pulling her up as he rushed them all into the kitchen and jerked the curtain closed. 'Not a sound.'

Magiere looked to Leesil for answers, but he shook his head, white-blond hair falling forward over his shoulder. The curtain swayed slightly as Clover Roll sauntered in, weaving through their legs away from Chap to settle beneath the kitchen table.

There was a knock at the inn's front door. Magiere hooked the curtain with one fingertip and peered out.

Byrd opened the front door, revealing a slender man. His wild black hair, dusky complexion, and silver earrings marked him as a Móndyalítko. When he turned his head, she noticed he wore the rings in only one ear. His other ear was missing, and only smooth scars remained.

Magiere didn't care much for these wanderers with their wagon houses. She and Leesil had encountered their traveling families over years on the road. They wore motley bright clothes and had open smiles for strangers, and their laughter came too easily to be trustworthy.

The man in the doorway was different. Closed and serious, with hard eyes, he showed none of his people's sly mirth. He was rather plainly dressed in a burgundy shirt, high boots, and a thin belt. As he stepped into the common room, several cats scurried out from hiding beneath tables. Even Tomato and Potato skittered around behind the bar in a strange panic.

'Bit late for a visit, Faris,' Byrd said.

'As if I'd make a social call here,' the man answered.

'Then what do you want?' Byrd shut the door but didn't follow his visitor into the common room. He stayed at the bar's far end near the front door.

'Lord Darmouth wishes to find a woman named Magiere. He's been told she's in the city.'

Magiere stiffened. Why and how had she come to that tyrant's attention?

Byrd merely shrugged. 'And what of it?'

'We were told she's a dhampir.' Faris offered a shallow smile of mockery. 'A noblewoman was assaulted outside the Bronze Bell last night. The story is that the attacker was a vampire.'

Faris waited for Byrd's reaction. When none came, he continued with a shrug of his own.

'Our lord wants to protect the city, of course, so he wishes to engage this hunter's services . . . for whatever fee. Put the word out and be quick about it. He wants her found tonight.'

'Of course.' Byrd paused. 'But which noblewoman was attacked?'

'Lady Hedí Progae. She is safe now, under our lord's protection.'

As Faris spoke the name, Magiere heard a breath sucked in behind her. Something clattered to the floor, followed by a hiss. She glanced back to find that Leesil had retreated back against the kitchen table, knocking off a carving knife and startling Clover Roll. Leesil's gaze was fixed on the curtained doorway, and he didn't blink.

The noise had surely attracted Faris's attention, and Magiere dropped one hand to her hip. The falchion wasn't there. She'd stowed it behind the bar while serving drinks earlier that evening.

Clover Roll scurried out from under the table. Magiere ducked back as the doorway curtain rustled in the cat's passage. When the fabric settled in place, she peeked out again. The cat sauntered around the bar's near end and out into the common room.

Byrd looked down at the cat and smiled calmly. 'Ah well, I forgot about my partner's late night nibble. My kitchen will be in quite a state for that oversight.'

Faris sneered in disgust. 'Just find the hunter – tonight.' He pushed past Byrd to the front door and left.

Magiere spun around, stepping close in front of Leesil. He didn't acknowledge her.

'What's wrong?' she said. 'That woman's name . . .'

Magiere stopped. Leesil's gaze wandered across the floor, eyes shifting quickly as if he was watching something. When she glanced down, there was nothing to see. Leesil remained silent, and at first Magiere thought she saw him shaking his head ever so slightly. Then she realized he was shuddering.

'Leesil? What has that woman to do with this?'

And still, he didn't seem to know she was there. She was about to grab him and shake him to awareness when Byrd stepped through the doorway curtain.

'You heard?' he asked.

Before Magiere could answer, Leesil whispered.

'A trap . . .'

Magiere slowly reached toward him and then stopped.

'If Darmouth knows of Magiere,' Leesil continued to himself, 'then he knows she's with me. He knows I'm here, and this is just a pretense to draw me out.'

'Don't be so quick,' Byrd warned.

'What if there is a vampire?' Wynn asked, looking to Magiere.

The little sage stood off to the side and couldn't see

Leesil's face as Magiere could. Leesil blinked, finally focusing on Magiere, then slowly tilted his head toward Wynn as if realizing she was there and had spoken.

'There are better cities to settle in,' he said, 'where prey is just as plentiful.'

Byrd's brow wrinkled at Leesil's response. Magiere wished Leesil hadn't been so quick to reveal their belief in such creatures. And normally he wouldn't have.

Byrd shook his head and answered hesitantly, his brow wrinkling as he eyed Leesil.

'Faris thinks it's all nonsense . . . but he believes Darmouth is convinced that your woman can deal with this . . . vampire, supposedly. Any truth to it?'

'Yes,' Magiere snapped, her self-control faltering. 'And call me "his woman" again, and I'll fix you so you've no interest in one of your own.'

Byrd didn't even react to her warning. 'Anyone before ever try to locate you like this? To hire you?'

'We spent years on the backroads, working the remote villages of southern Stravina,' she answered. There was no point letting Byrd know it had all been a ruse until last season.

'We never worked this far north,' Leesil whispered, 'No one here would've heard of her by rumor. Someone told him we were here . . . told him of Magiere.'

'And now Darmouth has invited me inside the keep,' she said, and instantly knew it was the wrong thing to say.

Leesil's gaze lifted to her face as if her voice had startled him. His eyes widened, and his head shook. Not truly in denial but more like the shudder within him had grown suddenly.

'This is over!' he tried to shout, but it came out harsh and grating rather than loud. 'You're not meeting Darmouth in that keep or anywhere else. We're leaving tonight.'

Before Magiere's anger fueled a retort, Byrd pushed her aside to face Leesil.

'Don't be a fool! She's fierce and clever, and she's been handed an invitation to the last place your parents were seen. She can handle Darmouth. I didn't think Nein'a's son would go belly-up so easily.'

Leesil tensed, and his features slackened for an instant before his eyes locked on Byrd. He started to lean forward as if ready to lunge.

Magiere shoved Byrd back. 'Shut your mouth and get away from him!'

For a second, Byrd peered straight in her eyes, waiting. He backed up to lean against a cutting block table at the kitchen's side wall.

'Am I right?' he asked her. 'You think about it . . . and maybe get him to do the same.'

Magiere's instincts rose like hunger in her throat. Leesil's self-control had slipped farther than she'd ever seen before, and it had something to do with the woman's name Faris had mentioned. Getting inside the keep might be her only avenue to help him find answers, but now Byrd was suddenly pushing too hard. Why had the man lost his temper the instant Leesil mentioned leaving?

Wynn stepped away from Byrd to the kitchen table, but she was watching Leesil as warily as the innkeeper. Leesil lowered his head, hands gripping the table edge as he clenched his eyes shut.

'I am coming with you,' Wynn said quietly to Magiere. 'So is Chap. We may recognize things of interest while you are negotiating services with Darmouth.'

'No,' Leesil said hoarsely. 'Wynn, don't —'

'We'll have Byrd feel this out,' Magiere cut in, 'and try arranging an audience. If it smells bad – or we don't like the way he handles it – then we're gone. All right?'

'Why ask me?' Leesil said coldly. 'You've made up your mind.'

He shoved off the table so hard it slid several inches, making Wynn jump back and Chap sidestep out of his way. As he swatted the doorway curtain aside and left, Magiere watched in stunned silence. Worse still was that she didn't know whether to leave him be or follow and force out of him whatever had just pushed him over the edge.

Magiere turned on Byrd. 'Set it up. Tell me as soon as you hear anything.'

Byrd's eyes were on the kitchen curtain, still swaying in Leesil's wake. He glanced at her, nodded with a frown, and left. It wasn't until Magiere heard the inn's front door slam shut that Wynn came up to her.

'Chap and I are going with you,' Wynn insisted, and grasped Magiere's arm. 'You will need us.'

Magiere looked at her, and finally nodded. 'Yes, Wynn, I know.'

Hedí sat at a mahogany table in the small common area of the Bronze Bell Inn. It was little more than a wide alcove just off the foyer and the main hallway running between the front and rear doors. She wore a midnight-blue velvet gown with a matching wide ribbon around her neck to hide her recent wound. She picked at an apple tart with a fork as she waited for Emêl's return.

The clop of hooves grew loud outside the inn, and the creak of the front door followed. Hedí was slightly surprised when Lieutenant Omasta strode through the foyer into view. Emêl was close behind, and the subtle widening of his eyes and clench of his jaw muscles told her something was wrong.

'What has happened?' she asked.

She stood up, her head barely reaching the top of Omasta's leather hauberk, and stepped around him to Emêl standing in the hallway. There were four of Omasta's guards waiting near the front door and no sign of Emêl's own men.

'I've been ordered to escort you to the keep, lady,' Omasta explained. 'Lord Darmouth will ensure your safety until this beast in the city has been dealt with.'

'I am safe enough here,' Hedí replied evenly, holding in her rising panic. 'I have the protection of Baron Milea's own contingency.'

Emêl shook his head slightly, just once.

'Baron Milea remains here,' Omasta said. 'I have my orders, lady. I've brought a horse for you.'

'She will need her personal effects,' Emêl said. He took Hedí's hand and walked toward the foot of the stairs.

Omasta fell in behind them. 'Of course. I will assist with the baggage.'

Hedí climbed the stairs with Emêl. It was clear that Omasta would not leave her alone with the baron. Something more had happened for Darmouth to want her locked inside the keep for her own 'safety.'

Emêl looked strained as he led the way to her room and began gathering her clothes and belongings. Omasta remained out in the upper hallway but kept the door open. There would be no chance for a single private word with Emêl.

Once Hedí was packed, her panic rose again. She tried to think of a way to postpone her departure and have even one moment alone with Emêl. When no ideas came to her, she was left with only the most cliché of feminine ploys.

Hedí put a hand to her throat, rolled her eyes closed with a soft exhale, and slumped to the floor in a heap.

She heard Emêl kneel beside her, felt him take her hand, and he shouted at Omasta, 'Get cold water and a towel . . . to the kitchen, man!'

A moment's silence followed, then heavy footsteps pounded down the hallway.

Hedí opened her eyes and pulled herself up by Emêl's grip, leaning close to him with a whisper. 'What has happened?'

'Shhhhh,' he answered, and there was as much fear in his green eyes as she felt herself. 'I should have told you last night. Darmouth has chosen you for a wife. He wants a legitimate heir.'

Hedí stared at him. Had she even heard him correctly? Too many thoughts raced through her mind, and Omasta would return any moment.

'Do not let them lock me up!' she insisted.

'We cannot refuse,' Emêl said quickly. 'I would end up rotting on the keep wall, and you would still be trapped.'

'I would rather be dead,' she answered too loudly, and

Emêl raised a finger to his lips, 'than be breeding stock for that aging savage! There must be —'

'Go with Omasta, and wait for me,' he said. 'Smile for Darmouth, flatter him, play the bride-to-be if you must, but do whatever keeps him pacified. I will find a way to get you out, and we will disappear, but we cannot let him suspect anything.'

Omasta came running back to the doorway. 'The maid is coming. Are you . . . all right, lady?'

He saw her hand clasped in Emêl's as she leaned close to him, and the concern vanished from the lieutenant's face as his eyes narrowed. A serving woman followed on his heels with a pitcher and towels. Emêl turned his back to the door and looked Hedí in the eyes.

Go, he mouthed silently, *and stay alive.*

Alone in the dark room upstairs, Leesil dropped on the bed's edge. He was awake, yet visions like nightmares thrashed about in his mind. There had been so many victims, and then so many years of drinking himself into unconsciousness just to forget. Sometimes he couldn't remember all of their names. Only those who came after him in his sleep.

Lord Baron Progae . . . Lady Damilia . . . Sergeant Latätz . . . the blacksmith of Koyva . . . Lady Kersten Petzkà. . . Josiah, the old scholar . . .

Leesil looked about for something, anything, to focus on rather than face his own rising memories. Magiere would come soon, but he half-hoped she would stay away. It took all his effort to fight off the ghosts, so how could he keep them from her?

Someone shifted in slumber beneath the bedcovers behind him.

Leesil lunged away, spinning about as he backed against the room's opposite wall.

The blankets and sheepskin cover were still neatly pulled up where he'd left them that morning.

The bed was empty. It was just his memories taunting him. But Leesil remained staring at the smoothed bed covers, uncertain that he could trust what he saw. He slid down the wall to lean against it on his haunches.

He should light a candle, or prepare for bed. Do anything to keep himself in the moment. But he remained there shaking in the dark, unable to forget . . .

Hedí Progae.

He'd seen her only once. No, in a way, it had been twice. One face among so many in his mind. And it had all been so long ago . . .

On the morning of his seventeenth birthday, his mother presented him with a gift.

The wooden box was as long as his forearm, less than half that in width, and no thicker than two hands stacked one on the other. Inside were items of unmatched craftsmanship. The sheen of their metal was brighter than polished steel.

Two stilettos as thin as knitting needles rested upon a coiled garrote wire with narrow wooden handles. There was a short curved blade strong enough to cut bone. Hidden behind a foldout panel in the box's lid, he found hooks, picks, and wire struts for opening locks.

No boy would have wanted this for his coming of age.

His mother slipped away as Leesil examined the items.

When he noticed she was gone, he clutched the box and went looking for her. On the house's second floor, he stopped at his parents' room, looking in through the half-open door.

Cuirin'nên'a . . . Nein'a . . . Mother . . .

She sat on the window seat at the back of the room, the lake and forest and gray sky all far out of reach behind her through the glass. Her perfect caramel skin, white-blond hair, and large almond-shaped eyes were mesmerizing. She was like an unearthly statue of smoothly polished wood, silent and unmoving, except for wet tracks of tears upon her checks.

Leesil backed away, unable to watch anymore.

Something tugged at his pant leg, and he looked down. Chap let go with his teeth and turned down the stairs. Leesil followed his only boyhood friend through the house to the kitchen. When Chap whined and pawed at the hatch in the corner, Leesil lifted it open. Chap jumped effortlessly down into the cellar and waited as Leesil followed.

He lit the lantern resting on the floor. The cellar was sparse, with no furnishings and few stores except a crate of dried goods, a barrel of excess fabrics and linens, and small sacks of whatever vegetables were in season. A small assortment of light and short blades and one buckler hung from the stone-reinforced walls.

Leesil opened the box, wondering at his mother's tears after all the training she had insisted he endure. He lightly fingered a stiletto blade as the hatch above him opened again.

His father climbed down the ladder.

Gavril always dressed in neutral colors, earthy and

dark hues. His brown hair hung to his shoulders, and soft down covered his chin. His refined hands looked as if they belonged to a musician or perhaps a silversmith.

Leesil lifted one wire pick, a bit thicker than all the others. 'What kind of lock would this open?'

His father held up both hands as a call for silence. 'Our lord has a task for you.'

Leesil blinked. He'd seen Lord Darmouth only once, four years earlier, as the ruler left his keep to lead a regiment out of the city. Gavril had been called to attend, and Leesil waited in the road with his father just beyond the gatehouse of the keep's stone bridge.

Darmouth rode out on a gray-flecked stallion so large that Leesil was certain he felt each pound of its hooves vibrate through the stone bridge and into the earth beneath his feet. Darmouth didn't dismount or even gesture to Leesil's father, but pulled up his horse under the gatehouse.

Gavril put a hand on Leesil's shoulder, telling him to wait, and stepped forward. Darmouth spoke down to Leesil's father in a low voice. The gray-flecked beast beneath him pawed the ground and snorted in the freezing winter air, its breath like belching smoke. Leesil never learned what was said, but Gavril was gone all that night and returned after the following dusk.

Seated on a crate in the cellar, Leesil looked at his father. The hatch in the kitchen floor above Gavril remained open, and light spilled down, deepening the shadows on his face. His skin seemed too tightly stretched over cheeks and jaw, as if he couldn't relax.

'What does Lord Darmouth want from me?' Leesil asked.

The tension of Gavril's face broke, leaving a strange exhaustion as he pulled a rolled parchment from the front of his shirt.

'Baron Progae is accused of treason. His influence is such that Lord Darmouth cannot risk arrest and a public trial. The death warrant has been signed by the council of ministers. I have a map of Progae's fortress and grounds. You will leave tonight.' He paused, not looking at Leesil. 'Scale the north wall to the rampart and enter through the northeast tower. I've marked Progae's chamber. He will be alone. All other family members are away with relatives. Make certain he is asleep. Do you understand?'

Leesil followed his father's words, but he did not understand . . . didn't want to understand.

'This is why we still live,' his father said, 'how we stay alive. It's your time.'

Leesil had undergone years of training, with many nights in this very cellar learning things he put out of his thoughts during daylight. Still, he wasn't prepared for this moment.

'Remember every detail,' Gavril continued. 'Lord Darmouth expects an accounting when you return. I've vouched for your skill, and . . . our lives depend on each other. Do what is necessary. Consequence matters not unless it comes. Remember your training, and it never will come.'

Leesil left that night with his toolbox, thick and short daggers for climbing, and a rope coiled about his torso. No one saw him in his dark cowl and clothes as he scaled the north wall, clinging below the rampart until the guards passed out of sight. The rest of the way, from the tower to the courtyard and on to the main manor house, seemed almost too easy as he slipped along walls, around corners, and through doorways. Some part of him waited for something to go wrong – wanted it to happen.

He believed he was alone, but while passing an archway, he saw faces peering out at him.

Leesil's muscles tightened. He forgot his training in an instant of alarm. He ducked his head and froze in a crouch, with the cowl shading his eyes above a black wrap covering the lower half of his face.

Through the archway was a room with hardwood chairs, a dark colored divan, and a russet carpet covering the middle of the stone floor. Long curtains by the window had been left open. The moon threw enough soft light into the room for Leesil's elven eyes to see a large family portrait hanging on the wall. He relaxed slightly. It was just a painting.

Everyone in the portrait had dark hair, perhaps black, from the man and woman to the three daughters, dressed in simple but refined attire. The father stood behind his seated wife and an eldest daughter, and the two younger girls sat upon the floor at their mother's feet. Behind them was a draped curtain for a background.

Baron Progae's chin beard and scant mustache accented a long face of narrow features but prominent cheekbones. A shelf of thin eyebrows over-hung his hazel eyes. He wore a white shirt beneath a plain brown vestment trimmed in black. His wife was austere in her cream dress with an overlaid vest of golden fabric, yet there was warmth and pride in her eyes. She had one arm around the eldest daughter seated beside her.

The daughter looked about fifteen, or at least a bit younger than Leesil himself. A mass of black curly hair fell past her shoulders. Her skin was pale, her nose and mouth small and delicate, making her eyes seem deep and dark. She had her father's nobility mixed with her mother's allure. Leesil had rarely been exposed to young women face-to-face, and this girl in the painting was quite pretty.

He flushed beneath his cowl and scarf at being so foolishly startled. He slowed his breaths and moved on.

Rounding the stairwell landing on the third floor, Leesil faced an empty corridor. The guards were all outside and the servants asleep. He spotted the third bedchamber door on the right. It wasn't likely to be locked, but he already had a pair of wire picks in his mouth.

Leesil crept down the corridor, quick and quiet, and found the door was unlocked. Progae had no idea his betrayal had been uncovered. Leesil took his time turning the latch, inching it down slowly to be certain of silence, then slipped in and closed the door. He took the picks from his mouth and locked it from the inside.

The room held a four-poster bed. It was so immense that at first he wasn't sure anyone slept there. From the dresser and chest to the window seat and side tables, all the room's fixtures seemed large in the dark. Leesil crouched, listening, and heard the long and low breaths of slumber. He crawled along the floor to the bedside.

Progae slept on his back, lips barely parted. A thick down quilt was pulled up high about his throat. Leesil hesitated. His mind went blank and he couldn't move – until he heard his father's voice in his thoughts.

*This is why we still live . . . our lives depend on each other
. . . do what is necessary.*

Leesil watched Progae take two more breaths.

He removed one silvery stiletto from his wrist sheath
and settled next to the bedside so his left hand could
reach Progae's face. In his right hand he held the stiletto
poised above the bed's edge. One of his mother's lessons
came to him.

A sleeper will roll away from a touch, even before waking.

Leesil reached out and brushed Progae's cheek with
his left palm. The man started in his sleep and turned
away, exposing the back of his neck. Leesil followed the
movement and wrapped his left hand across the man's
mouth. The rest took less than a blink.

He rose up, full weight behind his grip. The man's
head sank sideways into the yielding pillow, pinned by
Leesil's forearm. He drove the stiletto upward, and it
pierced the soft skin at the top of the neck. The tip
scraped over the first vertebrae and into the skull. The
blade stopped when the narrow hilt guard met skin.

Progae clenched and went limp.

A splotch of blood welled around the stiletto's hilt.
It looked black in the dark room.

Leesil remained there, pressing his victim's head into
the pillow. He didn't know how long, only that the
muscles in his left arm suddenly cramped, goading him
back to awareness. He jerked the stiletto out and rolled
the body onto its back again. He forgot to wipe his
blade before sheathing it.

Progae's hazel eyes stared up at the ceiling over a
gaping mouth. Leesil closed the mouth and eyes and
straightened the quilt. When he left, he locked the

chamber door from the outside with his picks before stepping softly down the hallway to the stairs.

In the years that followed, he never remembered leaving the grounds, nor whether he'd been cautious or run the whole way home.

He arrived before dawn, breath ragged in his throat and chest, to find his parents waiting. Nein'a was watching out the kitchen window when he stepped in the back door. He passed her without a word, but Gavril stood in the carved archway to the front room. Leesil had no choice but to stop.

He gave his report without looking at his parents' faces. When he fell silent, and it was clear he had nothing more to say, his mother quietly dismissed him. He sat alone on the floor of his room, the door closed, and barely heard Chap scratching from the outside.

Come dawn, Gavril took him to the keep. He was led to an alcove by guards to make his report in secrecy. Lord Darmouth nodded in approval.

'No one will even know he's dead until my troops seize his fief. You've done well, boy. Progae's treachery ended before he made his first move.'

Leesil told himself again and again that he had assassinated a traitor. The relief of justification stayed with him for almost a whole moon.

His mother was called to the keep for a celebration, and so his father decided to take Leesil out for the evening. Along the way, they passed a few nobles in their finery on horseback headed down Favor's Row to the keep bridge.

Leesil sat alone at a table in an out-of-the-way inn, nibbling on roasted mutton with herbs, while Gavril chatted at the bar with a man named Byrd. He couldn't hear much of what they said over the noise of other patrons. What he did hear was a name uttered by someone nearby behind him.

'Shameful,' one said. 'About Progae.'

Leesil lowered his fork.

He knew better than to get involved. Even in this inn, his father told him to keep his cowl up. His hair was too different from that of other people. Leesil kept his back to the speaker at the table behind him and toyed mechanically with his food.

'About Progae?' asked a second. 'I heard he was a traitor.'

'I meant his family,' answered the first.

'What of them?' asked a third, deeper voice.

'The wife and two youngest girls starved to death in the streets.'

Leesil stopped poking at his mutton.

'What?' asked the second. 'No one helped them?'

'They were outcasts,' the first said. 'Blood of a traitor and all, and they served no use anymore, I suppose. Not even their relatives would take them in, probably on their guard to see who was next. Only the eldest girl survived. Darmouth gave her to one of his loyal "nobles" as a mistress if I heard right.'

'Damn shame,' said the third. 'I saw them once, coming in for last winter's harvest celebration. Lady Progae was an eyeful, and that eldest daughter had the look of her. Hedí, I think. Why cast out women and children? It was Progae's treachery, not theirs.'

'Watch your mouth!' whispered the second. 'Just be thankful you and yours aren't blood kin to a traitor. I for one can't wait for spring. At least then I can take my goods and caravan away from this place for a while.'

Leesil stood slowly, dropping the fork before he realized it. He didn't look back to see the men's faces and said nothing to his father as he pushed out the inn's front door.

He walked quickly through the night streets. By the time he entered Favor's Row, he was running for the house. He slipped in through the kitchen door and stared out the window at the keep upon the lake.

'*Léshil?*' a soft voice called from behind him. 'What is it?'

Leesil spun about. His mother stood in the kitchen doorway with Chap beside her.

Only Nein'a called him by that name. His more common one was simpler, less memorable to any who overheard it. Her speech was tainted by her own native tongue and made anything she said both lyrical and guttural. Leesil wondered if this was just her or if all her people sounded this way.

And he wondered why she'd returned so early from her duties at the keep.

She wore a deep tan gown that matched her skin, its vine-and-leaf pattern wrapping about her tall form. A midnight-green cloak with ermine trim hung over her shoulders, its hood down.

Chap whined softly, staring at Leesil with perked ears. His tail stopped wagging.

Mother wasn't often affectionate, but when she stepped close to Leesil, her slanted eyes showed concern.

'What is it?' she repeated. 'Where is your father?'

Leesil still wouldn't speak, but the fear faded from her expression.

Nein'a's amber eyes looked into his. Her thin lips pressed together as a shadow of sorrow passed over her face. She finished a slow blink, and the sorrow was gone. She became her controlled and poised self once again.

'You have heard something, yes?' she asked.

She reached out with a soft hand. Slender fingers that seemed too fragile brushed Leesil's cheek, and her warm palm settled against his face. She seemed to know what churned inside of him.

'Never seek to know the fate of those your actions affect. We serve, and we survive. You, your father, and I live for one another. Think only of us and yourself, for now, and do as you are ordered. Let go of all else, for it will do you no good.'

She brushed white-blond hair away from his face, and Leesil nodded, showing his understanding and acceptance. That nod was the first lie he'd ever told her.

The next few days were quiet. He watched the street from his house or while wandering the city with his cowl pulled forward around his face. He left Chap behind when he went out, though the dog growled and barked each time he was locked inside. Leesil watched for the ones on horseback, fine men in armor or rich dress with their retinue. Days passed, and he began wondering if his mother was right. He headed home at dusk one day, passing before the mouth of the bridge gatehouse.

Coming out along the bridge was a tall man with red hair and lightly freckled skin riding upon a bay charger. Mounted men in leather armor and yellow surcoats followed behind him. Leesil crossed the way quickly, putting the gatehouse behind as he headed for home, but he heard the horses turn his way into Favor's Row. He ducked into the first house's walkway though it wasn't his own home. He didn't like having anyone at his back and waited for them to pass.

The red-haired noble ignored Leesil, as did his men. A smaller figure on a roan horse rode between them. Her fur-lined cloak was pulled fully around her, hiding even her hands, and her mount's reins were held by the nobleman. The man led the girl's horse under his own control. Anyone would have thought her a daughter. Anyone who hadn't seen the portrait of Baron Progae and his family.

Hedí Progae's vacant eyes were sunken in dark rings from many sleepless nights. Her cracked and dry lips were slack, slightly separated. Whereas the guards breathed clouds of vapor in the cold air, her breath came out in a slow, thin trail. The life in her simply leaked into the winter air.

The nobleman rode on, his property in tow.

Leesil stared after Hedí Progae. He went numb inside.

She was property. They were all property here. Obedient slaves who did what was necessary in order to live one more day.

The procession passed out of sight beyond the distant bend in the road.

Leesil didn't remember stumbling home until he stood in the kitchen. His mother didn't come to him, or even his father. There was only the sound of scraping claws on the floor, as Chap raced toward the kitchen to see who'd returned.

Leesil frantically looked about as he heard the dog

coming. He wanted no one near him. He lifted the cellar hatch and dropped through the hole, then jerked the hatch shut. With no light at all, it was pitch-black even to his half-elven eyes. He scurried to the cellar's back, far from the hatch, and huddled in a corner.

Chap clawed at the hatch, and his muffled whines filled the cellar. Leesil ripped his cloak off. He clamped his hands over his ears and sat shuddering in the dark, in the cold, waiting for numbness to spread from his flesh into his thoughts.

Until he felt nothing at all, finally numbed inside by his mother's counsel, and he could go on and . . .

Do what is necessary.

He had done it again, and once more, and then yet again. He'd kept on killing for Darmouth for another six years.

Silence surrounded him.

Leesil realized he was sitting on the bed in the room he shared with Magiere.

Everything became mixed and muddled as he broke out in a sweat. Was this Byrd's inn? Or was he still in the cellar?

Leesil backed away from the bed in uncertainty. It didn't make sense. Magiere hadn't been in the cellar in the dark. He couldn't hear Chap scratching overhead in the kitchen. He looked up to a timber ceiling. The floor under his feet was wood planks, not the dirt of a cellar.

Still, he should be in that cellar, where he could stay numb. He was so hot, and what he wanted was the cold. He pulled at his shirt clinging to his chest from sweat until it came off and chill air surrounded him.

The room was black, and his elvish night sight caught only the barest details.

And it was wrong. There was no crate, barrel, or sacks of vegetables. There was no narrow bed he had slept in with Magiere. He now saw dark columns of a large four-poster bed, and heard the deep breaths of a man sleeping there.

He had to protect the lives of his mother and father. He had to do what was necessary. Crouched in the corner, he wondered why the walls looked too close for a traitor's bedroom, but he knew where he was. He knew why he was always here in the dark listening to someone's last breaths.

It didn't matter what happened to Hedí Progae. It didn't matter what became of the mother and two younger daughters. He'd always do what was necessary.

Leesil jerked a stiletto from the sheath on his wrist.

Magiere stood in the upper hallway of the inn with a small lantern in her hand. There was no light coming from the crack under the door, so Leesil hadn't bothered lighting candles. If he was already asleep, she didn't want to wake him. Sleep was seldom peaceful for Leesil, but it was still some relief from all he'd faced in recent days.

She closed the lantern's shield to smother its light, then steeled herself as she quietly cracked open the door. The dim glow escaping the closed lantern revealed the shadowy form of an empty bed in the dark room.

'Leesil?' Magiere whispered.

Movement to her left. Something skittered, quick and low, to the bedside.

Magiere's sight widened instantly as her dhampir instinct surged up. A dim shadowed form became distinct.

Leesil crouched there, naked to the waist with a stiletto in hand, and his head snapped around at her voice. His amber eyes were bright sparks in Magiere's night sight. They focused on her without recognition, and his dark skin glistened with sweat.

Magiere's stomach clenched.

He pivoted in his crouch to face her . . . like a predator, with his head low.

'You weren't there,' he whispered. 'I have to finish this.'

'Leesil!' Magiere flicked the lantern open and thrust it out.

He lurched back as light struck his face, and raised an arm to shield his eyes. Leesil backed toward the corner, until his shoulders struck the wall, and held out the stiletto.

'You weren't there . . . here,' he rasped at her. 'Father . . . Mother are waiting up for me.'

Magiere's gaze shifted once to the slim blade held out at her, then back to his face. She grew more frightened with each breath as she watched him, his chest expanding and contracting erratically.

His eyes flicked once toward the bed.

What did he see that she couldn't? There was no one in the room but the two of them. Was someone else doing this to him?

She glanced quickly about the room, afraid to take her eyes off of him for too long. She remembered the night in which they'd each run into the Droevinkan forest. The undead sorcerer named Vordana had assaulted them with their own fears, trapped them each in a phantasm that masked the real world from their senses.

But Leesil did see her, knew who she was, though he didn't believe she was standing before him.

'One more,' Leesil whispered and jabbed the stiletto in the air at Magiere. 'Always one more. Always necessary!'

Leesil looked at the bed, as if he *had* to go to it, and if he didn't, it would cost him more than he could live with. But he held his place, cowering in the corner.

This wasn't sorcery or any magic. It was madness. And that was so much worse, Magiere almost rushed to him. Leesil was drowning in his past, and she didn't know how to follow and pull him out again.

Magiere realized she was shaking and set the lantern on the floor for fear of dropping it. Her mouth was so dry she couldn't swallow.

'You weren't there, and I have to do this,' Leesil insisted. Sweat now matted tendrils of hair to his face, and he closed his eyes so tightly his features twisted. 'Get out!'

'No!' Magiere growled back. 'I *am* here, Leesil . . . look at me!'

Leesil's eyes snapped open, anger plain on his face. Suddenly he became blurred in Magiere's vision, and she felt the tears drip off her jaw beneath her watering eyes. She inched forward toward him.

'I'm not leaving,' she insisted. 'We're alone. We are in our room at Byrd's.'

Magiere lunged in and snatched his wrist.

Leesil didn't try to bring the stiletto in at her, but every muscle in his body twisted against her efforts to make him lower it. He began shaking from the effort, pushing at her with his free hand. His strength was more than Magiere could counter.

Hunger rose in her throat until her strength matched his. And with it, her fear grew . . . of what she might do to him. Her jaws began to ache. She clenched her teeth, fighting back the change. Her dhampir nature was in her flesh, in her eyes, making Leesil's hair and amber irises searing bright in her vision.

All the pain Magiere felt in watching Leesil suffer – in losing him this way – turned her hunger to anger. She wanted to rend and tear every memory that tortured him.

'Don't . . . leave me!' she managed to get out. 'Come back.'

Leesil's eyes were so bright. For an instant the madness faltered, and he seemed aware of her as she struggled with him.

Magiere released his wrists and grabbed for his face with both hands, lunging in close. Leesil stiffened as she pressed her mouth to his.

She heard the stiletto clatter to the floor. His fingers closed tight on her upper arms, pulling and pushing to throw her aside, but she held on to him. Magiere didn't lift her face from his until he finally quieted.

Leesil looked at her. His expression was sad and wild, like he'd woken from a nightmare but still believed it was real just the same. Magiere slid her fingers up into his drenched hair.

He opened his mouth to speak and closed it again as his eyes searched her face. Then he was kissing her, but harder than he'd ever done before. He pulled her close as they slid to the floor.

Words weren't enough for Leesil at that moment, and Magiere wrapped herself around him. He buried his face in her neck, his arms tightening around her until she felt the muscles in his back clench beneath her hands. His mouth slid to the top of her shoulder, and Magiere began pulling off her own shirt.

She would not let him leave her again.

Hedí rode beside Lieutenant Omasta across the long bridge, the keep seeming to grow and fill the night as she approached. It was built like a gigantic square with a wide courtyard in its open center. Its four corners were reinforced towers rising above the main structure. Firelight from massive braziers atop the towers reflected across the water. As they crossed the lowered drawbridge, the double gates opened wide, and she passed through a long tunnel into the courtyard at the keep's center.

Omasta helped her dismount. He led the way across the courtyard as his men took away the horses. At the courtyard's far side, they entered through a set of wide doors and into the keep's main floor.

Hedí tried to remain impassive. She slowed her quick breaths and forcibly relaxed her face to show no expression.

Once inside, Omasta called for a servant. A middle-aged woman scurried out from a vast dining or common hall on Hedí's right. To her left was Darmouth's council hall, and straight ahead was a wide stone staircase leading upward. To the sides of the staircase were two corridors running in opposite directions, north and south.

'Welcome, my lady,' the woman said with a submissive curtsey. 'I am called Julia. I will show you to your room.'

Hedí scrutinized the woman. Her hair was tucked under a muslin cap, and she had a round face with reddened cheeks. Her expression was open and warm, if a bit simple, but the woman kept nervously twisting the edge of her apron with two fingers. She carried no keys. This was not what Hedí had expected.

Lieutenant Omasta sighed in relief. 'Well, then . . . I bid you good night, lady.'

He seemed glad to release his charge into someone else's care and turned toward the council hall. Perhaps he did not enjoy abducting women for his master and pretending to play bodyguard.

'Come this way,' Julia said. 'Are you hungry, my lady? Do you need water to wash?'

Her kind tone made Hedí waver again. What was happening here? If Omasta had dragged her to a room and locked her in, at least she would have known for certain that she was a prisoner.

They ascended the stairs. When they reached the third floor, Julia turned left down a corridor. She opened a door midway and stepped back with a polite bow of her head as she ushered Hedí inside.

A fire burned brightly in a small hearth to the right, and to the left stood a cherry-wood wardrobe and desk. Against the back wall was a matching bed with a thick mattress, covered by a deep blue comforter. Her chest of personal effects had already arrived ahead of her, likely by Omasta's men. Darmouth must have been quite terrifying in his orders for her careful retrieval.

'I hope this is acceptable, my lady,' Julia said. 'I prepared the room myself by our lord's instructions.'

He is trying to please me, Hedí thought. She remembered Emêl's words and smiled. 'Yes, it is fine. Your effort is appreciated.'

Julia's nervousness faded a little as her smile broadened. 'Can I bring you anything, or help you out of your gown?'

'No, I can manage myself. I would like to unpack my things. You may go.'

Julia hesitated, but Hedí remained poised and waiting. Ladies did not unpack their own clothes, but neither did servants refuse dismissal. Julia nodded, and Hedí watched the woman leave. She listened, her body tense.

No click or rattle followed after the door's lever settled. Waiting a moment longer, Hedí stepped to the door and opened it herself. It was not locked. Prisoner of the keep she might be, but it appeared her personal room was not to be treated as a cell. She took a slow, shaky breath, and her thoughts cleared enough to turn elsewhere.

She now had an exceptional opportunity to gather more details of the keep for Byrd. But how would she ever get such information to him?

And poor Emêl. He must be suffering by himself at the inn, worrying about her. Perhaps she could bribe a servant to take him a message? No. Their fear of Darmouth was greater than their desire for coin.

The hour was late, and Hedí opened her travel chest. She took out the heaviest nightdress and her robe. As she laid them upon the bed, someone knocked at the door.

'Julia?' she called out. 'I need nothing more. You can retire for the night.'

The door swung in, and Lord Darmouth stood in the opening.

Hedí froze at the sight of his tall and wide frame

filling the doorway. His cropped hair appeared more brown than gray in the dim light from the fire, but she still made out the faint scars below his left eye. He crossed his knotted arms over his leather breastplate.

'I wanted to be certain you were settled comfortably,' he said, voice low.

Hedí weighed her response carefully. 'The room is quite agreeable, but I did wonder why you had me escorted here. The baron's soldiers protect me at the Bronze Bell, and it was my own foolishness in leaving without them that put me in harm's way.'

Darmouth took one step inward. 'They should've attended you better . . . or you wouldn't be wearing that ribbon around your throat.'

She had no response to this, so she nodded graciously at his observation and presented her best worried front.

'Am I free to move about the keep? Or are there further concerns for security I should be aware of?'

His brown eyes softened, but this made her wary rather than relieved. He took another step toward her, now fully inside the room.

'You're my guest, here for your protection, Lady Hedí. The main floor and the upper levels are yours, but stay clear of anything below. Only prisons and stores are in the lower levels, and neither are of any interest to a lady.'

She felt dwarfed by his size and unnerved as he stepped ever closer. His eyes were fixed upon her face but occasionally drifted elsewhere. Hedí feared that if he touched her, she would grab for a war dagger at his belt and bury it in his guts. She stepped back, fussing with her nightdress and robe upon the bed.

'Thank you for your concern, my lord, but it has

been a long day and night. I am quite tired. Perhaps I will see you at breakfast?'

Darmouth hesitated.

Hedí knew her one real weapon. He wished to gain her approval and foster her affection for him. He would not force himself upon her if there was a chance he might yet win her willing consent. She had to keep him in his role of the hopeful suitor as long as possible.

Darmouth backed to the door with a curt nod. 'Good night, then.'

'Good night.'

Once the door closed behind him, Hedí waited until his footsteps faded down the hall. She ran to the door to fasten it, but there was no key for the lock on the inside. Hedí retreated to bed, still watching the door.

She hoped Emêl would come soon.

Welstiel walked the night streets of Venjètz, thoughts turning one upon the other, until he was barely aware of the shabby buildings slipping past him. He tried to focus upon his agenda.

Whatever was needed to move Magiere onward, it had to begin with Darmouth. Welstiel had dealt with a few warlords in his time. Most were petty tyrants of limited intellect. Darmouth might be a deluded pretender to a crown, uneducated as well, but he was no fool. And he was well guarded.

The best Welstiel might manage was to weaken the keep's security and assist once the assassination was under way. Once any such plan was in motion, it was a matter of days or less before the event took place; otherwise the risk of discovery in waiting further was too great.

All Welstiel had to do was keep Magiere diverted for that time, and then her and Leesil's motivation for coming to Venjètz would be gone. Hopefully this nonsense concerning the elven lands would fade as well. She would once again turn to finding the orb in order to stop *him* from finding it first. Magiere would become his unwitting bloodhound once again.

Welstiel shook his head at the irony. So much time had been lost since Magiere had left Bela. Thinking too much on it fed Welstiel's frustration. He paused in the street, realizing he had lost track of his destination. People still moved about the marketplace up ahead, drinking and talking even in this bitter cold.

Welstiel was surprised at the effort it cost him when he moved on. He was hungry, and an edge of fatigue crept in upon him. It had been too long since he last absorbed a life. He sidestepped into an alley out of reach of the street lanterns and watched the few people passing by. Most were inebriated or just tired at this late hour. Two voices engaged in an argument, and their words became clear as they drew closer.

'You know it's two coppers, Deni. It's always two coppers!' the woman nearly shouted.

'Not tonight it's not,' the man answered. 'I ain't got two coppers, but I'll catch you up next time.'

Welstiel flattened against the alley wall as they passed by.

A young woman with long, oily brown hair shrugged a tattered shawl up over her shoulders. It did not cover her scant cleavage, partially exposed by two unfastened buttons at the top of her bodice, and she coughed twice.

'You know I don't give credit,' she said.

The man trailing her wore a long leather hauberk, most of its sewn-on iron rings missing. He reached out to grab her waist from behind.

'Oh, come on, Alliss. I got a warm bed. Better than freezing out here, trying to find someone with coin at this time of night.'

She elbowed him, spinning away from his hold. The man threw up his hands with a disgusted huff and continued on without her. The girl snorted and headed back toward the marketplace.

Welstiel stepped out. 'Miss?'

She turned and looked at him, spite still lingering on her gaunt features.

Welstiel held up a silver penny. 'I can offer more than a warm bed.'

She sauntered toward him, a coy smile stretching her lips. Stains marred her faded lavender dress. With just this and a shawl, he wondered how she withstood the cold. Her skin was sallow.

'Looking for company?' she asked.

Standing in the alley's mouth, Welstiel lifted one side of his cloak. 'Come in for warmth.'

Her smile grew. Perhaps she saw luck in finding a gentleman, and she walked right up to him. He stepped farther back, determined to touch her as little as possible.

She followed him beyond the reach of the street lamps. Before she could speak again, Welstiel slammed his gloved fist into her face. The woman's head jerked sideways. Blood spattered the alley wall from her nose and mouth. Welstiel tensed in alarm.

He had struck with too much force, anger welling

inside him before he could stop it. If she died from the blow, his effort was wasted.

The woman toppled sideways, scraping down the wall to flop facedown. Welstiel's senses snapped open wide, and he felt a moment's relief upon hearing the muffled beat of her heart.

Her hair splayed out above her head. A trickle of blood ran out of her mouth across the frozen mud. Welstiel stared at the growing trail and the back of her exposed neck.

Anger at Magiere made him reckless. A drive to feed wormed through his mind as he remembered Chane ripping a woman's throat open.

Welstiel recoiled at his own savage impulse. He could not allow Magiere's actions ever to weaken his self-control again. Welstiel stared down at the woman, remaining still until his calm fully returned.

He knelt and removed an ornately carved walnut box from his pack and opened it. Resting in fabric padding were three hand-length iron rods, a teacup-size brass bowl, and a stout bottle of white ceramic with an obsidian stopper. He took out the rods, each with a loop in its midsection, and intertwined them into a tripod stand. The brass bowl's inner surface was etched with a pattern of concentric rings all the way to its lip. Between these lines were the characters of his conjury. He carefully placed the cup in the tripod.

The white bottle contained thrice-purified water, boiled in a prepared copper vessel whenever he had time to replenish the fluid. He pulled the stopper and poured just enough to fill half the cup.

Welstiel rolled the prostitute onto her back. So much

life was lost in bloodletting that little was actually absorbed by an undead who drank for survival. It was not blood that truly mattered but rather the leak of life caused by its loss. His method was far more efficient. He slipped out his dagger and dipped its point between her lips, collecting a puddle of her blood on its tip. Tilting the blade over the cup, he let one red drop strike the water.

It thinned and diffused. He began to chant.

The air shuddered before his eyes. He felt it grow humid and warm in the distortion. The woman's skin started to shrivel.

Her body slowly dried to a shrunken husk as her life drained away. When her heart stopped, Welstiel ceased his chant and the air around him became clear and crisp again. The woman was a brittle shell with sunken eye sockets.

The water in the cup brimmed to the lip, so dark red it appeared black — a red-tinged black like Magiere's hair. Welstiel lifted the cup from the tripod. He tilted his head back and poured the liquid down his throat so that he tasted it as little as possible. A last drop struck his tongue and tasted of ground metal and strong salt.

He set the cup back in place and flattened both hands upon the ground to brace himself. So much life taken in this pure form shocked his system. It burst inside him like burning sunlight and rushed through his dead flesh.

Welstiel waited for the worst to pass.

When he picked up the cup to put it away, it was clean and dry, with no sign that anything had been in it. He packed away the iron rods and white bottle as well. He stood up carefully under a lingering vertigo, but it passed, leaving him clear in his thoughts. Normally he would have found a way to hide the girl's body, but if her corpse were found, it would cause more panic. It would build Lord Darmouth's desire to employ Magiere. There were monsters to hunt down in his city.

Welstiel made his way to the Ivy Vine inn, wondering how Chane had fared all this time being trapped alone in his room. When he arrived, the lobby was empty. He headed up the narrow stairs to their room. He did not bother to knock and opened the door to step inside.

Chane sat on the floor in bare feet, feeding his robin crushed nuts and crumbled bread. He wore breeches and a well-tailored muslin shirt, and looked like any handsome young noble engaged in a pastime.

The parchment and quills still lay untouched upon his bed.

'I see you've fed,' Chane said in his rasping voice. 'You look better.'

Welstiel did not answer. Instead he rummaged through his pack and pulled out a small bag of black charcoal and a wad of tattered clothing that smelled of urine.

'Lord Darmouth has engaged Magiere's services,' he explained. 'You will keep her occupied by giving her an unusually savage beast to hunt.'

Chane blinked, staring at the rags in Welstiel's hand. 'What are those?'

'I bought them from a servant at the keep. If you are witnessed during an attack and described as a tall noble with reddish hair, Magiere may wonder. We must create some other creature for her to track. Sit, and I will cut your hair, then use charcoal and oil to dye it black.'

Welstiel took out his dagger and motioned to a chair. Chane hesitated.

'It will wash out,' Welstiel said.

'But will my hair grow back?' Chane rasped.

The question surprised Welstiel. Not by its vanity, but that it was the first time Chane had shown such concern over anything since crawling forth from his second death.

'Have you ever seen a dead body months after it was buried?' Welstiel asked.

Chane shook his head.

'The hair is longer. And I will not cut much off.'

He motioned again to the chair. Chane sighed but obeyed.

Late into the night, Leesil was still awake. Magiere curled against him, breathing softly, lost in deep sleep. He watched her pale face on the pillow. He wished he could join her in the oblivion of sleep, but he couldn't.

Nightmares wouldn't let him.

The name of Hedí Progae opened dark cell doors in his mind that he'd long been able to keep locked. He couldn't close them again.

Leesil tried to focus on the memory of Magiere's mouth, her body, both soft and hard, and her hands all over him. But whenever his eyelids drifted shut from fatigue, he saw the back of Baron Progae's bleeding neck.

Progae's hazel eyes opened where he lay dead as Leesil pulled the bedcovers back into place. Those eyes rolled to glare at Leesil, and his pale lips parted, speaking with Gavril's voice.

'Think only of your mother, father . . . of yourself . . . this is how you survive.'

Leesil's eyes snapped open.

He'd slipped into sleep for an instant, but he couldn't face it again. Not without smothering away the nightmares, drowning them as dead as his victims. He'd sworn to Magiere never to do that again, but the moment stretched as he watched her beside him. When his eyes drifted closed again, he snapped them open.

He couldn't stand the faces in his sleep anymore.

Leesil slipped from under the blanket. Magiere rolled, and he froze until she grew still once again. He pulled the blanket and sheepskin cover back in place over her bare body, and walked softly to the door. He stopped for a moment, looking back at Magiere's sleeping form, then stepped into the hallway and gently shut the door.

The inn was silent. The stairs were empty, even of cats. He crept downstairs, and two steps creaked lightly under his feet. All was quiet in the common room, and he stepped around behind the bar and found the cask of red wine Byrd stored there.

Leesil opened the cask and picked up a tin cup from under the bar. When he poured out half a cup, he stared into the red liquid. His hand shook slightly, and he gripped the cup with both hands.

He could put it down, go back upstairs to Magiere.

He knew this, even as he drew the wine to his lips and swallowed.

9

The next morning Wynn awoke from a deep sleep to a knock at her door. She opened her eyes, disoriented at first, and remembered where she was. 'Leesil?'

She sat up, wiping at her sleepy eyes, as the door cracked open. Byrd stuck his head in. Yellow scarf tied neatly about his head, he looked as if he had been up for a while.

Wynn pushed her disheveled hair out of her face, then quickly pulled the bed's sheepskin cover up to her neck.

'Yes?' she asked.

Byrd smiled as his gaze fell upon the fat form of Clover Roll curled up on the bed's end. Tomato and Potato lay tangled in sleep on a braid rug near Chap. Head upon paws, Chap was fully awake and glowering at the kittens.

'I sent Faris word that I'd located Magiere,' Byrd said. 'But I didn't tell him where. A messenger came back this morning. Lieutenant Omasta will meet her below the bridge gatehouse at noon. No one gets into the keep without an escort.'

Wynn took a deep breath, still trying to come fully awake. 'Have you told Magiere?'

'No, I thought I'd leave that to you.'

This was odd, but Wynn kept quiet about it. Byrd made her nervous, as she knew his polite front was an act. After last night's confrontation in the kitchen, it was obvious he wanted something from Leesil.

'Of course,' she replied, 'if you will close the door so I may dress.'

He pulled his head halfway out and then stopped. He leaned in again to eye Wynn curiously.

'You won't get out of Omasta's sight,' he warned, 'so watch carefully in the chambers or corridors you pass through. Don't just look the place over. Pay attention to the placement of guards standing watch and remember anything you overhear.'

Chap rumbled softly, and Wynn glanced toward the dog. His head was still down, but his crystalline eyes were on Byrd.

'Thank you,' Wynn said. 'Chap and I know what to look for.'

Byrd frowned. 'He's just a dog.'

'And your "partner" is just a cat,' she retorted, with a quick glance at Clover Roll.

'All right,' Byrd answered with a shrug. 'Just be careful. Darmouth would step on you without a blink.'

He closed the door.

Wynn scrambled out of bed and pulled her heavy coat on over her shift. Chap got up, shook himself, and followed as she hurried out the door and across the hall. This time she knocked, quietly at first. When no one answered, she knocked more sharply.

'Yes?' Magiere called from inside.

'It is I. May I come in?'

After a brief pause the door cracked open, and Magiere peered out. She looked haggard, as if she had suffered a long night with little sleep. The room smelled stuffy, even from the hallway, and an unpleasant scent floated to Wynn's nostrils.

'What is it?' Magiere asked.

'Byrd just came to me. Can I come in?'

Magiere hesitated, then stepped back. Wynn entered with Chap tagging along.

'Has someone been sick?' Wynn asked, wrinkling her small nose.

'No,' Magiere answered.

Leesil rolled in the bed but did not sit up. His eyes were closed, strands of his hair tangled over half of his face. Wynn quietly related everything Byrd had told her. Magiere's eyes sharpened as she listened.

'That gives us time to prepare.' She looked down. 'Chap, were you with Leesil on a visit to the keep? Is there anything I should know before we leave?'

He huffed once for yes.

'Fair enough. Wynn, get out the talking hide while I dress. I'll join you shortly.'

Wynn thought Leesil should be involved as well, but Magiere practically pushed her out the door, scooting Chap out behind her. Not until she was out in the hall did Wynn realize the sickly sweet smell had not grown stronger near Magiere. Which meant it had come from Leesil.

A scraping sound woke Hedí. She sat upright in the large bed.

Julia knelt by the hearth, working to start a fire. The maid wore the same housedress and apron from the night before, but now her hair hung down her back in a red-brown braid. She jumped slightly at Hedí's movement.

'Oh, I'm sorry, my lady. I was trying to be quiet.'

'Do not concern yourself. Is the sun up?'

Julia smiled. 'Yes, and breakfast is prepared in the lower meal hall, when you're ready.'

Hedí considered this. Yes, she was hungry, and she would be expected to appear. Better to hurry down now than to have Darmouth come looking for her again, alone in this room.

She climbed out of the bed, and Julia immediately opened the wardrobe. All of her clothes had been properly arranged there. It seemed Hedí had slept right through Julia emptying the travel chest.

Hedí normally did not like being tended at dressing, but she allowed Julia to help her into a pale blue gown. The maid arranged her hair in a twisted bun, leaving a few loose curls at her temples. The teeth marks on her throat were red and lightly scabbed, but they were healing. Julia neatly fastened the velvet ribbon around her throat to hide them again.

'Very fine, my lady,' Julia said. 'You look lovely.'

Hedí was uncertain about the bun but did not argue. 'Thank you. I can find my own way to the hall.'

Stepping out in the corridor brought relief, as if she needed a reminder that she was not a prisoner of her room. She followed the corridor to the stairs and wound her way down to the main floor and the vast meal hall, hoping Darmouth had already eaten and left.

She looked in to see several long tables and an enormous hearth. The household did not seem to stand on ceremony at breakfast, as several servants and four common soldiers were milling about, eating bread and sipping from pottery cups. There was no sign of Lord Darmouth.

Lieutenant Omasta stood with several of his soldiers, a large hunk of buttered bread in one hand and crumbs in his blond beard. He looked over when she entered and nodded, pointing to a chair.

'Here, lady, come and sit.'

Although Omasta was Darmouth's lapdog, Hedí still preferred him to his lord and master. The lieutenant was clearly most at ease in the company of other men. Simple as he was, he did not pretend to be anything other than a soldier. He was dutiful, perhaps with some semblance of propriety, and Hedí wondered what made such a man loyal to the likes of Darmouth. To the best of her knowledge, Omasta had no family. She sat down and poured herself some tea.

She took her first sip as Darmouth strode into the hall like a barbarian out of place in his polished and oiled armor. His men straightened to attention, but he ignored them and walked straight to her. She could smell him before he closed on her.

'Did you sleep well, lady?' he asked.

'Yes, very,' she answered with forced politeness, and put down her cup.

He seemed preoccupied and glanced once at Omasta as if some important matter kept distracting his thoughts. Then he asked her, 'Do you need anything more from the inn?'

This caught her unprepared for the opportunity, but she quickly took advantage.

'I have my belongings, but I did leave behind unfinished affairs. There are several letters to be completed and a few matters for the baron's family. If I could speak with Emêl, I am certain he could handle these for me. Could you send word to him?'

Her heart pounded as Darmouth stared at her. He did not say 'yes,' but he did not refuse either. Instead, he raised his eyes to the cluster of soldiers.

'Omasta! Come with me. You're to meet the hunter at the gatehouse by noon.' He looked down at the ribbon about her throat. 'We will finish the beast that did this to you.'

Hedí smiled sweetly with a shy nod. 'Thank you. That is a great comfort. Then I may be safely returned to the Bronze Bell.'

Again he did not answer, and turned to stride out of the hall. Hedí wondered who this hunter was, this 'dhampir' Viscount Andraso had mentioned.

Omasta dropped his bread on the table and followed his lord. Darmouth stopped in the arched doorway and looked back at Hedí. Omasta had to sidestep out of his way.

'I don't like your hair this morning,' Darmouth said. 'Don't wear it that way again.'

Hedí lowered her eyes in obeisance, and Darmouth left without further comment. Under the table, she crushed the fabric of her gown's skirt in her hand.

Perhaps she should shave her head and see how he liked it. She'd hated Darmouth more than any other person – except for the one who had murdered her father in his sleep. All eyes in the room were upon her now, and her appetite faded.

She stood up and walked out into the main entryway, wondering what to do with herself. Directly across the way was the council hall, where she had sat at dinner two nights before next to the true monster in this land. She had no intention of visiting there.

To either side of the staircase were corridors leading left and right behind the halls. As far as she could see, there were no other passages, and no stairs leading downward. She stepped around the central stairs and into the left corridor that headed north. It stretched a good way, then turned right. She followed it, stopping short of the corner to peek around the turn. At the end of another long passage, two soldiers stood guarding a door. She retreated and retraced her steps to the entryway.

The right-hand corridor heading south produced the same result — two guards standing before an identical door. Perhaps one or both doorways led beneath the keep. She was eager to search the keep's interior to expand Byrd's maps.

Darmouth had forbidden her to wander into the depths below, but there were still the upper levels. If anyone stopped her, she could always give the pretense that she had lost her way while returning to her room.

Hedí climbed the central stairs. She passed two servants along the way but no soldiers. As she reached the second-floor landing, movement caught her eye. Julia stepped from a room near the corridor's end with a tray of empty dishes.

Was someone else a 'guest' of the keep?

Hedí counted the doors to the one Julia exited and then circled around to the next flight of stairs upward. She waited out of sight, and then peeked cautiously back around the stone railing into the corridor. Julia descended toward the main floor.

When Hedí was certain the maid was on her way, she doubled back. As she approached the door, she heard soft and high singing. It sounded like a little girl, but Hedí could not imagine why a child would be here in the keep. To the best of her knowledge, Darmouth had no family or relatives, especially not a daughter or niece.

She knocked lightly at the door. 'Hello?'

The singing stopped, and an instant later the door opened. A small face looked up at Hedí.

The girl was no more than ten, and was small-boned and slender. She wore a simple cream-colored dress, and her thick, chocolate-black hair was tied in a white ribbon that made her dusky complexion look even darker. Deep brown eyes looked up at Hedí. There was something vaguely familiar about the girl's appearance.

Hedí smiled. 'Hello, I'm a guest here, but there is not much to do. Would you care for some company?'

The girl looked quite surprised and smiled. 'In my room? You want to come in?'

'Of course . . . unless you would prefer a walk instead?'

The girl shook her head, little face scrunched in a stubborn frown. 'I'm not supposed to go out without Julia and Devid.'

'Who is Devid?'

She rolled her eyes with a sharp sigh. 'He has a sword. He protects me from bad things.'

Hedí wondered why the little girl needed a bodyguard inside the keep. This was the first child she had ever seen here. The girl shoved the door wide with her small hands.

'Do you want to see my dolls?'

'Yes, I would like that very much.'

Hedí stepped into a pleasant little room quite out of place in the stronghold of a tyrant.

Austere stone walls were softened by small tapestries of fantastical creatures, from a serpentine dragon to strange, thin-lipped people covered in downy feathers with wings to hide their bodies. There was one of a small, dark-brown cat perched on the back of a stag of silver-gray hue, though its coat was longer than that of any deer Hedí had seen. Its horns were single long curves without prongs. A four-poster bed filled most of the room, but there was space enough for a bookshelf filled with dolls and toy animals. A large trunk with stuffed pillows atop it rested at the foot of the bed.

'My name is Hedí. I am a guest of Lord Darmouth. Are you a guest here, too?'

'I'm no guest. I'm Korey,' she answered, as if this should be obvious. 'I live here with Papa and Mama.'

Hedí looked into Korey's impish eyes and suddenly knew to whom the child belonged – Faris and Ventina, Darmouth's skulking attendants. Not only did Korey have the traits of a Móndyalítko, but hints of her parents' lean features were obvious in the girl.

'Come see Selina!' Korey said and grabbed Hedí's hand. 'She's my favorite. She has yellow hair, and I always wanted yellow hair.'

Hedí followed Korey to the bed. A beautiful doll with a porcelain head sat against the pillow. Korey reminded Hedí of her little sisters, always eager to show new guests their toys and dolls, like exotic treasures acquired by their father from faraway places. Hedí never told them otherwise, not spoiling their childhood fantasy that the world was a wide and inviting place awaiting them.

A fresh wave of grief passed through Hedí before she could stop it. She took a short breath, forcing back her soft smile.

'How often do you see your mother and father?' she asked.

'Often?' Korey frowned slightly. Perhaps time was still a difficult concept for her. 'Devid and Julia take me to see them. Sometimes Papa takes me out to the court-yard, but Julia has to come with us.'

So Darmouth never allowed the child out of sight, always under a watchful eye . . . even with her own parents? It sounded as if they were not even allowed in Korey's room, alone with her.

Korey was a hostage. This was no surprise to Hedí. Everyone in this land was a slave in some way, shackled by fear and the threat of death. Though it did make her wonder about Faris and Ventina. What services did they provide that Darmouth found so essential, that the bastard would lock up their daughter to ensure fealty?

Little Korey was eager for company, even that of a stranger.

'Do you have any games?' Hedí asked. 'We could play.'

'Games?' Korey's face brightened. 'You can stay for a game? I have cards. Papa said he would teach me, but he hasn't. Do you know how to play with cards?'

'I do,' Hedí assured her.

Korey's blossoming excitement made Hedí's sadness grow, but she kept it hidden from the girl. She sat on the bed's edge, smoothing the comforter, and began laying out cards facedown in a square pattern.

'The first game is called Catch the King,' she whispered with a smile.

Korey giggled back. They spent the day there, Hedí careful never to let Korey realize they were both prisoners.

Magiere stood anxiously waiting with Wynn and Chap before the gatehouse archway and the long bridge to the keep. She needed to prepare herself for what came next, but that damn keep filled up her sight.

It was daunting up close, though she'd seen larger strongholds. Four square towers shot up at its corners, adding to the impression that the whole thing had risen from the water one forgotten night to loom over the city shoreline. Suddenly her plan to play Darmouth so she could get inside seemed weak. She shouldn't be taking Chap or Wynn anywhere near this place. She braced herself for an audience with the despot, but the memory of Leesil's lost eyes and sweaty face, as he crouched with stiletto in hand, still filled Magiere's head. Especially when she looked at the keep.

She'd awoken in the night to find herself alone in bed and Leesil gone from the room. Before she could grab her shirt to go looking for him, he'd nearly fallen through the door. He tripped over his own boots on the floor, and she caught him and guided him to the bed. The stench of wine was thick on his breath. She pulled him onto the bed and covered him, holding him in silence. What could she say?

Magiere looked up at the keep towers. This land of Leesil's 'first life,' as he called it, haunted him with so many things she didn't know.

'Do you think someone will come soon?' Wynn asked, shivering. Frosty white breath puffed from her little lips with each word.

'Crouch down with Chap by the wall,' Magiere said. 'Put your coat around him and share some body heat.'

Wynn did as suggested, and Chap snuggled in close to the sage. Wynn's hair was neatly braided for this meeting, but the sheepskin coat pulled on over her torn short robe still looked shabby. Her pack was worse, weather-faded and mud-stained.

Magiere didn't bother checking herself. She wore her hauberk over a wool pullover on top of her linen shirt. The worn tip of her falchion sheath poked out beneath the hem of her hooded cloak. Unlike the snobbish elites of Bela, Darmouth wouldn't care what she looked like. He was seeking a hunter and would expect results by any means. The rougher her appearance, perhaps the better.

A loud creak called Magiere's attention, and she saw the keep's heavy gates begin to open.

'Is someone coming?' Wynn asked, and stood up to look.

A trio of men strode down the center of the long stone bridge. The lead man was obviously an officer. He was armed with a shortsword sheathed at his waist and wore a hardened leather breastplate. His face was covered with a blond beard a shade darker than his hair. The two flanking men carried spears taller than themselves.

'You're the hunter?' he asked with no introduction. 'The one named Magiere?'

'Yes,' she replied, but the officer now stared at Wynn and Chap. 'My companions . . . my assistants,' she added.

'I was told to fetch only you,' he said.

'She does not hunt without us,' Wynn said before Magiere could speak. 'Each creature is different. Each hunt must be planned. So we must be privy to all details.'

The tall officer seemed taken back by Wynn's manner. Magiere crossed her arms and waited, confirming Wynn's words. It was odd to have the sage playing the unbendable one, let alone playing this game at all.

The officer still looked undecided.

'I need them both for a successful hunt,' Magiere added. 'Perhaps Lord Darmouth wasn't fully informed before he sought me out.'

The officer looked Magiere over from head to toe, stopping at her face. 'I'm Lieutenant Omasta. You'll follow me to the inner courtyard and wait while I explain all this to my lord. He'll decide who stays and who goes.'

Magiere nodded. One step at a time was always how she got her way.

The two guards stepped aside, and Omasta led the way, with Magiere following. Wynn and Chap brought up the rear, and the guards fell in behind them.

Crossing the bridge, Magiere couldn't see the water directly below over the stone ledges to both sides. All she saw was Omasta's broad back as the man led her across the drawbridge and through the open gates. Entering the long tunnel was like being swallowed down the keep's gullet, and finally they came out in the inner courtyard.

Before leaving Byrd's, Chap had given Magiere instructions through Wynn on protocol. She was to keep her falchion sheathed at all times, and not hesitate to relinquish it if ordered to do so. He'd pawed out 'follow orders' and 'no threats.' Magiere ground her teeth, but she intended to follow Chap's counsel.

Omasta spoke quietly with two more armed guards

in the courtyard before turning to Magiere. 'Wait until I return.'

He crossed the courtyard to the far wall and entered through the heavy doors.

Magiere waited until he was gone, then looked about at the high walls, like four tall stone buildings between four towers, enclosing the open courtyard. It wouldn't hurt to wander here within sight and look the place over.

Before she finished three steps, the guards repositioned. They boxed in Wynn, Chap, and herself, standing to the courtyard's four sides. They stayed back far enough that Magiere was beyond a spear's reach, but it was clear that no one was getting near the inner walls.

Getting inside Darmouth's stronghold was becoming more and more futile.

Wynn shivered again, and Magiere hoped Leesil still slept in their warm bed. He was drunk for the first time since they'd left Bela, breaking his promise, but perhaps he'd have some rest without dreams to torment him. Wynn crouched next to Chap, and the dog huddled against her.

It wasn't long before Omasta returned and waved Magiere forward toward the open keep doors. She assumed that meant all of them, and pulled Wynn to her feet. The lieutenant stepped aside at their approach.

Warmth struck Magiere's face as they entered the wide entryway. Perhaps it wasn't warm so much as far less cold than outside. To either side were archways into large halls. The right one looked to be a feasting hall, and she heard a crackling fire somewhere at its far end. Omasta led them to the hall on the left.

Weapons and shields lined its walls between braziers, and one long thick table and ten sturdy chairs filled its middle. Two tapestries covered the far end wall. One displayed an ornate coat of arms – three mountain peaks with green hills below and a golden crown like a sun in the sky above them. The other was of a mounted horseman against a black background.

Two wolfhounds paced forward along the table's right side, sniffing the air. One growled at Chap's presence. He didn't growl back but positioned himself in front of Wynn.

Magiere's attention settled on the room's three occupants.

The first was the man who'd come to Byrd's last night. Faris sat in the right-hand chair farthest away, studying her in return. Behind him stood a slender, dark-haired woman so similar in features she could be his sister or close kin.

Magiere wondered why a pair of Móndyalítko served Darmouth. These mountain wanderers didn't strike her as people who'd willingly follow a warlord.

The hall's third occupant stepped forward along the table, coming up behind the wolfhounds with his arms crossed. The odor of stale sweat filled Magiere's nostrils. He wasn't as tall as Omasta, but he had presence. It brought all attention to him as he moved.

Darmouth had been but a shadow to Magiere, a faceless specter in Leesil's past, until this moment. She remained calmly indifferent as she studied the man who'd maimed Leesil's mind and spirit . . . and might have murdered his parents as the price for Leesil's freedom.

Magiere let her dhampir nature rise up, until her senses

opened wide, and tried to *feel* him out. His stench thickened sharply in her head. She felt a deep winter creep toward her with each step he took. The leather breastplate under his crossed arms was well oiled, its steel reinforcements polished to a gleam. His hair was cropped short and his face carefully shaven – not as Leesil had described him once. Lines of encroaching age marred his wide face, but his forearms were thick and powerful.

'You're the hunter?' he said, voice low and hollow.

Magiere realized this man could order her death, Chap's and Wynn's too, and forget them in the next breath. She'd never be able to lure him into talk of anything but the business at hand.

'Yes,' she answered.

'You believe in these creatures? These vampires?'

'As do you . . . or you wouldn't have sent for me.'

He stopped beyond arm's reach. 'I've heard of charlatans' shows for peasants. How would you kill such a creature, if it's already dead? Magic powders? Invisible spells perhaps?'

'Take its head off,' she answered bluntly. 'And burn the body.'

Darmouth paused, and Magiere wondered if her answer had been too simple for him. Or perhaps its directness had quelled his doubts. He looked at Chap and Wynn.

'And these two?'

'He tracks. She finds people and places for him to investigate. If you have clothing from the victim, it would help, as well as anything known about this undead.'

Darmouth appeared put off by her tone and roughly shoved one wolfhound back out of his way. 'It's an unnatural man drinking blood from the throats of noblewomen. Find him and be quick about it!'

Magiere didn't flinch. 'So it's male?'

Darmouth's face grew darker. Magiere realized he didn't care about the details. Maybe he didn't even believe it was more than a madman. He simply wanted to hire her services and be done with it.

Omasta stepped in from the archway. 'It happened in the alley behind the Bronze Bell Inn. Perhaps your dog might pick up a scent still there? Several of Baron Milea's guards got a clear look as it assaulted Lady Progae. They might tell you more.'

Magiere understood. Omasta grew concerned by his lord's mood and wanted this audience finished. He'd known her name when he'd come to the gatehouse, so he was more than just some office, perhaps someone in Darmouth's confidence. He was about in his midtwenties, so too young to have been in service while Leesil's parents were here. But he might know other things, such as why anyone fleeing the city would run into the keep instead of away from it.

Then there was Lady Progae, the one Faris had mentioned not long before Leesil lost all hold upon himself.

Magiere spoke directly to Darmouth. 'We should speak with Lady Progae, as she is the best witness.'

'No,' Darmouth snapped. 'Omasta will handle any more arrangements. Start hunting, if you expect to be paid. I'll double the coin if you finish this tonight and bring me the head of this *creature*.'

Magiere's revulsion increased. 'How did you know I was in the city?'

'It's my city,' he answered. 'You're dismissed.'

Faris rose, stepping around the table along with his slender companion. They came up behind Darmouth, one on each side.

Investigating the keep seemed folly in hindsight, but Magiere saw Wynn studying the walls, the shields, weapons, and tapestries, and the people present. Chap's eyes wandered as well, though he stayed close to the sage, standing between her and Darmouth's company.

Before Magiere could speak, Omasta took her arm, urging her toward the archway. She pulled free from his grip but followed, herding Wynn and Chap out in front of her. Chap trotted ahead into the entryway's expanse, looking about.

Magiere fought down frustration. What could he possibly see here that was of any use? As they reached the doors, Magiere heard footsteps behind. She stopped and turned halfway about.

Darmouth headed for a side corridor with his Móndyalítko lackeys dogging his heels.

'You should hear my fee,' she called out, 'before offering to double it.'

He didn't even glance back as he disappeared into the corridor.

10

Leesil trudged up the inn's stairs with a quiver of quarrels, two flasks of oil, and a wadded-up old towel he'd found in the kitchen. He opened his room's door to find his companions sitting on the floor around the elvish talking hide.

Magiere's expression was impossible to read. It could've been disappointment, anger, concern, or a mix of things Leesil couldn't guess – didn't want to guess. She hadn't said a word about it, though he couldn't remember how he'd gotten back into the bed. He'd no time for shame over what he'd done last night. At least he had slept. Neither memory of Progae nor a young Hedí disturbed him for a short while.

'There isn't any garlic,' he said, and laid down the quarrels. 'And it's too late in the season to bet on finding any at the market, but I have options we can try.'

'Sit,' Magiere said, and slid over where she sat leaning against the bed.

She was dressed as 'the hunter' with her black hair tied back in a thong. Two lanterns and several candles sent crisscrosses of warm light over her, setting off the bloodred glints in her locks. He'd always liked her hair.

But she was so composed. Magiere dealt with conflict in two ways: head-on in open outrage or with icy disregard that anything had happened. He wasn't certain how to interpret her new quiet watchfulness.

Leesil dropped down beside her, and his stomach lurched as if suddenly turned inside out. His body was no longer conditioned for nipping himself to sleep, let alone drowning himself into oblivion.

They'd managed to keep up idle conversation in front of Byrd after Magiere's return, and now they finally had privacy. Leesil's own feelings were mixed. Although desperate for any scrap of information regarding his parents' fate, he was still angry that Magiere, Wynn, and Chap had ignored his insistence to stay clear of Darmouth. Having to remain in hiding wasn't helping. The others did his work and took all the risks.

'We did not get far,' Wynn said, 'only the courtyard, entryway, and the council hall. There was a meal hall across the way, and a center stairway upward, with corridors at the base going both directions behind the halls.'

'You were right,' Magiere added, still studying Leesil. 'We won't learn anything from Darmouth. But this lieutenant — Omasta — might be of some use.'

'No!' Leesil said too sharply, and his head throbbed for it. 'Don't trust anyone in Darmouth's company. He holds something over each of them, or he'd never let them near him. This Omasta will act for his own preservation, and you won't know it until he's already betrayed you.'

A hint of Magiere's belligerent side filled her expression. Before she could argue, Chap barked and thumped a paw on the hide.

'What?' Leesil asked.

Wynn mumbled as she followed Chap's paw. 'He says "three" and "speculation" or "guess." Guesses for what?'

'For why my parents ran into the keep,' Leesil answered.

Wynn watched Chap's pawing and wrinkled her nose with a frown. 'This is difficult. The closest Belaskian would be "a thing for coercion." Perhaps your parents sought something to force Darmouth to spare their lives?'

Leesil nodded, his thoughts beginning to clear. 'But what? Darmouth has committed unspeakable acts for decades . . . and everyone knows he is responsible, one way or another. What could they have gone after that he would fear being revealed?'

Chap pawed again, and Wynn waited for him to finish. 'The next possibility is "escape" and . . .' She pursed her lips and sighed in frustration. 'The best translation is "path." Escape path?'

'The keep is surrounded by a lake,' Magiere said. 'Are you sure you're catching his meaning?'

'Of course I am,' Wynn retorted. 'It is just not making sense. Chap's dialect does not match my Elvish, and some concepts do not translate well into other tongues.'

Leesil cringed, adding another spike to his splitting headache as he waited for Magiere's irritable response. She simply raised her hands in resignation.

Wynn sighed and watched Chap spelling out Elvish, but this time she sat upright, tense. She wouldn't look at Leesil when she spoke.

'Last option – they tried to kill Darmouth themselves. I suppose this makes sense. If he were dead, others might hesitate, free of his influence, and your parents might be able to flee Venjètz.'

No one spoke for a moment.

When Leesil first fled the city in youth, the province was stable. There was little hint of outside threat beyond its borders, and he'd served well to uproot any insurrection from within. He suspected his mother might have considered this third option, but his father would've counseled for the least risk. The coercion option would be Gavril's choice.

Leesil shook his head. 'I don't see it. My parents gauged their actions quickly, and assassination on the spur of the moment is higher-risk than the other possibilities.'

'Oh, wait,' Wynn said, as Chap continued. 'He says there were men down the corridors near the main floor, and they were not there before . . .' She stopped to scowl suspiciously at the dog. 'How could you possibly know that? We were not close enough to —'

Chap bobbed his muzzle in the air, sniffing and snorting loudly.

'No, you could not,' Wynn argued back. 'The place reeked of men and sweat and food and a smoky fire. You could not smell people down those back corridors.'

'I think we'll trust his nose more than yours,' Magiere said. 'What's this about "before"?'

Wynn appeared only half-satisfied as she watched Chap's reply. 'He says there are doors at the corridors' ends, and they lead to passages to the lower level, but there were . . . When did you go down there?'

Chap continued pawing at the hide.

'He was there once with Gavril,' Wynn translated. 'But there were men, probably soldiers, down both corridors today.'

Leesil closed his eyes. These speculations were going nowhere. He found some comfort that his companions worked so hard to ask questions and consider any possible answers. The four of them had puzzled out parts of Magiere's past in the same manner, but this time they had too little to work with.

When he opened his eyes, Magiere was watching him. She no longer bothered with quick glances when she thought he wasn't aware.

She stood up, grabbed a lantern from the floor, and placed it up on the table. 'It's getting dark. If we want to keep our welcome at the keep, then we have a hunt to begin.'

Relief took the edge from Leesil's hangover. Getting out of Byrd's inn was a welcome escape. At least he knew how to run down an undead if he couldn't run down his own past.

'We start at the Bronze Bell,' Wynn suggested. 'Lieutenant Omasta said there were witnesses, and Chap may pick up a trail.'

'I think you should stay here,' Magiere said, but it wasn't an order or filled with any spite toward Wynn. 'It's not about what you . . . what happened in Droevinka. We don't have garlic for the quarrels, and you can't defend yourself otherwise. This is a straight-up hunt, and if Chap gets a scent . . .' Magiere stumbled over her words and turned blunt by nature. 'We can't get held protecting you.'

Wynn looked dumbstruck, and Leesil held his breath against the coming tirade. He agreed with Magiere, but knew he'd have to make Wynn see the sense of it. Chap barked once in agreement and stuck his nose into Wynn's neck. She exhaled and looked up at Magiere.

'Of course. I would just be in the way.'

Leesil pulled out a few quarrels and tore up the towel to wrap the heads with small bits of cloth.

'Wynn,' Magiere said, and crouched beside the sage. 'Spend some time on those drawings of Byrd's. Now that you've been inside the keep, maybe something will come to you.'

'Yes,' Wynn answered, gaze down. 'That sounds like a task for me.'

Leesil uncorked an oil flask, then dipped and drained each quarrel head so its cloth wad was soaked.

'What are you doing?' Magiere asked.

'Take a flask and some quarrels,' he said. 'If one of us gets a shot with a burning quarrel, the other might hit him with a full flask of oil. Soak his clothes or hair, and he'll go up in flames.'

Magiere frowned, clearly not caring for the idea but having no better substitute. 'We have to find him first.'

She fitted a quarrel into the crossbow, slipping the feathered end under the thin metal clamp on top of the stock that held the shaft in place. She slung the weapon over her shoulder and tucked the rest of her quarrels through the back of her belt, then checked that her falchion slipped freely from its sheath.

Leesil strapped on his winged punching blades, and readied his own quiver, oil, and crossbow. He pulled his hood up around his face and slipped on his gloves. Finally he lifted the topaz amulet out of his hauberk's neck to hang in plain view.

'Ready?' he asked.

Magiere nodded. 'Like Wynn said, we start at the Bronze Bell.'

Chap licked Wynn's cheek, then led the way downstairs. Leesil glanced back into the room before closing the door. Wynn didn't look up, still sitting on the floor like a small kitten locked in the house after everyone left.

Hedí worked on an embroidered pillowcase as she sat in the meal hall that evening. It was a proper thing for a lady to do. When young, she'd never found much use for such pastimes. But a woman sewing quietly in a chair was almost invisible. Few ever noticed her presence or realized she noticed them.

Servants and soldiers wandered in and out, but no one spoke to her. Dinner had been to her liking, a mutton stew and fresh bread served with dried fruits and nuts. Fortunately, Darmouth had not appeared for the meal. Omasta sat with her at supper, but they did not feel the need to talk. Hedí noted that he left once his bowl was empty, not sending a servant for a second helping. It was strange that he did not indulge like the others, having risen up to favor in Darmouth's eyes.

Hedí did not care to go back up to her room, though sometimes she felt more alone among people. She worked in tiny stitches on the pillowcase. Time passed, and the dining hall emptied. With no one left to observe, she thought of Emêl, hoping he did not worry too much and still sought a way to free her.

Low voices caught her attention. She looked up to see Faris and Ventina enter, walking with heads close together in whispers. They stopped at the sight of her, clearly not expecting anyone here well past the evening meal. Hedí stood up with a short bow of acknowledgment.

'I hope I am not imposing. I was not tired and had nowhere else to go.'

Her words were intended to put them at ease, but neither appeared moved or politely sympathetic in return. Faris stared at her with hard eyes and then lightly gripped his wife's upper arm.

'I must go. The hunt should begin soon.'

Ventina nodded, and her husband left the meal hall. She walked to the table and gathered leftover bread and dried pears. She was a slender, wiry woman with wild black hair. Golden bracelets dangled from her wrists, though Hedí doubted they were true gold, and a matching circlet around her head held back wisps of loose hair.

Hedí stepped around the table's end, approaching Ventina. She might never again have an opportunity to speak with this woman alone.

'Lord Darmouth gave me leave to wander the keep,' she began. 'I met your daughter today.'

Ventina looked up, her long features caught between caution and anger.

'Korey is a lovely child,' Hedí went on, 'with sweet manners and a gentle nature. You have raised her well.'

Ventina's features smoothed. 'You spoke with her?'

'Yes, we played at card games all afternoon, just children's games. She learns quickly. Catch the King was a bit too easy for her.'

Few mothers could resist hearing their child praised, and Ventina was no exception. 'How did she look? Was she well? Had she eaten?'

Hedí patiently answered Ventina's barrage of questions, assuring her of the girl's well-being. She watched Ventina's wariness melt, watched her shift slowly from the guarded servant of a tyrant to a mother starving for scraps of information about her daughter. Guilt flooded Hedí for what she was about to do, but she did not falter. When Ventina appeared most at ease, Hedí stepped closer, pitching her voice to a whisper.

'I know you must hate him . . . as I do.'

Ventina froze, confusion washing over her dusky features.

Hedí needed to break through Ventina's defenses, and pressed on. 'Darmouth uses your child against you – Korey's life for your obedience. What if he no longer had such a tool in his possession?'

Ventina's eyes narrowed with a threatening cock of her head. Hedí did not back down.

'Baron Milea prepares to come for me, so we can escape the city. You can move more freely here than I. Help me, and you, Faris, and Korey may come with us. Emêl has wealth and loyal men, and he will protect you. Help me and you will be free with your daughter.'

Ventina backed slowly away from Hedí, suspicion growing with each step. There was one moment where Hedí was sure she saw the woman's hope grow, but it vanished like a candle flame caught in an evening breeze.

'You do not know,' Ventina rasped, slowly shaking her head, 'how many years we have been here. You sat next to him at your fine dinner, and you think you know Darmouth?'

Hedí was about to answer when Ventina lunged at her. It was Hedí's turn to retreat, the embroidery needle clasped in her hand behind her back.

'Do you think Korey was always an only child?' Ventina growled, then paused to let her words sink in.

Hedí understood but did not let it show.

'There are many ways to die,' Ventina went on. 'Some *you* couldn't imagine for yourself, let alone for a child. Seek your escape, and Darmouth will know. I won't listen to this madness!'

She whirled and headed for the archway. There she stopped, still facing out of the meal hall.

'What keeps me from going straight to my lord with this treachery?'

'Because you know Darmouth,' Hedí answered evenly. 'Because I do know him. Any whisper that you were offered a chance to betray him will only raise his suspicion toward you . . . and it will grow. You are no fool, Ventina, if you have lived this long in his service. You will never speak a word of this to Darmouth.'

This was the catch, and Hedí's security for her gamble. Whether Ventina agreed or not, she would do nothing in spite or fear. Ventina remained a moment and then fled, her red skirts swishing in her wake.

Hedí closed her eyes, cursing herself. She had played her hand too soon or in the wrong way. Instead of an ally, she had made another enemy.

Chane walked the streets toward the Bronze Bell and his next victim. Welstiel had told the locals that vampires developed a 'taste' for certain kinds of victims. So why not support such a ridiculous lie? When he reached the more affluent district, or what passed for such in this city, he took to the alleys. It was unwise to try for a kill in the exact same spot, but somewhere close would serve well enough.

His tattered clothing reeked, and he was certain the cowl over his head was lice-ridden. The long, torn shawl was no better. Welstiel had jaggedly cut his hair, colored it black, and smeared coal dust on his face. He had left his longsword behind, as Welstiel said it did not fit Chane's new persona. He looked and smelled like the lowest dregs of mortal cattle, and this should have been humiliating or enraging, but Chane didn't care.

Standing at an alley's mouth, he scanned the main street beyond. Welstiel told him to pick a pretty noble-woman. Chane had no argument with this.

At first only soldiers in motley arms and well-dressed men passed by. There was one young man in reasonably fine garb, perhaps the son of a well-to-do merchant or local official. He was too young, and a woman would still be more effective for outrage and panic. Chane sank back in the alley against the building's side, wondering how long this would take. Perhaps his unsuccessful meal behind the Bronze Bell had left the local women reluctant to be out at night.

'No, Jens,' a feminine voice said from the street. 'I asked you to pack my red purse. How do you forget the smallest instructions, even when I write them down?'

Chane peered around the corner.

A lovely young woman with auburn hair and a dark green cloak headed his way with a pensive-looking manservant following close behind. The only other person nearby in the street was a peddler. The wares of pots, pans, and kitchen instruments dangling from his body clattered as he hobbled away in the opposite direction.

'Forgive me, m'lady,' the manservant answered. 'I don't recall your red purse in the packing list.'

They passed the alley's mouth.

★   ★   ★

Chane grabbed the woman's face, palm covering her small mouth, and clamped his other hand around the manservant's throat. He hurled the woman backward into the alley as the servant began to struggle. Chane clenched his grip. He felt and heard the man's windpipe crackle and collapse under his thumb. The manservant clutched at his own throat, face reddening in silence, and Chane dragged him into the alley.

The girl had tripped on her gown and fallen to the frozen mud of the alley. She sat up and opened her mouth to scream. Chane slammed Jens into the alley wall. The woman sucked in a shocked breath at the wet crack of her servant's skull against the brick. Jens's gaping mouth and eyes remained open as Chane released the body, letting it slide to the alley floor.

He closed in on the woman.

She crawled backward, and Chane stepped on her voluminous skirt to halt her retreat. He looked down at her, knowing she saw his eyes and teeth in a face not quite human. Chane put all the force he could muster behind his maimed voice, and said one word like the hiss of a snake.

'Scream.'

Her mouth opened wide and round like her eyes. All that came out were her own quick rasps.

Chane grasped the front of her cloak, pulled her up, and pinned her to the wall. He hardened his fingernails by will and sank them through her clothes into her chest.

She screamed, and a faltering wave of pleasure passed through Chane as he bit into her throat

Her flesh was soft and hot with fear, but he drank

only enough to weaken her. He slowed, licking at the wound to make the moment last a little longer, then pulled back and twisted his fingernails in her skin.

She screamed again, trailing into panting whimpers. This time the sound brought Chane only melancholy. When she tried to pull his hand away, he pushed his fingernails through layers of her clothes and flesh.

Her sounds of pain and horror would attract all the attention he wanted, but she wasn't putting up enough of a fight, barely a pretense of self-defense.

Chane didn't cover her mouth as he burrowed his face into her bloodied throat. He ripped her flesh open with his teeth, but took care not to collapse her windpipe. She cried out and began a series of moans as he dropped her to bleed out on the alley floor. Pounding footsteps in the street told him it was time to slip away. He scurried to a deep black doorway down the alley and paused to watch.

A soldier skidded on the wet cobblestones as he passed the alley mouth and hurried back to see the woman. He had no torch or lantern and nearly tripped over the manservant's body as he rushed to her. Another guard arrived with a torch held high, the light exposing both victims. Both guards stared at the woman.

Blood had stopped spilling from between her fingers clamped about her throat. It pooled about her head, slowly running along crevices between the cobblestones. Her brown eyes were still open.

'Get Lord Geyren – now!' the first soldier yelled.

The second guard dropped the torch beside his companion and ran back the way he'd come. Shouts and confusion followed.

Chane knew he should slip away, but a strange fascination kept him there. He watched longer than he should have.

Armed men and gasping townspeople began to collect at the alley's mouth. Chane heard an anguished shout.

A young man in polished boots pushed through the gawkers to stand over the young woman's corpse. He wore a royal-blue tunic and an open indigo cloak. When he crumpled to his knees, he took no notice of blood soaking into his fine breeches.

'Marianne?' he asked, reaching out for her red-stained fingers. He pulled them away, exposing her throat. 'Marianne!'

The second soldier had returned with the young nobleman and began pushing the crowd back. The first soldier turned on his knee toward the manservant, checking for life. In front of the guards and everyone else, the young nobleman sobbed like a child. He lifted her body and pulled it to his chest. Her blood smeared across the side of his face. He looked around wildly.

'Help me! Someone get help.'

Chane watched in puzzlement as the young man rocked the woman in his arms, back and forth.

It wasn't fair. He should still have the joy of the hunt and the kill, but it had come and gone in an instant. Euphoria eluded him, no matter how much warm flesh he bit into since . . .

That night in the Apudâlsat forest, Wynn, bleeding from a shoulder wound, threw herself in front of Magiere. Chane hesitated. Magiere took his head. And then nothing but waking in terror from that last instant, and thrashing free of the corpses thrown over him.

Watching the young nobleman, Chane felt no pity or regret, but there was an image in his thoughts, as he imagined . . .

Wynn collapsed across his own headless body. She sobbed upon his chest, her small face streaked with dirt and tears and his own black fluids.

Chane couldn't watch any longer. He slipped along the wall, deeper into the alley. No one noticed his departure. He kept seeing Wynn's face marred by his own second death.

The first long, eerie wail rang out through the night air, close enough that Chane froze. He stood in an open street, completely unprotected from the shield of Welstiel's ring.

Chap was hunting him.

Magiere walked toward an inn, and as they drew near Leesil's torch lit up the yellow-painted letters of its sign – THE BRONZE BELL. Hunger rumbled in her stomach, and the barest burn of it rose in her throat. She hadn't bothered to eat anything before they stepped out on the hunt. Her jaw muscles twinged, probably from all the tension she'd suffered in the last few days. She reached for the door handle to enter the inn.

'Magiere . . .' Leesil whispered from behind.

She turned and saw his face strangely lit up inside his deep cowl, but the clomping of heavy boots pulled her attention away. Two men in leather armor, short-swords unsheathed, ran by through the intersection they'd just crossed.

Chap snarled and broke into a full-throated wail.

Hunger sharpened in Magiere's stomach in response to Chap's cry.

'Damned dead deities . . . we're right on top of him!' Leesil said.

He pulled the crossbow off his back, a quarrel already fitted under its holding clamp as he cocked it. Magiere saw why his face was lit up within the cowl.

The topaz amulet glowed upon his chest.

'Chap, go!' she ordered.

The dog bolted down the street, wailing as he turned the corner after the running soldiers. Magiere followed as fast as she could with Leesil close at her side. Chap outdistanced them to the next cross street, but there he pulled up short.

Two soldiers held back a small cluster of people before the mouth of an alley. Chap paced behind the townsfolk, trying to look through their legs into the alley. When Magiere caught up, she and Leesil stopped as well. She pushed halfway through the crowd before she saw the spectacle that had drawn them here.

A torch on the alley floor illuminated a man in an indigo cloak rocking the body of a small woman – his face smeared with her blood and his tunic soaked from her torn throat.

Magiere's hunger burned her from the inside. She was too late.

Chap wormed out of the crowd and past the two soldiers. Leesil pushed forward to follow, torch and crossbow held up in one hand. One soldier stepped in his way.

Leesil planted his foot behind the soldier's without breaking stride and struck the man with his hip and shoulder as he walked on. The soldier's footing slipped, and he flopped to the cobblestones.

'Leesil, easy!' Magiere snapped as she followed.

Chap scurried deeper into the alley, head low and swinging with his nose just above the cobblestones. He stopped, shook himself, and looked back to Magiere and Leesil with a high-pitched howl.

The crowd's murmurs softened, and two armed men behind the noble turned at the sound.

Leesil trotted ahead. He was halfway to Chap as Magiere drew her falchion to follow. The second soldier turned his back to the crowd. Shortsword drawn, he tried to cut Magiere off before she got into the alley.

Magiere lowered her sword but kept it in front of herself. She held up her empty hand.

'We were hired by your ruler to deal with whatever did this.'

The soldier hesitated. She stepped along the alley's far wall, keeping well away from the kneeling noble. When she'd cleared the grieving man, the soldier appeared satisfied and turned back to holding off the townsfolk.

Armed men surrounded the noble and tried to take the woman's body from him, but he wouldn't let go of her, and clutched her tightly to his chest. There was nothing Magiere could say or do for him, and she ran after Chap and Leesil heading out the alley's far end.

An old woman in an olive shawl and brown cloak stood across the wide street where the next stretch of alley continued on. She pointed east along the street, peering hesitantly around the alley corner.

'He went there,' she said.

Chap was well ahead. So was Leesil. Magiere nodded to the old woman and ran to catch up. The dog howled out again, this time pitched to an almost human wail of anger.

'Go on!' Leesil shouted over his shoulder as he swerved right toward a cross street. 'Don't let him duck for cover. I'll try to head him off.'

Magiere ran after Chap, falchion in her hand. They would have to harry this undead closely to do as Leesil wanted. She caught sight of a tall man in tattered clothing running ahead and *knew* this was her quarry. She felt it, the same rage and vicious hunger that overwhelmed her each time an undead was close by.

The few people she passed on the street were a blur quickly left behind. A wide-bellied man called out angrily as she brushed past him. Magiere let her dhampir nature rise, and the night lit up in her sight. Hunger seeped into bone and muscle little by little, and she gained ground, coming up behind Chap.

The dog had the full scent of their quarry, and Magiere focused on keeping up. Buildings blurred by. Even if she hadn't felt this thing for what it was, nothing on two legs could stay ahead of Chap but a vampire. She spotted the city's wall beyond the rooftops and realized they were headed in the direction of the main gate.

The tattered man veered right into a side street.

Magiere tried to curse, but it came out a hiss. If Leesil managed to stay parallel to them in the next street over, that thing was going to run right into him. Chap let out a sustained howl as he turned to follow. She hoped Leesil understood they now headed his way.

The dog rounded a corner. Magiere swerved, and her

boots slid. She didn't have all fours and claws to run on as Chap did. Her feet wouldn't hold the turn at full speed.

She slammed sideways into the planking of a shop, spun on recoil, and fell. The falchion tumbled out of her grip. The drag of her hauberk against frozen mud brought her to a stop.

Chap wailed out ahead of her, and Magiere's anger cut away her control.

When she lifted her head, rising to her feet, her jaws pressed apart as her teeth elongated. The night grew so bright that tears leaked from her eyes.

The fleeing undead skidded to a stop in the next intersection, as if something blocked his way. Beyond him, in the next section of the street, a figure crouched behind a small flame.

Magiere saw a white brilliance around his face, and the amber glow of his eyes like tiny suns in the night.

Leesil had gotten ahead of them, crossbow aimed and the quarrel lit. He fired.

At the snap of the bowstring, Magiere charged, leaning to snatch up her falchion. Chap closed in on their prey.

The quarrel stuck. The vampire's tattered shawl ignited. For an instant Magiere's sight blurred painfully in the increased light.

She saw only the barest details. He was dressed like a poor city worker, and the stench of urine accosted her heightened senses. She bore down upon him, taking hold of the falchion with both hands.

The undead barely paused. He jerked the quarrel from his body and ripped away the burning shawl in the same movement. He flung them at Chap and ducked into another alley.

'Damn it!' Leesil shouted, as Chap dodged aside from the flames.

Magiere was first into the alley and didn't wait for her companions to catch up. Chap's wail came behind her as she ran; then he passed her by. She followed at the tip of his tail, hearing Leesil's angry breaths behind her.

Everything became instinct as Magiere's hunger focused on the undead fleeing through the dark ahead of her.

Chane saw the quarrel an instant before it hit him and braced for the flames. He did not have time to think or react. He was afraid . . . and this made him angry.

He dreamed so often of ripping Magiere's throat out, but he could not face her and Chap and Leesil all at once. And not on the run and unarmed.

The quarrel struck him with a sickening thud, and the air around his head ignited into flames. He jerked out the quarrel, stripping away the burning shawl as well. He flung these at the dog, and ducked into the nearest path to run.

He had to reach the Ivy Vine without being seen.

Chane fled down the alley. Even if he eluded his pursuers' sight, hiding would do him no good. That bitch dhampir or the dog would sense him, or the half-blood's glowing stone would reveal that he was nearby. He simply ran, twisting and turning into other paths wherever he could.

But he needed that instant out of their sight, and it came at the right moment.

Chane spotted the Ivy Vine inn ahead. One block

away, he cut inward to find the alley that ran behind it. He reached the back of the inn. The wailing grew louder as his pursuers approached. Chane clawed his way up the wall, digging hardened fingernails into crevices and cracks between wood planks. He hoped he would not have to make noise by breaking the window.

As he reached the second floor, the window swung open. A hand reached out and grabbed the back of his shirt. Welstiel heaved, and Chane toppled over the sill into the room. He heard the window close sharply as he spun around.

Welstiel crouched beside Chane, gripping his shoulder. They both froze and listened. Welstiel held up his hand with the ring of nothing on his first finger. It would hide them from the senses of the dog and dhampir, and even Leesil's amulet.

The dog's wailing stopped. Chane heard frustrated snarls outside in the alley. Welstiel put a finger to his tight lips.

Chane wrinkled his brow. He did not need to be told to keep silent.

Indeed, he was surprised at his own relief at being so well protected. Such a thought brought distaste and a thin edge of self-loathing. He longed for the rapture he had once known in the hunt and the kill.

But tonight, while Chane watched the nobleman sob in the alley, his mind finally conjured images to replace his missing memory . . .

Of Wynn weeping over his corpse.

Chap nearly burst with rage when the undead's presence vanished from his awareness. He could smell which way it had passed, and he ranged back and forth along the alley. The trail ended midway near the back of an inn, but it made no sense. If the creature were inside, he would feel it this close, like an aching wound in the Spirit of the world.

Frustration was one more annoyance of living in flesh, and he found it harder to face with each passing year. He snarled through bared teeth, trying to let it out, spitting it from between his teeth, but it would not pass from him as he turned in agitated circles.

Perhaps his kin, the Fay, were not wrong in their accusation. Taking on flesh had changed him.

'You lost it?' Leesil asked between pants.

He barked twice for 'no,' then three more, low and rumbling, for his uncertainty. He looked up to Magiere, wondering if she could still feel the undead's whereabouts. Frustration drained and tension grew in its place.

Her irises were pure black. Tear tracks stained her pale cheeks. Each breath she took hissed in and out through her teeth, and Chap clearly saw her elongated canines. She shuddered under her own strain to retain self-control.

Chap cautiously approached Magiere from an angle that would allow him to stop her if she suddenly turned on Leesil.

'Do you sense anything?' Leesil asked.

Chap looked briefly toward Leesil. But Leesil was not looking to him. The half-elf's face was clenched with concern, and he did not return Chap's gaze. Chap looked quickly back to Magiere and couldn't stop the growl that escaped him.

She glared at Leesil, breath deep and sharp. This was

not exhaustion but the heat of something else within her. Chap heard Leesil behind him take a step toward Magiere. Chap tensed on all fours, ready to take Magiere down.

'Magiere?' Leesil said softly. 'Can you sense anything?'

A startling change washed over her features. Her black eyes focused on Leesil.

The wrinkle of her brow faded. Her breaths became even and smooth, though her teeth remained unchanged. It was like seeing a feral animal suddenly look with longing at what stood before it.

Magiere dropped her gaze, reflexively covering her mouth with the back of her free hand.

'No . . . nothing,' she said, though the words came out like a loud whisper.

Leesil stepped around Chap, grasping Magiere's raised hand. He gently pulled it down.

'I've seen it before,' he said. 'You don't need to hide from me.'

Magiere clutched Leesil's fingers, blinking slowly. She looked tired now, as if the fading of her dhampir nature fatigued her more than the chase.

'I sense nothing,' she answered more clearly, and looked down to Chap. 'Where was the last place you smelled it?'

Magiere's teeth appeared to have receded, though her eyes remained unchanged. Chap whined again, and shook himself.

He relied on scent in some ways when tracking, but with an undead it was more that he felt its presence. He trotted back to the alley's center behind the building where the scent had ended. One second he had a strong sense of the creature, and the next, it was gone.

Chap saw that Magiere was as frustrated as he, gripping her sword tightly. It was hard to get this close and not make the kill . . . and more innocents might die as a result. His kin called this the way of things. Chap had long had his doubts that one small life of any kind in this world should mean so little, even in the balance of eternity.

Leesil crouched next to him. 'My fault. I should've hit him with an oil flask, but he pulled the quarrel out too fast.'

Magiere tried to catch her breath. 'How did you get ahead of us?'

'Shortcut. I grew up here, remember. Did you get a look at him?'

'No, but his clothes were stolen.'

'How do you know?'

'Because they smelled of the living . . . urine and sweat.'

Chap continued to growl and fret, barely listening to his companions. He had been on the undead's tail, but the battle had been stolen from him. He began to tremble.

'He's gone,' Magiere said. 'The amulet lost its glow, and neither Chap nor I can pick up anything. How is this possible?'

Chap snorted and pawed at the alley's dirt.

'Now what?' Leesil asked. 'Try again tomorrow night?'

Magiere frowned. 'I wanted that thing's head tonight, so I could take it back to the keep. Then maybe Darmouth might find me a more trustworthy servant.'

Leesil's expression darkened. Magiere reached out to touch his shoulder.

'If we haven't found something in the next few days, we should leave,' she said. 'Head up into the mountains and find our way to the elves . . . and hope Sgäile wasn't lying.'

Leesil dropped his head in silence.

Chap had pondered this option to the point of frustration.

When Leesil had fled Venjètz eight years ago, Chap's place had been at his side. That was part of his purpose. Chap had never questioned his kin in this.

Gavril and Nein'a had played no part in what would come, in stopping the return of the ancient one known by differing names to the different people of this world. Wynn and her sages called it 'the night voice' from the decayed Sumanese scroll they had uncovered. Ubâd, that abomination to life, had prayed to it by the name of *il'Samar*. Leesil's parents had been expendable in the plan of Chap's kin. Now, like Leesil, something pulled at Chap. Leaving this city with no answers . . .

It would feel as if he abandoned Nein'a and Gavril again.

He rumbled, then looked back at the two beings now in his charge, grunting once for their attention. Leesil stood up beside Magiere, and they began to make their way back toward Byrd's inn.

Dark streets caused little trouble for any of them, each with sight gifted in differing ways. Chap's thoughts were occupied with what he had seen in Magiere's feral expression as she looked at Leesil. Deep within her dhampir self, she still recognized him. Perhaps his presence and their bond now provided the strength she needed for control. It was comforting but troubling nonetheless. Chap had never intended that she delve so deeply, so soon, into her darker half.

Twice he heard small paws on wood across the rooftops. Somewhere out of sight, another odorous feline headed for the inn, and he paid it little attention. As they approached the door to Byrd's, he heard it a third time.

Chap turned to sniff the air. His nose wrinkled at the scent. In the dark he saw a black cat sitting on a barrel outside a tavern down the way, watching him.

'How about some late-night sausages?' Magiere asked him. 'After all that running, you must be hungry.'

Chap forgot the cat, and his ears perked at Magiere's words.

Oh, sausages!

11

Darmouth was lost in thought in the Hall of Traitors when Faris appeared in the far doorway and hesitated. Darmouth let him wait.

He disliked having his private thoughts interrupted. He'd been thinking of how best to approach Hedí.

He'd courted many women, but none like her. Polite and guarded and cold, she showed no interest in what he offered her. This was a far cry from the women of his early years, eager to please and beg favor. He could simply order the marriage to take place, and he expected it to go forward as planned during the winter feast, but he wanted more. He wanted the mother of his heirs to accept him by her own choice. He wanted the proper image of a royal family.

'What?' he finally barked at Faris.

The Móndyalítko quietly stepped in, passing between the stone coffins of Darmouth's father and grandfather. He stopped two paces away, and his attention shifted briefly to the back wall. Bare skulls leered within shadowy stone cubbies where the light of burning braziers around the room couldn't fully penetrate.

'Forgive me,' Faris said with a submissive nod. 'I followed the hunter as you asked. There was another disturbance. This one more public and not far from the Bronze Bell. Lord Geyren's mistress, Marianne a'Royce, was killed.'

Darmouth turned toward Faris, his anger growing.

Marianne a'Royce was an empty-headed and spoiled girl. However, she was a favorite of the other 'ladies.' Lord Geyren was excessively fond of her, and Geyren collected taxes and tribute from nearly a third of the province's lands north of Venjètz. This death had consequences Darmouth couldn't afford.

'The hunter told the truth about one of her companions,' Faris continued. 'The dog picked up a scent and tracked the killer. But by the time I caught up in the chase, the dhampir had lost her quarry in the alley behind the Ivy Vine.'

Darmouth stared at him. 'What of the girl in the sheepskin coat?'

'She wasn't there,' Faris answered, and the lilt of his voice suggested some private doubt had been confirmed. 'There was a man in her place with a glowing amulet on his chest. I never saw his face clearly, but he was quick, skilled, and knew the city well. He took shortcuts even a regular visitor might not know. When they returned to their inn, I followed.'

'You remained . . . in disguise?'

'Of course, and it seems they stay at the inn of the very man who found her for us – Byrd, one of your longtime agents. Convenient, isn't it?'

Darmouth disliked coincidence, though Byrd had been useful through the years. Such things often warned of betrayal in the making.

'What else?' he asked.

'I thought you'd want the news of Lord Geyren's mistress right away.'

Darmouth pulled one of his daggers and stepped in

close to Faris. 'Go back to the inn and get inside, you half-wit! Can you make yourself small enough?'

Faris went rigid but didn't back away. 'Yes . . . Byrd has a weakness for homeless cats. He wouldn't be concerned at one more.'

'Then get to it.' Darmouth added, 'Report back before morning.'

Faris glowered briefly as he bowed and backed toward the door. Darmouth didn't care if his servants hated him, so long as they obeyed.

Welstiel gripped the shoulder of Chane's tattered shirt so that both their presences were hidden by the power of his ring. He crouched below the window until he was certain that Magiere was long gone, then stood up. Chane did not move.

'Are you injured?' Welstiel asked.

Chane stared into the room's darkness with a blank expression. There was blood on his face and shirt. Welstiel took the basin and water pitcher from the table. He set them on the floor.

'Clean up and get out of those rags and back into your own clothes.'

'He wept for her,' Chane rasped, still staring at nothing.

Welstiel had no idea what this meant. 'Get up!' he ordered.

Chane blinked and a haughty, offended expression came over his long features. He climbed to his feet, picking up the pitcher and basin.

'I'm not leaving this room without my sword again, and I'm not wearing these rags. An old cloak with a heavy hood will do, if need be.'

Welstiel grew hesitant. If need be? Chane did not wish to go hunting again?

'What happened? Did Magiere catch you off guard?' he asked.

'The dog sensed me from a short distance,' Chane rasped back. 'I was unarmed and couldn't fight all three of them. I had to run.'

'You were not supposed to fight,' Welstiel threw back at him.

Chane set the basin back on the table. He poured water from the pitcher too roughly, and droplets splashed over the rim. He slapped a hand towel into the water and turned on Welstiel.

'And it occurs to me that I take all the risks to get Magiere to do your bidding, to move on in search of your *prize*, whatever it is. I won't wait much longer for you to tell me more. Or you can serve your own secret needs by yourself!'

He snatched up the wet towel, wiping blood and coal dust from his face, then stripped away the soiled clothing, dropping pieces to the floor. Welstiel saw the layers of lash scars covering Chane's back, a gift of discipline from his father in life.

Welstiel considered cowing Chane into obedience, but he did not. He was too relieved that his companion's ire appeared to bring back his former wits. In spite of Chane's haughty nature, he had once been resourceful and far more useful. Welstiel would have him so again, but he had no intention of revealing any more than necessary, and especially not about the patron of his dreams.

Chane dunked his hair into the basin, scrubbing with his fingers. He dried his hair out, soiling the towel, and then pulled on his shirt and breeches. His hair was jaggedly cut and a few patches were still black, but his own red-brown color showed through.

'When do you think this assassination attempt will occur?'

This was at least an intelligent question, rather than mindless muttering about some weeping man.

'Soon,' Welstiel answered. 'Perhaps in a few days.'

Chane nodded, and Welstiel began putting the room in order. He stuffed the more usable remains of Chane's peasant attire in a pillowcase and shoved them into his pack, in case the disguise might be needed again. He dumped the basin's blackened water out the window. When he turned around, Chane sat at the table with the blank parchment and feather quill.

He did not write but stared at the wall in front him, quill poised in his hand. Even so, the sight brought Welstiel another moment of relief.

The inn's front door creaked open, and a stab of winter-night air rushed into the common room.

Wynn lunged from her seat at the nearest table and ran to the door as Chap slipped in — and Magiere and Leesil. Waiting by herself had left her more anxious than was bearable.

'Did you find it?' she asked. 'Did you destroy it?'

One look at Magiere's face gave Wynn her answer. Chap grunted and dropped his rump to the floor. Leesil pulled the quarrel case and crossbow off his back, and Wynn tried to assist.

'Close,' Leesil said. 'I hit him with a quarrel, but then he just vanished.'

He looked haggard and sweaty, as if he'd run several leagues. Magiere was worn as well, but her fatigue seemed to come from within rather than from physical exertion.

'Go upstairs and put your things away,' Wynn said. 'I will find some food. You can tell me all while we eat.'

Byrd stepped out through the kitchen curtain, his yellow scarf slightly askew. 'Ah, you're back. Did I hear something about food? Come on, Wynn, and I'll dig something out.'

Leesil took the other crossbow off Magiere's back and set them both on the bar. Wynn placed the quarrel case next to them. She was about to join Byrd when she noticed Leesil's gaze fixed on something behind the bar.

'Wynn . . .' Magiere said slowly. 'Make us some spiced tea, please.'

Leesil lifted his eyes, but he didn't look at her. 'Yes, hot tea . . . and sausages for Chap.'

Wynn sensed that her companions needed to collect themselves before they could talk, so she slipped off to the kitchen as they headed for the stairs. She took her time with the late-night supper. Byrd cooked pork sausages while she loaded a bowl with dried fruits and some pickled vegetables from the vinegar barrel. They sliced day-old bread and stoked up the fire to boil water. Once all was ready, she and Byrd carried the hodge-podge meal out to the common room.

Magiere and Leesil were back downstairs again, out of their gear, and all weapons and equipment from the hunt stored away. They sat at the table nearest the front door, and Chap lay between its legs. Wynn took one of the tin plates she carried and placed two sausages on it.

When she leaned down, one sausage disappeared into Chap's snapping jaws before the plate touched the floor.

She did not scold him for bad manners and stood up to pour tea into the mugs Byrd had set out. Magiere took the first and set it down in front of Leesil. She seemed strangely sad beneath her usual dour air.

'Are you all right?' Wynn asked.

Magiere pulled another mug across to herself. 'A woman died tonight. I should have gone out sooner.'

Wynn sat down. 'Do not blame your —'

A sharp scratching at the front door made her pause, and Byrd got up. When he opened the door, a dark shape bolted through his legs into the room.

Everyone at the table shifted or tensed. Wynn jerked her feet off the floor, twisting quickly in her chair as she searched for what had invaded the room.

Across the floor near the bar sauntered a dark brown cat as large as Clover Roll. His eyes glistened like his fur. Everyone relaxed again.

'Another stray,' Leesil muttered before taking a gulp of tea. He had not yet touched any of the food.

Byrd's reply was cut off by hissing and spitting. They all looked over to see Clover Roll up on the next table, head low as he yowled at the newcomer. His dirty-cream fur stood on end, and his tail arched forward over his back with the tip quivering.

The few other cats about the common room slinked away in all directions. Only Tomato, sitting with her brother at the bottom of the stairs, stood her ground. Her mouth widened in a hiss, and she resembled a tiny orange porcupine. But Tomato was too small to be heard over Clover Roll's raucous noise.

'Clover, stop that,' Byrd scolded. 'You know what it's like to be hungry, so mind your manners!'

Wynn remembered Chap was right below the table, and she leaned sideways to peek at the dog. Chap watched the new stray without a blink but stayed in his place. Wynn breathed easier. At least Chap had resigned himself to being a guest in this place with so many four-footed patrons.

Clover Roll lowered his voice to a grating rumble.

Byrd tore up small bits of sausage and dropped them onto a plate. 'Here, boy,' he said to the cat. 'Come and eat this.'

The newcomer strolled over to nibble on the tidbits Byrd offered. At the quick lick of the animal's tongue, Wynn noticed that it was dark like the rest of him rather than pink.

'All right, what happened tonight?' Byrd asked, hunkering down in a chair. 'You all look like you've seen the backside of cheer.'

As far as the hunt was concerned, they had no secrets from Byrd. Magiere started with the bodies of the woman and servant in the alley. Wynn listened intently to all, down to the vanishing of their quarry.

'This ever happen before?' Byrd asked.

'No, not without leaving some trace,' Leesil answered.

'Not only did we fail to protect the people here,' Magiere added, 'but I took this bargain with Darmouth so we'd have an excuse to get back into the keep. We're no closer to that, either.'

Tomato still made a great show of hissing. Wynn walked over to pick her up, softly petting the kitten's head as she returned to the table.

'You will find this undead,' she encouraged, looking Magiere straight in the eyes. 'We can still take its head to Darmouth and reenter the keep. And you must get this vampire, Magiere. It is a terrible danger to the people here.'

Magiere remained quiet.

'There may be another avenue we could attempt,' Wynn continued. 'Concerning why Leesil's parents ran for the keep. Magiere . . . could you not befriend Lieutenant Omasta? From the way he looked at you, he appeared quite interested. Did you notice how he looked at you?'

Leesil spit tea back into his cup. 'What?'

'Wynn . . .!' Magiere snapped but was too shocked to finish.

'That's enough!' Leesil shouted, standing up. 'All of you stop thinking you can toy with Darmouth.'

'Well, then, lad,' Byrd put in, his voice rising, 'why don't you come up with a way to get inside by yourself?'

Wynn was not fond of shouting matches, but after time in Magiere's company, she had hardened to them. Her dislike of Byrd grew more and more, and she looked away in disgust. She noticed that the plate of sausage scraps on the floor had hardly been touched, and the new stray was nowhere to be seen. Clover Roll sat on the front window sill, rumbling, as he peered out through the half-open shutter.

Magiere's tone was low and threatening as she turned on Byrd. 'And what exactly are you up to? You think this coy routine —'

'The new cat is gone,' Wynn said.

Byrd looked around. 'Maybe he was just a neighbor out for a stroll and headed home.'

The diversion quelled the brewing fight, and Leesil dropped back into his chair.

'We are all tired, and it is late,' Wynn said, putting Tomato up on her shoulder. 'We should sleep and talk tomorrow.'

Magiere was the only one who nodded agreement and began piling dishes back onto the wooden serving tray.

Before Wynn headed for the stairs to retrieve Potato, she stepped to the front window and scratched Clover Roll's back. He purred in answer but remained vigilant. Wynn looked out to the empty street as cold night air struck her face.

Hedí gave up on sleep and climbed out of bed. It was late, perhaps well past midnight, but the bed's heavy coverings felt stifling. She decided to walk the halls, if nothing else. No matter that she could leave at any time, this room was still her cell and the keep no more than a prison. If she tired herself enough, she might return later and sleep. She pulled her cloak over her cotton shift and fastened the front.

The corridor was as cold and stale as her room, but she breathed in relief nonetheless. The passage was deserted, as expected, and she headed toward the stairs down to the main level. Perhaps there was still some wine about – or ale, if she were desperate – to help calm her into slumber.

Hedí stepped off the stairs into the main entryway and turned toward the communal meal hall. She was halfway to its arched entrance when she heard low voices behind her. Someone was talking in the counsel hall on the other side of the wide entryway. She paused, remaining still to listen more carefully.

'You're certain?'

Hedí recognized the low voice as Darmouth's growl. She backed toward the stairs, staying clear of sight, and then crept toward the council hall's entrance with soft steps.

'Yes, my lord,' Faris answered from within. 'The traitor you described and the one who attacked our men at the Stravinan border. One and the same. His companions called him "Leesil." He is with that woman you hired. They stay at Byrd's inn, and Byrd took part in their discussion. The half-blood and his companions spoke of getting back into the keep.'

A long silence followed. When Darmouth answered, his voice grated with strangled rage.

'Take them all – now! Use as many men as you need. I want his corpse on the keep wall by dawn!'

'No, my lord,' Faris warned. 'If he's half of what you claim, soldiers might not be able to capture him. We could catch his woman and the others, but he would slip away in such an insecure area. And taking this hunter by force in public is no better. Word has already spread among the nobles from Geyren that you personally hired her to protect them. How will it appear if you arrest her only a day later?'

'I don't give a damn what it looks like,' Darmouth snapped.

'Wait until tomorrow,' Faris advised. 'Send her word that you require another audience. The death of

Marianne a' Royce is reason enough. Once she is within these walls, we can hold her quietly. When she fails to return to the inn, the half-blood will come for her.'

'Why, when he already abandoned his own parents?'

'He will, my lord. I saw him look at her. He will come . . . and we will deal with Byrd later.'

Hedí stood frozen in place.

Booted footsteps inside the council hall approached the archway. Darmouth or Faris would step out in a moment. Hedí hurried up the stairs, keeping her steps light. Upon reaching the third floor, she walked more calmly.

There was little relief in returning to her cell of a room. How could she warn Byrd?

12

Wynn dressed as Tomato and Potato wrestled on the rumpled bedcovers. The door was ajar, and Chap was gone. She gathered up the kittens and headed downstairs.

The common room was empty except for Clover Roll, curled on a table near the window. A strange rattling came from the kitchen, so Wynn set the kittens down and pushed aside the doorway curtain.

Magiere and Leesil rummaged about, gathering sausages and hard biscuits and tea leaves. Their hair was in loose disarray, and Magiere's muslin shirt hung out of her breeches. Chap whined as he paced and wove between them, getting in the way more than anything else. A late night and morning had made them all miss breakfast, but Chap's exaggerated complaints were far too dramatic.

'Did you see Byrd when you came down?' Magiere asked.

'No,' Wynn replied. 'Have you been up long?'

'Not long,' Leesil said, and placed a kettle on an iron hook arm above the hearth's embers.

Physically he looked improved. His eyes were no longer bloodshot but still held a hint of the haunted withdrawal that Wynn had observed since the night of Faris's visit. Something in the Móndyalítko's words had upset Leesil, even horrified him, but Wynn hesitated to ask.

And it unnerved her that Byrd was suddenly missing.

Leesil should pay more heed to her concerns about that man's involvement with the *Anmaglâhk*. He did not seem to understand what would happen to the common people if Darmouth were assassinated.

'Do you suppose Byrd might . . .?' Wynn began, then thought better of it. Byrd would hardly be meeting with the elves in broad daylight. 'So what do we do for today?'

Leesil glanced her way and then returned to staring at the kettle not yet boiling.

Wynn immediately regretted asking. He wanted a course of action to follow but objected to all of their suggestions. And she feared her sympathy would only make him feel worse. Magiere dropped a few sausages into the iron pan settled among the hearth's coals, and they began to sizzle. The smell made Wynn slightly nauseous.

'You had the only option last night,' Magiere said. 'Take the vampire's head to Darmouth for bounty.'

Leesil's face clouded. Any denial he was about to spit out was lost as Byrd swatted the doorway curtain aside and stepped in.

'You won't need it,' he said. 'Darmouth wants to see you – now. He wants a report about last night. The dead woman was the mistress of Lord Geyren, a younger noble growing in favor.'

'Why?' Leesil asked, and his tone was cold. 'Geyren's men were there, as well as two city soldiers. There's nothing Magiere can add that they haven't already reported.'

Byrd shook his head. 'He wants to hear about the hunt itself. That's all I know.'

'Very well,' Magiere said. 'Back in Bela, even Councilman Lanjov wanted word on our progress. And he couldn't stand being in the same room with us.'

'That's not all he's after, I'll wager,' Leesil said, and closed his eyes. 'You don't know who you're dealing with.'

Wynn had no wish to cause Leesil distress, but it was he who did not understand. She had no intention of leaving Venjètz until they knew what Byrd was planning.

'There are two choices,' she said. 'Continue the search, which means getting back into the keep, or leave for the mountains to find a way to the elven lands.'

Wynn expected Leesil to lose his temper again over her so bluntly stating the obvious. It seemed the best way to force him to choose, instead of resisting every suggestion.

Leesil slumped as he covered his face with one hand.

Wynn almost choked for what she had just done and looked to Magiere with silent regret for hurting Leesil further. Wynn expected little more than Magiere's fury, and this time felt she deserved it.

Magiere simply frowned and nodded her understanding.

Chap licked Leesil's hanging hand and barked once, confirming Wynn's words. Leesil slid his palm over the dog's head.

'You want to go back in?' he asked.

Chap again barked once.

Magiere pulled Leesil's other hand from his face and gripped it tightly. 'Can you give us any plan, any ruse to try? Once we're inside, are there people to speak with, bribe' – she shrugged – 'threaten?'

'No,' Leesil said, but he appeared to be thinking. 'Servants and guards won't know anything and couldn't be bribed anyway. Darmouth holds something over everyone he keeps close, like Faris or Omasta. Nothing you'd offer could outweigh that.'

'Well, then,' Wynn said as the smoky smell filling the room began to sting her nose. 'We will have to find an opportunity once we are inside.'

Byrd had remained silent throughout this exchange, but now added his own admonishment. 'And you're forgetting one thing, lad. If Magiere doesn't report, Darmouth will simply send soldiers to retrieve her. He's given an order, and she has to go.'

'I know that!' Leesil glared at him. 'And I haven't forgotten that you talked her into —'

Chap bellowed, turned a quick circle, and shoved his way between Magiere and Leesil to the kitchen hearth. A yowl followed, and Wynn stood upright, wondering if he was hurt. Both Magiere and Leesil looked at the dog.

Smoke billowed into the chimney from out of the pan on the embers. The stench burned Wynn's nose. She barely made out the blackened shrivels of sausage remains in the pan.

Chap let out an angry series of yips as he shuffled before the hearth.

'Oh, stop it!' Magiere snapped at the dog, and pulled Leesil toward the curtained doorway. 'Come and help me get ready. Wynn, get your cloak and your pack. We'll meet you back here.'

'My good pan!' Byrd growled, and rushed for the hearth.

He grabbed an iron poker and speared the pan's handle loop. When he lifted the pan, it toppled to dangle from the poker's end. The sausages' charred remains tumbled into the coals with a sizzle and puff of ashes.

'You people are the worst patrons I ever took in for nothing,' Byrd grumbled.

Chap whimpered and shoved his head into the hearth. He began hacking and sneezing with smoke billowing around his face. Wynn grabbed his haunches and jerked him back.

'Both of you be quiet!' she shouted, and grabbed Chap's muzzle in one hand. 'And you – stop acting like a drunkard at the bottom of an empty keg!'

She snatched a hard biscuit off the table and shoved it into Chap's jaws. Chap bit it in half and spit the pieces on the floor.

'Fine,' Wynn said. 'Then go hungry.'

She stomped out of the kitchen and did not slow until she reached the upper hallway and the door to her room. Across the way, the door to Leesil and Magiere's room was shut tight.

Magiere wanted Leesil alone for a moment, and Wynn understood. She slipped into her own room to bundle up for winter weather. She was pulling on her gloves when the door opened and Leesil stepped in. He held two small daggers in makeshift sheaths, each with dual straps attached.

'Give me your arms,' he said.

'Where did you get those?'

'I bought the makings back in Soladran,' he answered. 'I pieced them together the night we stayed in the barracks. Now give me your arms.'

Wynn was uncertain. Leesil pushed up her coat sleeves and began strapping the sheaths to her forearms, the dagger hilts held downward toward her palms. He pulled her sleeves down to cover them.

'Reach across for one,' he said, 'or fold your hands into your sleeves against the cold to grab both. Don't do it until the last moment, or you'll lose the advantage of surprise.'

Wynn looked up at his tan face and amber eyes. His concern touched her, and she leaned her head against his chest.

'We will be fine,' she whispered. 'You will see us soon.'

Leesil closed his arms around her shoulders, holding her tightly.

'Am I interrupting?'

Wynn stiffened and lifted her head.

Magiere leaned against the doorframe with arms folded, her hair pulled back with a leather thong. Her hauberk was buckled down over her thick wool pullover, and the falchion was strapped to her waist. Hood down, her cloak was pushed back off her shoulders.

'Or should I come back later?' she added.

There was no anger in her voice and her serious expression was marred by one cocked eyebrow. When it came to Leesil's affection, Magiere had nothing to fear from Wynn. She had nothing to fear from anyone. Leesil had eyes only for her. Magiere's humor was as caustic as everything else about her.

Wynn blushed, quickly holding out her arms to divert attention. 'Look what he did.'

'I know,' Magiere replied. 'I suggested it. You ready?'

Wynn nodded. She grabbed her pack loaded with

scholar's wares to maintain the front they had first established in Darmouth's presence. When they returned to the common room, Chap paced before the bar, still whining. Leesil opened the front door and remained there as Magiere led the way down the street. No one said good-bye.

Wynn pulled her hood forward and lowered her head a little against the cold breeze. They walked without speaking, Chap trotting beside her. He finally quit mourning the loss of his sausages.

Wynn barely noticed the city around her until the keep appeared ahead between the buildings. They passed a few soldiers loitering in the street near a dry-goods shop. Magiere glanced at them and kept on walking. She had not bothered to pull up her cloak's hood, and Wynn wondered how she could stand the cold.

They passed more soldiers milling about. Rather than patrolling, they stood outside of homes and taverns as if they had nothing better to do.

Magiere reached the crossing of Favor's Row and stopped. Ahead of them, Lieutenant Omasta waited in the archway of the bridge gatehouse. No soldiers accompanied him, but three came slowly down Favor's Row from the right.

Magiere remained still, and Wynn wondered at the delay. Omasta waved them forward, and Chap growled.

'Start backing up,' Magiere whispered.

Wynn stepped up next to her. 'But . . .?'

Magiere was expressionless. Snowflakes landing upon her pale face seemed to disappear before melting.

'We run,' Magiere said quietly. 'Find a place to hide until dark and make your way back to Byrd's.'

Wynn glanced back the way they had come.

Two cross streets back, the soldiers who had been hanging about only moments before now walked toward them at a quick pace. One drew his shortsword. Lieutenant Omasta stepped off the bridge's end onto the cobblestones, walking casually toward them.

'It's all right,' he called out. 'My lord wishes to speak with you.'

Wynn knew right then he was lying.

Magiere jerked out her falchion. 'Wynn, to your left. They don't want you.'

'But what about —'

'Run!'

Chap snarled, spinning about to face behind them.

Wynn bolted to the left down Favor's Row. She ran as fast as her short legs could without slipping on frozen cobblestones. She glanced back once over her shoulder.

Magiere headed the other way toward three soldiers charging to meet her. Chap was close behind her.

Wynn looked ahead and veered toward the first street away from the lakeside. She turned the corner and slammed straight into something.

Hard bumps ground against her face and forehead on impact. She recoiled and stumbled, barely keeping her footing. All she saw for a moment was a wide torso covered by a studded breastplate of hardened leather.

'Where you goin', girl?'

The soldier was more than a head taller than Wynn. A cap of quilted wool with earflaps covered his head and framed a square face of ruddy windburned cheeks and beard stubble. His eyes looked too small for his face. Another came up behind him.

All Wynn could think to do was scream out, 'Magiere! Chap!'

'Not gonna happen,' the soldier said, and grabbed the front of her coat.

Wynn gripped his wrist with both hands, trying to pull him off. He jerked hard, curling his arm, and spun her around. Her pack ended up crushed against his chest. He closed his other arm around her, and the ground dropped from under her feet as she was lifted.

Wynn's arms were pinned and she kicked wildly, but the soldier's hold would not give. She felt something grinding through her coat's bulk and her short robe into her ribs.

A dagger – the one on her left wrist.

'Be still, you little whelp,' the soldier warned. 'Malik, get over here and grab those legs.'

Wynn focused on only two things. She pushed panic aside and folded her left leg up high. She kicked sharply downward.

Her boot heel ground down the soldier's thigh and hit sharply on his kneecap. His leg buckled, and he barked out a curse. When her feet touched down, she thrashed free of his grip, but he grabbed the pack before she could get clear.

Wynn slipped her arms from its straps and reached up her left sleeve. As her hand closed on the dagger's hilt, a booted foot struck her hard between the shoulder blades.

She toppled forward and slid. Her right cheek grated across the street's cold stones. Panic took hold as she scrambled to her knees, swinging blindly back with the dagger.

Its tip grated along a leather hauberk instead of a breastplate. The second soldier half crouched above her. His eyes widened at the blade's passing, and he lashed out with his hand.

His palm cracked against the side of Wynn's face, and her head whipped sideways. Wynn's vision turned white, and she vaguely heard a metallic clatter.

She lay facedown in the street, but the white still blurred her vision like a blizzard enveloping the world. What little she made out looked as flat as a picture – her left eye would not focus at all.

Something thin and biting circled her wrists. A sharp pain in both Wynn's shoulders cut through the dull ache in her head and eye, as her arms were pinned back and tied.

'Lucky day, girlie,' came a voice she barely heard. 'We're supposed to bring you in one piece.'

Wynn's arms jerked upward, her shoulders twisting back as she came off the ground. She exhaled sharply. Her feet dragged on the stones as she was carried away.

'You half-wits!' someone shouted. 'You were to stay out of sight until they were on the bridge.'

It took all Wynn's strength to turn her head. She looked up with only her right eye.

Lieutenant Omasta glared down Favor's Row and slowly shook his head. Wynn tried to focus.

Bodies lay in the street. Soldiers were Wynn's best guess. Magiere and Chap were gone. They had escaped – and she was alone.

Wynn could not feel afraid. She was too tired. She wished the soldier would just drop her so she could sleep on the cold stone. She remembered Leesil holding her as she told him that everything would be fine.

Omasta turned about and looked down at Wynn. 'Take her in and wait for me. The rest of your contingent had better bring that hunter back.'

Wynn's head sagged. A salty taste filled her slack mouth, and every few paces a dark red droplet spattered on the snow-dusted stones of the keep's bridge.

Magiere heard Wynn cry out. She faltered in her flight and stopped to look back. Chap whirled about as well.

Three soldiers closed behind them. Three more were coming out ahead. Magiere couldn't see Wynn, and anguish only made her furious that she'd led the young sage into this trap.

Chap lunged back down the road toward the trailing soldiers.

'No!' Magiere shouted.

The dog skidded to a halt with an angry snarl.

'We can't help her if we're caught,' Magiere said.

Chap barked twice in denial, but he turned back, lunging ahead of her toward the soldiers in their path. Magiere rushed after him.

The soldiers were fully focused on her, and the first was caught by surprise when Chap grazed his leg in passing. The man stumbled sideways, and Magiere slashed into his side with the falchion as she passed. She didn't look back to see if he went down. The next two slowed.

Chap swerved right, snapping and snarling as he passed one soldier's flank. The man spun about at the dog's circling attack, and Magiere charged straight for his companion.

Every fast breath Magiere took fanned her hunger. She no longer felt the cold. Her opponent cocked back his shortsword, and Magiere swung downward while still running. For that instant the soldier seemed to slow in her vision, yet her own movements retained speed.

The shortsword had barely finished half its swing when Magiere's falchion collided with it. His force seemed weak, and Magiere's strike broke through his guard. The falchion's curved end bit through his hauberk's shoulder, and he crumpled. She turned away before he hit the ground.

Chap's jaws were clamped on the third soldier's ankle. He set all fours and jerked backward. The soldier slipped and fell, his boot tearing between Chap's teeth.

The soldier's skullcap helmet clanked on the stone. Magiere kicked his head as she passed, and his body spun a quarter turn on the cobblestones. He went still, arms splayed out like a rag doll's. Chap pulled in beside Magiere as she ran on, with the trailing soldiers closing from behind.

Chap rushed ahead and swerved down the first side street, and Magiere followed. The dog turned again into an alley. He wove his way between the crates and barrels, and Magiere toppled as many as she could in her passing to slow their pursuers. A few steps ahead she spotted a half-open door in a building of weather-bleached planks.

'Here!' she shouted at Chap.

The dog spun around, running back. He leaped through the opening, and she followed, slamming the door behind. She quickly heaved a pivoting wood bar into its braces, sealing the door.

'Help! Murder!' someone screamed.

Magiere flattened her back against the door.

A portly woman holding a dripping ladle stood gasping in wide-eyed panic near a small stone hearth. Brown stew bubbled within a cast-iron pot hanging over the weak flames, and spatters of the same color stained the woman's greasy apron. There were stacks of tin and wood plates and mugs on a squat side table, and crates of potatoes were piled in the corner under plucked chickens dangling from wall hooks. Magiere was in a back scullery and kitchen.

'No,' she said, lowering the falchion. 'Ma'am, be quiet.'

She must look horrifying to a commoner, rushing in armed with a large dog at her side. Magiere put one finger to her lips. The squat woman stared at her with wide round eyes.

The door bucked against Magiere's back as something struck it from outside. The woman screamed again.

Magiere shoved past her, kicking open the far plank door. She ran out and startled a skinny girl with a haggard face carrying a wooden tray of brimming tankards. Magiere stood in the common room of a small tavern. Clusters of townsfolk stared at her in surprise as another squealing scream came from the kitchen.

'Murder!'

The skinny girl stumbled, and the tray of tankards toppled to the floor with a splashing clatter. A stocky man in a floppy leather cap stood up in alarm.

Chap lunged out before Magiere, letting out a deep snarl. His muzzle and teeth were stained with blood.

'Wolf!' cried the stocky man.

Patrons toppled drink and food, chairs and tables, as they scrambled in any direction away from the dog. This left a clear path to the front door, and Chap raced for it as Magiere realized what he'd done. She slammed her palm into the chest of the man in the cap, knocking him aside as she followed the dog.

She stopped briefly in the street to look both ways. Another soldier rounded the far right corner, coming straight for her with his shortsword out. He was young, probably less than twenty years.

He came at her too fast, and she sidestepped him neatly. As he passed, she slammed the butt of her sword into the back of his head. He went down face-first in a crumpled heap and didn't move. Hunger worked its way throughout Magiere's body, building to an ache in her jaws.

Chap barked, and she spotted him across the street before a set of wide doors. She joined him, jerking one door open, and they both hurried inside. She hadn't seen any other soldiers in the street, but some townsfolk across the way had surely watched out the windows. They would point out where a 'wolf' and a fleeing woman had gone. She looked about her new surroundings.

A long row of stalls ran down one side, and near the doors was a ladder up to an overhead loft. At the stable's far end were bundles of dried hay. She didn't see a rear door, but there was a wide window with shutters closed and barred from the inside.

A soft whine from Chap echoed through the stable. Magiere glanced about but didn't see him. He whined again, and she followed his sound to the back and around behind the hay. He scratched at the dirt floor.

'What are you doing?' she whispered, but words felt difficult in her mouth. 'We have to go.'

A straight crack in the floor appeared where Chap clawed. He kept at it, and exposed a thin rope loop, Magiere grabbed it and pulled. A hatch opened, spilling back loose hay and dirt. Magiere hesitated for two breaths.

She stepped to the window, lifted the bar and tossed it away, then slapped the shutters wide. When she turned back to the floor hatch, Chap had shoved a hay bundle over to rest against the hatch's top. Magiere pulled the hatch up halfway. Chap wriggled through the opening and disappeared. She followed and dropped down into the dark. The hatch slammed shut under the weight of the hay bundle.

Anyone following in haste wouldn't see the line in the floor beneath the hay . . . but would see an open window. A risky gamble, but better than trying to outrun Darmouth's soldiers through streets she didn't know.

The cellar – or whatever purpose this pit served – was empty except for two large barrels near a ladder she hadn't seen before jumping in. Magiere moved to the back to crouch and wait with Chap.

Her teeth still hurt, and she was so angry over losing Wynn that her dhampir half wouldn't recede. She tried to breathe quietly and push the anger down.

Loud voices and footsteps burst into the stable above. Magiere closed her eyes and tried to block out the shouts overhead. Musk and leather, sweat and lingering beer or ale filled her nostrils beneath the scent of dirt, hay, and horse manure.

'Quiet!' someone yelled as a pair of heavy boots stepped through the stable above.

It was Omasta's voice. There were perhaps three or

four men with him, by the different positions of shifting feet that Magiere heard. A lighter set of footsteps followed.

'Can't your men follow simple orders?'

Faris.

Chap rumbled once softly.

'That's none of your concern,' Omasta fired back.

'Yes, this was *your* task, not mine,' Faris answered. 'And all you have to show for your bungling is one little scholar, who may mean nothing to the half-blood. You can explain that to Lord Darmouth, and not I.'

Another set of footsteps ran in. 'She's not in the alley, sir.'

'Well, look again!' Omasta answered. 'It's clear she climbed out the back window. Spread out and search the connecting streets, as she can't have gotten far. I will go to our lord. The rest of you keep hunting until I send word otherwise.'

A dull thunder of footsteps headed toward the stable doors. Magiere remained crouched in the darkness with Chap.

Faris knew about Leesil, and though she wondered how, there was no doubt that he'd told Darmouth. She shivered with a need to run to Leesil, and flattened her palms on the dirt floor to get up.

Chap stepped down on her hand with his paw, growling softly in warning.

Magiere settled back. They had to wait for darkness and hope it was not too late.

Hedí spent the morning in Korey's room.

At breakfast she had asked Julia for brightly colored

yarn and needles. She went up to teach the girl some basic knitting. Korey was so excited by this new project she could barely sit still at first. She finally settled down, and the hours passed quickly as they chatted and worked.

Past noon, Julie came with a tray. She was shocked to see Hedí sitting on the bed with Korey. 'My lady . . .'

Clearly Hedí was not supposed to be here, but Julia would not dare give orders to anyone of favor or nobility.

'Don't leave,' Korey said to Hedí. 'Please.'

Julia's mouth opened and closed, and suddenly she looked frightened.

Hedí had no wish to cause a simpleminded servant unnecessary trouble. She stood and picked up her sewing bag.

'I have some things to attend to,' she told Korey. 'But I will see you tomorrow. We can play at cards again.'

Korey's face fell, and she shot Julia a glowering pout. Hedí kissed her on the head and swept past Julia out of the room.

She went to eat her own lunch, and stayed in the meal hall to work on the embroidered pillowcase. Working with her needle, she busied her thoughts with how she might get a message to Byrd, but all possibilities seemed blocked. She considered bribing Julia to carry a note, but if by chance the woman agreed and then faltered in any way, the repercussions would be disasterous – and brutal for Julia.

Heavy boots on stone echoed in from the entryway outside the meal hall. Hedí set down her work and stepped to the archway to see what the commotion was about.

Omasta was there and looked both angered and

worried. He was always on edge, like all those around his pig of a master, but he looked more troubled than ever before.

Two soldiers followed him in, dragging a young woman in a sheepskin coat by her bound arms. One of them limped and clutched a canvas pack in his free hand. They dropped the woman, and she landed with her cheek flattened to the floor. The limping soldier dumped the pack's contents out, and Omasta watched impatiently as his men rummaged through the woman's belongings.

There were small roles of parchments bound with string, two leather-bound journals, and some charcoal and quills. A small bottle of ink cracked open on the floor.

The woman, or perhaps girl, was small, with olive-toned skin uncommon for the people here. Her eyes were closed. The left side of her face was reddened and swollen, including her left eye. Her slack lips were blood-stained on the left side.

Parchment, books, and quills – a scribe, perhaps? No, even a journeyman of that profession would have found a place to settle and ply her skills. And what would Omasta want with a scribe badly enough to have her beaten, bound, and searched?

Some type of scholar seemed the only other possibility, but such were rarer than an act of kindness in the Warlands. In Hedí's limited travels with Emêl, she had met only two, and both were in service to noble houses. Even an apprentice would be under the guidance of a master, so why was this one dressed for the winter travel . . . and so young?

'Where's that pasty-skinned hunter?' Darmouth boomed.

He stepped from the counsel hall across the way, a tall pewter tankard in his grip. Hedí ducked back a step.

Darmouth's breastplate was recently oiled and cleaned, and he looked freshly shaved. Omasta stood at attention, but Hedí noted no fear in his eyes. Rather, he expressed deep regret. Hedí had never seen this in anyone facing Darmouth's anger. Omasta genuinely did not wish to disappoint his lord. She could not imagine what would foster such a willing sense of duty to this tyrant.

'She escaped, my lord,' Omasta said. 'The men closed in too soon. But the search continues, and we may yet find her. I'll keep the men at it, even into the night.'

Darmouth's eyelids drooped halfway as he stared at Omasta for a long moment, but there was none of the brutal anger he showed to others who failed him. He stepped forward to stand over the small woman and hooked his boot toe under her shoulder to flip her over.

'Where would Magiere hide from my men?' he asked.

The girl did not respond and simply lay prone below him. Darmouth poured the tankard over her face.

She choked on the foaming liquid filling her mouth. Her head rolled, and only her right eye blinked to clear the fluid.

'Magiere,' Darmouth repeated, 'where is she?'

'I do not know,' the woman mumbled. She tried to shake her head, but the gesture was feeble.

Darmouth's expression darkened. He lifted his boot over the woman's face.

'My lord!' Hedí shouted, and stepped into view. 'She is a scholar, not just some commoner.'

It was a desperate guess, and all Hedí could think of to halt any further abuse.

Darmouth lowered his foot at the sight of Hedí. He swallowed hard and took a deep, slow breath, perhaps not wishing to appear the beast that he was in front of her. In any other moment Hedí would have found this sickeningly humorous. She consoled herself: As long as Byrd breathed, one day this tyrant would choke and squirm in his own blood.

Darmouth glanced down at the young woman, then back to Hedí.

'Of course,' he answered, and turned to Omasta. 'Secure this prisoner in a room on the first level – not the lower cells – and put a guard on the door. I'll speak to her later, when . . .'

He trailed off, watching Hedí. The rest of his orders were not for her ears. He headed back into the counsel hall, motioning Omasta to follow. Omasta nodded to his men and joined his lord.

Hedí had no doubt that Darmouth would order Omasta to organize a raid on Byrd's inn.

The girl on the floor slowly rolled her head to look at Hedí with her good eye. One soldier shoved her belongings back into the pack, and both hoisted her up by the shoulders and dragged her up the stairs.

Hedí followed from a distance.

The guards took their prisoner up the stairs and down the corridor of the second level. Hedí watched long enough to see which room they placed her in. One remained outside the door. Hedí hurried quietly up the stairs to her own room. Once inside she could not sit still, and paced the floor.

A fire burned in the small hearth. She looked about at the cherry-wood desk and wardrobe and the thick quilt upon her bed. Darmouth took pains to have this room made comfortable for her. Such thoughts made her hate the surroundings even more. The same man thought nothing of stepping on the face of a helpless girl for answers she might not even have.

Hedí did not know why she had put herself at risk for this stranger. It was a foolish act that gained her nothing.

'Mrowr.'

The sound was so soft that Hedí was not certain she had heard it until scratches followed outside her door. What was a cat doing inside the keep? She twisted the latch, opened the door, and a dark little form bolted around her skirt into the room. Hedí twisted about.

A small, brown-black cat, with eyes of matching color and a bobbed tail, hopped up on the bed. It stared back at her and let out a soft 'purr.'

In spite of everything Hedí had just witnessed, she almost smiled. 'There are wolfhounds below, you little fool. How did you get in here?'

Perhaps a soldier or servant had brought it in to hunt vermin in the lower levels, but this one looked too small for such a task. It was barely beyond a kitten. Firelight glimmered off the fur across its ears and face.

Hedí approached the foot of the bed, reaching out. 'Very well, come here. I will have Julia fetch some milk. If you are lucky, there might even be cream.'

A ripple swelled through the cat's shoulders.

Hedí jerked her hand back.

A larger swell passed down its back as it craned its neck and crouched low. It issued a grating yowl, digging its claws into the bedcovers as its eyes rolled up in its head.

Hedí backed away as the cat flopped on the quilt, twitching.

Its face flattened and its round muzzle collapsed inward upon a skull that bloated from within. Shoulders widened to grotesque misshapen mounds about its thickening neck. Black-brown fur thinned, and pale flesh showed beneath. Forelegs elongated. Ears shriveled inward around its stretching face. Eyes rolled back down and irises shrank, as its whole body began to grow in size . . .

Hedí almost cried out as she whipped around, lunging for the door.

'Hello!' a small voice called.

She sucked in a breath she could not let out, and flattened her back against the door.

Sitting in the middle of her bed was a naked little girl with dark eyes and skin and long wavy hair.

'It's me,' Korey said with a giggle, then waved happily at Hedí.

Hedí panted in short breaths as she slumped to the floor, unable to even blink.

Korey crawled off the bed's side and dropped to the floor in her bare feet . . . bare everything. She started to run across the room but stopped and smothered another giggle with her hand.

'Whoops! I forgot again,' she said, and with a sigh scurried back to pull at the quilt with all her strength. 'My clothes don't come with me.'

Hedí tried to speak. 'H-how . . .'

Korey struggled to pull the quilt around herself. It

was too big, and half of it wrapped around the bedpost. She stopped struggling long enough to look at Hedí.

'Papa taught me,' she said, as if it were obvious.

'Your father . . . taught you that?' Hedí whispered.

'Uh-huh. Mama can do it too . . . I think, but I've never seen it. Papa can do great big ones, when he wants.' Korey frowned and tried to look over her shoulder at her own bare buttocks. 'But I can't get the tail. Just a stubby thing!'

As a child, Hedí had heard stories of shifters. Most were too wild to be anything but superstitious nonsense, folklore forgotten as the fancies of youth.

'Can . . . can all your people do this?' she asked.

Korey finally heaved the quilt free and wrapped it about herself, but most of it dragged across the floor as she came to plop down before Hedí.

'Papa says some, but not all. It's a family thing. Mama says Auntie Balalee − I never met her yet − sees things that aren't there but are somewhere else. I don't understand that part. Are you sick?'

'Sick?' Hedí's breathing slowed, but her heart still pounded against her ribs. 'No, I . . . I am fine.'

She touched the ribbon about her throat. Faris could turn himself into a great cat, perhaps something like a mountain lion. It was no wonder that Darmouth wanted control over this family of Móndyalítko. Her heart tightened in fear for little Korey.

'You should not be here,' Hedí said. 'What if Julia finds you gone from your room?'

Korey shrugged and rolled her eyes. 'She won't come till dinner; then she'll just leave the tray. No one ever comes to visit but you. You like to be with me. Mama and Papa love me . . . but you like to be with me.'

Hedí took a deep breath and let it out. 'Oh, Korey.'

Hedí's own mother had liked nothing better than to visit with her daughters, play at cards, and braid their hair, even late into the night. Hedí never realized the wonder of a mother's companionship until it was gone. And Korey's own parents were never allowed that close to her for too long.

Hedí did not like using a child, but unless Darmouth was assassinated, Korey would grow up trapped here, until he used her like her parents – or killed her. Korey did not appear to know of the lost sibling that Ventina had viciously hinted at. If Byrd was not warned, he would be arrested, and everything they had worked for would be lost, even the life and future of this girl. And it appeared Darmouth did not know Korey shared her parents' ability, or he would have taken extra precautions with the child.

She grasped Korey's shoulders. 'Lord Darmouth has captured a young woman and locked her in a room one floor below us. He calls us guests, but that is a lie. I am a prisoner here – as are you. Do you understand that?'

Korey pulled back suspiciously. 'Papa says we aren't supposed to talk about that.'

Hedí felt a twinge of guilt, but there was too much at stake to stop now. 'Your father is afraid of Lord Darmouth, and he should be. You are a good girl for your papa, but I must get a message to a friend in the city, or we could all . . . get hurt, including your parents. Can you sneak out as a cat and take it to where I tell you? Stay in the shadows on the bridge, and you will be small and dark enough that no one will notice.'

'I don't know the city. I've never been,' Korey said, and now she looked frightened. 'I'd get lost! But you know the city, and you could do it.'

Hedí released Korey's shoulders, sinking limply back against the door. 'Lord Darmouth will never let me out. You have to —'

'I can show you,' Korey said, and grabbed Hedí's hand. Unfortunately, this caused the quilt to slide off and she was once again naked. Hedí pulled the quilt up as Korey leaned forward, whispering. 'You don't talk to me like everybody else, like I'm too young . . . too stupid. I know things! Papa tells me.'

Hedí sat upright. 'What things?'

'One time Papa played a trick on Julia and Devid when Lord Darmouth was gone away. He put stuff in their food, and they went to sleep. Julia snores like a dog! Papa said when they woke up, they wouldn't tell or they'd get in trouble for sleeping. He told me to change into a cat, and hid me in a big sack, and took me down and down under the keep, with places like cages with iron bars for doors, and showed me a piece of wall . . .'

Korey paused to catch her breath.

'We went through it and found a thing he called a "portal," and he opened it. He showed me, and he said, "Just in case." Then we hurried real fast to get me back to my room. He told me if I went through the portal door, I'd find a secret to take me to the woods way over on the other side of the lake.'

Hedí remained as calm as she could. If Korey's tale was true . . .

This was more than a way to send Byrd a warning.

Could it be what they had spent years searching for — a way to breach the keep? How could she get into the lower levels? She had seen guards at every post that might lead below.

'Korey, what is down there? How could I get across the lake to the woods?'

Before Korey could speak, a knock sounded on the door.

'Quick,' Hedí said, and lifted the quilt off Korey. 'Under the bed.'

Korey scurried away on all fours and wriggled out of sight, and Hedí spread the quilt roughly over the bed. She returned to the door and opened it a fraction.

A middle-aged guard stood before her in the corridor. He looked distraught.

'Forgive my disturbing you, lady,' he said. 'Baron Milea has arrived and is waiting in the meal hall. Our lord sent word last night that you wished to see the baron. But all this happened before —'

'Before today's commotion,' Hedí finished for him.

'Yes, my lady. Our lord has granted the baron a *short* visit.'

'Thank you. I will be down in a moment.'

She closed the door and rushed to the cherry-wood desk, grabbing a scrap of parchment and a feather quill.

'Korey, come out,' she said, and dipped the quill in the inkwell, scribbling a note. 'You must get back to your room quickly. Wait . . . how did you open and close the door with paws instead of hands?'

Korey scoffed with a roll of her eyes. 'I don't do it while I'm a cat! I take my clothes off in my room, wait till no one's in the hall, then go out and change. No one notices a cat around here 'cause they're supposed to be catching rats and mice.'

Hedí shook her head. If only she had met this little one years ago. 'Hurry back to your room. Julia may be there soon with your dinner. I will come for you later, and you can show me how to find this portal.'

'I'll wait up for you,' Korey agreed.

Hedí fought down guilt again. What she did was for the sake of her people – her lost mother and sisters, and her father, and even for Korey.

'Good girl,' she said. 'Now, change.'

Korey's body began to shrink, darkening with fur that sprouted from her soft skin.

Hedí watched the reverse process with fascination instead of horror.

When it was complete, she cracked the door open, and Korey, the little black-brown cat, scurried out and down the corridor. She closed the door and folded the note she had written until it fit into the palm of her hand. When enough time passed that Korey would be well on her way, Hedí left and went down to the meal hall.

Emêl stood within the archway in his green tunic and watched her enter. She almost smiled at the sight of his face. Then she saw Darmouth standing further into the hall.

'My lady,' he said, and the tone made her feel like property.

She ignored him and held out her hands to Emêl in greeting. Confusion replaced the sadness in his eyes as he returned her polite gesture, taking hands. His brow creased when he felt the folded paper she pressed into his palm.

'It is good to see you,' he said calmly. 'Lord Darmouth tells me you left unfinished business at the Bronze Bell?'

'Yes, I have not paid Mistress Dauczeck at the dressmaker's. It is two streets west of the inn. She will be waiting for the coins. Also, I never got to the letter for your sister regarding plans for the winter feast. Would you see to that for me?'

Emêl nodded politely.

The following moments of inane chatter were torture, standing so close to him. Hedí wanted to touch him and to ask how he was or assure him of her treatment. Darmouth remained vigilant at the rear of the hall. When she ran out of conversation and imaginary tasks for Emêl, Darmouth became restless and approached.

'Is that all?' he asked.

She could think of nothing else. The note in Emêl's hand was urgent, and hopefully he would understand and follow her instructions. She studied his reddish hair and kind eyes, wishing she were leaving with him.

'Then I've other matters,' Darmouth said. 'You're dismissed, Emêl.'

He crossed his arms over his breastplate. Emêl nodded his good-bye to Hedí, his subtle sadness returning, and left the meal hall.

Hedí was left angry and adrift as she heard the entryway door clunk shut. It strained her to remain polite and submissive in Darmouth's close presence.

'Perhaps you think me harsh,' he said, 'to lock up that scholar.'

Neither denial nor confirmation would please him, so she remained silent.

'Your scholar girl is bait for a dangerous criminal,' he

continued. 'Another traitor to be dealt with. You even know something of him, as I suspect you've never lost interest in what happened to your father.'

Hedí was now confused. She remained passive, and answered truthfully, 'I do not understand, my lord.'

'His name is Leesil,' Darmouth answered slowly. 'Son of my former servants, Gavril and his elven wife, Nein'a, who betrayed me.'

He looked her up and down, watching for her reaction – or something else. She wanted to spit bile in his face.

'I do not understand,' she repeated, doe-eyed.

'That half-blood drove the stiletto through the back of your father's skull while he slept.'

13

Shortly past dusk, Chane and Welstiel stepped into the Ivy Vine inn. They retreated to the privacy of their room, their task completed. Chane had awoken Welstiel after the sun dipped below the trees. The two had gone in search of the inn called Byrd's, where they knew Magiere hid with this would-be revolutionary. Chane had only to glimpse the location to hold it in his mind for later use, and Welstiel shielded his presence from Magiere's or Chap's awareness. Still, Chane was relieved to be back in their room.

Removing his cloak, he dropped to his knees beside the robin's cage and carefully lifted out his bird. Welstiel stood silently as Chane opened his hands and watched the robin fly into the night.

Chane closed his eyes and guided his familiar.

Leesil's anxiety grew through the afternoon. When he put on his cloak to leave in search of Magiere, Byrd stepped in his way.

'I'll do it,' Byrd said. 'I'll put up my "closed" sign, and you lock the door after me.'

'I'm sick of sitting here. They take too many risks just because I might be seen by someone who knows me. That's over. I'm making the decisions now.'

'Then make the right one,' Byrd argued. 'I know who to see and what questions to ask. And someone has to stay here, in case they make it back.'

Leesil remained poised to force his way past Byrd. His father's old 'friend' was right, which only angered him more.

'Then go,' he said.

Byrd left, and Leesil reluctantly latched the door behind him.

When dusk finally came, anxiety turned to panic, and Leesil paced through the common room. Twice he found himself leaning on the bar, staring over it at the wine and ale casks behind. He was on the verge of grabbing his cloak again when he heard a creak from the kitchen. He jerked the doorway curtain aside as Byrd came through the back door alone.

'Where are they?' Leesil asked.

'Calm down,' Byrd said, but his stoic expression had no such effect. 'I can't get a straight answer from any of my contacts, but there's been gossip among the towns-folk about a skirmish near the bridge. Soldiers chased a tall woman and a wolf through an eastside tavern. No one knows what happened after that.'

'What?' Leesil grabbed Byrd by his thick wool vest-ment, and anger and fear made his stomach burn. 'You're the one who was all for her going to Darmouth!'

Byrd's expression darkened as he tried to pull away and step past.

Leesil shoved him back. Too many things had gone wrong since they'd come to Venjètz. For all Byrd's cunning – plotting against Darmouth and still serving him, allied with the *Anmaglâhk* yet still alive and unsuspected – why did this man always know so little when it mattered most?

The back door slammed open, and Magiere and Chap rushed in.

Her hair had broken loose from its thong, and both she and Chap panted from exertion. Leesil released Byrd and grabbed Magiere in his arms. She let him hold her for a moment and then pushed him back. Her face was smudged, and her clothes marred with dirt and strands of hay.

'They took Wynn,' she said. 'You were right. It was a trap . . . and they caught her instead of me.'

Leesil hadn't thought of Wynn amid his relief over Magiere's return. 'How long ago?'

Magiere shook her head. 'Not long after we left. We had to run, and I sent her the other way, thinking the soldiers would follow me. I heard her call out but couldn't go back for her.'

Chap's sudden growl startled Leesil. The dog wrinkled his jowls, half exposing clenched teeth as he inched toward Byrd. When Leesil lifted his eyes again, he found Magiere's irises had flooded black.

'You two-faced bastard!' she snarled, and lunged around Leesil.

Leesil heard the crack of her fist before he could turn his head. Byrd reeled into the kitchen's hearth, then pivoted around, raising heavy fists before Magiere closed again.

'You sold us out!' Magiere shouted.

Leesil grabbed Magiere's waist but only slowed her enough for Byrd to shift out of her reach. Chap circled around the table's other side, blocking Byrd from reaching the kitchen doorway.

Byrd's innkeeper persona vanished. All emotion drained from his face, and the blinks of his eyes came further apart as his gaze hardened upon Magiere. He slid his left foot slightly back so that he was angled well enough to charge at either Magiere or Chap. Byrd slipped his right hand behind his back where Leesil had once seen the man pull out an infighter's fist-knife from under his shirt.

'Darmouth is strangling my people,' he said, 'but I wouldn't give you up to him. It would gain me nothing.'

'How else would he know?' Magiere continued shouting. 'Wynn is Darmouth's prisoner. And you're in league with those murdering *Anmaglâhk*. I won't swallow any more of your lies!'

Byrd held his guard, watching Magiere and Chap, but his answer was to Leesil. 'I told you before, my goals have nothing to do with you.'

'Faris knows about Leesil,' Magiere continued. 'He may even know where Leesil is . . . and that means Darmouth knows. Why else would his men try to take me, except to get to Leesil?'

Leesil didn't know how Magiere had learned all she knew, but events were starting to add up. He'd half-heartedly tried to believe that Byrd wasn't using him – yet. He'd dragged Magiere, Chap, and Wynn into danger. Even when he'd wanted to get them out again, he'd given in to their risky plans on the thin hope of finally learning what had happened to his parents. And Byrd was the one who'd pushed for that plan to proceed.

Leesil ached inside as he felt his past bleeding into the present. His selfish weakness had put Wynn into Darmouth's hands. But there was also more at stake than a search for two long-missing people. Much more.

'You think killing Darmouth will help anyone here?' Leesil asked, now that Byrd was forced to listen. 'You'll start a bloodbath. The other provinces and even his own officers will tear one another apart to take his place. Are you prepared for "your people" to get caught in the middle? Warlords and petty tyrants fighting each other at the front gates of Venjètz? You're deluded if you think you can stop it. As bad as things are, Darmouth holds this province together.'

Before Byrd answered, someone rattled the inn's front door as if trying to open it. Loud banging followed. Byrd started for the curtained doorway, but Chap snarled until he stopped.

'We're getting Wynn back,' Magiere said. 'And you're going to help.'

'And if she dies,' Leesil added to Byrd, 'so do you.'

Magiere glanced his way. Even with irises deeply black, Leesil saw her anger falter.

'I need to see who's come,' Byrd replied flatly, unaffected. 'It might be news of your friend.'

Leesil hesitated, then motioned Chap out of the way. The dog reluctantly backed up and Byrd headed out. Leesil followed to the curtain, watching through the crack.

Byrd paused at the front door with his hand on the latch. 'Who's there?'

'Baron Emêl Milea,' a muffled voice answered. 'I have a message for someone here.'

Byrd unlocked the door, and a slender man stepped inside. His open cloak exposed a green tunic and a straight saber sheathed on his hip.

Leesil knew him.

Older now, with thinning hair, this red-haired nobleman had chased him through the forest beyond the city walls. Eight years ago, Leesil had barely eluded the baron among the night trees. He also remembered Emêl leading the mount of a young girl given to him by Darmouth — an orphaned fifteen-year-old girl. Hedí, the only survivor of Leesil's first service to Darmouth, had been Emêl's reward for constant loyalty.

'You are the proprietor?' the baron asked.

Byrd nodded.

Tentatively, Baron Milea held out a folded parchment. Byrd took it and, upon opening the first fold, stopped to read something. He then opened the sheet completely and read further what was written on the parchment's full page. The barest hint of surprise crossed his features.

'Where did you get this?' he asked.

'Lady Progae. She is held at the keep . . . for her protection. Explain what this is about.'

'Leesil, Magiere,' Byrd called. 'Get out here.'

Leesil pushed the curtain aside, and Magiere and Chap followed him into the common room. Clover Roll perched on a table and only blinked as Chap passed by. At the sight of Leesil, Emêl's mouth opened slightly.

'You?' he breathed.

'This is Baron Emêl Milea.' Byrd gestured toward his guest. 'He brought us something interesting.'

'I know who he is,' Leesil answered with a glare. 'Lady Progae — Hedí Progae — is your mistress.'

Magiere glanced at him in alarm. Perhaps she remembered the name Faris had spoken before Leesil's night of madness.

Baron Milea nearly snorted in disgust. 'Do not feign concern for her welfare. I can guess what you are.'

Leesil jerked a stiletto from his left wrist. 'You won't have to guess.'

'Both of you stop it!' Byrd stepped between them, but it was Leesil he faced. 'Magiere, make him see some sense . . . if you want to help your little sage.'

Leesil remained where he was, and all Magiere did was step in next to him.

'What's this about?' she demanded of Byrd.

Byrd folded the parchment in half and handed it to Leesil. A few lines were scrawled in Belaskian on its back.

Take this to the farthest inn south of the merchant district. I will join you soon.

Leesil flicked the sheet fully open. More was written therein, obviously intended for Byrd.

Leave the inn, or you will be arrested shortly past sunset. I have learned there is a way to escape the keep from the lower level. I do not know more, except that it will take me to the woods on the lake's far shore. Take the bearer of this note, and go there to watch for me tonight. If my guide is correct, we have our way in.

Leesil stared at the parchment. Hedí Progae, the baron's slave consort, was no fool. She had purposefully kept all names out of the message, in case it was found.

'A hidden path from the keep,' Leesil whispered to no one in particular. 'With the city gate closed and outer wall alerted against escape.'

This was why his parents had fled there on the night he'd abandoned them.

'What?' Magiere asked. 'Leesil?'

She couldn't read well, so he read the note aloud to

her, pondering the words again as she listened. When he finished, she grabbed his arm, and her words were hurried and anxious.

'I know how much this means, that your parents might have escaped. That's why Byrd's informants never learned more of what happened to them. But Darmouth's soldiers will be on their way. We have to go now!'

Leesil sidestepped to the bar, watching Byrd, and lifted the glass off a lantern. He lit the parchment and dropped it on the floor, watching it burn black before grinding it with his boot.

Movement in the shadows below the tables and chairs caught his eye. Chap crept within lunging distance behind Byrd, his jowls quivering short of a snarl. Leesil looked away, so as not to draw anyone's attention toward the dog. Magiere thought only of getting him out of here, but Chap understood what she'd overlooked in panic.

'You're not leaving my sight,' he told Byrd.

The baron looked at the stout innkeeper. 'Who are you, and why would Hedí go to such lengths to send you this information? I know she has certain . . . proclivities for commoners, but what have you dragged her into?'

Instead of answering, Byrd glared at Leesil.

It now seemed possible that Leesil's parents had found a way out. He should've found relief in the thought, but he didn't. Hedí Progae must have worked a long time for the scattered pieces of Byrd's unfinished drawings. How ironic that she'd finished her desperate service this night, in the same note that brought Leesil his first hint of what had happened. That note would pull this province apart.

Byrd might have found a way into the keep for his *Anmaglâhk*.

Leesil could restrain him, but what of the man's elven conspirators? They might come for the innkeeper, and he would tell them everything. Even if Leesil killed Byrd, he couldn't be certain whether his father's old friend had betrayed him to the elves, to Darmouth, or both. The *Anmaglâhk* could be watching all of them, following everything Leesil did.

For any choice or none at all, Byrd's plot boxed Leesil in on all sides. And it had trapped Wynn in the worst place in Leesil's world.

'Do you want your lady back?' Byrd asked Emêl flatly, and looked at Magiere and Leesil. 'Do you want Wynn back?'

No one replied. No one had to.

'No matter what Hedí uncovered,' Byrd continued, 'her chance of reaching the lower levels and escaping are slim to none. Wynn's odds are worse. When Darmouth's men don't find Leesil here, he'll dangle the little sage piece by piece until you give yourself up.'

Magiere pulled on Leesil's arm. 'Then there's still time —'

'I said piece by piece,' Byrd repeated. 'Wait too long and not much of her will be left.'

Chap lunged with a loud snap of his jaws.

Byrd sprang away toward the bar's end. Baron Milea turned white, hand on his saber's hilt.

Leesil lifted his hand to Chap. The dog held his place, but his growls came in sharp, fast breaths as he watched Byrd.

'Whatever Lady Progae thinks she's found,' Byrd

continued, 'it has an entrance within the keep and an exit on the far shore. Leesil and I are the only ones who might locate a hidden exit in the forest. If you want my help, there'll be no more questions. Now, get your things . . . before the soldiers kick in my door.'

The baron scowled, looking at each person present as if finding himself in the worst of company. He clearly wasn't used to ultimatums, but his hand dropped from his saber hilt in surrender.

'I must get Hedí out of there,' he said.

The nobleman's determination puzzled Leesil. Why would one of Darmouth's remaining loyals risk so much for his bed slave?

Chap barked once, and Magiere pulled on Leesil's arm. 'Gear up, and I'll get our belongings. We're not coming back here, no matter how this ends.'

Clover Roll hissed loudly from his tabletop and arched his back. Leesil followed the cat's eyes to the window.

One shutter was open no more than a hand's width. A large robin rested upon the sill, its head stuck through the space.

Clover leaped across the tabletops, straight for the window. In a flurry of feathers the bird vanished from sight. Clover hit the shutters, knocking them wide as he tumbled into the street with a yowl.

'Better let out all your cats,' Leesil said to Byrd, and headed for the stairs behind Magiere.

Welstiel waited, observing Chane impatiently.

Chane looked deceptively peaceful, sitting cross-legged on the floor, hands on his knees. He'd finished washing the black from his hair and wore dark breeches and a tailored muslin shirt. The change brought the illusion of the young Noble Dead that Welstiel had met back in Bela.

The illusion shattered as Chane gasped and fell forward, catching himself with his hands.

Welstiel crouched down. 'What's wrong?'

Chane looked about, disoriented. It wasn't uncommon when he roused from sinking his awareness within that of a familiar.

'Cat . . . large cat,' he rasped, and looked at Welstiel with feral anger in his eyes. 'Darmouth has Wynn and he will torture her to get Leesil. We are getting into the keep – *now!*'

'Control yourself,' Welstiel ordered, 'and tell me what you heard and saw.'

Chane leaned forward on his hands, and for an instant Welstiel grew wary that his companion might lunge.

'Leesil . . . and your precious Magiere are going to try to breach the keep,' Chane whispered, 'and go after Wynn. Soon they may all be inside with Darmouth and his forces.'

'What? Magiere should be preparing to hunt you.'

The shadow of a thin smile crossed Chane's face, but his eyes held no amusement. He recounted all he had seen and heard through his bird, from the moment of Emêl's arrival, to Leesil reading Lady Progae's letter aloud, to the paunchy stray cat diving for the familiar.

Welstiel settled on the bed's edge.

An assassination attempt would be made on Darmouth, leaving Leesil with no other avenues to search for his parents. He would leave, and therefore so would Magiere. But now she was hunted by Darmouth and running straight into the warlord's hands.

'We go now,' Chane repeated. 'Either to the forest to trail them or . . .'

Welstiel shook his head and ran a hand over his face, pulling back his hair.

'No. If they find the exit for this rumored passage, we could not follow unseen and unheard. I will go to the bridge gatehouse and say that I have information regarding Magiere's whereabouts. Darmouth will be eager to hear this. You will pose as my manservant and keep your hood up. Once inside we will break away, but no bodies must be left visible. We assist Magiere from the shadows, as we did in Apudâlsat.'

Chane stared into the dark corner of the room. It was obvious his addled mind was not on Magiere's safety but rather on Wynn.

Getting out of the city gates wasn't as difficult as Magiere had expected.

She paid the stable bill for Port and Imp, packed their belongings in the wagon, and everyone climbed in. With their hoods up, almost no one gave them notice on the night streets. A small band of soldiers tried to question them, but Baron Milea pulled his hood back and ordered them off. The sergeant in charge nodded respectfully and waved his men out of their way.

Their first stop was the Bronze Bell. Emêl went up to his room while Magiere took everyone else to wait with the wagon at a nearby stable. She was slightly surprised when he returned with a chest and several canvas sacks of soft goods.

He'd gathered all of his belongings.

The bleary-eyed stable master brought out the baron's

horse and a second mount with a lady's flat saddle, likely intended for Hedí Progae. There was no sign of personal guards or retainers.

This confirmed Magiere's guess. Emêl planned to take his consort and run, likely for the Stravinan border. For all the worthless elites she'd met, it was strange in this fear-filled land to see a nobleman ready to abandon his way of life for someone else.

Emêl gathered canvas tarps and loaded them in the wagon's back. He looked up at Magiere.

'Soldiers at the city gate are looking for a dark-skinned man with white-blond hair.' Emêl didn't look at Leesil, but a grimace of distaste crossed his features. 'And now they will be on watch for a black-haired woman with a wolf. Some may know Byrd. I will ride up front with you, but the others must hide in the back.'

He held out a wool dress, and Magiere stared at it.

'Hedí is smaller than you, but you should still fit into this,' Emêl added. 'At least enough to pass with your cloak over it. The gate watch will hesitate to question a noble escorting a lovely woman out of the city.'

Leesil nearly hissed. 'It pays to be among Darmouth's favored, doesn't it?'

'Better than doing his dirty work,' Emêl returned with equal venom.

Leesil sat up but only returned Emêl's glare.

'That's enough from both of you,' Byrd snapped. 'Magiere, put on the dress, and Leesil, you keep quiet.'

Magiere wasn't certain how much the baron knew of Leesil's past. If Emêl had been a member of Darmouth's inner circle in Leesil's youth, he would certainly have his suspicions concerning Gavril and Nein'a, and thereby their son.

She unbuckled her sword and laid it under the wagon's bench, then took the dress from Emêl, not caring for how all this was playing out. Since the moment Wynn had been captured, Magiere had felt out of control. Leesil hadn't been himself since entering the Warlands, and pain emanated from him no matter how silent and cold he might act. Now they trusted their lives and Wynn's to one of Darmouth's inner circle and a two-faced spy with a soft spot for cats.

'Aren't you bringing your men?' Byrd asked Emêl. 'The gate guards might find it odd, your leaving without an escort.'

'Involving my men would make things too political,' Emêl answered. 'A lone noble with a woman only gives the guards something to snicker about. They will assume I'm returning later, but Hedí is all that matters to me now.'

Magiere climbed down and walked into the stable's back stall. She tried to slip the dress over her clothes. It caught on the hauberk, so she removed that and tried again. The dress was too tight. She took off her wool pullover, then had to remove the shirt as well. Glancing nervously over the stall's partition, she shivered in the cold air. She pulled the dress over her head, leaving her breeches and boots on. The dress was too short and barely closed in front, but with her cloak on and perhaps a blanket over her legs, it might do.

When she returned and stuffed her clothes behind the bench, she pulled a blanket out and placed it on the seat. Leesil, Byrd, and Chap concealed themselves beneath a canvas tarp in the wagon's back. Emêl shifted his sacks toward the rear, giving the illusion that the wagon was merely packed with stores.

'I hate this,' Leesil whispered from beneath the tarp. 'I'm sick of hiding.'

'We don't have a choice,' Magiere murmured back, and climbed onto the bench next to Emêl. 'Now, for the last time, be quiet!'

She draped the blanket over her legs, hiding the short skirt. Emêl took the reins and steered them into the open street. They followed the main way through Venjètz.

As they left the upper-class district, Magiere looked back to be sure Leesil remained covered. A spark of light glinted from somewhere to her left, and she twisted around.

Magiere looked at the buildings as the wagon continued on its way. Perhaps she'd only seen the light of the sparse street lanterns reflecting off something. A glass window?

Another quick glint came from farther behind on her left.

'Stop the wagon,' she whispered.

Emêl pulled up. 'What is it?'

She peered along the row of buildings – a narrow two-story inn, two smaller structures she couldn't name, and then a tanner's shop. All appeared quiet and dark. She felt foolish that her nerves had gotten the best of her.

'It's nothing,' she said. 'Move on.'

Emêl glanced back once with a frown, examining the street, then flicked the reins.

When they finally approached the main gates, none

of the soldiers even questioned Emêl as he ordered them to open up. One in a well-worn chain vest over quilted padding gave Magiere a long glance. His eyes drifted downward from her face, and he turned away with an amused smile and a shake of his head. She breathed a sigh of relief as they left Venjètz behind.

Emêl clucked to Port and Imp and turned them onto the main road. Magiere kept her eyes forward, not caring to see the rotting decorations upon the wall's outer iron spikes. It was bad enough that she smelled a thin stench and heard the low metal creak of a crow's cage swinging slightly in the low breeze.

The forest thickened around them as the city fell farther behind. The near-full moon shed some light on the open road. Frozen mud ruts made the wagon lurch and jerk too often. Magiere stayed quiet, finally risking a glance back to see that the city walls had disappeared behind them.

'Where to?' she asked.

'This road heads west into the foothills,' Emêl answered. 'We'll stop soon, and go on foot through the forest back to the lake.'

'Can the cargo get up now?' asked Byrd, voice muffled beneath the tarp.

'Yes,' Magiere answered. 'I doubt anyone travels the roads on so cold a night.'

Thrashing in the wagon's bed made her look back. Byrd, Chap, and Leesil shoved blankets, tarps, and other covering aside. Byrd rose up on one knee, looking into the forest.

'We're close enough,' he said, and pointed toward a spot ahead. 'Hide the wagon and horses there.'

Emêl steered the wagon in between two trees to a small brush-filled clearing. Everyone climbed out, and Leesil gathered blankets from the back. He held one up, and Magiere changed clothes in moderate privacy. Once she had the dress off and her shirt on, he strapped on his blades and lashed his toolbox to his back with a length of rope.

Magiere buckled down her hauberk. Leesil handed their two lanterns to Emêl and Byrd. He looked more like himself, now that he had something to act upon. He handed her a sheathed dagger, which she tucked into her belt. As soon as all were ready, Byrd led the way deeper into the forest.

It was a short walk before they emerged to moonlight shimmering upon the lake. Across the water was the black silhouette of the keep, its towers' crowns marked by the red-orange glow of their top braziers. Chap began sniffing the shore.

'It is a sound design,' Emêl said. 'Anyone approaching across the water would be picked off by archers, and the city itself makes for a difficult frontal assault. Either way, the keep is out of the reach of most siege engines.'

Magiere gazed out across the lake.

'Don't light the lanterns yet,' Leesil warned. 'They might be seen from the ramparts. Moonlight will serve us for now.'

Emêl frowned. 'What exactly are we looking for?'

When Leesil didn't answer, Magiere began with her own questions. 'How could any escape route from the keep allow Lady Progae to cross the lake? Would there be a boat hidden in the lower levels, something small that might go unnoticed? That won't help us get in, not until she's already out.'

Byrd shook his head. 'Too risky. Any escape route in case a siege breached the defenses would have to provide protection for those fleeing. If an enemy force took the keep, their own archers could pick off those in flight across the lake. No, it has to be something created when the keep was built, back in the days of King Timeron.'

Leesil approached the lake, and Magiere watched him stare at the water, lost in thought.

'Not across it,' he whispered, watching the soft ripples of water. 'But under it.'

'What nonsense have you got in your head?' Byrd asked.

'The keep was built on a flat depression in the land,' Leesil answered. 'The lake came afterward.'

Magiere didn't follow this. 'No one could swim the lake all the way underwater, and especially in the cold.'

'That's not what I meant,' Leesil replied.

'Oh, bloody deities,' Byrd whispered.

Magiere was about to tell him to shut his mouth, but Byrd stared at the water with Leesil's same knowing expression.

'If the keep was here before the lake,' Leesil continued, 'then what else might Timeron have built down there, hidden beneath the water?'

Byrd shook his head slowly. 'It's been right here in front me . . . all these years of searching.'

'A passage?' Magiere asked. 'Under the lake?'

Leesil didn't even nod. 'We have to get in the water and search below the surface.'

Emêl finally joined in. 'If it is under the lakebed, what could we possibly find?'

Leesil cast a scowl toward the baron but remained

civil in his reply. 'Anything that would hold up under that water over decades would have to be strongly reinforced. I wouldn't bury it, since flooded water would hide it well enough. And I'd make it out of thick stone that wouldn't decay.'

'Yes, but this winter is so . . .' Byrd paused, at a loss, looking at the thin ice over the lake's edge. 'All right, we'll try it.'

They all began stripping off gear, and Leesil was chosen to stay onshore to watch their weapons. Magiere stepped into the lake, its fringe ice cracking as her boots sank into the water. Byrd and Emêl followed.

Icy cold burrowed into her legs before the water even topped her boots. Both Byrd and Emêl began panting quickly as they too felt the cold. She'd expected the water to be bitter, but it was on the verge of freezing. She stepped back out as her toes became numb.

'This is insane,' Emêl said. 'Even if we find something, we will not be fit to breach the keep if we are half-dead with cold.'

Leesil stepped past Magiere into the water. He hurried back out, bending to rest his hands on his knees with a moan of frustration. When he looked up at Magiere, there was more doubt in his face than discomfort.

'When you're in . . . your other state,' he asked, 'do you feel the cold as much?'

Magiere didn't like where he was going with this. 'Not as much, sometimes not at . . . But I can't just make it happen. That level of . . . hunger . . . it has to start, before I can do anything with it.'

'Then think of something – anything that gets to you.' He grabbed her forearm. 'Wynn is in that keep, and the rest of us don't stand half the chance you might in that water. You have to try.'

It wasn't that he was asking her to do something difficult. Magiere would do anything for him. He was asking something she didn't know how to do.

'Remember the schooner to Bela,' he said, cocking one white eyebrow. 'You gave me coin to buy wine, because I was seasick, and I lost it all gambling with sailors. Then you got attacked by thugs, and I was so drunk that . . .'

Magiere crossed her arms and glared at him. Yes, and it was still one of the stupidest things he'd ever done, but not exactly the kind of thing that would accomplish what he asked of her.

'What?' Emêl asked blankly, and looked at Byrd. 'What has this to do with anything?'

Byrd shook his head and threw up his hands in disgust. 'Why are you asking me? Leesil —'

Leesil shot him an angry glare, and Byrd rolled his eyes, grumbling under his breath.

'This isn't going to work,' Magiere said.

Chap loped over, his long, silver-blue fur glinting in the moonlight. His crystalline eyes locked on hers. She felt a tickling at the edge of her thoughts.

Memories began to surface.

The dark world around her flashed white, as if someone had shoved a torch in front of her eyes. She blinked hard to shield her vision.

And there she saw the graveyard of Chemestúk, her home village. The memory was so strong, it blocked out the lake and forest around her for the moment.

Adryan had hated her since childhood, whispering

his lies to the other villagers. They'd shunned her, tormented her, and she'd grown up alone but for Aunt Bieja. She saw Adryan's greasy black hair and scarred face as he swung an iron-shod staff in his madness and spite. And she was afraid of him, as she scurried across the damp ground of the graveyard.

Hunger boiled in Magiere's stomach, and rage heated her flesh. She grabbed for her falchion, but it wasn't there.

The night sharpened as her sight expanded. The ache in her jaws brought tears to her eyes. She kept her lips tightly pressed together.

Adryan wasn't truly there, and she wanted something to kill.

'Hold on to it,' Leesil ordered, 'but don't let it take you. You take it instead. I'm right here with you, always, and Wynn needs us.'

Chap's summoned memory of Adryan faded, and Magiere saw only Leesil's narrow face. His hair burned with moonlight, and his amber irises were two suns that pained her eyes. But this was a pain she wanted, and it made her long for him. She clung to his presence, holding him in her awareness against the hunger burning up her throat.

Magiere looked to the lake. She tore at the hauberk with her fingers, and Leesil stepped close to help. He barely had it off of her as Magiere stepped into the water.

'What is she doing?' Emêl said, and stepped toward her. 'The lake is too cold.'

Magiere pivoted toward him and tensed, waiting to see if this were some *thing* she could fight.

'Get back!' Leesil warned, and shoved Emêl away. 'Magiere?'

She snapped her head toward him. His face brought clarity again. She nodded and stepped farther out, water rising past her waist and up her rib cage. The wet feeling left a distant sting upon her skin. It balanced the hunger, and she waded in until the water lapped over her shoulders.

'I'm right here,' Leesil called. 'Don't go under until you're ready.'

Magiere kept moving, listening to Leesil's voice. She let hunger stay with her, stronger than she'd ever allowed it by choice.

'Has she found anything yet?' Byrd asked from a distance.

'It has been too long,' came Emêl's voice. 'Get her out of there. She is in danger.'

A slight wave of cold passed through Magiere.

Had it been a long time? She shut out their voices. There was only Leesil, and hunger, and Wynn waiting. The cold passed away, and she took another step.

Her boot scraped across something hard. A boulder in the lake bottom?

Magiere let Adryan's face return . . . then the image of Welstiel standing over her mother's bed, watching Magelia bleed to death . . . and Chane stalking them into the Apudâlsat forest.

Rage spread the hunger into her limbs, until she felt its heat in her face. She dove under, her night sight fully open.

Scant ripples of moonlight danced across the lake bottom, making mud, water weeds, and stones quiver before her eyes. She saw a clear patch that appeared to be made of stone, but when she scraped at the mud around it with her boot, she couldn't be certain it was more than boulder. Magiere swam deeper toward the lake bottom, clawing through mud with her hands.

She uncovered a flat panel of stone, too flat and smooth to be natural. When she dug away more silt, she exposed a clean edge. It ran level out into the lake, where it was too dark for even her eyes. She faced along the direction of its line and pushed off the bottom.

Magiere shot up through the lake's surface to see the braziers of the keep dead ahead. She thrashed around toward the far shore.

'Here!' Magiere tried to call, though she couldn't be certain the word came out. Her teeth hurt, and speaking was difficult.

'Come back,' came Leesil's voice.

He looked small and far away in Magiere's sight. And he began to fade, as if the darkness suddenly grew deeper. Coldness began burrowing into her limbs and chest.

'Magiere,' Leesil shouted. 'Come back – now!'

She couldn't feel the lake bottom and started clawing at the water's surface to pull herself toward him. He became clearer again as she grew closer.

He looked afraid, staring at her with wide eyes, and he stepped forward until she heard his boots crack ice and splash into water. Why was he afraid?

Hunger vanished, and the water felt like ice shards being dragged across her skin.

'Magiere!'

Her legs and arms went numb. She found the lake floor when her legs stopped kicking and her feet hit something solid. She forced herself toward Leesil, and the water receded to her waist. Then she started to sink again, and couldn't stand up anymore.

Leesil splashed toward her and grabbed her wrist. The last thing Magiere saw was Emêl dashing in beside him to take her other arm.

Magiere opened her eyes again and found herself looking up into the dark forest canopy. Leesil's face was above her, his hair glinting in the moonlight. She tried to reach his face and found she was wrapped in wool blankets, lying in his lap.

'That was foolish,' Emêl said. 'You could have died.'

Byrd stood a way off, staring out over the lake. 'But she found it.'

'Yes, she did,' Leesil said, his eyes remaining on her.

'How . . . long?' Magiere asked, and heard the chatter of her own teeth as she shivered.

'You were out for only a moment,' Leesil whispered. 'And you need to stay awake now.'

Her teeth kept chattering. 'It's . . . a tunnel. Straight line from where I stood . . . in the water. Exit must . . . behind us.'

Leesil looked up at Emêl. 'We need a fire, somewhere out of sight. Now!'

Emêl nodded, crouching down. 'I will take care of her. You help Byrd find the exit.'

Leesil looked down at her uncertainly, and Magiere felt his arms close tight around her, not wanting to let her go.

Magiere closed her eyes and saw an image of Wynn. 'Go,' she said to him.

★   ★   ★

Leesil headed into the trees behind Byrd, with Chap loping out.

He didn't like this. He should be the one to watch over Magiere.

Perhaps Emêl's concern for Hedí Progae was genuine. Perhaps he wasn't a complete toady to a tyrant. And he'd run into freezing water to help save Magiere. None of this meshed with what Leesil knew of would-be nobles, who sat and nodded agreement like bobbing crows on Darmouth's council.

Byrd, on the other hand, hadn't been remotely concerned about Magiere, and now he trotted through the forest in search of the tunnel's hidden exit.

'Here,' he called from beyond a tall fir tree. 'If the tunnel runs straight from the keep, the exit will be along this line.'

Leesil checked the sight line, shifting about until he caught a glimpse of the lake through the branches. Chap began sniffing the ground.

'Search for anything that doesn't smell natural,' he told the dog. 'Anything that might be man-made.'

Chap licked his nose with a rumble, as if to say he didn't need to be told.

Leesil dropped to the ground. They could be looking for anything. It might even be buried, the opening unearthed from the inside only when the exit was finally used. Or it could be covered with decades of forest mulch.

Byrd dropped down beside him. 'Timeron was quick-witted, from what I've heard. And remember that he was trying to hold off men like Darmouth's grandfather, which was no small feat. He'd have found craftsmen and builders clever enough to create more than just a hole in the ground.'

Leesil nodded, still wondering what they searched for. All nobles holding a keep or castle made certain of an escape route for the family, but this was by far the most elaborately planned route he'd ever heard of. A water-tight tunnel constructed before the plain was flooded.

He'd breached more than one stronghold in his life, but not like this. Scaling a wall or opening a hidden bolt-hole was simple by comparison. The tunnel had to emerge where the ruler and any retainers might rea-sonably escape assaulting forces. Looking around, all Leesil saw were trees, brush, and half-frozen ground.

'It has to be right here somewhere.' Byrd scraped traces of snow and brittle mulch to expose the earth beneath. 'Give me Magiere's falchion. You use the narrow wing on one of your blades.'

They took a position five paces from each other and worked their way across the forest floor. Every two paces they rammed steel into the earth to probe for anything hidden below. Chap circled through the area around them, sniffing everything.

Leesil found nothing. In several places, the space between the trees was too narrow for any exit. Byrd's countenance was calm, but Leesil sensed that he grew anxious.

'We're missing something,' Byrd finally muttered.

Leesil hesitated. 'This is why my parents ran into the keep. The exit has to be here.'

Byrd sighed. 'One of them must have known.'

Leesil thought back into the past. 'They would have fled through the exit, perhaps exposing it somehow, but there's no sign of escape here. Did they get away or not?'

'Pay attention.' Byrd stood up, looking around. 'All right, if it's not in the ground, where could it be?'

Leesil looked about and saw nothing but snow-dusted earth, trees, and brush. He'd found bolt-holes within the walls and towers of strongholds. Here in the forest there were no designed structures to consider. Then he stopped and looked up at the trees rising into the air.

Towers – forest towers of wood.

Three thick and massive gnarled oaks stood on a direct line to the keep across the lake. At this time of year they were bare of leaves, but the one in the center seemed . . . wrong. He stepped closer, running his hand over each tree. The middle tree was wider than the other two. Some of its bark crumbled in his hand. This center one was old. Perhaps dead?

'Chap!' Leesil called. 'Come here.'

The dog loped over to his side. Chap circled the trees, his nose tracing exposed roots up to the trees' trunks. He stopped and leaned his forehead and snout up against the center one as he closed his eyes.

'Is it dead?' Leesil asked.

Chap looked up and barked once.

'Yes,' Leesil whispered.

Byrd raised his eyebrows at this exchange. 'So? What of it?'

'I'd guess it hasn't been alive for a long while, but it's still upright because it's soundly lodged between the other two.' He pointed from the tree's base toward the lake. 'Look. That's where Magiere came out of the water.'

'A tree for an exit?' Byrd scowled and circled around, studying the triple trunks.

Leesil circled as well. Stopping at the back, he felt the bark for knots and crevices. He found nothing.

'If you think it has a door or hatch,' Byrd said, with a doubtful shake of his head, 'the latch or bar would be on the inside. The engineer wouldn't want anyone getting in . . . only out.'

'That doesn't mean I can't find a way in,' Leesil answered.

'All right then.' Byrd stepped back and hefted Magiere's falchion to swing.

'No! That'll leave the keep wide open,' Leesil warned.

Byrd whirled toward him in anger. 'Then what would you have us do?'

Chap rumbled, moving in on Byrd. Leesil shook his head at the dog.

An open back door would serve a rebellion – or an assassination. He'd have to watch Byrd carefully, but short of killing him, there was only one answer in the end.

Wynn had been right. This province was headed toward conflict, and the removal of Darmouth would sink it – and perhaps all of the Warlands – into blood-shed. Darmouth or those close to him had to be warned before Byrd's *Anmaglâhk* allies could act.

Leesil's stomach knotted. He had to save the monster who'd made him kill again and again for the lives of his parents.

'Wait,' he snapped at Byrd, and stepped close to the dead oak. He doubted they could hack through with only a sword. There had to be some sign of where the opening might be. The darkness made it difficult to see any detail, but he felt along the rough surface for anything odd.

At the place where the curve of the center trunk met its companions was a line. Some of the dead bark had broken away over the years. The more he inspected, the more a pattern emerged. A definite crack of decay ran vertically along the crevice.

'Here,' he said. 'Chip away lightly along this line. But be quiet about it.'

Leesil stepped back, and Byrd chipped at the crevice with the falchion's point. The noise made Leesil flinch. They were far from the city, but he still turned about to glance in all directions through the forest.

At first Leesil saw nothing and held up a hand for Byrd to stop. When he ran his fingers across bare wood where the bark was gone, he found a thin crack in the exposed surface. He pulled one of his winged blades, sank its tip into the crack, and levered it to the side. Byrd joined him, pushing with the falchion's blade. They worked in turns, one prying so the other could slip a blade farther in.

A crack of splitting wood answered. Leesil pushed his blade deeper, and they both heaved again. A louder crack and snap came this time.

Byrd stumbled sideways into Leesil before righting himself. A piece of the tree's wood broke away, and Leesil stared into a jagged dark hole the size of his fist. He braced his foot on the tree's roots where they met with the trunk, and stepped up high enough to slide his hand in.

The hole's depth was about half his forearm's length, and then he felt nothing but open space. The dead oak between its siblings was hollow.

Leesil felt along the inside surface and touched a narrow but thick strip of metal. When he wiggled it, it spun sideways, mounted on some nail or pin at its midpoint. Nothing happened, and he sank his arm farther into the hole. He felt around the inside, found two more metal straps within reach, and twisted each one.

A large oblong piece of the trunk fell outward against him, and he jumped back out of its way. It toppled, thumping against the tree roots, and Leesil stared into a dark opening large enough for a crouched man to crawl through.

The builders couldn't hide hinges and had simply used the lines of the tree to cut a hidden hole in the trunk. They'd secured the panel from the inside – bark and all – with simple pivoting straps of metal that braced against the opening's inside.

'That's it,' Byrd said. 'I'll get Magiere and Emêl.'

He walked away. Byrd's eagerness roused a sickening knot in Leesil's stomach. He and Magiere could get Wynn back, but they still had to keep Byrd in check.

Leesil leaned into the opening, and looked down. In the dark, he barely made out metal rungs forming a ladder down to a stone alcove deep beneath the triple trees. There was no wall on the alcove's side facing in the direction of the keep. This would be the tunnel they sought.

For a moment, Leesil imagined the panicked faces of his parents appearing in the alcove to look at him.

Byrd hurried through the trees toward the road rather than to the small fire where Emêl and Magiere waited. When he had the wagon in sight, he took out the strange small mirror the *Anmaglâhk* had given him and stepped to where he could clearly see the near-full moon. He tilted the mirror and aimed its reflected light toward where they'd left the horses.

He'd done the same thing as the wagon had headed for the front gates of Venjètz. Carefully shifting in the dark beneath the canvas, he peered out the back and used the mirror. He wasn't even certain if they were nearby, but they always seemed to appear whenever he wanted to contact them.

Anxiety built as he waited. Then a light sparked in the night woods. Byrd took a deep breath of relief.

At least one of his allies had escaped the city and understood this was an opportunity that might not come again. He signaled his acknowledgment and ran back through the forest to find Magiere and Emêl.

The *Anmaglâhk* would follow.

14

Wynn's feeble pounding on the locked door received no answer. No food or water had been brought, and her thirst grew with the pain in her head. She crawled back onto the narrow bed with no blanket and huddled in her sheepskin coat, trying to keep warm. Her right eye opened only halfway. The inside of her cheek felt raw where it had ground against her teeth when she was struck down.

Wynn was alone and imprisoned.

The soldiers had searched her before leaving and found the other dagger strapped to her wrist. They took it and both sheaths and her pack. After they left, she put her hands into her coat pockets for warmth and touched the one thing they had missed — the cold lamp crystal. She had left behind her working journals and notes at Byrd's inn, as well as Chap's talking hide.

She hoped that Magiere and Chap had escaped, and felt ashamed for screaming out the instant she was in trouble. Her companions would not be able to get her out. Darmouth knew who they were and had set a trap for them. She saw no way for her companions to reach her without being captured. And she did not wish that to happen, even to save her.

Footsteps grew loud out in the hall. Wynn was uncertain whether to approach the door or hide behind the bed. Frozen, she remained huddled upon the bed, waiting.

'How dare you?' said a haughty female voice outside the door. 'I am bringing the prisoner her supper.'

'Lady Progae, I . . . I can't,' replied a young male voice, stuttering with uncertainty.

Wynn sat up. The woman's name was familiar, but she could not remember where she had heard it.

'I've orders not to open the door,' the man continued, 'Lieutenant Omasta said —'

'Do you know who I am?' the woman asked. 'I will soon be the matron of this keep. I do not forget a face. Now open the door!'

A moment of silence followed, and then a rattling at the lock. The door swung inward.

Grasping its handle was a young soldier no older than twenty, and likely less. A small-boned woman stood in the opening. She had pale skin with dark hair cut above her shoulders and a velvet ribbon around her throat. She held a wooden tray with a clay bowl and pewter tankard.

It was the same woman who had stopped Darmouth from stepping on Wynn's face.

Lady Progae stepped past the anxious guard, and her glare encouraged him to close the door quickly. The instant it was shut, she put the tray on the floor and fumbled beneath her voluminous skirt.

Wynn watched closely but stayed on the bed. Lady Progae removed a canvas sack tied about her waist with a bit of rope and placed it on the floor with gentle care.

'We have little time,' she whispered. 'That boy outside may be easy to cow, but if I stay too long, he will call for a superior.'

Wynn stared at her. Who was this woman?

Lady Progae crouched and carefully opened the canvas bag. A small brown-black cat crawled out. It plopped its hind end down, twitching its stub of a tail, and looked up at Wynn. The cat lifted its tiny muzzle with a soft mew for Lady Progae, who answered with a 'shush' and pulled a heavy brass candlestick from the bag.

She stood up and stripped off her velvet gown to expose a plain muslin dress beneath. She removed this and began pulling her own gown back on.

'What are you doing?' Wynn asked.

Lady Progae took the tankard from the tray and handed it to Wynn. 'It is only water, but I assume you need it.'

Too thirsty to question, Wynn gulped down the chill liquid. The cat meowed, and the woman glanced down at it.

'My name is Hedí Progae,' she said to Wynn. 'Do not be alarmed or cry out, no matter what you see.'

The cat hunched down on the stone floor, and a rippling swell passed through its shoulders.

Wynn stopped drinking, tankard poised at her lips.

An undulating ripple cascaded down the cat's body, and its torso swelled in lurches.

Wynn backed into the bed's headboard.

The cat's feet grew, then its legs. Black-brown fur receded to expose bare flesh. Its body continued to expand at a rapid pace, and fur on its head elongated to shiny hair. Its front paws became hands.

Out of the grotesquely writhing form appeared the face of a girl with dark eyes and a smooth dusky complexion. She stood up, slender and naked, and Wynn's mouth dropped open, dribbling water down her chin.

Hedí Progae retrieved a short cotton shift from the bag.

'I am sorry I could not bring anything more,' she whispered to the girl. 'I was afraid my skirts already looked too bulky.'

'Oh, this is fine,' replied the girl, and looked at Wynn with a wide grin. 'Hello!'

Wynn wiped her chin, mouth still half-open.

'This is Korey,' Hedí said. 'Some of her family are . . . have certain abilities. We are here to help you.'

Fatigue and pain kept Wynn's scholarly instincts from rising up. All she noted was how much the child resembled the Móndyalítko she'd encountered during the journey into Droevinka with Leesil and Magiere.

'We must hurry,' Hedí said. 'If we can get to the lower levels, Korey says there is a way to escape the keep and reach the forest across the lake – outside the city.'

This was happening too fast. Wynn was desperate, but she hesitated to blindly trust someone she had just met in the company of this strange child.

'A way to escape?' Wynn whispered. 'We cannot swim through freezing water, and a hidden boat would be spotted by soldiers walking the keep walls.'

Hedí's face flattened in quiet anger. 'This child's father took a great risk to show her a door he called "a portal" and promised she could escape through it, if need be. That is all I know, but we have to go down and find it.'

'If she knows a way to escape,' Wynn asked, 'why come for me? Why not just leave?'

'Because I might need assistance,' Hedí answered bluntly. 'And I do not care to leave anyone in Darmouth's hands, if possible. You would not last long in any further "conversation" with the lord of this keep.'

Perhaps Wynn had spent too much time in this threatening land, with Leesil seeing plots and ploys all around. Or maybe she began to see things from his perspective. In the end, she had no choice.

'How do we reach the lower levels?' she asked.

'Then you are with us?'

'Yes.'

'Good. The corridors running north and south on the main floor end at doors that must lead below. There will be guards to get past, which would be more difficult to deal with by myself.'

The thought of facing more of Darmouth's soldiers made Wynn reluctant again, but she nodded. Hedí picked up the discarded muslin dress and held it out to her.

'Put this on,' she said. 'At present, Darmouth and Omasta are distracted. No one else will take notice of a servant in my company.'

Wynn stripped off her coat and short robe to put on the maid's dress. Hedí pulled a white cloth out of her gown's sleeve and wrapped it about Wynn's hair, then stuffed Wynn's coat and short robe into the bag.

Hedí appraised Wynn, nodded in approval, and snatched up the brass candlestick. 'I will call in the guard. Stand before the door, just as you are, and let his suspicion draw him in. Korey, it is time to be a cat again.'

Something about Hedí reminded Wynn of Magiere. Perhaps it was the way she took charge, as if it were her natural role. That thought vanished as Wynn stood in wonder, watching Korey revert to her previous form.

Thin fur sprouted from the girl's soft skin. Hands and

feet became tiny paws. Her body shriveled and shrank until the shift dropped around her to the floor. The small brown-black cat squirmed out of the shift's neck. Hedí shoved the girl's clothing back inside her bag, then picked up Korey to tuck her in as well. She handed the bag to Wynn.

'Ready?' she asked, and stepped back beside the door.

Wynn was not remotely ready.

Hedí kicked the tray with its bowl, and Wynn jumped at the racket as pottery clattered across the floor.

A key rattled. The door swung open. The young guard looked in, one hand on the hilt of his sheathed shortsword.

'Lady?' he said.

Wynn's small hands closed tight on the bag's scrunched opening.

The guard's eyes widened at the sight of her changed attire. He took one quick step through the door.

Hedí swung. The candlestick's wide base caught the young man squarely in the back of his head. He crumpled to all fours, but started to rise. Hedí swung again, and the soldier went down, eyes rolling closed.

Wynn knelt, feeling the man's throat and listening at his mouth.

'What are you doing?' Hedí asked.

'He is still breathing,' Wynn answered with relief.

'He is a servant to Darmouth. Save your concern for yourself.'

Hedí crouched, setting the candlestick down, and took the guard's key ring from his belt hook. She pulled his shortsword as well, tentatively lifted the weapon, shook her head slightly, and set it back down. In its place, she drew the dagger on the man's belt.

Wynn watched with growing concern as Hedí eyed the blade's sharp tip and glanced down at the defenseless young soldier's exposed back. Perhaps Hedí was not so like Magiere after all. Wynn grabbed the candlestick off the floor, holding it in one hand and the canvas bag in the other. She stepped over the guard to stand above Hedí.

Hedí glanced up at her once with a frown and then rose. Wynn followed as the woman stepped out of the room and locked the door behind them.

Welstiel rode ahead of Chane as they approached the gatehouse before the keep's bridge. They could have walked, but he had decided to pay the stable bill and retrieve their horses. This delayed them for some time, as the stable master had retired and had to be sent for. Looking down on the gatehouse soldiers from horseback would give him a more noble and imposing air. Welstiel had also taken time to dress carefully, appearing exactly as he had on his first visit, with a black cap covering the white patches at his temples. Chane wore a cloak with the hood up and remained silent as he rode behind.

Four soldiers were stationed before the bridge gatehouse. Welstiel halted his horse and waited for one to approach him. A middle-aged man with a heavily scarred face came up – the same one who had escorted Welstiel inside on his first visit.

'Your business?' he asked gruffly.

'I met with Lord Darmouth a few evenings past,' Welstiel said. 'I have come with further news of the hunter he hired. Inform your lord, as he will want to see me.'

Welstiel had the appearance and manner of an outland noble, and the guard studied him for only a moment before turning around.

'Open the way!' he called out, and the gates swung wide as the scarred soldier waved Welstiel onward. 'Follow me, sir. You'll wait in the inner courtyard until my lord has been informed.'

They crossed the bridge behind the soldier. When they passed through the keep's main gates and tunnel into the courtyard, Welstiel dismounted. Chane followed his lead and stood behind him. They left their horses with the courtyard soldiers and trailed their guide to the keep's wide doors on the far side. The soldier had already opened one of the doors when he realized his visitors were still following.

The scarred soldier raised a hand for them to wait as instructed, but Welstiel did not wish for Darmouth to know of his presence.

'What is your name?' Welstiel asked.

The soldier appeared taken aback. 'Devid, sir. I'll announce your arrival, if you'll wait here.'

Welstiel guessed most of Darmouth's men would be out looking for Magiere. He stepped back from the door compliantly and glanced about. Aside from one man leading their horses off, there were three others in the courtyard. Welstiel was hesitant to use the mental tricks of an undead in the open, but so long as the target was calm, any onlookers would be none the wiser. Chane shifted closer toward the doors, watching him curiously.

Welstiel motioned for Devid to join him with a curt wave of his hand. Devid scowled, but stepped forward. Looking into the man's eyes, Welstiel spoke in a low thrum that carried his suggestions into the man's thoughts.

'Perhaps we could wait inside, out of the cold?'

Devid blinked twice. 'Yes . . . it is cold out . . . but you're not to leave the entryway.'

Welstiel leaned closer, glancing toward the tunnel to the bridge. 'Your lord called you to the Bronze Bell Inn, did he not? He needs your service even now.'

He focused an image in his mind of Darmouth ordering Devid to the inn. He did not even look at Devid, but waited.

A moment passed. Devid took two steps into the courtyard toward the tunnel. He looked back once at Welstiel. The man's blank expression clouded with confusion, then settled into a stoic urgency. He hurried off across the courtyard.

Welstiel watched him leave, holding the image of Darmouth in his mind until Devid was far into the tunnel and approaching the keep's outer gate. He waited for Chane's usual comment. Every time Welstiel used any ability as a Noble Dead, it elicited some sardonic remark from his companion. He had become accustomed to it, but this time Chane remained silent.

Welstiel looked back. The door was ajar, and Chane was gone.

He hurried inside to find the wide entryway empty. Welstiel looked up the stairs ahead.

Chane had run off to save his little sage once again.

Welstiel's anger passed quickly. He might be better off alone in watching over Magiere, especially with Chane's obsession constantly distracting him. It would certainly be easier to move about the keep. Welstiel could see that a time would come when a choice might be necessary: either to be rid of Chane, or to remove the object of his distraction once and for all.

The sounds of male chatter carried from the meal hall. He hurried along the opposite wall away from the voices, and ducked through the archway into the counsel hall. Before he looked back to be certain no one saw him, he sensed something warm and alive within the hall.

Two wolfhounds with wiry gray fur lay at the hall's back beneath the tapestries. Both stood up at the sight of him.

Welstiel felt the long-dormant predator within each of them, a trace that decades of domestication had not fully erased. He could guide that instinct with purpose. He had done so once to bring a wolf within Chane's reach for the making of a familiar. Dogs were easier to seduce, already pliant to human masters.

He projected a sense of calm toward them. The taller one walked over and licked his hand. Its back nearly reached Welstiel's hipbone.

Welstiel looked around the large room. Nothing had changed from his first visit. He examined the table, chairs, and tapestries, annoyed that he had been forced to step into a place with no other exit.

The voices across the entryway quieted for a moment. He listened carefully, hoping for a chance to leave and locate Magiere. A deep male voice said something unintelligible. Two . . . no, three people stepped into the entryway, footfalls growing louder as they approached the counsel hall.

Welstiel glanced about the room once more. He could

handle Darmouth but did not want to be exposed just yet. And Darmouth was not alone.

Hurrying along the side wall, Welstiel ducked low behind the table and chairs as he crossed to the tapestry of a lone horseman, hoping there was room to hide behind it. When he lifted the edge, he found an opening built into the stone wall. Stairs led downward, and he stepped inside, trying to still the tapestry's swing as footsteps entered the council hall.

Welstiel took two steps down the stairs and then remained silent. He did not move. Something brushed his leg, and he looked down. Both wolfhounds had followed him. The taller gazed up with liquid hazel eyes.

He could not risk sending them back and attracting attention and placed his hand on one dog's head to quiet it.

The tunnel beneath the lake was narrow. Leesil took the lead with a lantern. Chap came next. Magiere followed with Emêl behind her, and Byrd brought up the rear. The passage wasn't a straight line as expected, and Leesil wondered about the long, gradual curve. The stone walls were cold and watertight, but even so, the lantern's light glistened off their damp surfaces.

Leesil had made certain that Magiere was recovered enough to continue. Her hair was nearly dry, and she no longer shivered, but she was obviously fatigued, either from cold or her dhampir state, or both. He knew she was troubled about Wynn, about this search for his parents . . . and about him. He glanced back.

'Are you all right?'

She held their other lantern low at her side. 'Yes, but we left an undead loose in Venjètz.'

Leesil frowned. He hadn't given the undead another thought since their failed hunt. There was truth enough in what she said, but it wasn't what was really on her mind. It was just one more thing that had gone wrong in this fool's venture into his past.

'We can't save everyone,' he answered, and focused on the tunnel ahead. 'Sometimes we can only save ourselves.'

A sentiment expressed by his parents for many years. He didn't like hearing it from his own lips, but right now he had enough to deal with, as did Magiere.

The tunnel kept on for so long that Leesil became anxious. Then the lantern's light hit upon a surface straight ahead, and he spotted the end wall.

'Leesil!' Emêl called out.

He looked back, holding up his lantern, and Magiere turned as well. Emêl stood alone, facing back the way they'd come.

'What?' Leesil asked. 'Where's Byrd?'

'Gone,' Emêl said, his voice low. 'I thought he was right behind me all the way, and now he's gone.'

Leesil stepped around Chap, but there wasn't enough room to get by Magiere and Emêl. 'When did you last see him?'

Emêl let out a sharp exhale. 'I don't know . . . a while. I didn't hear anything. I looked back once I saw the tunnel's end, and he was gone.'

Leesil cursed himself for letting Byrd take the rear. Watching over Magiere and hurrying to Wynn had distracted him.

'Why would he leave us?' Emêl asked.

Magiere blinked several times before she looked at Leesil. 'You'd better tell him. I don't know what to do, and he might be able to help.'

This wasn't a good idea. The baron was well-favored in Darmouth's circle. How else had he survived all these years, in addition to being gifted the daughter of Progae for his loyalty? Still, who better to give Darmouth warning of an assassination plot than a trusted noble? However, in the end, that might also lead to mass arrests of anyone who'd ever been seen inside Byrd's establishment.

'Tell him,' Magiere insisted.

'What is this about?' Emêl demanded. 'I have had enough secrets for one night.'

Magiere answered when Leesil remained silent. 'We think Byrd is planning to assassinate Darmouth.'

'Magiere!' Leesil snapped.

'And he has a good chance of succeeding,' Magiere continued, 'with some skilled assistance.'

Leesil sighed. There was nothing left for it but to tell Emêl everything. 'Your tyrant master has to be warned . . . and protected. If he dies now, your petty nobles will slaughter everyone in their paths in trying to take his place. Or the other province rulers will swarm in, trying to do the same.'

Emêl was silent for a moment, his gaze shifting suspiciously between Leesil and Magiere. 'You should have told me this earlier, before we left the city.'

'Don't tell me you could've done something,' Leesil snapped back at him. 'You wouldn't have lived long enough. Byrd's not some penny-grubbing informant, and he wouldn't have given you one blink to draw your sword.'

Magiere leaned back against the tunnel wall in frustration. 'The only reason he helped us was to find this tunnel. He's gone, and that means he's in a hurry to put his scheme into motion.'

Emêl fell silent, watching both of them with a bit more confusion than suspicion, but he finally glared at Leesil alone.

'You!' he said. 'I can guess the things you did for Darmouth in your day – no worse than what's whispered of those Móndyalítko always in his shadow. Why would you care what happens to anyone here?'

Leesil's head felt like it would split. The pressure vented at Emêl.

'All you want is your prized consort,' he shot back, his voice growing more strained with each word. 'How many times did you close your eyes and grovel for Darmouth, while others suffered and died? Don't you dare question my motives.'

Emêl's features became more pronounced in the lantern light as every muscle in his face clenched and held tight in suppressed anger.

'Is there anyone inside we can trust?' Magiere asked abruptly, and Emêl's hard gaze shifted to her. 'What about that lieutenant, Omasta?'

'Omasta?' Emêl blinked and pushed reddish hair back off his forehead. 'Yes, he would see to his lord's safety.'

'And what's Darmouth holding over his head?' Leesil asked bitterly.

'Nothing,' Emêl replied in kind. 'He is Darmouth's bastard son.'

Magiere stood up straight. 'What?'

'Darmouth brought back some woman from a raid into the west, the province of Lùkina Vallo,' Emêl said, and waved aside any more questions. 'This was long ago, and I do not recall her name. He put her up in a cottage and eventually lost interest in her. One night I went with him to her home to reclaim personal items left behind. We found only the boy, Omasta, for his mother had died of fever. I persuaded Darmouth to take the boy to the barracks, let him live there as a servant for the lower officers. Years later he distinguished himself in the ranks, and he still sees Darmouth as a savior . . . because of what I did. Any mention of assassination will set him to protecting his father at all costs. He will close the city down and start making arrests, including any outsider who warned him.'

Magiere closed her eyes. 'That's the end of it. We are on our own.'

Leesil turned away. It wasn't surprising for a bastard son to crave any favor or position of note in place of a father's open recognition.

'We can't go after Byrd,' Leesil said. 'Once inside, we'll do what we can to leave a warning or stop him ourselves. First we find Wynn . . . and Hedí Progae.'

Chap was quiet during this whole exchange, and Leesil found the dog sniffing about the tunnel's end.

Rather than a hinged door, the entire end wall was thick solid wood beams held together with iron straps lightly marred by rust and age. It seemed too solid, perhaps having been replaced over the years. A quick inspection revealed that it slid down along grooves in the tunnel's side walls and was raised into a ceiling slot by a set of chains dropping out of holes in the ceiling's stone.

'Too easy,' Magiere said over Leesil's shoulder.

'No,' he answered. 'Just a draft-door . . . something to pass through quickly . . . and maybe block off afterward.'

He knelt down with the lantern and heard Magiere step closer. He tipped the lantern to direct its light to the lower left corner of the wooden portal. A bar of aged steel was mounted against the bottom. It was so dark it melded with the wood and stone without the light shining upon it.

'Slide bolts,' he explained. 'On both sides. Easy to kick into place and seal the door. Most wouldn't notice these, if they didn't already know they were here. Pursuing forces have to batter down the portal from the inside, should they find it.' He ran his hand over the wood. 'The passage beyond is likely steep, narrow stairs leading up, making it difficult to use even a small ram to bring it down. A simple and efficient design.'

Leesil stood up, gripped the dangling chain, and pulled. It came down more easily than expected, and the wooden portal scraped along the wall channels up into the ceiling. Somewhere in the ceiling or walls there was a counterweight doing most of the work.

As he'd guessed, a steep stone staircase on the other side led upward and was just wide enough for one person. Each step was deep enough for only his boot, from toe to heel. He climbed upward, and Magiere followed. Farther behind he heard Chap's claws on the steps and glanced down once to see Emêl's glowering face in the lantern's dim light as the baron followed last.

At the top, Leesil came upon bare stone blocking his way.

'Now what does your *expertise* tell you?' Emêl whispered.

'Just wait,' Magiere replied, and her slipping patience was plain in her voice.

Leesil traced the mortared stones with his fingers. However it opened, it had to be simple for anyone fleeing the keep. Any mechanism had to stand the wear of moisture over the years. Rails, hinges, and mechanized devices wouldn't work, and would be visible from his side of the wall. He pulled out a stiletto and tested the cracks.

The stones were chiseled to fit like huge bricks. He found a crack between two at the left side where there was no mortar at all. He checked the top of the wall. The line between the top row of stones and the ceiling was completely unmortared.

Leesil handed Magiere his lantern, and she pulled his toolbox out of its makeshift rope straps on his back. He removed a thin hookwire from the foldout panel lid and handed the box back to her. She tucked it into the ropes again. Leesil slipped the wire into the crack above the top row of stones.

The wire strut slid all the way in until he held its end with only his fingertips. He worked along the crack, slipping it in and out again and again. Then it jammed to a stop, sinking only an inch or more near the wall's midpoint.

Leesil shifted the wire back and forth, feeling it scrape on something metallic. He pulled the wire out and tucked it into the back of his wrist sheath.

'It pivots,' he said. 'Get ready. We won't know what's on the other side until it's too late.'

Leesil put his shoulder against the wall's left side and pushed. At the sound of grating stone, Magiere reached around his chest and flattened her hand against the wall to assist.

It pivoted at the center, just as he'd expected. A thick metal rod must have been run through the wall's mid-point. The side he pushed spun inward while its opposite end turned outward. He dropped to a crouch, stiletto in hand, and looked through the opening on his side.

There was an empty room with more stone walls. It was so small there was barely enough room to lie down on the floor. In the far wall was a stout wooden door with a metal-shuttered peephole. This room was most likely a cell for prisoners.

Magiere leaned out the opening on the rotated partition's other side. She stepped into the small room with her falchion drawn. Leesil followed, heading straight for the door, and found it locked or somehow barred. Even worse, there wasn't a keyhole.

'Now what?' Magiere asked.

Byrd shortened his stride so no change in the rhythm of his steps would be heard. When Emêl had slipped from sight around the tunnel's gradual curve, Byrd headed back the other way.

He listened carefully with each step. When certain that no one noticed he was gone, he picked up his pace. He reached the tunnel's end, climbed up the rungs in the stone wall, and crawled through the hole in the dead tree. He'd barely emerged when two tall figures seemed to materialize from the darkness.

Both wore cowls over their heads and wraps across the lower halves of their faces. They'd tied the trailing corners of their cloaks across their waists. All of their attire was a blend of dark gray and forest green.

Though Byrd knew them, he moved cautiously until close enough to see their large amber eyes. Strands of silvery hair hung down across the leader's dark-skinned forehead. Brot'an was Byrd's main contact.

'You have a way into the keep?' Brot'an asked.

Though elves were reputed to be tall and lanky, Brot'an was solidly built for his height and almost a full head above Byrd. Even in the dark, faint lines around the man's large eyes marked him as an elder of his people. His most distinguishing markings were the ridges of straight and pale scars upon the right side of his face. Four lines ran through his feathery eyebrow, skipped over his eye, and continued through his cheek, disappearing under his face wrap. Staring into the elf's eyes, it was if those large amber irises burned through cage bars made of scarred flesh.

Byrd had seen Brot'an's companion only twice. He was younger and slight of build, and the few tendrils of hair visible beneath his cowl might have been light blond. Daylight would likely lighten them further. Byrd had never caught the younger man's name.

'Yes,' he confirmed at Brot'an's question. 'How did you escape the city?'

'At your signal, we intercepted the wagon and crawled underneath. We were with you for most of the passage into the forest.'

The younger elf stepped up to the dead tree, leaned into its hole, then looked back to Brot'an. '*Bithâ cœil-leach slighe vo lhohk do dân'gneahk.*'

'Where does the tunnel come out?' Brot'an asked.

'Somewhere in the keep's lower levels,' Byrd said. 'There's already one of you inside. Well, not exactly . . . he's the half-breed of an elven woman who —'

'*Cuirin'nên'a?*' Brot'an whispered.

Byrd paused, for the name was only half-familiar. 'If you mean Nein'a, then yes. Her son's name is —'

'*Léshil,*' Brot'an finished.

'If you mean Leesil,' Byrd added, 'then yes.'

At the mention of Gavril and Nein'a's son, Brot'an's companion stepped closer, casting a suspicious glance at Byrd before silently watching his superior. Brot'an's gaze drifted away, and he looked about the dark forest as if lost in memory.

Byrd saw only the man's eyes, but was certain a flicker of hardness passed over Brot'an's expression beneath the scarf. Apparently this elder *Anmaglâhk* knew of both Nein'a and Leesil. Byrd hoped this wouldn't affect the many years of work that had led to this night's good fortune.

'Why is he here?' Brot'an asked suddenly.

'He's trying to discover what happened to his parents,' Byrd answered. 'And I'd guess he might try to stop you as well.'

Brot'an let out a sigh and sagged under some hidden weight.

'Do you know something about Leesil's parents?' Byrd asked, and it was a slip he immediately regretted.

Brot'an glared back at him, and Byrd wondered if he

saw an instant of pain in those amber eyes – just before they hardened with a hatred that put Byrd further on edge.

'*Uilleva mì so óran Aoishenis-Ahâre,*' the young one said to Brot'an. '*Ge mì faod vorjhasij leanav âg trú, Léshil!*'

'*Na-fuâm!*' Brot'an snapped.

His companion flinched and did not answer, but apprehension was plain in his stance. The final word the young elf had spoken was far too close to Leesil's name, and Byrd suspected these two argued over how to deal with Leesil. Brot'an clearly didn't care for whatever fervent suggestion his subordinate had made.

'Is Leesil's presence a problem?' Byrd asked, careful not to let his anxiety show.

Brot'an looked into the tree's dark opening. 'No. Darmouth will die tonight.'

'Then my people thank you.' Byrd nodded and grew more businesslike. 'It's become harder over the years to bribe information from servants, but from what I've heard, Darmouth will go to his family crypt in the lower level if he needs a secure place. I don't know more than that. Perhaps it is the best-fortified room.'

Byrd casually backed away while he spoke, as if all this were but parting comments he thought of as he was leaving. Brot'an watched him with eerie, slanted eyes, and Byrd's sense of danger grew.

Without another word, Brot'an crawled into the dead tree, and his companion followed.

Byrd trudged through the forest beyond sight of the lakeshore, heading toward the city. Come sunrise, he could slip in with some band of merchants or farmers. He would rouse the Vonkayshi, the rebels of his cause, and word would spread quickly to prepare for a better day.

Secrecy was essential to Brot'an and his kind, but it didn't matter to Byrd how many servants or guards died this night, should the elves encounter such accidental witnesses. A higher purpose had to be served, and freedom never came free of cost. Unfortunate deaths didn't weigh against the lives of a whole province. Darmouth must be removed at any price.

That was why Byrd had first become part of the tyrant's far-reaching eyes and ears. In turn, he watched and learned Darmouth's ways as much as he could. The Vonkayshi fought for the people as a whole, and anyone unfortunate enough to fall in their cross fire was a casualty of the silent war waged here for many long years. What Byrd did, he did for all the people in this land.

Byrd shivered in the slow-falling snow, but he warmed himself with the image of Brot'an's slim stilettos piercing Darmouth over and over. If only he could be there when it happened.

15

Wynn flattened against the wall next to Hedí in the small alcove at the head of the north-side corridor.

Fortune favored them more than Wynn hoped, as they met no one along the way, even when sneaking off the main stairs and through the keep's wide entryway. They kept to the side of the staircase and inched along the rear wall down the north corridor, all the way to the corner.

'Take that scarf off your head,' Hedí whispered. 'Crouch down and peek around the corner. I saw guards by the end door the other day, and they appeared less than attentive.'

Wynn sank to her knees, still holding the candlestick and bag, and kept her head near the floor as she looked. Two guards stood before a door, apparently talking, but the corridor was so long that she could not catch what was being said. She pulled back and stood up.

'They will see us the instant we step out,' she whispered.

Hedí gave her a hard glare as she handed Wynn the key taken from the young guard.

'Then we will let them,' Hedí returned. 'Follow me like any attentive servant. When the moment comes, be ready with that candlestick. If you still want your freedom and your life.'

Before Wynn could reply, Hedí tucked both hands

behind her back, still holding the dagger, and stepped into the corridor.

Wynn's breath caught in her throat and her thoughts froze upon the only plan Hedí could have in mind. It was too dangerous, but Wynn could not stand there alone in the corridor. She tucked the candlestick behind Korey's bag and followed.

Hedí stepped smoothly down the corridor, and Wynn could not help but duck her head. She glanced up every few steps, until Hedí halted just out of arm's reach of the guards.

The one to the right appeared the most tired, with the half-closed eyes of someone too long on duty. Tall and lanky, he wore a leather hauberk that was at least clean and well made. The other on the left was an overweight, bristly-jawed soldier who smelled of ale even before he spoke.

'Lady?' he said. 'Did you lose your way?'

Wynn saw only Hedí's back and the dagger behind it. Hedí turned her head toward the fat soldier, and the tall one became nervously alert. He straightened to attention with a worried side glance to his partner, who swallowed hard and cleared his throat.

'Lady,' he repeated. 'No one goes below without us being told to allow it. And there's nothing down there anyway.'

Hedí lunged at the heavyset guard.

Wynn dropped the bag, and a muffled yowl came from within as it hit the floor. She glanced down, remembering Korey was inside. When she raised her eyes again, everything happened too quickly.

The bristly-jawed soldier toppled toward the corner

with a strangled yelp. Hedí followed so close that she leaned into his chest. Her hands were tucked between herself and the soldier. His eyes filled with shock – then pain. Sharp whimpers escaped through his gritted teeth, and he clawed at something between himself and Hedí.

The lanky tall guard took a fast step toward Hedí's exposed back, reaching for his shortsword.

Wynn cocked back the candlestick with both hands. He turned toward her as she swung. For an instant the candlestick's wide base arched straight for his head.

It passed before his face, never touching him.

Wynn's good eye widened. The pain in her swollen one brought a sinking realization. Panic and hampered vision made her misjudge the swing.

In one movement the lanky soldier jerked out his shortsword and swung hard with his free hand. Wynn did not see the fist that caught the blind side of her head.

Magiere stepped back from the stout door to let Leesil study it further. Emêl had already shoved the twisting wall section back into place. She glanced at it repeatedly, half expecting it to grate open again with gray-clad *Anmaglâhk* lunging out, stilettos in hand. Foolish, since Byrd had to get back inside the city before he could even contact them. She tried to shake the feeling off.

'I do not recognize this place,' Emêl said.

Leesil didn't look up. 'Most who see its inside don't live long enough to return for another look.'

'I meant I have been in the lower levels but not here,' Emêl growled back.

Magiere studied the door once more. There was no lock, only a peep slot with its metal panel closed from the outside. The door would swing outward, and so the hinges weren't accessible either.

'Shouldn't the keep's occupants have easy access back inside if needed?' she asked.

'Yes,' Leesil answered, then sighed. 'I'm missing something here.'

He was frustrated, and Magiere wished she could help, but she didn't have his experience and skills. Even Chap could sniff about the room, checking every corner and crevice. All she could do was wait, and keep Emêl from breaking Leesil's concentration.

Chap rumbled and traipsed over to Leesil's side. Two low woofs said he had found nothing worthwhile.

Leesil dropped to his knees and fingered the door-frame's stones. He finally sat back on his haunches, clenching his fists. When he reached around behind his own back, Magiere crouched to help him pull the toolbox from its makeshift harness.

'There has to be a proper way through this door,' he said, opening the box. 'But we've no time.'

Magiere still didn't care for the sight of the silvery garrote lying therein amid his spare stilettos and a thick curved blade. She heard a muffled curse from behind her. Emêl had seen the box's contents as well. She looked over her shoulder at his feet rather than into his eyes, making certain he kept his distance.

'If I can't open it from within,' Leesil continued, 'then I'll have to reach out somehow.'

He took out the thick, curved blade and folded the box closed. Magiere returned the toolbox to its harness as Leesil stood up. He set the blade's point against the door above its handle and gripped the hilt with one hand over the other.

'Time to call attention to ourselves,' he muttered.

Emêl stepped close – too close for Magiere's taste.

'You are not serious?' he asked. 'You will never cut an opening with that thing.'

'Better hope otherwise,' Leesil answered, and threw all his weight behind the knife.

He pulled the blade sideways toward the frame. The blade scored into the wood, and it made more noise than Magiere liked as it tore through the grain. Leesil cut a line slightly longer than the width of his hand. He repeated this several times, deepening the cut with each stroke, then moved up to work another cut a hand's length above the first one. Finally he used the blade's tip to chip and peel the wood's top layer with the grain, digging out a rectangle between the two cuts. The process was difficult and noisy, and Leesil's brow began to sweat.

Magiere understood what he was up to and took the blade to relieve him. She worked inward until she'd gouged halfway through the door.

'Enough,' Leesil said, and took the blade from her.

This time he worked at the top and bottom cuts without chipping more wood from the hollow they'd created. He finally stopped, tucked the hooked blade in his belt, and drew one of his winged blades. He set its tip into the hollow's center.

'If that didn't attract attention,' he said, 'then there's no one out there to hear this.'

He slammed his weight behind the blade's crosswise handle.

The crack of wood made Magiere flinch as Leesil's punching blade sank in sharply. He jerked it back out, and Magiere leaned down to look into the hollow.

The wood had broken away on the outside, leaving a rectangular hole. Leesil crouched and slipped his arm through the hole and nearly up to his shoulder. Magiere heard scraping metal, followed by a *click*.

Leesil pushed the door open but stood there with a scowl, not stepping out.

'What's wrong?' Magiere asked.

'Nothing . . . just another obstacle I've removed for Byrd's *Anmaglâhk.*'

'No other choice,' she said, and stepped past him.

The cell they exited was one among a row along a double-wide passage. They had been trapped in the last one at the back end. What passed for a lock was a metal slide bar with a pin, just enough to keep a prisoner inside but not requiring a key to the door. The place was silent, but Magiere still opened two of the other cells. Both were empty, and the door handles were thickly grimed by dust and damp air. This place had been left unattended and unused for a long while.

Leesil closed the cell door behind them and sheathed his winged blade. He did his best to press the popped chunk of wood back in place. It didn't stay, and Magiere grimaced as he licked the piece's rough side and smeared grime from the floor on it. He pressed it in again, and it held. No one would notice at a quick glance, unless they opened the door and the piece fell out.

Leesil walked ten paces to the far-end door with a larger barred window. The outer room beyond was dimly lit.

'Locked?' Magiere whispered, growing anxious.

Leesil gently pulled on the latch. The door opened, and Chap slipped by them into the next room, sniffing about with his nose in the air.

'Who taught you . . . your skills?' Emêl asked.

By his tone Magiere suspected he already guessed the answer.

'Does it matter?' Leesil returned.

Magiere glanced back at the baron. Emêl watched Leesil carefully, but his gaze shifted to her.

Leesil stepped into the outer room and stopped. Magiere saw him roll a shoulder as if fighting a brief spasm of muscle.

'My parents taught me,' he finally answered. 'Shutter the lanterns and leave them inside the door. We'll want our hands free.'

Magiere did as he asked and followed him into the long room.

Crates, barrels, and other goods were piled end to end with narrow paths and small spaces between. The far wall held another door, and more closed portals were along the back wall to the right. The long wall to her left was a series of stone pillars forming archways, and beyond these she saw a parallel passage running north and south. Two braziers in that passage's far wall threw dim light through the arches into the storage area. Magiere stepped through the center arch and looked both ways down the passage.

Both far ends met with stone staircases leading upward, one to the north and the other south. In the center of the passage's wall was a door she hadn't spotted while standing within the storage area. Its dark wood was bound with polished leather strips and iron straps, all mounted with steel studs. The handle and mounting plate were steel as well and didn't show the same signs of age as the brazier mounts. Unlike the slide-bolted cell doors, it had a keyhole. A few paces along the wall to either side were outlines in the stone wall where two more openings had been filled in and closed up.

'Why isn't anyone down here?' Magiere asked as she rejoined Leesil in the storage area. 'The cells were empty, so where would Darmouth keep Wynn?'

'There are no prisoners,' Emêl said. 'Except for your friend and my Hedí. Darmouth beheads traitors immediately. Petty criminals and captives are killed unless they swear fealty. Our forces grow thin, and every able body is pressed into service. His paranoia mounts by the year, and no one stays within the keep unless he has a hold on them. Anyone who does is kept under watch, though there are few men to spare for that.'

'Then where is Wynn?' Magiere insisted.

'I am not certain,' Emêl said. 'Hedí is not officially a prisoner, so she would be given a room above. It is possible your Wynn is up there as well, awaiting questioning or —'

'You let us think she was locked down here.' Leesil turned on Emêl. 'Why didn't you tell us this back at Byrd's?'

'I did not know if you would still assist me!' Emêl snarled back, but a flicker of guilt passed across his features. 'I must get Hedí back, and I needed your help. I used you no more than you have me . . . but I will find your companion.'

A chill ran through Magiere, as if she'd just crawled from the winter lake. She was sick of this land. Amid all the lies, truth was held concealed like a weapon to be used in the right moment. Anger swelled, and though she tried to quell it, her words were spiteful.

'Are you so cowed that your wits have festered? We can't search above without being seen!'

'I can,' Emêl answered, though he looked less than certain. 'Few in the keep will know I have not been summoned. And fewer still would question a trusted noble in Darmouth's confidence.'

'You'll just come up out of the prison?' Leesil asked. 'Look around you. The braziers are lit, but there's dust everywhere. Few ever come here, and not without permission.'

Emêl fell quiet, as if he hadn't considered this.

Magiere bit back any further viciousness before she spoke. 'We'll search this level first. No one goes up until I'm certain Wynn isn't down here somewhere. Maybe we can find another route that . . .'

She stopped as Leesil spun away. Losing himself in the middle of something this dangerous wasn't like him. He was coldly quick and calculating when necessary, but little he'd done since they'd come to Venjètz was like the Leesil she knew. He stood there with his back turned, and she reached for him.

'Emêl, if you know so much of Darmouth,' Leesil blurted out, 'what do you know of my parents?'

Magiere stopped before she touched him.

Everything these two said to each other was laced with poorly hidden accusations. Leesil didn't like speaking to Emêl, much less asking anything of the man. Emêl turned his gaze toward the ornate door beyond the archways.

'I knew of them,' he said with hesitation. 'I saw Lady Nein'a at a few of Darmouth's gatherings. She was often . . . in the company of some noble or officer.'

Magiere stiffened. Emêl's implication brought a low rumble of displeasure from Chap. She wondered if the dog had known of Nein'a's 'duties,' and she looked back to Leesil. Again, she wanted to touch him, to stop him from asking anything more that might shake what little hold he had on himself.

'The tunnel,' Leesil said. 'It has to be why they ran for the keep. Do you know if they escaped?'

'I do not,' Emêl answered quietly. 'I oversaw western fiefs at the time and did not return to Venjètz until your parents were gone. By then, Faris and Ventina already hovered in Darmouth's shadow. Questions concerning Lady Nein'a and her husband were treated as impudence. No one inquired further.'

Magiere slowly came up behind Leesil and laid her hand upon his back. It took a moment to speak, but she needed his help . . . needed him to put his questions aside for the moment.

'Start looking,' she said, and felt his back swell with a slow breath.

Leesil pulled away from Magiere's touch without looking at her. There was no time for her to soften his pain. She pointed to the ornate door beyond the arches.

'Where does that door lead?'

Emêl hesitated. 'Darmouth's family crypt. He holds private counsels there sometimes . . . with certain individuals. It is locked, but no one would ever be held there.'

Magiere nodded. She took one of the three doors in

the long back wall. Leesil took another, and Emêl the last. She found only empty cells and an abandoned room at her passage's end. She returned to the storage area as Leesil came out of his passage and shut its door.

'Some stores tucked in the cells,' he said coldly. 'Nothing more. The keep is being stocked up more than is normally needed.'

She hurt for him every time he spoke.

Emêl returned with a concerned frown. 'Weapons, bundles of quarrels, and a rack of arbalests.'

'Maybe Darmouth prepares for a siege,' Leesil said.

Emêl's silence was confirmation enough; he'd not known before now. It seemed Darmouth kept even his closest nobles in the dark, not that they couldn't see the turmoil of the province for themselves. And so much the worse if its leader suddenly died.

Magiere went to the door in the storage area's far end. The room hadn't seen use in some time. There was a wooden chair and a table with old quills scattered upon it. A tapestry hung from an iron rod across most of the back wall, so faded and worn she couldn't make out anything of its image other than the oak leaf pattern along its tattered border. She stepped back out.

'Some kind of office,' she said. 'No one has used it in a long while. So now what?'

Emêl shook his head. 'It is time I bluffed my way onto the main level. We will try the south staircase. I believe Martin and Kêrev are on night duty there, sometimes Devid, but they all know me. I can claim to be inspecting stores in lower levels.'

'Except they never saw you come down here in the first place,' Leesil said pointedly.

'If asked, I will say I went down the north staircase,' Emêl explained. 'None will be the wiser, as they will not run into the guards from that position until off duty at sunrise.'

'And what about us?' Magiere asked, as she didn't care to leave Wynn's fate in Emêl's hands. 'We just wait here?'

'For now. Stay below the landing within hearing . . . in case my ruse fails.'

Magiere followed Emêl with Chap at her side, though she glanced back to be sure Leesil was there. His expression was as cold and emotionless as the first day they entered Venjètz.

They made their way up the south staircase, which was longer than Magiere had expected. The lower levels were deep. When they reached a landing before a door, Magiere stayed back with Leesil and Chap some five or six steps down the stairs. Emêl reached for the latch, and a frantic female voice rang out on the other side.

'Devid! Are you there?'

'He's at the bridge gatehouse tonight,' answered a deep male voice. 'Something you need, Julia?'

Emêl froze as the woman's voice grew louder and nearer the door's other side.

'Oh, Martin,' she said. 'Lady Progae and Korey are missing. So is the woman locked up in the north side. Ventina found young Mikhail out cold in the woman's room, and now Faris is in a fit. He sent word to our lord and Lieutenant Omasta that the keep's been breached and then he went off on his own. He blames Devid, and I came to warn him.'

The woman's words came out in a rush. Little made

sense to Magiere except for the mention of a prisoner. It had to be Wynn. The voices continued, but Magiere waved Emêl back down the stairs.

'We go back down,' she whispered. 'If Hedí and Wynn are missing at the same time, they may be together. Hedí's note said she'd try for the lower level. We need to be ready, in case they're followed.'

'There's no time,' Leesil said softly. 'If Faris thinks the keep has been breached, that means . . .'

Leesil paused so long Magiere became anxious. They couldn't stand about in the stairwell, waiting to be found. He glared down the stairs.

'Byrd,' he whispered.

'What of him?' Emêl asked.

Magiere followed Leesil's gaze and saw nothing, but realization followed quickly. She knew what occurred to Leesil. Her voice rose almost too loud.

'That two-faced fat rat used us!'

Byrd had slipped away once they'd discovered the tunnel, but it hadn't been long enough for him to take advantage of his new information. Unless the elves had followed them from the city.

Magiere remembered the strange flashes of light she'd glimpsed as they'd left Venjètz – signals in the dark. And now they'd let the *Anmaglâhk* in. She didn't see how the elves could pass through without notice, but it wasn't the first time one had managed such a feat. Sgäile, the one who'd come to Bela, had entered the barracks of sages without even Leesil realizing until it was too late.

'Emêl, there are assassins in the keep,' Leesil whispered. 'Elves.'

The baron paled as he too looked down the stairwell.

'Byrd has planned this for a long time,' Leesil added. 'I thought I could leave a warning and be gone before they made a try for the keep. But if they're already inside . . . The guards are too busy searching for escaped prisoners to stop assassins, even if they could.'

'We cannot let this happen,' Emêl insisted. 'No one would mourn Darmouth's death, but the raids across our borders are growing. Now he has begun stocking the keep for a siege. If the nobles and officers go into a frenzy, fighting to take his place, the province will be overrun from outside.'

Leesil took a stiletto from his wrist sheath. 'I know.'

Magiere gripped the hilt of the falchion, squeezing it tightly until her hand ached. She hated feeling responsible for the people here. And worse was risking Leesil's life to save the man who'd maimed him in so many ways.

'Get those guards to open that door,' she told Emêl. 'Don't bother bluffing your way through.'

Chane had never been inside the keep. Straight ahead was a wide stairway leading up. To either side of its base were passages running north and south, and in the entryway's side walls were arched openings into wide chambers.

And where exactly was he to find Wynn in this place? There were too many options, and Welstiel would not be far behind once he dealt with their escort.

Chane approached the stairs. Voices came from a distance, and he stopped. Someone was in the corridor above on the next level. Two men, one louder than the other and angry. He could not tell if they were headed for the stairs. He slipped around the base of the stairs and into the small alcove at the head of the north corridor. He crouched low against the wall as he opened his senses wide.

A pained whimper and crack came up the corridor behind him.

He glanced up at the stairs, then retreated down the corridor. When he reached a sharp turn in the passage, he paused to spy around the corner with one eye.

At the far end, a woman in a gown was backed against the side wall by a tall soldier. He held a shortsword pointed at her chest, and she stood rigid with a bloodied dagger in her hand. A second fat and unshaven soldier was crumpled in the corner beyond them. The man breathed in quick whimpers while clutching his stomach, and blood seeped between his fingers. None of them looked Chane's way.

Someone else lay on the floor. A woman in a plain muslin dress rolled to her side. Light brown hair toppled from her face, exposing a reddened cheek and jaw below an eye swollen half-shut. A brass candlestick lay just beyond her open hand.

Chane's senses sharpened at the sight of Wynn's beaten face.

There was blood between her lips, and it ran in a thin line of saliva out the corner of her mouth.

He rounded the corner at a run.

Every fragment of life energy he'd stolen welled through his cold flesh. When the tall soldier and the woman heard his footfalls and turned, he'd already closed the distance.

The lanky soldier raised his sword.

Chane grabbed the man's throat with one hand. With the other he snatched the soldier's grip on the sword, closing his fingers over the man's own. Chane squeezed tightly as he drove the soldier to the floor.

He barely heard the muffled pop of cracking bone. He kept squeezing, tighter and tighter, with the image of Wynn's battered face wedged in his mind until it was all he could see. It clouded the guard's reddening, silent face . . . gaping mouth . . . swelling tongue.

'Ch . . . ch . . .'

Chane froze at the sound of her voice trying to say his name. The soldier's eyes were wide and blank. Blood ran between Chane's fingers, and he felt the split skin of the soldier's throat beneath them.

'Wynn?' he rasped, and turned his head.

She lay with her face toward him, one eye half-open. It closed slowly.

Chane scurried to her on all fours. He reached to grab her, saw his hands soaked red, and shrank back. He heard Wynn's even breaths, heard her heart beating evenly. She was alive, only slipping into unconsciousness, but he could not tell how badly she was hurt.

A scuffling behind him snapped his head around instinctively, and he lashed out with his boot. It connected with the fat soldier's throat. The mute crackle of the man's windpipe mixed with his choking, and he sagged in the corner, still and silent. Behind that sound Chane caught the soft pad of feet and swung back around.

Rage rose up in Chane on the tail of his fright. For an instant he saw Magiere waiting for him with dark hair and pale features. His muscles tightened.

Her skin was not quite pale enough.

The woman in the gown stiffened, halting her reach for a canvas bag between Wynn's feet. Something squirmed within the bag.

Memory surged in on Chane – a woman behind an inn.

He remembered the taste of her blood and fear . . . smelled that fear on her now, though there was little of it in her hard expression. This was the one who had been spying in the keep. Chane shifted on all fours, crouching protectively over Wynn.

The woman stepped slowly back, holding out the dagger.

Chane's thoughts began to clear. Wynn had been trying to get below this keep, and this pale woman was with her. He lowered his head like an animal suppressing its urge to spring, and locked his eyes upon the woman's own wary gaze. His voice rasped within the narrow passage.

'Do you still wish to live?'

Leesil gripped a stiletto and waited behind Magiere as Emêl pounded on the door.

'Open up. It is Baron Emêl Milea.'

'Baron Milea?' a deep voice called, and after a brief jangle of keys, the door opened.

Leesil saw a perplexed soldier standing in the opening with a hauberk of large leather scale. He stared at Emêl and then turned his eyes upon Leesil in the stairway below.

Magiere shoved past Emêl and drove her fist into the soldier's face. The man teetered backward, and a second soldier leaned in from beyond the door to grab the tail of her hair.

Chap rushed in, sinking his teeth into the second man's inner thigh. Before the guard cried out, Emêl smashed the man's face with a fist and shoved his way through the door. The second guard's grip held on Magiere's hair, and she toppled out of Leesil's sight.

Leesil rushed out and found himself face-to-face with a stunned housemaid with reddish hair tucked under her cap and an empty serving tray clutched in one hand. Her shock turned to fright, and she swung the tray at him.

He ducked aside, and the tray caught Emêl in the face. The baron toppled back through the stairwell door.

Leesil hissed under his breath. He, Magiere, and Chap should have taken these guards down in two breaths, and with far less racket. The only fortune was that neither guard had been able to draw a sword. From his crouch, he swerved around behind the maid. When she opened her mouth wide to shout, he had no choice and struck the back of her head with the butt of his stiletto. The tray clattered out of her grip to the floor, and he caught the maid under the arms and lowered her down.

Chap had one guard pinned. Magiere had pulled her hair free and now grappled with the other.

'Leesil, go!' she called to him. 'Get to Darmouth. I'll find you.'

Leaving her in this of all places wasn't something he'd ever imagined doing. But it was his only choice.

The corridor was open before him, and he ran cautiously in a half-crouch. He knew part of the main floor well enough, and there would be few places to hide.

When he reached the end of the long south corridor and entered the alcove, he crawled forward to scan the wide entryway. There was no one about, and he hurried to the nearer archway. The meal hall was empty, and he ducked inside.

His thoughts drifted for an instant to what Emêl had said.

He'd called his mother 'Lady Nein'a,' seen with nobles and officers here in this keep. Leesil had wondered in his youth why she was required at Darmouth's few evening events. Had his father known all along? Only a naïve boy wouldn't have imagined . . .

'What — Lady Progae is gone? And what breach? Make sense!'

Leesil saw no one in the entryway, but Darmouth's deep voice carried from inside the council hall across the way. His grip tightened on the stiletto.

For all the years since he'd heard that voice, it sank him into all the shadows of his past. He closed his eyes tight, then snapped them open again when memories leaped at him from the dark in his own mind.

He would do this. He would save Darmouth from the *Anmaglâhk*.

'Where is Faris?' Darmouth boomed. 'Where is that useless trash? Find him!'

As if to answer this question, Leesil heard the entryway's doors swing open. He glanced around the archway's side.

Faris entered, wild-eyed and half-mad with anger, and behind him was a woman who resembled him closely. She panted, looking panicked. The two hurried toward the council hall, and Leesil stayed low, still watching.

Faris paused short of the archway, seeming to prepare himself to face Lord Darmouth.

A distant shout echoed from the south corridor, and Faris turned.

Leesil ducked back. If these two followed that sound . . . He looked back carefully.

Faris and Ventina were gone. Leesil heard running footsteps fade down the south corridor, headed straight for Magiere and Chap.

All Leesil's instincts screamed at him to go back to them.

'I want the mongrel Móndyalítko and his bitch found!'

Darmouth's voice echoed across the entryway, and Leesil pulled back into hiding.

The only way Chap could silence his adversary was to rip the man's throat out, but he hesitated. Killing made the predator instincts of his animal body rise up. It was unsettling, and he needed to remain aware of all around him. The soldier he had pinned kept swearing and swinging, and Chap ducked and snapped at the man's face.

Emêl appeared at Chap's side, and smashed the hilt of his straight saber down on the soldier's forehead. The man dropped unconscious, and Chap wheeled away toward Magiere.

He grew anxious the instant he saw her.

Her irises were black, and it seemed her nails had lengthened. The soldier she fought looked openly horrified. Magiere sank her fingernails into his hauberk and slung him sideways into the corridor wall. Before he could right himself, she rushed in. She punched him so hard in the face that his head slammed back into the stone wall. The shortsword toppled from his grip as he slumped down to the floor.

'Magiere?' Emêl said, stepping toward her. 'Are you all right?'

Chap advanced quickly as Emêl looked into Magiere's face. The baron had seen her change at the lake while diving in the icy water. But here, up close, she was a disturbing sight to anyone who did not know what she was.

Magiere breathed hard, and Chap wished he had time to give her calming memories he had gathered from her thoughts over the years. He heard footsteps down the corridor and looked.

Faris appeared with Ventina on his heels.

'You?' Faris snapped at the sight of Magiere.

Chap growled. These two had expected to find someone else here. Faris eyed Emêl, and his expression filled with contempt.

'I knew your head would end up on a spike,' he said. 'No one sincere can grovel that well. Where has your consort taken my daughter?'

Ventina stepped close behind Faris, and her voice cracked with hysteria. 'Where is she, Emêl?'

'I do not know,' Emêl answered, 'I came for Hedí.'

Faris shook his head slowly. 'Your lord and master will clear that foggy memory. Move toward the counsel hall!'

'I don't think so,' Magiere said.

Chap sidestepped in front of Magiere, hearing her breath coming hard. She was fighting for self-control, and there was nothing he could do to help her. He kept his eyes on Darmouth's servants. Anyone unarmed who gave orders so easily made him wary.

The first ripple passed through Ventina's flesh.

Her face darkened as short brown-black hairs sprouted across it. She dropped to all fours. Hands and feet swelled, and fingers shortened into heavy paws with sharp claws. Her shoulders arched, filling out until her shirt and dress split. Faris writhed and changed beside her.

Chap heard Magiere's falchion slide from its sheath. He now faced two great predator cats taller than himself. They were black in color, but wherever the hallway's brazier light touched them, their fur shimmered a deep brown. Their large eyes were the same hue as their fur, and the only way Chap could tell them apart was by Faris's one missing ear. For an instant, they stood like two sentinel statues blocking the passage, then Faris snarled, exposing yellow-white teeth and long fangs. A yowl of rage rolled out of his throat and reverberated off the stone walls. It struck Chap's ear like the combined roll of thunder and the crack of lightning splitting the air.

'Into the stairwell!' Emêl shouted, backing up. 'Get behind the door.'

Ventina roared, and Chap whirled, trying to shove Magiere back. Magiere ran for the door. She shot through it, and Chap followed.

Emêl tried to slam the door closed. It bucked against him before he finished, and Chap ducked aside as the baron pitched backward, nearly knocking Magiere down the stairs.

'Down! Down!' Emêl yelled.

Magiere descended, taking the steps three at a time. As they rushed into the lower corridor, Chap ducked into an archway along the passage and whirled about, looking for Emêl.

The baron ran down the corridor toward Chap, and then he pitched sharply forward to sprawl on the stone floor.

Faris crouched atop him. Out of the dark passage, Ventina leaped over her mate. Her front paws touched down, and she swerved through the first archway toward Magiere.

Chap let his canine nature take hold. He bared his teeth and lunged forward into Faris's snarling face.

Darmouth couldn't remember a night of so much stupidity. Even Omasta had failed him, and he was one of the few to whom Darmouth gave his full trust. The raid on Byrd's inn found the place empty. Now some lackbeard guard from the bridge burst in with a muddled message of escaped prisoners and a breach of the keep.

'What – Lady Progae is gone?' Darmouth shouted. 'And what breach? Make sense!'

The young man cowered, lowering his eyes. 'Faris came running out to see if we'd admitted or released anyone. I told him Devid brought in that count and his manservant, but they never came back out. When Devid came out, he rushed off into the city, saying that you'd sent for him.'

'How, if I'm still here?' Darmouth asked, and his voice grew louder in frustration. 'Where is Faris? Where is that useless trash? Find him!'

Omasta stepped to the hall's archway, looking out.

'My lord, if the keep is breached, we must get you to safety.'

'No – I want Andraso,' Darmouth growled. 'That outlander and his servant are the only breach here. Andraso must be working with the hunter, and Emêl will answer for it. And Devid will be crows' food on the city wall!'

Darmouth pushed past Omasta toward the archway. A bestial roar and hiss echoed through the keep from the south corridor.

Omasta raised his arm in front of Darmouth. 'My lord, please. If Faris . . . He wouldn't take such action inside the keep, in plain sight, without great need. We must get you to safety.'

Omasta's concern did move Darmouth. It was the reason he'd never punished his lieutenant, even when the man faltered. And his bastard son's failures were rare. Omasta was sensible and skilled, like his sire.

'Take six more men off the keep walls,' Darmouth said. 'You'll need them.'

'And you will let me secure you away?' Omasta insisted.

'In time! Now call those guards.'

When Welstiel felt certain he was safe from discovery, he silently stepped down the stairway behind the counsel hall's tapestry. The wolfhounds followed.

At the bottom was an opening covered by a heavy cloth. He touched it, realized it was the backside of another tapestry, and let his senses reach beyond the fabric. He detected nothing living beyond and lifted the tapestry aside. The hounds trotted out ahead of him.

Welstiel stood in an empty room with a door in the

far wall. There was only an old wooden chair and a table strewn with broken quills. The tapestry was too faded and worn to make out anything but the oak-leaf pattern along its border. Then he heard snarls and cries, and the roar of a predator.

Welstiel reached the door and slid open its metal peephole shutter to look out. He tensed at the scream of a raging cat. It took two blinks to truly grasp what he saw.

Magiere rolled across a stone floor between stacked crates and barrels, tangled with an enormous brown-black cat. Leesil was nowhere in sight, but to the right through a set of archways, Chap lunged into a second feline. The two animals tumbled off the back of Baron Milea.

Welstiel looked back to Magiere.

She snarled as savagely as the beast that grappled with her. One upper arm bled through claw tears in her wool sleeve beneath the hauberk. She had abandoned her sword and stabbed at the cat with a dagger. The cat thrashed so rapidly it countered every swing of her blade.

The baron regained his feet but looked unsteady.

Welstiel could lose Magiere here and now, but he could not allow himself to be seen. He looked about the room for anything he might use, and his gaze fell upon the wolfhounds.

They might not last, but they could give Magiere time and advantage.

Welstiel focused, calling upon the dogs' dormant predator nature. That latent ancestry lay suppressed beneath generations of domestication, but some spark of the beast buried within them was necessary for his effort to work.

He built an image of the great cats in his own mind.

One hound bared its teeth with a growl, and the other quivered as it inched toward him.

Welstiel ducked behind the door as he pulled it open, and the hounds rushed through.

Hunger burned strength into Magiere, and instinct was all that kept her dodging Ventina's quick and fluid strikes. Each time Magiere lashed out with the dagger, Ventina's muscles shifted rapidly, and the cat aimed another slash of her claws.

Magiere heard Chap's snarls, but Faris yowled with equal rage from beyond the storage room's archways.

She twisted right on the floor, as Ventina slammed a large paw down toward her face, then whipped back and stabbed for the cat's throat. Her dagger sank into Ventina's shoulder, and the cat squalled in pain. Magiere rolled free, scrambling to her knees with the dagger poised. Ventina tried to lunge, but her foreleg wouldn't hold, and she stumbled.

Growls rang out behind Magiere, and she glanced toward the sound.

Two wolfhounds rushed between stacked crates, and despair crippled Magiere's rage. She heaved herself backward to her feet.

Emêl was up again, and Magiere shouted, 'Watch Chap's back!'

She steeled herself as the lead hound charged toward her.

It barreled straight into Ventina, and the second dog leaped to the top of a wide crate. As Ventina roared and twisted about at her new attacker, the second hound leaped from the crate toward Faris.

Magiere hesitated in confusion.

Ventina's hindquarters became exposed when she turned on the hound, and Emêl stepped in, straight saber gripped two-handed. He rammed the blade through her back.

Its point came out the bottom of her rib cage. She squalled and crumpled to thrash wildly upon the floor.

Magiere rushed out the nearest archway into the passage. Faris faced both Chap and the second wolfhound, but Magiere saw no way to join in the narrow space. Chap looked as feral as he had the day at the Stravinan border. He snapped like a wild animal.

The wolfhound had landed behind Faris, and the cat was boxed between the two dogs. It clamped its jaws on Faris's hind leg. As the cat twisted back to snap at the hound, Chap lunged in. His teeth closed on Faris's throat just below his jaw, and Chap thrashed his head wildly.

Blood spattered the wall and floor as Faris's throat tore away. Chap leaped to the side, the silver fur of his face stained red and dripping.

Faris's panicked yowl ended in strangled choking. He collapsed, squirming, with the wolfhound still tearing at his leg.

Magiere saw Faris's fur begin to recede.

His body writhed within his skin as if another form hid within it and struggled to emerge. Fur on his head grew to dark hair as his one ear slipped down the side of his elongating head. The more he changed, the feebler his movements became.

Faris's naked body lay dead before Magiere, with the

torn muscle and sinew of his throat still leaking blood across the stone floor.

'Stop,' Magiere shouted at the wolfhound.

Her voice sounded clear to her own ears, and her teeth had shifted halfway back to normal. With the change came returning fatigue and a burning ache in her left arm where she'd been clawed.

Someone coughed.

Magiere stepped through the archway toward the strangled weeping among the crates and barrels. Ventina had changed as well and lay naked with Emêl's blade through her back. She tried to gasp air while tears ran down her face.

This wasn't what Magiere had wanted, and she knelt down at Ventina's side. These people were slaves just as Leesil had been. Emêl knelt beside her, his expression troubled.

Ventina grabbed Magiere's forearm, glaring up with a strange mix of panic and lingering hate. 'Korey . . .' she choked out, and her eyes shifted to Emêl. 'You know what he'll do to her.'

Emêl sagged with a slow sigh. 'I will protect your daughter, as best I can.'

Ventina's breathing slowed as she stared wide-eyed up at Emêl. When her breath stopped altogether, her eyes remained open. Her grip was still tight on Magiere's arm, and Magiere went numb, peeling the dead fingers away.

'Are you badly hurt?' Emêl asked.

'I'm all right.' The slashes were bleeding but not deep, and she would heal quickly enough.

'Look away,' he said. 'I have to free my sword.'

If he had any idea what horrors Magiere had witnessed in her life, he would never have said such a thing to her. Magiere found his strange chivalry curious. He jerked the blade free of Ventina's body with a sickening wet sound.

Something nudged Magiere's side. She looked around to Chap's blood-soaked face. The sight no longer bothered her as it once had, and she stood up.

'We have to find Leesil.'

Chap barked once.

'Hide the bodies first,' Emêl said. 'Even with the blood here, it's best their deaths are not discovered too soon.'

For the first time Magiere could remember, a sweet coppery scent filled her head. Her gaze shifted to the red pool spreading around Ventina's corpse. The sight made the smell even sharper, but there was no time to ponder why this new awareness plagued her now.

Both wolfhounds had ceased growling and trotted back toward the far end of the storage area. Magiere ignored them and helped Emêl drag Faris and Ventina through the last of the three doors at the room's back. She sheathed her dagger, picked up her falchion, and followed Chap to the south stairway with Emêl close behind.

Welstiel put a hand to his face in quiet relief. Magiere's injuries were minimal. There was nothing more he could do at the moment to drive her from this place. He watched quietly until he was certain that she and her companions were gone, then slipped out to follow. He ignored the wolfhounds and crept up the south staircase.

The door at the top was closed, and he crouched upon the landing. With his senses fully open, he picked up voices as far away as the keep's wide entryway. This was as good a place as any to wait for opportunity. He had yet to drive Magiere from this land.

16

Hedí stared at the pale man crouched over Wynn, his hands wet with the soldier's blood. Her stomach still lurched from what she had seen him do. She tried not to shake as she held the dagger out at him.

He looked familiar, but she could not think of where she had seen him. The cloak he wore was well-made, and his even features were distorted in a feral expression. He might have been handsome, if not for the predator's crouch on all fours. Hedí did not trust handsome men.

'Do you still wish to live?' he rasped.

His words were little more than a harsh whisper, as if injury or illness had crippled his voice.

'Who are you?' she whispered back, trying to be both quiet and forceful. 'What do you want with her?'

He glanced down at Wynn. When he looked up again, Hedí felt cold. His strangely beautiful eyes were like crystallized ice.

'You are Lady Hedí Progae,' he rasped, merely stating a fact. 'You seek to escape from the lower level of this keep. An innkeeper named Byrd is to wait for you on the lake's far side. I suspect you assume Baron Milea will be there as well.'

Hedí lowered the dagger only an inch. 'Are you with Byrd? Did he send you?'

Such contempt crossed the man's face that her hope

died instantly. She backstepped, trying to keep fear from overcoming her wits.

'Your plans are nothing to me,' he said. 'Help me get Wynn to her companions, and I will protect you.'

There was a thinly veiled threat in his words. Any disagreement and she would need protection from him. Hedí did not respond well to threats, but the man crouched in her way, and she doubted a dagger would be enough to get her to the door.

'What happened to her?' He looked down at Wynn, and his rasping voice softened.

'She arrived at the keep beaten and restrained. I found her locked in a room. I helped free her, and we came here. The guard we left behind might awake or be discovered at any moment.'

He jerked his chin up, all traces of gentleness gone. 'Her guard is only unconscious?'

'Your friend did not care for killing an unconscious man, regardless of the risk for leaving him.'

He looked about, then leaned over to wipe his hands on the dead soldier's breeches. Not all the blood came off.

Hedí wished she did not need his help. She had feared for Wynn when she realized Darmouth used the scholar as bait for the assassin who murdered her father and left her mother and sisters to starve. Wynn had to be Leesil's next target, and Darmouth tried to lure him in. She would not let what had happened to her father happen to Wynn.

And Leesil, who had ruined her life, would not fall into Darmouth's hands either.

Hedí would find him first.

Black wishes grew in her mind until they seemed within reach. When Byrd's assassins came for the warlord, they would bear Hedí's token. The lecherous savage would know she had committed his final betrayal, as the elves presented Darmouth with Leesil's severed head.

'Your note to the innkeeper spoke of a guide,' Wynn's guardian said, and lifted her limp form in his arms where he knelt. 'I see no guide.'

Hedí was startled from her thoughts. 'What do you know of my note?'

'Where is the guide?' he demanded.

Exposing Korey troubled Hedí, but she had no alternative. She could not find the way out without Korey's assistance, so she crouched to open the canvas bag's mouth.

A small dark brown cat hopped out. She hissed at the tall man, and the fur on her back stood up.

'What is this nonsense?' the man asked.

'It is all right,' Hedí said to the cat. 'Change. He will help us.'

Korey backed away, ducking behind Hedí's skirt. Her fur receded and her body grew. The man watched with fascination as Korey transformed into a little girl. Hedí pulled the cotton nightdress from the bag and covered her immediately.

'He's bad!' Korey whispered. 'Cold and bad.'

'We have a long way to go,' she said to Korey. 'This man will protect us and carry Wynn.'

Korey remained half-hidden behind Hedí.

The man gently shook Wynn, whispering in the little scholar's ear, 'Can you move? Wynn, wake up.'

But Wynn did not awaken. Her breathing was regular, and other than her battered face her color was normal.

'She will recover,' Hedí said.

He stood, holding Wynn against his chest as if she weighed nothing. Hedí grabbed the bag and took a step closer. Her head barely reached the man's collarbone.

'Get the keys off the guard,' he ordered.

It took a moment, partly because Hedí could not bear to look at the soldiers' faces as she searched their bodies. Finally they were ready to descend. A skilled fighter was a stroke of luck Hedí had never counted on – but at what cost?

Deep inside, it felt like she had struck an unwilling bargain with a demon.

Chane waited until Hedí finished unlocking the door. 'I will go first.'

The little girl glowered at him from behind Hedí's skirt as he stepped past through the doorway. He carried Wynn down the dark stairwell, and the descent was longer and deeper than he had expected.

'Can you see?' Hedí asked from behind him.

'Yes.'

He did not care for this Hedí Progae, another social elite only Welstiel would value. She had spirit enough to take on the soldiers and even put one down, but she looked too much like the worthless noblewomen of Chane's childhood. And she was no thaumaturge, by his judgment.

Thaumaturgy, the magic of the physical realm, was one he had never witnessed. Even if Hedí Progae was such a mage, she certainly was not old enough to have mastered transmogrification, the changing of one living thing into another. Which meant the child had done this herself.

Wynn murmured in his arms, and he held her closer. Even in the dark stairwell, his sight made out the curves of her oval face, the swelling around her cheek and eye . . . the stain of congealing blood in the corner of her mouth.

He worried and hoped she would wake soon. Wynn had purpose: to study, to learn, to build upon all that she was even now. She was not part of the cattle that was humanity. She needed to be preserved.

When they reached the bottom step Chane paused and listened for any sounds of movement ahead. He heard nothing and he stepped along the passage until he reached a set of archways that opened into a long room filled with storage. There were doors at either end of the space and along its back wall. And one heavy door behind, in the passage itself.

Chane thought he felt something nearby.

Young Korey scurried past him, caught up in her childish pursuit of an adventure.

'Oh, we're on the far side,' she said, and nodded. 'Papa took me down the other stairs, the . . . the south one. But we're on the other side.'

Chane stared along the passage the other way and saw another staircase leading up.

'What are we looking for?' he asked.

'The portal,' she answered, as if this told him everything. 'I know where it is.'

Before Chane took another step forward, he picked up something on the edge of his senses again.

The smell of forest and fresh earth . . . decayed leaves? Sweat and wool? The thin scents were all mixed in the stale air here. Thin but fading, as if someone had recently passed this way. And even more powerful was the smell of blood.

Chane's awareness widened, and he turned around. He found himself staring at the ornate door in the passage wall across from the center archway. It was thick and solid, but in the moment of silence he thought he heard heartbeats beyond it.

'We are not alone,' he whispered. 'Start moving . . . quietly.'

Hedí took Korey's hand, and as they moved on Chane saw and smelled dark spatters of blood on the stone walls and floor.

Magiere and Leesil should still be across the lake looking for the passage's exit. He wanted to send Wynn through to them, but they must have found their way in first. There had been a fight in this room, and Chane picked up the scent of a dog and some other animal he could not place.

Hedí slowed to step around the blood. Korey scurried past into the storage area and pointed at the door to the room's far end.

'That one. I remember now.'

Chane followed with a glance to Hedí. 'Check the door.'

She did so, and when it opened she looked surprised. A trickle of anxiety ran down Chane's neck, but he stepped through the door, and Hedí closed it softly behind them.

Chane stood at the head of a short corridor with wooden doors every three paces on each side. Each had

TRAITOR TO THE BLOOD 417

a small metal-shuttered peephole. These were cells for prisoners, but he heard and smelled nothing, sensed no one locked away here.

'Now?' he asked.

Korey ran to a cell on the left. 'This one.'

Chane came up behind her. The door had a slide-bolt-and-pin fixture in place of a lock.

'Open it,' he said.

Korey pulled and a piece of the door above the latch fell out.

Chane backed away. Korey stared at the rough piece of wood on the floor. She bent over and picked it up, peering curiously through the hole.

'What does this mean?' Hedí asked, and took the piece of wood from the girl.

Chane had no answer. He shifted Wynn higher in his arms, stepped carefully to one side, and looked through the half-open cell door. The tiny room beyond was empty.

It seemed certain that Magiere and Leesil had found their way in, and their dog as well, for who else but Chap would have left a dog's scent in the outer chamber. He grew wary, wondering if they had come and gone, but he doubted they would leave so quickly without Wynn. Which meant they were still in the keep, searching for her. Eventually they would have to leave, if they wanted to survive. How could he be sure they would find Wynn if he left her outside?

Chane entered the cell and looked about. He saw no hint of any secret opening. He returned to the hallway, looked up and down, and noticed two shuttered lanterns on the floor beside the door. It brought some relief.

Leesil and Magiere planned to return this way, though it appeared they had not yet done so. Hopefully for Wynn, they would make it. Chane need only leave Wynn in Hedí Progae's charge within sight of whatever exit they might find. Either Wynn's companions would return, or Hedí's baron would come looking for her.

'Someone has already broken in,' Hedí said, still fingering the piece of wood.

'Yes,' Chane answered. 'And now we are breaking out.'

'The door's right there,' Korey said, pointing to the cell's back wall.

'Where?' Chane rasped.

Korey slapped the side of the wall with her little hand and frowned at him. 'Push it. It's right here.'

Chane set his shoulder against the wall and pushed. It gave just a little, pivoting at the midpoint. He shoved until the section turned all the way, leaving a narrow opening on each side of the rotated wall section.

'I have to go back now,' Korey said.

'No!' Chane turned on the child then glared at Hedí. 'Deal with this.'

He would not have the girl discovered wandering the keep and be questioned.

'I've been gone a long time,' Korey added, innocently unaware that Chane would stop her if Hedí did not. 'Papa is going to be so mad at me.'

Hedí glanced at Chane and knelt down. 'Korey, you must come with me. The keep is no longer safe. If you escape, your mama and papa will be free to leave. Your father knows of this secret way out. He will know where to find you.'

'No!' Korey half shouted. 'I can't leave. Papa said if I did, I'd never see him or Mama again.'

Hedí's voice hardened. 'Yes, and Darmouth told them that if they left, he would kill you.'

Korey's little eyes widened.

'Understand?' Hedí continued, grasping the child's arms. 'Leave now, and they will be free. All of you can come with me and Emêl, far away. You will never have to stay in your room, and you can be with your mother and father always.'

Korey's jaw was trembling. 'I don't have any clothes or shoes, just this nightdress.'

'Emêl has my things,' Hedí reassured her. 'And I have Wynn's other clothes in the bag. Here, let's put the coat on you now. We will find you other clothes once we are out of here.'

'We must go,' Chane said impatiently.

Hedí looked at him with suspicion as she draped the sheepskin coat around Korey. 'You said you would just take us to the lower levels, to help us escape.'

'Plans change. Now move.'

Chane knew Welstiel would be furious. Not that it mattered. There was nothing else to be done. He could not risk reentering the keep with Chap and Magiere inside. Hedí rose up, glaring at him.

'Yes?' he rasped. 'You wish to say something?'

'Let me get one of the lanterns,' she said.

'No, leave them. I need no light,' he said.

'We do.'

Chane was becoming tired of these two. 'Check Wynn's clothing, her coat, all of her pockets. See if you find a crystal.'

Hedí frowned in puzzlement but did as he asked. To Chane's mild relief, she pulled out a small cold lamp crystal.

'Rub it between your hands,' he instructed.

She did so, and when the crystal's light sparked, Hedí dropped it.

'Oh!' Korey said, snatching it up in wonder. 'Pretty!'

Chane could not suppress his groan – ladies and peasants, imbeciles all. 'You have your light; now move on.'

Korey scurried through the opening, crystal in hand and coat dragging on the floor. Hedí followed, casting a dark scowl at Chane. They climbed down more narrow stairs, and the walls grew damp. When they reached the bottom, there was a wooden partition blocking their way.

'Here,' Korey said. 'This is the portal. We have to go through.'

The crystal's light revealed a chain dangling through a hole in the stone ceiling. Chane nodded at it, and Hedí took hold and pulled with all her meager weight. The portal rose enough for Chane to duck under. He found another chain on the other side. Supporting Wynn with his forearms, he gripped it to hold the partition up. Korey came out behind him, waiting as Hedí followed. Chane released his grip, and the portal ground along the wall grooves back into place. He turned about to look down a dark passage that glistened with moisture in the crystal's light.

'A stone tunnel,' he whispered, almost in awe. 'Under the lake.'

Korey headed onward, and Hedí grabbed the girl before she got too far ahead. The tunnel curved gradually, and soon the wooden portal was out of sight behind them. The farther they went, the more Chane heard Korey's teeth chattering. They walked beneath a lake in the middle of winter, and her feet were bare.

'It should not be far,' he said.

He had lost track of distance and wished only to keep them moving. Hedí Progae was likely colder than the child. She had shoes but otherwise wore only the velvet gown. Wynn wore some sort of maid's dress, and Chane realized his own body provided her no heat. He held her close just the same, and rolled his shoulders, trying to wrap her in his arms beneath his own cloak.

The stone tunnel ended in an alcove barely wider than the passage. By the crystal's light, Hedí grasped the first of a set of iron rungs in the wall and began to climb. For a moment Chane wondered if the child could follow, but Korey managed awkwardly. Chane hoisted Wynn over his shoulder and climbed.

Above him, Korey clambered out an opening. At the top rung he realized he was inside a hollowed-out tree. He looked into the night forest, listening intently, but he detected no one except for the woman and the girl. He climbed out and rolled Wynn off his shoulder and back into his arms.

It was still snowing lightly. The ground was covered with white where falling flakes made their way through the forest canopy. Hedí rubbed her hands up and down Korey's arms, trying to warm the girl. She lifted the child, raising her bare feet out of the snow.

Chane carried Wynn a short way into the trees. He found an older fir that had lost its lower branches, and where the ground was bare of snow. He settled Wynn there, and pointed for Hedí and Korey to take their place beside her.

'Pull Wynn close and keep her covered,' he said, and stripped off his cloak to drape over the three of them. 'I will find kindling.'

He scavenged beneath other trees until he gathered handfuls of dead needles and leaves that might ignite. He searched for substantial fuel and added a pile of loose branches he snapped in proper lengths. Then he realized he had no flint to strike on his sword.

Wynn would freeze out here if he did not do something. He focused his attention upon the half-dry mound of needles and leaves.

'It's too wet to light,' Hedí said.

'Be quiet.'

In his mind Chane drew lines of light, slowly crafting symbols within his thoughts. First the circle, then around it a triangle, and into the corners between these two shapes he scrawled glyphs and sigils, stroke by stroke. The mesh of lines overlaid his sight, and he stared through it at the pile of kindling.

A small flame erupted. It sizzled and crackled with moisture. He held the flame there with his concentration as he added snapped twigs and waited until the fire held on its own.

'Thank you,' Hedí said warily, though she still shivered. 'The fire should help Emêl find us when he searches the lakeshore.'

Chane crouched and pulled the cloak tighter around all three of them. Wynn was still unconscious, but they had her positioned in the middle. He dug in the bag and found her short robe and draped it over her alone.

'I believe your baron went inside to look for you,' Chane said, and pulled a pile of snapped branches within Hedí's reach. 'He is welcome in the keep and privy to most news. Once he learns you are missing, he will come to find you. Keep a watch on the tunnel exit. Do not let the fire burn high enough to be seen across the lake.'

'You are leaving?' she asked.

Chane could not decide if her voice held worry or relief, but he did not care. If he stayed, he might end up fighting for his regained existence.

'Keep watch over Wynn,' he instructed.

'I will take care of her,' Hedí Progae said. After a long pause, she said again, 'Thank you.'

Chane turned away, gradually slipping from the firelight's reach among the forest's trees. He looked back more than once to Wynn's sleeping face, until he walked too far into the cold dark.

Crouched within the dining hall, Leesil grew desperate.

Snarls down the south corridor died away. A tall blond-bearded soldier stepped into the far arch across the entryway and shoved out a younger soldier, ordering him to bring more men in off the keep walls.

Leesil guessed this was Omasta. Soon his men would be rushing about the keep.

The coming confusion would work in the *Anmaglâhk's* favor. Omasta might secure Darmouth someplace safe, but the elves would find him. Leesil had instigated chaos inside strongholds a few times in his youth for exactly this purpose. The larger the place, the better it worked.

Omasta stepped back into the council hall.

Leesil had to do something quickly to warn Darmouth or Omasta. Voices shouting in the courtyard grew louder and closer, and he had only one option. If he didn't get his message out quickly enough, it would mean his own death, and possibly Magiere's and Chap's.

He rushed across the entryway before anyone came through the front doors, and crouched beside the council hall's arch. He left his weapons sheathed and spun around the archway into the council hall.

Omasta stood to the left of the table's near end. At the sight of Leesil, shock crossed his features, and Leesil shifted to the table's right side.

Leesil still wore his cloak, but the hood was halfway down, and his white-blond hair hung loose. His skin, eyes, and oblong ears were so different from those of the sturdy men who lived in the Warlands. Leesil could imagine how startling he must appear.

And then he saw Darmouth at the table's far end.

Leesil's throat tightened.

A sickening surge of revulsion rolled in his stomach. The very real presence of the tyrant made any surging memory but a shadow.

Darmouth's face was clean-shaven and his hair was cut short, but he still wore the steel-reinforced leather breastplate. Two long war daggers were mounted on his belt, and he wore a heavy shortsword sheathed at his hip. He took more care with his appearance than in the past, but Leesil saw only the murdering, self-obsessed dictator who'd made him kill over and over. Darmouth, who'd used his mother for . . .

'You!' Darmouth shouted.

Omasta reached for his shortsword. 'Guards!'

'I'm here to warn you,' Leesil said with great effort. 'Assassins are inside the keep.'

'Yes,' Darmouth answered. 'That's plain to see right here.'

Beneath the aging tyrant's anger, Leesil saw an eager hunger in Darmouth's glare. Omasta charged.

Leesil rolled across the table. He started to reach for a stiletto, but it would be no defense against a sword, unless he was willing to duck inside Omasta's guard and kill him. He pulled his right punching blade instead.

Omasta vaulted the table and came down swinging. Leesil blocked and ducked away at the clang of metal. He leaned into the wall and kicked up into Omasta's chin.

The solid impact whipped Omasta's head back, but he kept his feet, staggering against a high-backed chair. Darmouth drew his own sword and charged around the table's end. Leesil dove across the table again before Omasta could right himself.

'Listen!' he shouted, and words stuck in his throat for an instant. 'I'm not the one who's come for you. There are elven assassins inside the keep.'

He believed that deep inside Darmouth was a coward, like any who saw deceit and betrayal everywhere and beat down dissention wherever it was perceived. Leesil hoped the man's own paranoia would plague him enough to listen.

'Liar,' Darmouth growled, holding his sword out. 'Traitor and liar, like your mother. I'll gut you alive on the west wall while the whole city watches.'

Leesil's hatred for Darmouth began eating him up inside.

Omasta sidled along the table toward the archway, while Darmouth backed to the far end, circling to Leesil's other side. Blood trickled from Omasta's mouth into his beard.

Leesil tried to think of some way to convince one of them of the truth. Five soldiers appeared in the archway. His panic and fury made the dim room sharpen in his sight.

'I want him alive!' Darmouth shouted.

Magiere ran down the south corridor with Chap and Emêl following behind. She skidded out the corridor's end in time to see five armed men come up to the archway of the council hall. Darmouth's voice echoed out into the entryway.

'I want him alive!'

Magiere glimpsed Leesil at the hall's right side, and her breath caught. He looked desperate, sweating in the keep's cold air. The lead soldier in the archway rushed him, and Magiere raced across the entryway.

Leesil sidestepped so quickly that the soldier stumbled, then he pivoted in a complete turn. His winged blade sliced through the guard's side. The man toppled against two chairs and fell in a heap. Two more guards surged forward as Omasta waved them on.

'Leesil!' Magiere shouted.

He saw her and then ducked as the next guard came at him.

The soldier closest to Magiere started to turn toward her. She hammered the falchion's hilt into his skullcap, and he toppled into the man in front of him. Magiere kicked out into her target's back, and both men fell to the floor at the table's end.

Magiere spotted Omasta, and for one breath he seemed ready to come for her. But he turned, running down the table's side. Magiere saw Darmouth at the back of the council hall. Omasta grabbed the tyrant's arm, pulling him toward the back wall even as Darmouth tried to jerk away.

Chap leaped over the men Magiere had downed and landed atop the table. He wheeled about, snapping and snarling at the two soldiers closing on Leesil. One of the downed men rose up to face Magiere while the other fumbled for his fallen sword. Emêl ducked around Magiere.

'Try not to kill them,' he barked, and closed on the rising man.

Magiere swerved around the table after Omasta. As she passed Chap, a soldier turned from Leesil and swung down at the dog's head. Magiere faltered, ready to lunge across and block with the falchion.

Chap hopped aside. The soldier's shortsword bit into the table's edge, and before the man could pull it back, the dog launched into his chest. Magiere's gaze flicked about the room.

Leesil managed his one opponent. Emêl backed another soldier into the room's corner. She spotted a skullcap rising over the table's end – the first man she'd struck down. She stepped back and brought the flat of her blade down with a clang. The skullcap vanished from sight as she heard the soldier slump to the floor.

When Magiere looked back, Darmouth was gone. Only Omasta stood at the room's far end near the swaying tapestry of the lone rider. She rushed toward him.

'Leesil!' she shouted, and dodged Omasta's first thrust. 'Behind the tapestry!'

Leesil dodged away from his opponent. Omasta turned from Magiere to intercept him, and she felt a wave of dread. Leesil would kill Omasta if the man didn't get out of his way. Magiere slapped down his sword with her own, and threw herself at him.

They both hit the back wall beside the tapestry and recoiled to the floor. Magiere rolled blindly away and scrambled to her feet.

The tapestry swayed wildly and Leesil was gone. Omasta climbed to his feet to face her.

Only three soldiers were still conscious. Chap rolled on the floor with one. Emêl still battered steel with another in the corner who wouldn't give up, though the man made no headway in getting clear of the baron. Omasta tried to rush for the tapestry. Magiere slashed across his path with the falchion's tip. The lieutenant backed away.

'Move!' he yelled.

'Leesil is trying to protect Darmouth,' she snarled back.

Omasta glanced to his left. The first soldier who'd assaulted Leesil lay huddled on the floor with his side split open.

Magiere's last hope faded. Omasta would never believe her.

Emêl sliced his opponent neatly across the right shoulder, and the guard dropped his blade, crying out. The baron followed with his fist, and the man twisted and dropped to the floor. Chap had bitten both wrists of the soldier he fought, and the man retreated against the table, weaponless, as the dog snarled every time he tried to move.

The guard Magiere had bludgeoned twice was rising again at the table's far end. Emêl raised his boot and stomped the man down.

Omasta saw all this and seemed appalled by Emêl's actions. He looked back at the tapestry and Magiere.

'Don't,' she warned. 'It's over. You have to believe what I told you.'

He inched forward. There was no fear in his eyes, but he didn't come at her immediately. 'Move, Magiere . . . now.'

She didn't want to hurt him, and it was clear he'd rather not harm her. She had to keep him back if Leesil was to protect an entire province.

Magiere mirrored Omasta's slightest move. His face filled with anger. This time he swung hard. When she blocked, the force between their blades made them both stumble. Magiere's frustration became rage, and her vision sharpened.

The room brightened before her as the ache filled her jaws.

Omasta hesitated as he looked her in the eyes.

Magiere feinted with the sword, and he caught it on his own blade. At the instant of contact, she lunged low.

Her shoulder caught below his rib cage, and she drove

him back into the wall. He slammed against the stone, and she hopped back before he could rake her with his shortsword. One of his feet slipped, but he didn't fall. He grunted and swung at her. Magiere twisted aside and brought her blade down on top of his.

Both swords' tips hit the floor, and the impact of steel on stone echoed off the walls. She stomped down on his blade, rising up on her own force with her fist cocked back. Omasta stumbled as his weapon jerked from his grip. Magiere struck downward, sinking her weight into the blow.

Her fist cracked down the side of his face and collarbone, and Omasta crumpled, unmoving.

The only guard still standing was Chap's. Emêl grabbed him by the throat and pounded his saber's hilt into the man's forehead.

Panting, with hunger burning her insides, all Magiere could do was shove the tapestry aside and assume the others would follow.

Darmouth fled down the stairs from the council hall to the old sergeant's office. One moment he'd been eating supper with Omasta in the safety of his own stronghold, and now his keep was breached by the one traitor who'd ever escaped him.

He'd never forgotten. When Leesil hadn't been found, anger grew inside of Darmouth like consumption. He couldn't abide such a useful tool in service to anyone else, most particularly any other province ruler in the Warlands.

Emêl was in league with this half-blood. Darmouth was surrounded by betrayal, with only Omasta to depend on. He slapped the old tapestry aside at the bottom of the stairwell and emerged into the old sergeant's office.

There were his wolfhounds asleep on the floor. Kana, the taller, raised his head and blinked, looking dazed and tired. With no time to stop, Darmouth hurried out the door into the storage area. He headed straight through the archway for his family's crypt.

The Hall of Traitors had the heaviest door in the keep.

Darmouth pulled out the key to unlock the ornate door, but he fumbled for a moment. Once it was open, he stepped inside.

Warm orange light washed over him from small braziers on the columns that were always kept lit for the dead. There were iron braces on each side of the door, and he reached for the oak bar resting against the wall. The door swung sharply inward, catching his shoulder, and Darmouth stumbled back.

He caught himself on his father's crypt, and his shoulder throbbed from the impact.

Leesil – that mongrel traitor – stood in the doorway, panting.

He looked like some mad creature out of the forested hills below the mountains. His hood was pushed all the way back, and white-blond hair framed a narrow face that glistened with sweat. His amber eyes sparked in the braziers' glow.

Darmouth's rage faltered. He knew what Leesil was capable of.

Leesil took a step into the room, and his gaze shifted between the crypts of Darmouth's father and grandfather. His eyes grew calm.

Many years had passed, and Leesil's face had changed. A strange realization occurred to Darmouth.

He looked so much like his mother . . . born out of treacherous blood.

17

Shouts and footfalls echoed into the council hall from the main entryway as Magiere headed down the concealed stairway. She heard both Chap and Emêl close behind her.

Her eyesight was still sharp in the darkness. At the bottom of the stairs she saw the opening covered by a hanging cloth and swatted it aside. She stepped out into a room with a chair, table, and broken quills. They had returned to the abandoned office adjacent to the storage area.

The two wolfhounds slept near the door. Both dogs looked drained and tired. Magiere ignored them and hurried out into the storage area.

She glanced about, searching for Leesil. Stepping between the piled crates, she saw that the ornate door through the center archway to her right was open.

Leesil stood with his back to her just inside Darmouth's family crypt. And Magiere saw the tyrant beyond two raised stone coffins.

The sight brought only partial relief. Leesil had cornered Darmouth in a place they could secure. They need only lock the warlord in and wait for the keep's contingent to eventually flush out the *Anmaglâhk*. But Magiere wasn't about to leave Leesil in there alone. She reached the center archway, only steps from the door.

Two gray forms dropped from the ceiling inside the crypt and landed to the outsides of each coffin.

Magiere froze. Both were dressed alike in tied-up cloaks, cowls, and face wraps a color between charcoal gray and forest green. The one to the right was taller than Darmouth.

Anmaglâhk. They'd been waiting there. Somehow they'd known Darmouth would come to this place.

The sound of distant voices and feet echoed from the north and south stairwells. Magiere couldn't tell if they came this way or not, and there was no time to make certain. If Darmouth's soldiers interfered, trying to take Leesil, she wasn't sure how far these elves would go to finish their mission. The soldiers' misguided efforts would make things worse.

Magiere glanced at Emêl and Chap coming up behind her. The color in Emêl's face drained when he looked past her and into the crypt.

'Keep out anyone who comes down,' she said, and hoped the two of them could.

'Wait —' Emêl began.

Magiere darted inside the crypt and slammed the door shut. The last things she saw as it closed were Chap's perked ears and astonished face.

All eyes in the room flicked toward her once.

With her back against the door, Magiere spotted the wooden bar. She grabbed it and slammed it down in the braces, locking them all inside.

Leesil pulled one punching blade and held his empty hand out toward Darmouth. 'Get back.'

The two *Anmaglâhk* shifted toward the tyrant along

the outsides of the stone coffins. One might get to Darmouth the moment Leesil committed to going after the other. And behind him was Magiere.

He knew how strong she was in her dhampir state, but he was afraid it wouldn't be enough in close quarters against one of the elves. She needed more room than he did to wield her blade.

Leesil took in the lay of the room. To the left and right were archways between plain and stout stone columns. He'd seen the two blocked-up doors outside, and there had once been three separate rooms here. The spaces beyond the archways were dark, as the braziers upon the columns spilled most of their light into the center space holding the coffins. Perhaps Darmouth's hunger to legitimize his rulership extended to this room, where he would lay to rest the dead who would mark his descendants as true kings.

The far back wall was dimly lit, and Leesil saw a series of black pockets, row upon row of stone cubbies. Each one contained something the brazier light couldn't quite reveal.

Darmouth remained poised, watching everyone in the room. Then his gaze settled on Leesil.

Leesil went hollow inside when he saw any sign of fear fade from the man's eyes.

Darmouth gripped the stout hilts of both war daggers on his belt, and pulled the long blades from their sheaths.

'Come on, boy,' he said. 'I'll send you to your mother!'

Leesil's thoughts ground to a halt in confusion. His mother was with her people. What did Darmouth mean?

The warlord's weapons were as long as his forearms, the blades' bases wider than a hand's palm. Their edges ran straight to pointed tips, with a tapered ridge along the middle of each blade to reinforce its strength.

Darmouth was older now. Leesil couldn't see the man holding his own against one *Anmaglâhk* in close quarters, even in his prime, let alone two. Leesil's panic rose as he realized Darmouth was now ready to die . . . just to kill him.

Both elves watched Leesil out of the corners of their eyes, but their prime attention remained upon their target. Leesil couldn't see their mouths, but the tall and solid one had strands of silver hair hanging down his forehead from under his cowl. There were long scars around one of his eyes.

'Stand aside,' he said to Leesil and pointed at Darmouth. 'This one's life is forfeit, and you, of all who breathe, should have no reason to save him.'

His manner was different from Sgäile, the *Anmaglâhk* whom Leesil had encountered in the city of Bela. This one was cold but polite, as if making a request and waiting to hear Leesil's reply. The tall elf spoke in perfect Belaskian with his lilting accent. His words struck Leesil.

This one knew him – knew at least who he was – knew some small part of his life enslaved to the tyrant.

'I can't,' Leesil answered, with a fleeting hope that reason might work. 'Kill him, and the people here will suffer more in the following conflict than they suffer under his rule.'

The elder one spoke quick Elvish words to his companion and then fell silent. Leesil knew that the time for talk had ended. Both elves ducked through the archways into the dark spaces beyond.

They were trying to close in on Darmouth from both sides.

Magiere raced by Leesil on his right, heading after the elder *Anmaglâhk*, and Leesil almost cried out. He didn't want her facing the one so obviously the superior. The younger elf lunged at Darmouth from the far archway on the left, and Leesil had no choice but to run to the tyrant's defense.

Magiere slashed at the elder elf, hoping to turn him aside, to block him from Darmouth.

He did turn, but only for an instant. As her blade dropped low, he leaped upward.

His foot touched halfway up the column. One fist clenching a stiletto braced against the ceiling.

Magiere passed under him in her rush and heard him drop down behind her. She couldn't turn quickly enough and blindly swung the falchion back. It clanged against the stone column as she finished her pivot.

She caught only a glimpse as he ducked through the previous archway into the room's center section. Magiere twisted back the other way and stepped through the archway to get between the elf and Darmouth.

She knew he'd try to break inside her guard with his stilettos. She knew he would underestimate her strength.

This wasn't an undead she fought, but if she didn't kill him, he would kill her. Leesil would be alone against two of the *Anmaglâhk*. More than he could face himself or to save Darmouth.

Rage fed her strength and speed, and she needed both to keep up. The tall elf charged her from between the columns and the nearest stone coffin.

Magiere spun the falchion low, cutting upward in the narrow space. As she'd hoped, he leaped, stepping off the coffin to plant his other foot sideways at the column's top. He twisted aside as her blade passed before his face. Before he could come down on her, Magiere reversed her swing downward.

The falchion's tip sliced through his cloak's shoulder and his vestment, and she felt it go deeper and drag for an instant.

She spun around, following with a level swing across the coffin's top where he had to land. But he wasn't there.

Pain pierced through her left shoulder.

From the corner of Magiere's eye, she saw a dark hand wrapped around a stiletto hilt. Half its blade length was buried through her hauberk. He had ducked under the archway, landing around the column, and stabbed her before she'd spotted him.

Magiere flicked the falchion across at his arm. When he jerked his blade out and stepped away into plain sight, she threw herself into him. More pain flooded her left shoulder as she struck his chest, and they both collided into the next column.

Magiere rolled away, stumbling, and brought the falchion up again. A flash of gray passed in the dark beyond the archways. She lunged along the coffin's side and set herself in front of the next opening before he could reenter the room's center section.

How could she fight him if she couldn't keep him in sight? Her shoulder hurt but hunger slowly masked the pain. Somewhere behind her, steel scraped on stone, but she didn't dare take her eyes from her opponent to look for Leesil.

In the dark beyond the archway, she saw the elf face her in a half crouch. A dark stain was spreading through his tunic around a slash in the fabric over his collarbone. She had wounded him.

Magiere's jaws ached under the shift of her teeth. When she separated her lips to relieve the pressure, a flash of uncertainty passed across the elf's eyes.

'Dead thing!' he whispered.

He had seen her teeth, her eyes – both surrounded by her pale skin.

'No,' Magiere answered with effort, 'much worse.'

He moved toward her, slower than before. As she raised the falchion to block his slash with one stiletto, he leaned back and kicked up. His boot caught her sword hand.

The falchion tore from Magiere's grip. Before it hit the floor, his foot came down and he staggered slightly. Blood loss or pain had made him falter.

Magiere jerked the dagger from her belt and made a lunging slash at his face. Like smoke in the dark, he simply wasn't there when the blade passed. Before she reversed her swing to follow, he struck.

His stiletto slipped inside her hauberk's right armhole. She felt its slide, cutting her instead of piercing her chest. The pain was still sharp enough to make her buckle, and she dropped to one knee, losing hold of the dagger.

The hunger inside of her made his movements suddenly appear slow. She lashed out with her left fist into his midsection.

The movement cost her, as the pain in her wounded shoulder sharpened. She didn't even feel her strike hit, but his body snapped backward, and he tumbled into the space beyond the arch.

For a long moment they both knelt there, panting, bleeding, and glaring at each other.

Magiere saw faint lines of age around the elf's large eyes. Beneath her pain and hunger, she wondered what had just happened.

He'd found an opening, and she couldn't stop him. He could have stabbed into her chest. Had he failed? Had his grip slipped in the last instant? Or had he tried only to disable her dominant arm wielding the dagger?

His eyes suddenly widened with fright as he looked beyond her.

'*Grôyt'ashia* . . . no!' he cried out from beneath his face wrap. '*Mortajh wearthasej-na Léshil!*'

Magiere turned in panic to follow his gaze.

'Darmouth, stay back!' Leesil yelled again.

He raised his punching blade and pulled the second one as he rounded the coffin's far end. He still hoped the warlord would stay out of the fight. A foolish, stupid hope, like wishing a rabid dog wouldn't attack anything that moved.

The young elf switched one of his stilettos for a match of the bone knife Leesil still carried in his belt. His gaze traced Leesil's punching blades, studying them in a blink. Then his body became a blur of hands and feet as he charged, striking in short, controlled movements.

Leesil hadn't expected a straight-on attack. He scissored and slashed his blades to keep the elf at bay.

A flash of steel came at him from the side.

He ducked down against the coffin's end and heard

metal grate on stone. To his side he saw heavy, thick legs. One booted foot lifted, about to crush down on him.

Darmouth had come at him as well. The man wanted him dead more than he wanted to preserve his own life. And still Leesil had to keep him alive.

From his crouch, Leesil lurched sharply sideways with his shoulder into the sole of Darmouth's boot. He then struck upward with the top of his arm into the back of Darmouth's knee and shoved against the man's foot with his whole body. Darmouth toppled back, his shoulders landing heavily on the stone floor.

The elf's bone knife came instantly for Leesil's face. He twisted his head, and the silvery blade passed through his hair near his ear.

Leesil braced both his blade points into the floor. He pivoted on his left knee away from the elf and whipped his right foot backward.

His heel sank into the elf's abdomen. Momentum spun Leesil the rest of the way around. The elf was bent over from the kick, and Leesil slashed out with his right winged blade.

The young elf leaned away, and the winged blade's tip tore through the side of his cowl, level with his throat.

Leesil rose up. He'd missed doing any serious injury, but the wrap across the man's face was cut through below his chin. A shallow line across the side of the elf's neck began to bleed. Leesil heard Darmouth struggling and glanced over at him.

The warlord rose on one knee, both war blades ready.

'*Trúe!*' the elf shouted like a curse.

Leesil's eyes flicked back. The elf's hooked knife was

gone, but there'd been no clatter of it dropping to the floor. Something glinted around his palm and between his narrow fingers.

'*Grôyt'ashia* . . . no!' a lilting voice shouted out. '*Mortajh wearthasejna Léshil!*'

A name . . . and some command? These words had come from the other *Anmaglâhk*, but Leesil heard no one coming up behind him. Magiere must have found a way to hold the elder elf at bay.

The young elf's gaze lifted, looking beyond Leesil toward the room's far side. He shook off whatever he'd been told, and his smooth tan brow wrinkled as he glared back at Leesil.

'*Trúe!*' he spit again, and rushed in.

Leesil slashed an upward arc with his left blade. The elf dodged, one foot rising to step lightly upon the coffin's end. Then he was gone from sight.

A flash of thin silver passed before Leesil's eyes.

Panic filled his chest as the wire tightened suddenly around his throat. He was jerked upward, and his back slammed against the coffin's end. Darmouth came at Leesil with both blades raised.

Leesil released his punching blades, reaching back for the elf's hands behind his head. And he kicked up between Darmouth's legs.

The warlord hunched over with a grunt. Leesil was stunned when he saw the elf's foot shoot out to strike Darmouth's face. The warlord flopped away out of sight as the wire pulled tighter.

The toolbox on Leesil's back grated across the coffin's edge. Before his feet were pulled off the floor, Leesil kicked off, throwing his legs over his head. He rolled back over his opponent atop the stone slab and came up on top of the elf.

His knees pinned the elf's shoulders, and the man's amber eyes glared up with pure hatred from between Leesil's folded legs. The elf hadn't lost his grips and twisted the wire tighter.

Leesil couldn't breathe anymore, and he couldn't break free.

He fumbled for the bone knife tucked in his belt.

'Grôyt'ashia, stop it!' the same voice shouted. 'Léshil . . . do not kill one of your own!'

The room dimmed before Leesil's eyes. He slapped down between his knees, grabbing for the elf's face.

Only the bright spots of the braziers remained clear as he ground the elf's head to one side. He finally slipped the curved short knife from his belt and thrust downward to just beyond his other hand.

The blade sank into resistance, and he ripped it sideways.

The wire around his throat slackened instantly.

Leesil choked, not yet able to take in air through his bruised throat. The elf's body bucked beneath him. He heard a sound like someone drowning in water as he gasped in air. His hands felt wet and hot as if covered in warm oil. The room brightened bit by bit.

He sagged and his gaze dropped down. His hands and thighs were splattered in blood still gushing from the elf's slashed throat.

Leesil fell back, heaving air in gulps, and rolled off the stone coffin. His legs buckled and his vision spun from too quick a movement. He dropped to his knees on the crypt floor.

Magiere knelt across the room before an archway. Blood soaked through the left shoulder and sleeve of her wool shirt. Another dark stain spread down her right sleeve from the armhole of her hauberk. Her face was covered in sweat, and her irises were full black. She simply stared at him, unmoving.

Beyond her and barely within Leesil's sightline was the elder *Anmaglâhk*. His tunic below his cowl's collar was stained with blood. He held his side as he looked at Leesil and at the body of his companion sprawled across the stone coffin.

Darmouth crawled to the back wall of dark cubbies. Still grunting and hunched, he clawed up to his feet, clutching one of his war daggers. Leesil pulled himself up and stumbled toward the warlord, but his eyes remained on the elder *Anmaglâhk*.

The elf lurched to his feet. When he skirted the far side of the archway to get around Magiere, she hurried to get up as well.

'Magiere, stay where you are,' Leesil said.

The words came out as a hoarse rasp that hurt his throat. He side-stepped more toward the elf as he neared Darmouth at the back wall.

'Léshil!' the elf said, winded but harsh, and he turned his eyes briefly toward the warlord. 'You spill the blood of your own for *that*?'

'How do you know me?' Leesil rasped. 'Where did you learn my other name?'

Darmouth turned around to face them. War dagger held out, he appeared confused. 'Get out of my way . . . both of you!'

The *Anmaglâhk* cast his gaze toward the back wall.

He took a stumbling step forward and was silent for a moment. Then he turned to Leesil once more.

'Look to the wall,' he whispered. 'See if you find your own there as well.'

Leesil didn't let down his guard. He turned his head enough to see the cubbies and still keep the elf well within his vision. He was close now, close enough to see what rested in the rows of cubbies lining the back wall.

Skulls.

These weren't the rotting heads of criminals or innocents stuck on spikes upon the city wall. These bones were boiled clean and polished, collected like trophies, and one double-wide edifice held a paired set.

The nearest was no different from the others, human in all ways, but the second nestled close to it was distinct. A touch oblong. Even with its flesh gone its face was more triangular than its human companion and ended in a narrow jaw and chin bone. Its eye sockets were disproportionate – larger, tear-shaped. It was slightly smaller than the first.

A human – male – and an elf – female. Paired together in death.

Leesil heard banging upon the crypt's door behind him. The room around him dimmed again, and all he saw clearly was the mated pair of skulls.

Two together . . . his parents . . . always together.

'I'll add your head, mongrel,' Darmouth growled with effort. 'Soon enough. Now step aside!'

'Was it worth the price?' the *Anmaglâhk* asked Leesil, a vicious and spiteful edge in his voice. 'Is one human, or a thousand, worth what you have lost?'

Leesil had protected Darmouth — but for what? He looked at the man.

The warlord glared back at him. There must have been something in Leesil's face. Darmouth's expression turned coldly pleased, as if watching another of his supposed betrayers suffering before death.

'Leesil . . . no,' Magiere whispered.

He looked at her. Her eyes were locked on him, no longer black but filled with apprehension. He remembered a time when she was all that mattered. Just her. He would have his life be so simple again.

In his mind he saw his mother, Cuirin'nên'a . . . Nein'a . . . sitting in the bedroom window seat of his parents' room as she combed her brilliant hair. Beneath her stoic expression there had always been a sadness Leesil couldn't take from her.

If he could now just cut out the pain from his head and his heart.

Leesil lunged at Darmouth.

The warlord thrust the wide war blade dead center at Leesil's chest.

Leesil saw it, seeming so slow and weak with age. He turned his torso sideways without stopping, and the dagger slid along the steel rings woven into his hauberk. Leesil slammed the hooked knife into Darmouth's throat. From somewhere behind, Magiere screamed at him to stop.

Magiere watched Darmouth fall.

Leesil stood silent over his victim like another cold stone column in the crypt.

Darmouth clutched at the blade as he hit the floor.

It was in so deep that half the hilt was buried in his throat. It took so long for him to stop choking and become still. Leesil didn't move.

Magiere went numb. All feeling drained from her. Everything they'd done this night – the deaths of Faris and Ventina, injured or dying soldiers, abandoning the search for Wynn – had been to save this tyrant. All of it was lost.

Leesil had murdered Darmouth.

She wanted help. She wanted Chap. Her shoulder and side began to ache again.

And someone kept thudding against the crypt door.

Magiere made a stumbling run across the room. She jerked up the wooden bar and dropped it. The door swung sharply open.

Chap and Emêl stood there, the baron's hand still holding the door latch. No soldiers were in sight beyond them. Perhaps without their lord or Omasta they were still in confusion.

'Oh, merciless saints,' Emêl whispered as he looked beyond Magiere to the room's far end; then he closed his eyes tightly. 'We have failed.'

Magiere turned back, leaning into one stone coffin as she passed between them and the dead body of the younger elf. Shé couldn't bring herself to go all the way to Leesil. He still faced the paired skulls in the one wide cubby in the wall.

There was strange satisfaction in the elder *Anmaglâhk's* eyes and then he looked toward her.

'Touch her,' Leesil said, 'and I'll kill you and everything you love.'

Magiere kept silent. She already believed this *Anmaglâhk*

wouldn't try to kill any witnesses here. He hadn't tried to kill her, even when she refused to get out of his way. Why, was another matter.

'Do not think this changes what you have done,' the elf spit back at Leesil. 'You spilled the blood and life of one of your own. *Tríe* . . . traitor!'

Chap lunged around Magiere toward Leesil, his attention fully upon the *Anmaglâhk*. His growl rolled into a hiss that Magiere had never heard from the dog before. Leesil shuffled to the back wall and the wide cubby.

'Liars and butchers,' he whispered, 'all of your kind . . . and that's all I share with the likes of you.'

The elf's brows knitted at the sight of Chap, and his voice turned quiet. '*Majay-hì*. . . And we are not such liars as you assume.'

He edged around Leesil, and Chap circled to stay between them. The elf went to his fallen companion, rolling the body off the coffin and onto his shoulder. He gave no notice of the blood that soaked into the back of his cloak. Magiere wondered how he was still on his feet, much less bearing the weight.

Before he turned toward the door, Chap lunged to the top of the coffin, snarling at him. The elf backed away.

Chap's crystalline eyes locked onto the elf's amber ones. The dog went silent as his ears pricked up. The two remained in that stare for so long Magiere started to wonder what was happening. Chap's ears flattened, and a low rumble between his teeth started to rise in volume.

'Chap?' Magiere said.

The dog leaned toward the *Anmaglâhk*, jaws shuddering,

as if he were about to tear the elf's face with his teeth. The sound pounded in Magiere's ears as it echoed through the chamber, a snarl half of rage and half like a yowl of mourning.

'Chap!' Magiere shouted over his din. 'Leave him be!'

The dog flinched into silence. The elf shook his head and moved on, inching sideways toward the door to keep his eyes on all in the room.

Chap watched the *Anmaglâhk* until Emêl stepped aside to let the man out.

Emêl came in, behind Magiere, looking at Darmouth's body with a deep sigh. 'I know you two did your best to stop this, but we are ruined. Within days the blood-shed will begin, and when word of this spreads to other provinces —'

'We have to go,' Magiere whispered, then raised her voice with difficulty. 'Now. We can't stay here.'

'What of Hedí and Wynn?' Emêl asked.

'We hope they made it out,' she answered, watching Leesil. 'It won't be long before the soldiers spread their search into the lower levels. We can't fight anymore and there's no hope now of searching the upper levels.'

Emêl was no longer listening. He watched Leesil as well.

Leesil pulled off his cloak. He picked up his mother's skull and placed it carefully in the wool cloth. He did the same with his father's.

Magiere silently willed Emêl not to ask what had happened or she wouldn't be able to answer. She didn't realize Chap was beside her until he licked her hand.

He whined, took several hurried steps toward Leesil and barked twice. When Leesil merely clutched the bundled cloak to his chest, ignoring the dog, Chap kept barking, two at a time in rapid succession.

Emêl flinched at the sound. 'Tell him to stop that. He does not listen to me.'

'It means "no",' she said, but she didn't know what Chap was trying to tell them.

Without Wynn and the talking hide, there was no way to understand what upset Chap so much. Magiere could only guess. He refused to accept that Nein'a had died years ago.

Chap whined, thrashing his head, side to side.

'Enough,' she said, putting a hand on his back. 'We must leave.'

Magiere retrieved her falchion and dagger and headed for the door. The others followed, and Emêl secured the crypt behind them. No one would find Darmouth for a while. Leesil carried his bundle, but he wouldn't look at her.

She didn't care. She didn't want to look at him or speak to him, and merely led the way to the small cell block and the lanterns they'd left there. They passed through the cell and rotating wall, down the stairs, through the portal, and into the tunnel, not bothering to close the way behind them. As she walked along the tunnel, Chap remained deeply agitated at Leesil's side.

Welstiel heard noise in the lower level below him and crept to the base of the south staircase. The passage was long, but he could see all the way to the far end where the north stairwell ran upward. There was no sign of Magiere or her companions.

He could just make out the ornate door before the storage area. It opened.

A tall, cowled figure emerged carring a similarly dressed body over his shoulder.

Anmaglâhk. Welstiel sank back a ways into the stairs.

He heard the elf breathing, but his companion was dead. The elf stepped out through the arches into the storage area, and Welstiel lost sight of him.

He sat and waited and was on the verge of getting closer to the door to peer in.

Magiere and her companions came out, heading the same way as the gray figure. Baron Milea paused long enough to close the door.

Leesil was with her, but Welstiel could tell something was wrong. He was nearly catatonic, clutching a bundled cloak to his chest and walking so slowly that the baron passed him with a troubled glance. Magiere led the way, not looking back even once for Leesil.

Her shoulder was bleeding, and she looked haggard, but she was still on her feet. Welstiel felt only a slight relief. He was curious, even anxious, about what had happened in that room.

All four disappeared from his view.

Welstiel waited a little longer, then quietly walked to the leatherbound door and opened it.

At first he saw only two stone crypts between dark archways to either side. One was coated in fresh blood across its middle. Small shadowed edifices filled the back wall, and a body lay upon the floor. Welstiel stepped between the stone coffins.

Darmouth lay dead in a pool of blood. The back of a knife hilt protruded from his throat. There were skulls in most of the holes in the back wall.

Welstiel was at a loss even to guess what all this meant.

Had Leesil learned anything of his parents' fate? Would he abandon his plan to head for the elven lands? Welstiel turned back to the door.

A voice shouting out orders carried from the north stairwell. It was Omasta, and Welstiel rushed toward the end of the storage area where all the others had gone. There was no way he would be able to leave through the front bridge.

He looked carefully through the half-ajar door to find an empty passage between the cells. And no one he had seen leave was there. He didn't even hear footsteps. There was a hole along the side of one door just above its latch. He opened that door.

Before him was the twisted back wall of the cell, and beyond a narrow staircase.

Magiere needed time to get well ahead on whatever path lay below.

At least now, perhaps she would leave this place, although Welstiel grew anxious again in the uncertainty of what her next step would be.

18

Hedí kept the fire low and pulled the cloak tighter around Korey and Wynn.

Wynn coughed and opened her eyes. The young scholar rolled her head to look about, and fright washed over her face.

'You are safe,' Hedí said. 'We are all safe.'

'Ch . . . Chane?' Wynn stammered. 'What happened?'

'Your strange friend brought us out,' Hedí answered. 'He carried you all the way. I gave him my word that I would watch over you until your companions came. He left us here and would not stay. How do you know such a man?'

'Then it was real?' Wynn asked. 'He was there in the corridor . . . with the soldiers?'

Little Korey frowned and muttered, 'He was cold – bad man,' and snuggled closer to Wynn beneath the cloak.

'How do you know him?' Hedí repeated. 'Is he a foreign soldier of some kind? I have seen him before but cannot remember where.'

'Where are we?' Wynn asked, and glanced about as if truly noticing her surroundings for the first time. 'Where is your baron?'

Hedí tried to be patient. 'Your friend thought Emêl went into the keep, looking for us. I hope he did not, and that he will come for us soon.'

If only poor Emêl had known what would happen. In hindsight, she should have told him everything from the start. Byrd must have located the tunnel's exit, or Emêl — far too chivalrous for Darmouth's domain — would never have gone in after her. Soon enough, Byrd's associates would be sent to finish Darmouth, but not before Hedí dealt with Leesil.

'And Papa and Mama will come, too?' Korey asked.

'Maybe not tonight, but soon,' Hedí said.

Rhythmic scraping sounds came through the forest behind her.

Hedí leaned around the tree and looked toward the opening in the dead trunk. She started to pull herself from under the cloak.

A tall, cowled man stepped out into the forest with someone draped over his shoulder. Both were cloaked, and the one standing had a cloth wrapped across the lower half of his face. He turned his head, looking about, and Hedí barely made out large eyes in a dark-skinned face. He staggered in weariness, as if it were an effort to remain on his feet and still bear his burden.

Hedí pulled back out of sight and put a finger to her lips, signaling Wynn and Korey to be silent.

The dagger taken from Wynn's guard lay by her side, and she gripped its handle. As she looked at the small fire, her fear rose sharply. Its light could not be missed by anyone so close. If this was one of Byrd's elven assassins, then they had closed in on Darmouth more quickly than Hedí had thought possible. And this one might not care to be seen by three women in the forest.

She leaned slowly back to peer toward the tunnel's exit.

The elf was gone. She scanned the darkness between the trees. After long, tense moments, Hedí relaxed again.

'What was it?' Wynn whispered.

'I thought I saw something, but . . . no, nothing.'

Disturbing Korey or Wynn over this strangely fortunate near-miss would serve no purpose. They huddled in silence, letting the fire burn lower. Wynn appeared lost in thought. Angry dissatisfaction filled Hedí in realizing Leesil would not die before Darmouth. Then she heard another soft scuffling in the direction of the dead tree.

A tall woman crawled out of the opening, dressed in a leather hauberk and wearing a sword on her hip. The sleeves of her shirt seemed torn or tattered, though it was too dark to be certain. One shoulder looked stained, and she held that same arm against her chest. Hedí turned on her knees, holding the dagger ready.

Emêl crawled out next, his face smudged and dirty, and Hedí rushed out of hiding.

'Emêl! Here!'

He saw her and held out his arms. Then her face was in his chest, and he pulled her close.

'Magiere!' came a cry from behind.

Hedí caught a glimpse of Wynn rounding the tree that blocked the fire, steadying herself with one hand on its rough bark.

'Wynn?' the tall woman said, her tone melting to relief. 'You got out.'

Before the woman named Magiere took a step, a large silver-gray dog lunged out of the tree. It rushed to Wynn, and the little scholar sank to her knees. The animal licked her swollen face with a whine.

Another figure rose up in the hollow of the dead tree.

Slender, with brown skin and white-blond hair, his eyes were like amber. Clearly he was an elf, but Hedí was confused. Had Emêl joined with the assassins? The man's face was expressionless as he held a bundle to his chest with one arm.

'Leesil,' Wynn cried. 'You're safe.'

Hedí went cold.

Leesil. The son of Gavril and Nein'a. The one who had murdered her father in his sleep. And now, of all sick twists . . . Wynn was his companion and not his target?

He did not acknowledge the little scholar and stared into the darkness, slowly blinking now and again. Everyone else began speaking at once.

'Ah, look at your face!' Magiere said, kneeling beside Wynn. 'What are you wearing? Where's your coat? It's freezing out here.'

'Magiere, you are bleeding!' Wynn returned. 'Let me see your shoulder. What's wrong with Leesil?'

Emêl whispered softly in Hedí's ear, but she did not hear his words. Korey came out next around the fireside tree, the hem of Wynn's coat dragging around her bare feet.

'Are Mama and Papa with you?'

Hedí was barely aware as Emêl's mouth opened and then closed. He crouched, dropping from her sight. Hedí's gaze turned on Leesil alone.

'No,' Emêl answered to Korey. 'They are not with us.'

'We have a fire back here,' Wynn said. 'Magiere, I need to look at your wounds.'

'Not now,' she said. 'You go sit down.'

Hedí still had the dagger in her hand — she felt the hard hilt and the strain of her aching fingers.

Someone passed through her sight. Was it Emêl carrying Korey? She heard the others move away toward the fire, and the only one left was Leesil . . . his hands and thighs stained dark with someone's blood.

He blinked rapidly as if waking, and turned his head toward her. There he stayed, motionless with his eyes upon hers. She understood his expression — recognition.

'Assassin!' she hissed, and charged him.

He did not try to block her swing but only retreated and stumbled. The dagger's tip skidded across his hauberk, clicking across its iron rings as he fell to the forest floor.

Hedí threw herself onto him, where he sat clutching his bundle. She raised the dagger.

'Leesil!' someone shouted from far away, and the voice grew ragged and snarling. 'Get off him!'

'Murderer,' Hedí whispered. She ripped the bundle from Leesil's arms, and her voice rose so loud it tore at her throat. 'Do you know what happened to my mother? My sisters!'

She drove the blade down.

Leesil's eyes awakened — hardened. But not at her. They followed the tumbling bundle she had taken from him.

'Hedí, no!' This time it was Emêl's panicked voice.

Leesil reached for the bundle, twisting beneath Hedí. The dagger's tip slid off the hauberk's side and sliced through the inside of his shirtsleeve. Leesil whipped his other arm across her, and Hedí fell away as he lunged for the bundle. She righted herself on her knees, looking at the one man she wanted dead more than Darmouth.

Leesil knelt on the ground with his back to her, gathering the cloak into a bundle against his chest. He stayed there, not turning to face her, not even trying to defend himself. Hedí rose up, turning the dagger point down as she approached Leesil's exposed back.

A figure landed in her way like an animal pouncing from the dark, and its growling words were barely intelligible between distorted teeth.

'Get . . . away . . . from him!'

The woman named Magiere crouched, nearly on all fours, in Hedí's way. Her face was so pale it looked white in the darkness, but her irises had no color at all – only black, like her sweat-tangled hair. Her fingernails were pointed like claws. And in her mouth, upper and lower fangs extended beyond sharpened teeth.

The large silver-gray dog leaped through the brush behind Leesil and crept forward with its head low, watching Hedí with crystal eyes.

There were tears running down Magiere's cheeks, but her feral features held no sorrow, only rage slipping beyond the edge of reason.

Hedí looked into the face of a monster and did not care. All that mattered was that Leesil died, here and now. She inched forward, ready to gouge out this monster's eyes.

'Hedí, get back,' Wynn cried out. 'Magiere! Don't hurt her!'

Hedí rushed at Magiere, and someone grabbed her wrist.

'Stop it,' Emêl snapped, and jerked her back against

his chest, closing his arms around her from behind. 'You do not understand.'

'Yes, I do!' Hedí shouted, but no matter how she thrashed, she could not break free of Emêl's hold. 'He is the one! He took my life and did not bother to kill me for it.'

'He was a slave,' Emêl said. 'Like all those who serve Darmouth. Like his parents, Nein'a and Gavril. No different from that girl you brought out with you. What would have happened to Leesil's parents if he refused to obey Darmouth? You know the answer. You of all people know how Darmouth works, just as he used you against me for years.'

Hedí stopped struggling, but she had no outlet for the hate inside of her.

Leesil huddled on the ground with his back turned and would not move at all.

The monster, Magiere, backed toward him, torso and inhuman jaws expanding in deep, agitated breaths. Her appearance slowly changed, becoming more human as her lips closed. She crouched over Leesil and took hold of his shoulders. By the time she had him on his feet, Hedí saw only a pale, tall woman in leather armor and long black hair.

Hedí kept her eyes on Leesil until Magiere led him out of sight beyond the tree shielding the fire. Then she saw Korey huddled in terror in Wynn's arms. Hedí could only think of what she had lost long ago.

'No more killing,' Emêl whispered. 'There will be more blood in the days to come than any of us can bear.'

She did not understand and did not care.

Hedí crumpled. Rage's heat and anguish bled out in tears as Emêl gripped her in the black cold of the forest. There had been nothing but deceit and betrayal living under Darmouth. Slaves murdering one another to live one more day.

But Hedí had no pity for Leesil, and wished his life filled with all the suffering forever buried within her.

Magiere sat on a fallen log near the newly built campfire. All of them had returned to the wagon and then traveled northeast along the road. Not far, but enough that they'd never be spotted from the keep upon the lake. Far enough that she would never have to look at it again. Yet Leesil was still here to remind her of what she'd learned of his past in that place.

What she'd learned about him.

Emêl gathered canvas tarps from the wagon's back and busied himself constructing makeshift tents. Korey scurried about in wool footings Wynn had fashioned from part of a blanket. By her hair and coloring, it wasn't hard to guess who were her papa and mama. The girl busily helped Emêl with his work, which amounted mostly to getting in his way. Magiere wondered how long the baron would wait to tell Korey the truth about her parents.

Hedí assisted Emêl as well, keeping her head turned away from Leesil. Magiere didn't believe so much hatred would ever die, and kept her eye on the woman when she strayed too far toward the trees beyond the camp.

Out there, at the edge of the fire's orange light, Leesil sat against a tree, gripping the bundled skulls. Chap paced back and forth at the camp's edge, watching him. The dog was still unsettled. Magiere had not forgotten Chap's maddened outcry in the crypt. It worried her almost as much as Leesil's silence.

Wynn took a blanket from the pile Emêl set out and walked with a bit of a wobble to drape it around Leesil's shoulders. Returning to the camp, she retrieved a second blanket and came to drop wearily to her knees in front of Magiere. She dug in her pack and pulled out a cloth and the jar of healing ointment.

'Take off your hauberk and that wool pullover,' she said.

Magiere did so, and Wynn began cleaning and bandaging her wounds.

'Is Leesil injured?' she asked.

'He's not bleeding,' Magiere answered, though she'd seen the welt line around his throat. 'I don't think there's anything to be done for him – for now.'

Not in the flesh, at least. Wynn's attention wouldn't heal the real wounds he had taken.

Wynn finished bandaging Magiere, and firelight reflected off her oval face, still swollen and battered. Her injured eye was half-open.

Magiere was grateful that the little sage was still with them. Wynn suddenly turned her face away and settled to the ground, leaning against the log beside Magiere.

'I have something to tell you,' Wynn said. 'And it should not . . . cannot wait.'

Magiere frowned as Wynn swallowed hard, reluctant to continue.

'Chane is still alive . . . or exists.' She pulled the blanket tighter around her shoulders. 'I cannot remember much, but I *saw* him come for me in the keep. Hedí says he carried me out and helped her and Korey escape. Then he left us.' She paused. 'I needed to tell you. I want no more secrets between us.'

Magiere absorbed Wynn's words. A Noble Dead loose in Venjètz, wearing stolen clothes? It made sense, and for an instant her instincts made her consider going back. Chane, loose in a city soon to see war at its gates, in its streets, and no one would ever notice his victims.

'Hedí said he cannot speak properly,' Wynn whispered, 'as if his throat was injured.'

Too many thoughts filled Magiere's mind from this long night. She dropped off the log to the ground beside Wynn and pulled the blanket around both of them without a word.

'There is more,' Wynn said. 'In my journals and notes . . . the ones I sent back to the guild . . . Not everything I wrote was about the people and lands we passed through.'

'You mean about me,' Magiere said flatly.

Wynn glanced at her. Some color drained from the sage's olive face.

It hadn't been hard to guess. From the very start at the Guild of Sagecraft in Bela, Wynn and her mentor, Domin Tilswith, had been quite curious about a woman born of a Noble Dead father.

'You're not very good with deception,' Magiere said with only a touch of ire, and as her gaze drifted to Leesil, her voice dropped to a whisper. 'Not like the rest of us.' She took a long, slow breath before she looked back at Wynn. 'It's all right . . . writing about me, that is.'

Wynn sighed, huddling down closer to Magiere. 'And how do we help Leesil?'

Magiere didn't know how. He had ensured more death and suffering in his homeland. And all he had to show for it were the last remains of his parents.

Leesil had lived with years of wine-smothered nightmares over what he believed had happened to his parents when he fled his first life. She had held him in the night, felt him twist and mumble in his sleep. Then in Bela, the *Anmaglâhk* named Sgäile had given Leesil a spark of hope that at least his mother had survived. Along the way he'd chosen to go looking for his father as well.

He'd returned here to have his worst guilt-driven fears become real. This night, hope had died in that crypt more quickly than Leesil's last victim.

'Leave him be for now,' she said to Wynn. 'Darmouth is dead.'

'Emêl told me. You did what you could, but I cannot imagine what this has done to Leesil, trying to save a man who abused him in youth . . . only to fail.'

Magiere gazed into the fire, not looking at Wynn. There was still a secret between them. Magiere could tell no one what had truly happened in the crypt.

Korey and Hedí laid out remaining blankets in the tents as Emêl came to join Magiere and Wynn. Magiere had never been one to give manners much notice, but beneath his noble arrogance, there was something worthwhile in the baron. Perhaps.

'I want you to take Hedí and Korey north for me,' he said quietly. 'To the fief of Lord Geyren. His people know us and will protect them for me.'

Magiere pulled away from Wynn to sit up on the log again. 'What about you?'

'I am staying. You were wise to leave Omasta alive. I will try to get him to listen.'

'Are you mad?' Magiere said a little too loudly. 'He'll execute you on sight.'

'I do not think so. Lord Geyren is in Venjètz even now. He's young but a good man, and we can both give credence that Omasta is Darmouth's son. Most of the soldiers will be desperate for someone to follow – anyone with a true claim as heir. If we act quickly and keep our heads, we might avoid civil war and stand against what comes at us from outside our borders.'

Wynn sat upright. 'Omasta is Darmouth's son? How many know of this?'

'Not many, but enough. Most of the officers.'

'Careful, Emêl,' Magiere warned. 'Make certain Omasta learns all this before you get near him. I suppose he's preferable to his father. And you might curtail a civil war.'

She looked over at Leesil, wondering whether he'd heard them.

'Both of you get some sleep,' she said. 'Emêl . . . you, Hedí, and Korey take one tent. We'll take the other. Go on to bed, Wynn. We'll be along soon.'

Wynn nodded. She left Magiere the blanket and followed Emêl to the tents.

Magiere sat by the fire awhile longer, watching Leesil. She finally got up and headed through the camp. As she passed Chap, still pacing, the dog whined and huffed twice. She crouched and put her arms around his thick neck, then leaned her head into his.

'I know,' she whispered. 'You lost Nein'a and Gavril, just as Leesil has.'

Chap pulled away, snapping out two sharp barks for 'no.'

Magiere didn't know how to make Chap accept the loss. Or how she could deal with Leesil's grief in the face of what he'd done in that crypt.

She stood up and headed for the tree, coming up beside it to look down at a man she still loved but was no longer certain she truly knew. She knew only that when he suffered, she suffered as well.

Magiere sank down along the tree. She reached over to grasp his face, and leaning close, held his head to hers. Then she gently touched the bundle he held.

'I am sorry,' she whispered, 'for this.'

Leesil trembled. He buried his face into Magiere's neck in silence. She felt his tears against her skin as they ran down across her collarbone.

Chap watched Magiere hold Leesil while the half-elf trembled in small, steady intervals. Chap's anger grew upon one name stuck in his mind.

Brot'ân'duivé. . . Brot'an . . . the elder *Anmaglâhk* in the crypt.

Chap could recall any memory he had seen and bring it back to the surface of the owner's mind. A crude way to communicate – or influence – that gave Leesil fits of anger. But he could not give the memories of one person to another, and Brot'an's memories had revealed much.

For the first time Chap truly longed for the power of speech. Elvish was more subtle and useful than Belaskian, but there was so much to relate. A frustrating amount depended on Wynn's translation. Even attempting to explain the truth would require a long night of pawing at the hide.

Brot'an had triggered Leesil's vengeance with a lie.

Chap padded softly up behind the tree, drawing ever closer to Magiere and Leesil. Before either noticed him, he swerved around the trunk and snatched the bundled cloak in his teeth. With a quick lunge, he jerked it from Leesil's arms.

Magiere sucked in a sharp breath. 'What are you doing?'

Leesil gasped and clawed after the bundle, but Chap dragged it beyond reach. He shook the cloak until the skulls fell out upon the forest floor and then set his front paws around the one of the elven female.

'Give them back!' Leesil cried.

Chap snarled and added a loud snap of his jaws.

Magiere grabbed Leesil about the waist and pulled him back, staring at the dog in shock. Chap locked his gaze on Leesil's eyes and called forth memories of Nein'a, one after another. He sharply barked twice for 'no' as he nosed the skull of the female elf.

'Stop it!' Leesil shouted, and curled into Magiere's arms, cringing under the assault of memories.

Chap could not stop. Leesil had to understand.

When Chap locked gazes with Brot'an in the crypt, the scars on the elder elf's face confused him at first. Brot'an had had no scars on the long-ago night he accompanied Eillean carrying a young Chap across the cold mountains. Disjointed memories twisted through the elf's mind like autumn leaves caught in a whirlwind. And like catching those leaves in the order they fell from the trees, it had taken time for Chap to understand all that he saw therein.

Brot'an had been there eight years ago, the night Nein'a and Gavril fled from the keep . . .

Eight years in the past, Brot'ân'duivé walked out of the Crown Range beside Eillean and entered the woodland foothills of Darmouth's province.

Aoishenis-Ahâre, Most Aged Father, had grown impatient with Cuirin'nên'a and requested that she be returned. Brot'an and Eillean had been sent to Venjètz to bring her home — along with her half-blood son.

The request had been quick and sudden — with a hint of challenge.

Brot'an feared that Most Aged Father now questioned his allegiance and that of Eillean. He said as much to her once on the journey. Her reply was a glower laced with concern.

Disloyalty was unheard of in their caste. No *Anmaglâhk* was ever doubted for the sacrifice each made in service to their people. Alone in faraway places, they relied on their own judgment to solve any complication in their assigned tasks. Brot'an knew he now walked a line as thin as a web's strand and half as fragile. There was no choice but to comply.

The journey was long, and passage through the mountains was bitter. Winter was not far off, and the return home through the hidden ways of the Crown Range would be worse. On the fifth night after entering the foothills of Darmouth's province, he stepped across the road running south to the gates of Venjètz. Amid the trees beyond, he quickly held out a hand for Eillean to stop.

Harsh footsteps moved fast and stealthless through the

forest. He glanced at Eillean, saw that she heard them too, and they separated to hide within the forest's underbrush.

From out of the trees came Cuirin'nên'a and a human male, both sweat-soaked and breathless. Brot'an did not understand. Why and how had she run from the city straight to this happenstance meeting?

He stepped out in their way as Eillean reappeared at his side.

Cuirin'nên'a slid to a stop on the forest mulch, a pair of silvery stilettos clenched together in one hand. She stared at them, and her eyes settled upon Eillean as the human male looked frantically back the way they had come.

'Mother?' she said.

'Where is your son?' Eillean asked. 'We must take both of you back with us.'

Cuirin'nên'a fumbled for a reply. 'No! Leesil must never come under Most Aged Father's influence.'

'Why are you here?' her mother continued in demand. 'Where is *Léshil*?'

'Leesil is gone,' the human answered. 'And we are pursued!'

A grating snarl rose from among the trees, and a dark form leaped into view, followed by another.

The human shoved Cuirin'nên'a toward her mother. 'Go!'

Two great cats with dark, shining coats prowled forward in the moonlight, each as large as a mountain lion. Their eyes fixed upon their prey, but they hesitated at the sight of Brot'an and Eillean.

Cuirin'nên'a's husband crouched with a stiletto in

each hand, even as she twisted away from Eillean and separated her own blades. She tried to step in behind him.

Brot'an snatched her cloak and jerked her back toward the nearest tree. One cat leaped for her husband.

'Gavril!' she cried out, and swung back at Brot'an with one blade. 'Mother, help him!'

Brot'an ducked Cuirin'nên'a's swing, and Gavril glanced back when she shouted.

The lunging cat landed on the man, one forepaw against his throat, and he went down. When he hit the ground, the animal's claws raked open his throat and the underside of his jaw.

Gavril's stilettos rolled from his hands. Blood spattered his face. He lay twitching with his eyes still open.

'No!' Cuirin'nên'a cried out.

She tried to jerk her cloak free from Brot'an's grip as Eillean rushed at the cat perched upon Gavril.

The second cat leaped for Cuirin'nên'a's back. It slammed her down upon the mulch.

Brot'an stumbled as her cloak tore from his grip, and Cuirin'nên'a's head bounced hard against the earth. The animal's large paws ground into her back. Its claws bit through her cloak and shirt into her skin. She neither cried out nor moved.

Eillean called out from somewhere to Brot'an's right. Before he looked for her, twin stilettos tumbled through the air at the cat atop her daughter. Neither struck true, and both fell away, but the animal twisted its head with a snarl. Brot'an took in everything in that instant and hope died.

Eillean thrashed beneath the cat that had killed the

human male. Leaves and twigs flew up around her as she tried to fend it off without her blades. Her dark cowl shredded beneath its claws. The cat upon Cuirin'nên'a swung its head back to its own prey.

Brot'an could not save them both.

He leaped upward from the earth and pushed off a nearby tree with his left foot. High in the night air, he watched the cat atop Cuirin'nên'a turn to look frantically about, trying to find him.

Brot'an became still and silent as his ascent slowed above the animal. Stiletto hilt gripped hand over hand, he focused upon the cat's neck just behind its skull. He began to descend on top of it.

The cat glanced upward.

The tree that Brot'an had pushed off from was too far out of reach. The cat pivoted to get from under him. He had to fold his left leg before his foot struck its back. His knee and shin hit instead.

He drove the blade down, but the cat twisted sideways under his weight. The blade seemed to skim off of its head. The animal slapped at him with a forepaw as it screamed out in pain.

Brot'an saw claws pass before his face. He toppled from the cat and pushed off against its side to throw himself clear. He landed atop Cuirin'nên'a, rolled away, and came up crouched above her. The right side of his face stung, and his heart pounded as he steeled himself for the cat's lunge.

Instead, it writhed upon the ground, screeching.

The sting in Brot'an's face grew to a burning as he saw that the cat's left ear was completely gone. The fur around that side of its dark head glistened as if wet, and dead leaves and pine needles clung to it. Something warm and wet ran down Brot'an's face into his own right eye.

For an instant he thought it was sweat, blinking his eye to clear it. But this only darkened and blurred his vision more. There was blood running into his eye.

He had not escaped the claws altogether and felt searing lines in his forehead and right cheek. He crouched and heaved Cuirin'nên'a over one shoulder then ran back through the trees at the road's edge. Within the thick branches of a fir tree, he crawled up along its trunk.

The cat's screaming subsided to a rolling yowl that he heard coming closer.

Brot'an braced himself among the branches, with Cuirin'nên'a's limp form draped over his bent legs. He pressed the branches slowly apart enough to see out and wiped at his right eye with the back of his hand.

The maimed cat pounded about the forest below but never found where he had gone. It turned back to join its mate, and Brot'an watched in anxious fascination.

The two felines writhed upon forest mulch beside each other.

Their bodies rippled into two naked forms – a man and woman of dusky skin and dark hair. The male held the side of his head, still kneeling in pain. They whispered to each other, gestures wild with panic, and both stared at Eillean's torn face and body. When they set upon her, Brot'an went rigid. His back pressed into the tree's trunk, and it ground into his spine.

They sawed at her neck with one of her own blades and severed her head.

Eillean had thrown away her life trying to save a human who was already lost.

They severed Gavril's head next and ran off into the forest with their trophies.

Brot'an saw no more of them. By the time he could bring himself to climb down, he no longer heard their running feet. He set Cuirin'nên'a's unconscious form on the ground. He crouched over Eillean's headless corpse, at a loss over what he could do for her so far from their homeland.

Chap understood what Ventina and Faris had done. In fear of punishment, they stripped the skulls of flesh and presented these tokens to Darmouth. Their lord knew of only one elven female, and an elf's skull was proof enough of the couple's success.

This token of death had deceived Darmouth. And Brot'an had used it again to goad Leesil's rage. In turn, master and slave set upon each other. All for the skull of the wrong woman . . .

The last remains of Eillean, Leesil's grandmother.

In the aftermath of the crypt battle, the memory of Most Aged Father's withered face surfaced in Brot'an's memory . . . along with the request made by the patriarch. Brot'an knew he could not fight his way past both Leesil and Magiere to reach Darmouth. Magiere had wounded him too badly. But he was determined to preserve Most Aged Father's trust. The only way was to force Leesil to murder the warlord.

Chap shook off Brot'an's memories and snarled again. He could not give these memories to Leesil and only recalled Cuirin'nên'a's — Nein'a's — face over and over as he barked twice for 'no.' Leesil cowered away, covering his ears.

'Enough!' Magiere ordered. 'Stop this – now, Chap!'

Chap glared at her. He kept his eyes locked straight into hers, then nosed the skull toward her. He barked twice for 'no' and slowly swung his head back and forth.

Magiere held Leesil close in her arms, but anger faded from her face. She looked down to the skull between Chap's paws.

'No?' she whispered, her head shifting slightly side to side, mimicking Chap's own. 'Not . . . Nein'a?'

Chap barked once for 'yes.' He lay down, his head upon the skull of the woman who had first brought him to Leesil, and closed his eyes. Magiere's dawning awareness of the truth was no relief to him.

'Wynn . . .' Magiere said, voice hesitant, and then she shouted in panic. 'Wynn, get the talking hide . . . get it now!'

As dawn approached, Chane crawled into a forest thicket and buried himself with dead leaves, tree needles and snow-crusted earth. He had tried to get back into the city, but the gates were sealed in the night. Soldiers openly patrolled the rampart with loaded crossbows.

Hunger kept him from settling into full dormancy. Even hidden and shielded, the sting of sunlight crawled over his flesh like biting insects as he thought of Wynn. He lingered in discomfort until the sun finally set, and then crawled out shuddering, as if once again rising from that second grave. He was covered in cold earth and mulch. It was no less unsettling. When he neared the gates of Venjètz once more, hunger squelched his unpleasant memories.

But he could not release Wynn from his thoughts. Had she even truly seen him in the keep?

A few wagons and peasants on foot gathered before the city's main entrance, but the gate was still shut tight. A soldier upon the wall beside the gatehouse shouted down that 'Captain' Omasta had closed the city until further notice. No one was allowed in or out.

Chane did not know what had become of Wynn. Or his horse. Or Welstiel, for that matter.

He stepped back into the forest. Wynn had his cloak and, except for his sword and the clothes he wore, everything he owned was still at the Ivy Vine inn. He lingered behind a tree and searched the gathering of wagons and people for an opportunity to feed.

Most of those on foot stood before the city gate, arguing and pleading to be let in. A few remained behind among the wagons and carts. One was alone, sitting on the lowered gate of a wagon with a small lantern.

She was young, perhaps not yet in her teen years. It was hard to tell with the blanket draped over her head and pulled tightly about her. She had folded her legs beneath the covering as well, and only her face was visible. Lean cheeked, with a nose blushed by the cold, she looked down into her lap.

Chane crouched low, darting to the next closest tree. He could take this one and drag her into the forest. A feeble peasant girl was easy enough to smother into silence until he was done with her.

She struggled with the blanket to free one slender hand, and turned a piece of parchment in her lap.

Chane froze behind the tree.

It was not a parchment, but the page of a book. He

saw it clearly now. When she turned the next page, Chane saw lines of faded writing on the yellowed paper, stained with age.

Hunger's ache reminded him they were only mortal cattle, breeding and toiling, and living out their short existence in such ignorance that their deaths were no loss to the world. No loss at all, but . . .

The girl was reading.

Chane clenched his teeth. Where and how had this peasant whelp become literate? As he was, as Wynn was?

'Skulking?' someone whispered behind him.

Chane turned, ready to satisfy himself with whatever fool had managed to catch him unaware. A few paces into the woods, the shadowed silhouette of Welstiel stepped from between the tree trunks.

'How did you get out?' Chane rasped.

'Most likely the same way you did.'

There was something akin to defeat in Welstiel's voice.

'What's wrong?' Chane asked.

Welstiel gazed toward the city gates. 'It is probable that Magiere still follows Leesil into the elven territory.'

Chane did not care, but he had nowhere else to go. 'Then we find our horses and a way to retrieve our possessions, and we follow – as always.'

'We cannot.'

'Why?'

'She and her companions can enter that land. She travels with a half-elf and a *majay-hì*. We do not. If we tried to enter, we would fail. The dead cannot walk in to those lands.'

Chane stood there, absorbing his companion's words. There were too many times Welstiel revealed knowledge and awareness of things only when it suited him. Chane was growing very tired of this.

'And we cannot reenter the city,' Welstiel continued. 'Now that Darmouth has been assassinated, there is no telling how long before the gates will be unsealed, if at all.'

'Our money, clothing, my bird . . . my books are still inside!' Chane rasped at him. 'We have no horses. We have nothing, and now you tell me we cannot follow Wynn . . . Magiere any longer? There has to be a way to get to the inn.'

Welstiel shook his head. 'Omasta knows my face, and yours will be remembered as well. I have coins with me, and we will find horses and make our way.'

Chane could scarcely believe Welstiel's calm demeanor. 'To where?'

Welstiel looked him in the face. 'The Crown Range. I have my own notion of where to look, and for the moment there is nothing more to be done with Magiere. If we find the location of the object I seek, we may better drive her to it once she finishes this nonsense with Leesil. She will have to pass through the mountains again when she leaves the elven lands. If we cannot follow Magiere, we must wait and make her come to us.'

Chane leaned back against the tree.

Wynn would go north with Magiere to play interpreter, a human thrown in among elves who despised her kind. Welstiel had once again bungled his attempt to control Magiere, and once again Wynn walked a hazardous road. This time Chane could not follow.

'Leesil will protect her,' Welstiel said, guessing his

thoughts. 'I believe he has much to answer for. He will look out for her, as will Magiere.'

Such sentiment was unexpected – and unwanted – but Chane saw no choice but to follow his companion yet again. Sooner or later he would make Welstiel answer many questions . . . answer for the way he played with Wynn's well-being.

And Chane had not forgotten Welstiel's slumbering mumbles. *To never feed again.*

If whatever Welstiel sought possessed such power, Chane now wished to pursue it as well. Once this journey ended, Welstiel was to write him letters of introduction to a sage's guild. In the smallest part of Chane's mind, he imagined Wynn might yet . . .

He shook his head. Such a possibility was far from his reach, if he ever came within its grasp at all.

'We should find horses,' Chane whispered.

Welstiel nodded and turned away. Before Chane followed, he looked back once through the low branches at the peasant girl reading an old book.

Two evenings later, Leesil drove the wagon into the courtyard of Lord Geyren's stone manor. A soldier, or perhaps just a house guard, greeted Hedí politely. He looked a little surprised at how she traveled and the company she kept.

Magiere sat beside Leesil, their shabby clothing badly in need of washing. The wagon was packed with chests and blankets and canvas tarps. Korey sat on one chest, her curly hair in a tangle. She wore one of Hedí's wool gowns and Wynn's sheepskin coat – both too large – and struggled to keep her hands free for the apple she munched. Wynn huddled with Chap upon a pile of canvas. She had donned breeches and her short robe but also wore Chane's cloak, much too large for her small frame, and it hung about her like a blanket.

Leesil remained quiet for most of the journey. His throat ached, and hurt worse when he tried to speak, but this wasn't the reason for his silence. Wynn and the others were unaware of how Darmouth had truly died. Magiere had told no one.

'My lady,' the guard said to Hedí. 'I am at your service. Lord Geyren sent word that you would come.'

No matter what the man thought of Hedí's ragtag arrival, he treated them all as guests. Servants unpacked their chests and took Port and Imp to a stable. The guard led the weary travelers inside the manor. Hedí put her arms around Korey. She did not look at Leesil or acknowledge his presence as she turned to the guard.

'We would prefer food brought to our rooms,' she said. 'We are tired, and my young charge needs rest. Please put the two of us in the same room.'

The guard nodded.

Hedí had decided it would be too much for Korey to learn of her parents' fate along the road. Now she asked for time alone with the girl. Or perhaps she didn't care to eat with the man who had destroyed her loved ones, her family. Leesil felt sorrow for Korey, but at least she would have a place with Hedí and her baron, Emêl.

Chap and Wynn were shown to a room on the second floor, and a servant opened up a thick wooden door across the hall for Leesil and Magiere. Leesil carried in their travel chest and set it down at the foot of the bed.

A plush carpet covered the stone floor between a cushioned chair and dresser with polished brass handles. The painting on the far wall showed sun-drenched mountains in the early dawn. On the bed, large enough for three, was a cream comforter decorated with lace fringe.

Magiere settled a smaller chest upon the one Leesil had set down. She walked around the bed's side and brushed the comforter with her fingertips. She stood there, staring blankly at it, as if uncertain she could trust such luxury.

Leesil opened the small chest, one that Emêl had emptied of other possessions and given to him. Within, carefully padded with a blanket, were the skulls of his father and a grandmother he'd never known.

His mother was still alive, and right now the thought brought him no relief. He touched his father's skull, and looked at that of his grandmother. Chap had called her Eillean. She had been an elder of the *Anmaglâhk*.

Civil war now spread through Droevinka. A bitter and weary fear of the same had been spoken by the tall captain of Soladran at the border of Stravina. And now the Warlands would begin to burn with it.

He had sparked that last fire himself in one moment of overwhelming anguish.

Chap hadn't said as much, with Wynn and the others present, but it now became clear to Leesil just the same.

Though he had opposed his mother's caste, in the end, he had served their purpose.

Leesil's gaze shifted back to the skull of his father as Magiere stepped in behind him.

'My mother will want to bury him herself,' he whispered. 'If we can find her . . . get to her.'

Magiere's hand brushed his shoulder quickly and then the touch was gone. 'Let's get your boots off.'

This was the role she'd adopted over the past days — politely detached caretaker. He stood up and went to sit on the bed, taking off his cloak and boots. As he pulled the shirt over his head, he shuddered. It smelled terrible. Hopefully they'd have time to wash their belongings before heading into the mountains.

Magiere sat down beside him, pulling off her own boots. A dried bloodstain covered the rip near one shoulder of her shirt.

'We'll find her, Leesil. We'll start tomorrow.'

He nodded without speaking.

'Lie down,' Magiere said quietly.

Leesil lay back, watching her pull loose the leather thong that held her black hair back. He saw the stain on her shirt under her other arm.

She let the thong drop, not seeming to care where it fell, and shook her hair loose across her back. There was too little light in the room to spark its red depths.

Magiere remained faced away for so long that Leesil wondered if a father was all that he'd lost . . . if opposing his mother's people was not the only betrayal he'd committed in coming home. She turned so suddenly that he didn't see her pale face as she lay down next to him on her side. In another moment she slowly reached her arm across his chest.

He was barely able to put his hand atop hers, fearing how she might react.

'Are you all right?' he asked.

She slid her hand up to his shoulder, pulling herself closer, until her face pressed into his hair and cheek. Her answer was long in coming.

'We will be,' she whispered.

EPILOGUE

Aoishenis-Ahâre – Most Aged Father – felt the call of Brot'ân'duivé from within the massive oak in which he rested. The tree had lived almost as long as him and was the eldest in the great forest. He rested his aged body and too-long-extended life in a bower formed of living wood within the tree.

In the earliest days, the tree's hollow had been carefully nurtured to fulfill his future needs. He had lived so long that even the clans' elders no longer remembered the scant tales of where he had come from or why he had led his followers into seclusion in this far corner of the world. Wise in the way of the trees, he no longer walked among his people. His body clung to life only by the efforts of the great forest that sustained him through this ancient oak.

Through the tree's roots, touching others within his people's land, he reached out with his awareness to wander and watch within the elven forest. He heard and spoke with his *Anmaglâhk* in other lands as well, whenever they placed smooth slivers of 'word wood' taken from his own oak against any living tree.

He listened now, considering each word until Brot'ân'duivé had finished, then answered.

I am pleased. Come home.

The human warlord, Darmouth, was dead and his province left unprotected. Bit by bit, the humans turned on one another, and in the decades to come, the blood-shed would mount.

Most Aged Father sighed with relief, his breath a thin trickle between his shriveled lips.

He would protect his people. The ancient enemy grew stronger, turning in its slumber. He felt it in the earth, in the air, and the whisper of the trees. It would return one day, but it would not have the human hordes it had used the last time. He would see to this.

Not all that Brot'ân'duivé told him was good. Another of the *Anmaglâhk* had passed into the earth, and tonight the people would mourn in the proper ways. But Brot'ân'duivé's last words had been the most disturbing and left Most Aged Father uncertain.

He let his awareness weave through the roots and branches and leaves of the forest until coming to a glade. There sat a woman of the people, alone and isolated. The forest had been told she was never to leave this place.

Humans found her alluring, and this served her. Her own kind called her beautiful as well, even those few who had seen the scars of claws on her back. White-blond hair hung loose around her tall, lithe frame where she sat against the trunk of an elm. Her large amber eyes were hard, and her triangular caramel face was void of emotion. She stared out into the forest, not even knowing she was watched.

Most Aged Father knew her sorrows, but his sympathy was smothered by her treachery. Even now, he was not certain of all she had done, let alone why.

Each dawn, one of the *Anmaglâhk* brought her food and clear springwater. The glade was kept warm and dry by sentinel trees. Clothing or simple amenities were provided to her as needed. Beside her was a basket of butterfly cocoons with which she whiled away her days making shimmering *shéot'a* cloth. She wore a cloud-white wrap of the fabric, fashioned by her own hands, rather than give anything she made to her people.

Most Aged Father spoke to her, using the chatter of leaves in a light breeze for a voice.

Cuirin'nên'a . . .

She sat upright. Almond-shaped eyes narrowed with spite, as she searched the trees to find where the voice came from.

Your traitor son comes home.

PRIESTESS OF THE WHITE

Age of the Five Book One

Trudi Canavan

When Auraya was chosen to become a priestess, she could never have believed that a mere ten years later she would be one of the White, the gods' most powerful servants.

Sadly, Auraya has little time to adapt to the exceptional powers gifted her by the gods. Mysterious black-clad sorcerers from the south plague the land, and rumours reach the White of an army being raised. Auraya and her new colleagues work tirelessly to seal alliances and unite the northern continent under their banner, but time is running out.

War comes to the lands of the White, and unless Auraya can master her new abilities, even the favour of the gods may not be enough to save them . . .

Trudi Canavan, author of the bestselling Black Magician Trilogy, embarks upon a wonderful new fantasy series set in a classical world of magic, heroes, gods and forbidden love.

DEVICES AND DESIRES

The Engineer Trilogy Book One

K. J. Parker

When an engineer is sentenced to death for a petty transgression of guild law, he flees the city, leaving behind his wife and daughter. Forced into exile, he seeks a terrible vengeance – one that will leave a trail of death and destruction in its wake.

But he will not be able to achieve this by himself. He must draw up his plans using the blood of others . . .

A compelling tale of intrigue and injustice, *Devices and Desires* is the beginning of a brilliant new fantasy series from K. J. Parker, the acclaimed author of The Fencer Trilogy.